A Certain Romance

A NOVEL BY

To AnneMarie and Adam, for cleaning up my literary messes

Copyright Ciarán West, 2017. All rights are reserved by the author.

One

Last Year, London, Emma

The taste of soap in my mouth has stopped being strange or disgusting; it's just part of the routine now. Soap, shampoo, sometimes that special shower gel 'made from 100% natural ingredients'. The lemon one's my favourite, I can pretend it's meant to be in my mouth, with a bit of imagination. I scrub the rest of me, hard, same as every other day. Especially the fingers and the beard – that's where the smell sticks the most, and she'll notice it. She still kisses me, and my hands are always on her. Anyone might get the impression we're in love.

I pat my face dry with one of the towels she bought for the new house. Not our house, her house. I just live here. I look at the clock, a vintage train station one, which is like everything in this place (and the last place); part of her own unique style. So unique you can find it in every copy of *Living Etc.* she keeps neatly stacked in the downstairs toilet, along with *Crap Towns, Eats, Shoots and Leaves,* and other things that Middle Class people think are hilarious. It's nearly five. I need to start preparing dinner soon. Something that feels a little like happiness pops up in me, for a second, then it's gone. I like it when she likes the food I cook. I like it when she likes anything I do.

The queue at the shop across the street isn't long, but none of us in it are sure who's next, cos of the strange layout, and the way people on the tills randomly decide if they're serving or not. I just need some ginger and a bag of cashews. I've already been in earlier. I feel okay. Sober and lucid. There's a headache on its way, but I've already had the ibuprofen before I got in the shower. The girl in front of me moves forward, stopping for a second to see which server she should go to. Outside is sunny, but it isn't too hot. She'll be on the tube now though, where it's always hot, and cramped. I'm going to make Chinese. That always makes her happy. Even though these days she's never really happy. Best I can ever do is stop her hating me for a while.

The knives are sharp, but I'm used to them. I love sharp knives, and the power you feel using them. I should've chosen a different one for the chicken breast, but I like the way the curved one moves in my hand against the board. I could've chopped the veg first, but the meat needs to sit in its marinade for a while, and I don't have time. So, I just wash it in between, with a little of the Fairy that she tells me I use too much of. It says a lot about her power over me that I'm nervous about things like that when she isn't even here. But I'm used to that too. I slide the pink flesh into a small bowl. Some corn flour, a little rice vinegar, a good splash of soy. The rest of the taste will come from the sauce I'll make. I wash my hands to get rid of any traces of raw meat from under my nails. The garlic is fresh and wet inside, smells good. The iPod shuffles on to the next Bowie track. It's *Quicksand*. Always so quiet at the start that I feel the need to turn up the speakers. It's half past five. I think about sending a text. No service on the underground, but she'll get it when she comes out of the station.

Everything is chopped and prepared, sauce made, wok on the stove, rice measured out. I pick up the dog bowls and put them on the counter. The sound of plastic hitting granite makes them run in from the living room. The dogs are my favourite company. They don't judge, and they can't criticise. They're loyal, even if it's mostly down to their own stupidity. I wonder if I should start the rice, but she hasn't replied to my text. It could end up being one of those nights where she goes for drinks with people from work, and we'll have another stupid non-argument where I sulk, and she doesn't say much, but I know she hates me for stopping her doing what she wants. We're always on the edge of a fight. It's never been any different, right from the start, but we carried on. Something keeps us together, and it doesn't always feel like something good. You don't get addicted to healthy stuff.

My head feels okay; my mind is probably not as quick as it could be. If she came back right now, asked too many questions, I'd probably give the game away. I test myself sometimes, try to remember something specific about a piece of trivia, and see how long it takes. I remember, years ago, playing quiz machines in pubs, when the drink would slowly make me less able to get the answers right. I turn the music down to more of a background volume. She'll turn it down again when she comes in; I think she needs to feel some control whenever she comes back to her house, even something as tiny and meaningless as that.

There was never a period of settling. I've been in that 'first few months' stage with her for three years now. Never moved on the stage where I'm her long term thing. She's got better at it; she brings me out with her friends, and down to Plymouth to see her family. But, even then, I always feel more like some freak show than their future son-in-law. I used to be open minded about going out with people from different classes, but that was back in Ireland. English middle class people are the real deal, and they're definitely better than me. They're like a different species, and they look it.

Still no word, which usually means she's coming. She's always so stressed by the commute, morning or evening, that I've learned not to push her on stupid things like getting back to me in texts or emails. She's obsessed with the idea of not having enough hours in the day to do the things she wants, outside of work; that's why she hates me. I'm the one with all the spare time, and the one who does nothing with them. Nothing she knows about, anyway. It makes her angry at the worst of times, gnaws away at her for the rest. I can feel it sometimes, coming off her like a haze. She loves me, though. That's the weird bit. I believe her when she says it. I just don't think she knows what it means. Or she might just think it means something different than it does to me. I don't know.

It's been a quiet enough day, inside my head. Sometimes the noise is so loud that I have to do something to quieten it, or give in and listen to what it says. When I do the first one, it's touch and go as to whether the day ends well or badly. When I do the second, it always ends well for me, and badly for someone else. It's been like that for a long, long time, and I used to let it eat away at me. I used to let it keep me up, and drive me mad with guilt, and shame, and bad feelings. And then one day I just accepted it. Accepted myself, and the things I have to do sometimes. But it's been a quiet day today, in that respect, so I don't want to think about that now.

Love was always something I reckoned I understood more than whomever I said it to. They didn't get it, I did. That's what I thought. I was a love snob. This relationship isn't that different, but at least now I know of the root of the problem. My parents split up when I was fifteen, and I've been trying to find the perfect relationship ever since, as if doing that will fix the past. It's nonsense. Looking back, I realise that it didn't matter who I was with, just that they stayed with me. That I kept them. That I didn't fail like Dad did. When I met her it felt different. Didn't feel like I was settling. I'd found the one. Perfect for me in every way. That's how it felt. But it could've been wishful thinking. I'd been single for five years. It could be I just met someone who wanted me, and changed myself to make her fit me better. It didn't go both ways. She hasn't changed a bit for me. A text from her. She isn't coming. She hopes I haven't started cooking yet. She'll get something in the pub. I shouldn't wait for her. I walk to the cupboard where my fags are hidden, behind the toolbox. It'll be hours, I can do the soap thing again before she comes back.

It's getting dark; I spot an empty can in the garden from earlier. I'll have to take it out to the bin in the street, ours is a no-no. I pull long and hard on the ciggie, nice to have one after I thought I was finished for the day. After a lifetime of being unable to go two hours without a puff, I've now trained myself to stop in the early evening, and be fine without them until she leaves around eight the next morning. I can do it easily, unless we have a fight. Sometimes I think the nicotine demon inside me causes the fights, just so I'll storm out of the house and light one up. Immediately after, I regret it, and have to go to the shop on the corner to get chewing gum, or a lemon drink, to hide the taste, in case she stops me before I've had a chance to go to the bathroom and brush my teeth. Sometimes I think that I'm already halfway to quitting, if I'm able to go so many hours without a fix. But I know that it's just a deal I make with the demon to feed him again in the morning, and that he knows I won't go back on it.

I'm someone who has always been okay with keeping secrets. A secret is different to a lie, in my mind. I hate lies. But if I have to tell one in order to keep a secret, then I don't count it. That's not a real lie. A lie is something you tell to make yourself look better, or to stop someone's feelings being hurt. A lie to keep a secret isn't selfish in a nasty, horrible way, like some other lies are. It's just self-preservation, and we all need to do that. It's not a real sin; it's just a way of keeping afloat.

The bins are half way between the house and the shop. I feel the pull as I walk down with the can and few fag ends I picked up from the grass out back. Whenever I have some time to myself, especially when she isn't going to come home for the night; she's away for a weekend, or I'm house sitting for someone else, the feeling grabs hold of me, and it's hard to shake. It's never a question of just one drink. I'm not interested in drinking. It isn't a social thing. You can't be social with yourself, even if you have the internet and Facebook. I only ever want to get out of it. To get smashed. To have a little break from my own thoughts. Calling what's wrong with me 'depression' is misleading. I don't wake up with feelings of doom, and I don't get sad for no reason. The way it affects me is apathy, and no motivation. I hadn't written a word in months before I landed the gig at the Screen Passions website. And, even now, I need my editor to give me a deadline before I care enough to get anything done. Same as with the novels, I'm full of self-doubt, which goes away for a bit when I show my stuff to people, and they say good things. There's no snowball effect, though. Every morning I wake up again and feel like I can't do it. She doesn't help. I can feel her lack of faith in me. Every time (and it's rare) I talk to her about writing, her face takes on a look that says,

'That's all well and good, but when are you going to get a proper job?'

It isn't the whole reason for the writer's block, but having the person who loves you be supportive feels like it should be a given to me, and I hate her for not even pretending.

I go in for just one can. To take the headache away. At the big fridge, the names on the cans mean nothing, just the percentages. I don't like beer. It's just gas and water, never strong enough. There's one there that's 9.5%, but I can't stomach it. It tastes like stout with cheap whiskey in it. The black cans of cider are the strongest. Kestrel at 8.4%, or Union Black, which is the same thing, but cheaper. I take two, cos one is never enough. I'm sober, they won't get me so drunk as to be stupid or slurring when she comes in. And I can eat. I might eat. I can cook what is there, for one; or for two, and pack some of it away for her. I don't know. Thinking about it makes me nervous. Thinking about her makes me nervous. Three years now, and it's never changed. I don't wait to get home before I crack open the first one. It tastes like hot vomit. I never got used to how it makes me gag the first time it goes down. There's no pleasure in this. It's the opposite of a refreshing pint of suds in the beer garden on a sunny day with your friends. It's fuel, to get me away. But I never quite get away. Not for long. When it's over, I'm always back where I started, and usually feeling even shittier.

The laptop's still open. Something's paused on the media player from earlier. It's some episode of a show we've been watching together. That's one trick I have to stop the tension and the fighting. Get her interested in some American drama that we can fill those three hours in the evening with, and while we eat. Sometimes a new recipe, to make her a little happier. Sometimes an old favourite, to comfort her. I don't have any favourites anymore. Hers are mine, now. I don't enjoy doing anything she doesn't like too. At least while she is around. She hasn't seen this one yet. I sometimes watch ahead, as it's me who has the free time to do it, and anything is better than doing what I'm supposed to be. I won't tell her, she hates watching anything with me that I've already seen. I don't understand why, or need to. With her, it's enough to know that a thing annoys her. The only fix is to not do it again. There's no sense or logic to it. It doesn't matter who's right or wrong. What matters is who pays the rent.

The first can is nearly finished. I remind myself to get rid of it later. The veg is still on the chopping board. Doesn't look like it's going to be cooked, but God knows what I'll decide after can number two. Drink always seems like a choice to me, but after enough of them, it's the drink that decides. And it never decides something smart. It's like letting a blind guy walk me through traffic. Then again, I'm letting her steer us through our relationship, and she isn't qualified to do it. Ability isn't ever an issue for people like her. She's in management, where the people holding the reins aren't the ones with the aptitude or the knowledge; they're just the biggest bastards. I smile uncomfortably as I remember a conversation we had a few years back, where she told me she would have preferred to be with someone who didn't already have a child. When I asked her why, she looked at me with a combination of arrogance and doubt, and said:

"Well, you've already done it before, and I'd have preferred to experience it all for the first time with someone. That's important to me."

"Yeah, but I've been through all the scary bits too, and I'd be able to reassure you about things. Like when we think there's something wrong with the baby's skull, and it turned out all babies have-"

"See? That sort of thing. I don't want to already know. I don't want you to be the one who knows best. I want to find out by myself, and have someone else on the same page as me, do you not understand?"

"That's just bloody ridiculous."

"How is it ridiculous?"

"Well, cos you're saying screw all the benefits you'd get from having someone around who is already qualified to bring up a kid, who can put your mind at ease about stuff, who can let you know that it's not always gonna be like this, that or the other. You're saying balls to all that, you'd rather risk the baby's health and stuff, just so no one else gets to be better than you at something?"

"That's not what I said. At all."

"It is. What the hell is wrong with you? Are you that much of a control freak? Really?"

"Look, if you're going to be like that, let's forget it."

"Am I not a good parent?"

"What? What has that got to do with anything?"

"Huh? It has EVERYTHING to do with everything! For Christ's sake. Jesus, if I have to sit here and compete with some imaginary future husband of yours who comes baggage free and ready to dive head first into the exciting world of being a bloody clueless parent with you, I think it's only fair that I-"

"This is exhausting. Can we just stop, please?"

"For God's sake. It's always exhausting when you're losing the argument. Every bloody time."

"That's not true. I just… it's tedious, all right. I work hard, I travel three hours a fucking day, and I do NOT need my evenings filled with arguing with you about shit I don't care about. I've had enough of it!"

And then the tears start. Hugs and sorries from me. A half hour later she'll be tired and relaxing into my chest, and I'll be okay, and blissful, and happy again. Cos she won't be talking, so we won't be fighting.

And she'll need something from me, that hug, and I can give it to her. And that's where all my happy begins and ends. I finish the second can and think about a third. I need to go out anyway, to smoke, and drop things off at the bin. It isn't even eight yet. Plenty of time.

There are more drink options. The cupboard always has gin. She doesn't check it. She isn't anal like that. Sometimes I take too much, and go down Sainsbury's and buy their brand, to top up the Gordon's. She never notices. And the new bottle always has too much in it, so I treat myself to a few doubles, and it carries on. I don't think I've become better at drinking. Spirits are tricky. In my head they're stronger, but a single shot is the same as a half of lager. Less water though, so it's quicker to down, and the percentages are bigger. The 'half a lager' thing doesn't make much sense at the end of a long day in the pub, when the rounds of shots start. Those things mess you up a lot more than any glass of Bud does, cos you're already messed up. I pour a few fingers into a glass. The tonic is flat. I'll get her a fresh one from the shop later. I take a sip. That first taste always reminds me of something, but I can't place it. It's more a feeling than a memory. I think of one just then though. A morning on a day off from when I had a proper job. I'd bought some Cork Dry Gin, and drank it at 10.00am, while watching The Commitments and wishing I was back home. It isn't a sad memory, but I feel sad, anyway. Gin is some emotional shit. I try counting the units I've had already today, but it's pointless, cos I don't know what units they were, and I'm not sure if I can include that morning's session. That seems like a whole other day now. I'm drunk again, I can feel it. A fuzzy sense of everything being all right, which is what I'm on board for in the first place. I started to wonder when exactly my expectations of life dropped so much, but it starts to get me down, so I move on.

I go outside for a cigarette. There's always some paranoia, even here, where we know none of the neighbours yet. It's ridiculous. I'm 36. No one's going to tell tales on me. Still, I don't stay on the step. I walk down, maybe to the shop, maybe not. I take a route I'm sure she won't be coming back via, off her train. Even though I know she won't be home for hours. It's a work day tomorrow; she won't be any later than midnight. But you never know. It's best to be cautious. The sky is twilight, but the air is still warmish. I'm in a t-shirt. Coming up past the chip shop where they serve massive portions for a handful of change, I stop to pick up a used scratch card. I have no shame. While we were broken up for five months last year, I was poor, and got into a habit of checking them. One morning, I saw one inside the bin in front of a shop, and reached in to pick it out. It was a £20 winner. After that, any feelings of embarrassment at acting like a tramp disappeared for good. I'm already regularly wandering the streets off my face on cheap cider, sometimes I pick up half-smoked fags, when I have none of my own.

I'm in the queue again. By now, any choice in whether or not to continue drinking has gone out the window. The only say I have is in whether I go for the slightly weaker type of cider, and even then it's a struggle just to let my body walk away with the 6% stuff. One will be enough. One is sometimes enough. The rest of the drink hasn't hit me yet, and won't for at least a half hour. While I'm still in the position to be careful, I'm going to try. I need cigarettes too. There's only one left, and I'll want some in the morning. I think about washing my mouth out again, when I get back to the house. It needs to be done before she comes home, but another scrub in the middle of everything can't hurt. The bloke at the till looks past me with the usual London disconnect. If there's anything I miss about Ireland it's the way people in shops and cafés seem to genuinely mean it when they ask you how you are. Going back there, after a seven year break, it took some time to shake the feeling that they were up to something. London shopkeepers are Asian or Middle Eastern, and the amount of ignorant racist shit and constant robberies they have to put up with makes them put up a wall that people like me can't break with small talk or smiles.

I light up again outside, ducking into a doorway when her bus passes. She isn't on it. Well, I don't think she is. It's just an in-built reaction to the numbers on the front. I've no idea why, but fear is one of my main feelings about her. That, and love, whatever the hell that means anymore. It's more like adoration. People in the old days used to fear the gods they adored. I adore her, she loves me. My mum loved my dad when she left him. She probably loved all those pet dogs of mine she had put down too. Love's no guarantee. People still hurt you. They crush you. They walk away from you. I don't ever walk away, even when I should. I let things go to shit, rather than ending them, cos I'm a coward when it comes to confrontation. She is too. That's why we've lasted so long; she can't finish it, and I don't want it to end. I don't even know if that's true. When you're the only one holding things together, it's impossible to know if you'd be happier somewhere else.

I take a different way back. A little walk will be good, and I've been going in and out the door too much, it's pissing off the dogs. All the roads here look the same; I've been lost a few times since we moved, drunk and sober. It's all Victorian houses and council flats. A little panic sets in. The street names are familiar, but we looked at plenty of places around there before she made the offer on the house, so me remembering them doesn't help. It's got darker without me noticing. I light up another cigarette and pick a direction. It isn't like wherever I'm going is home. Home is a long way away, and a long time ago. I must be pissed. I'm being all poignant.

Back at the house, nothing's getting done; on an artistic level, anyway. I either start strong, and pile through all day, or I just hit the wall from the beginning, and it's already over until tomorrow. It's disappointing for me, and for her. But it's the way I am. It's not all I am, of course. I'm lots of things, and some of them she knows nothing about, thankfully. Some of them she doesn't want to know about, and she never will. She doesn't have to; it wouldn't make her life any better. There's a me that I keep just for me, and it's not a lie if you're just doing it to keep a secret safe. It's just self-preservation, and we all need to do that. It's not really a sin; it's just a way of keeping afloat.

Two

This year, Limerick, Orla.

She's the one that got away. I've thought about her more than anyone I've ever liked, over the years. We never even kissed. It was always the wrong time, or the wrong place. Or other people in getting in the way. Whatever it was, she was just out of my reach, and it killed me. I often wish we'd just had one moment; because no matter how good it might have been, it would have been easier to move on from than what was in my head – and what was in my head was what-ifs and what might-have-beens, and they were always going to be much better than reality. When you're worried about something, you always fear the worst, and when it happens, it's never as bad as you thought it would be. This feeling is kind of the opposite. I've been crazy about this girl for fifteen years – for thirteen and a half of them, we haven't even lived in the same country. All that time we hadn't said a word to each other, not even on social media. But here I am now, about to meet her in person for the first time since I left. And I'm shitting myself.

It's been a bit of a slog to get to this point. She's married now. No kids, but she wants some, she said. I like that there's no kids, because it feels less dirty that way, but I'm not sure it would stop me if there were. Stop me doing what exactly, I don't know yet. I'm sitting in a weird pub, up William Street. I chose it, because it's the sort of place no one either of us know would come to. Problem with that is that me sitting here on my own with a drink is sticking out like the proverbial. It's eleven in the morning, so there aren't many in, but the ones who are in are definitely regulars, and I feel like an invader. I've got a Guinness. That's all I remember about this place, from back in the day – they do the best pint in Limerick. I was going out with a girl – Holly – and it was her 21st weekend, so we were on a batter that lasted a few days. We were coming down off pills at about this time in the morning when a mate of mine suggested we come in here. We must have had the druggiest heads in Christendom that day, but the barman didn't seem to give a shit. I remember Holly went to phone her mother, to check in and let her know she wasn't dead. The mother was giving her some spiel that I couldn't quite make out, then she asks Hol to hand me the phone. She said to me:

"Listen, I know it's Holly's birthday, and it's a special one. And I know ye've probably had a few drinks and it's got a little crazy, but listen – don't be doing anything ye might regret. Do you understand me now?"

She was literally asking me not to take her 21-year-old daughter's virginity. I hadn't, in fairness. She'd lost that ages before she met me. Me and her had already tried anal. I didn't tell her mother that though; it would have spoiled the birthday atmosphere.

Some guy wanders in, looking like a Sunday Tramp. I mean, a normal tramp, just sort of polished and straightened up enough to go up for some Holy Communion. Still smells like piss, though. Or maybe Brut. I avoid eye contact, cos I'm a magnet for psychopaths; whether it's just in general, or my love life. Birds of a feather and all that.

I can't wait to see her. Except I can. I'm dreading it. But not in a bad way. I don't know. I'm thinking back fifteen years, when I was going out with her friend, and that was good and everything, but every time we happened to socialise with Orla, how much better everything was. How I used to get this itch about her. Clichéd as it sounds, there really was an electricity between us – the sort of electricity I didn't really understand back then, and I never felt again with anyone. Not until I met Emma. But Orla was different from Emma. There was no downside to Orla. It just felt like it was all good. Except I was with her friend. And she was with mine. Well, he started off as my friend, anyway. After a while, well, that's another story.

I feel like I should get up and leave, even though that sounds mental. It's just that… we've never – it's never been – The best thing about me and Orla is that we never fucked it up, and I'm sick of looking back at all the other things in my life that I've fucked up, or that just got fucked up by themselves, and there's a part of me that knows I could just keep this one perfect. If I don't pick at the scab. But it's perfection based on… fantasy. Or on something that never happened, and stuff that never happened, well, it's easy to see that as perfect, because it's never been tested. I don't even know if we're going to test it now. Or later. Or ever. She's not coming here to do anything with me. She's married. That's such a weird word to say in my head, especially about her, because it makes us all seem like adults, and maybe she is one, but I'm definitely not. And anyway, she's frozen in time in my head as the girl she was fifteen years ago. And she hasn't changed a bit. In my eyes anyway, and maybe they have a sort of filter on them from my lifelong obsession with her that just makes her eternally look like a pretty young thing to me, but that's not a bad thing. If someone had that for me I'd be well chuffed. A weird old couple come in the door, look around, she punches him on the arm, he calls her a cunt, and then they leave. Love comes in all shapes and sizes.

I go to the bar for another drink. I'm really early. Because I'm really keen, but she'll never know that. Who am I kidding? She knew that fifteen years ago. She's the only girl I've ever been completely unable to play it cool with, or keep anything from. And I am keen. We have social media now – we have Facebook – everyone is contactable. But when I moved to the UK, and the internet was still a bit niche, and your mum hadn't discovered it yet, I was looking for her. Friends Reunited, myoldmate.com, all the sites that existed. The first time lived somewhere with internet, after I moved to Britain, I was straight on that Freeserve dial-up, trying to find her. Cos I was single, and had no one to answer to, and maybe she was single too now, for once, and over there, possibly giving a shit if I cared. No one has ever fucked me up romantically like Orla Keane, and I mean that in a good way. She's without equal. She's my lobster, kind of, except I never told her. But maybe I did. But that was a long time ago. And now is different. Now is now. And I'm still thinking about all that nonsense, waiting for the old guy with all the nasal hair to pass me over the best pint of Guinness in Limerick, when she walks through the door, just dressed like any married woman in her 30s would dress on any occasion that wasn't special, and she still knocks my socks off, cos it's Orla Keane, and I'm powerless against that, and she just made my whole a world a little warmer by being here.

Three

Last Year, London, Emma

I wake up panicked, which is normal. A headache, so whatever happened last night, I didn't eat enough, or take some painkillers either. I see an empty water glass on the stool she uses as a bedside table. That might be hers though. She's over there, by the dresser. Freshly showered, putting on the plain black knickers she wears for work. They aren't in any way flattering, but her body is as great as her face is… whatever her face is. I sometimes wonder if that's why I cling on so desperately, in the face of everything. She's put on a few pounds since we first met, especially in that period we were apart, but she's still something. She's aware of it, but my compliments to her never go unappreciated. I make her feel pretty, she says. It's something she needs. And I love giving her what she needs. I lie there for a bit, half gazing at her, half trying to remember last night. In a minute, she'll feel my stare, and turn around. I'll know then if I've done something awful. There's nothing specific in my mind, which is good. Maybe I was just asleep when she came in. Properly asleep, tucked up in bed. With the dogs given their treats and locked in the kitchen, and everything tidied up. The other asleep has happened a couple of times in the last few months. Once before we'd left Hackney, which pretty much ended us. And another time a few weeks back, which was another final straw, but I'm still here. The other asleep involves her coming in to find me passed out on the couch or bed in an alcoholic stupor, smelling of cigarettes and surrounded by empty cans. I surreptitiously sniff at my fingers under the duvet. No fags, just a soapy smell. A good sign.

"Oh, hello."

Her tone in the morning is never particularly pleasant. It's understandable, as she's usually gearing herself up for the 90-minute commute on a packed tube, and her boyfriend is lazing in bed, with another day of doing nothing ahead of him. I do try to wake up with her, to get up with her. Anything to diffuse it. But, whatever I do, she gets used to it in time, and I have to think of another way to move the goalposts. She doesn't seem particularly angry with me. I got lucky. I wondered should I talk to her. Sometimes, in the morning, I start conversations with her in my usual (what I used to consider likeable) way, spitting out sentences at an alarming rate, tangenting from one topic to another, and forget that she doesn't like listening to me at length. Especially when she is doing something else, which is almost all the time. She can't cook or prepare food while I talk to her, or even push a shopping trolley and pick out the groceries. Whatever the other action is, the only constant is that my nattering is secondary to it, and can be done without. She's been very vocal about not wanting me to be too vocal, from the very first day. In the car, after we'd met at Stratford, one of the first whole sentences she said to me was:

"Do you always talk this much?"

It cut me in two, far more than it ever should have, which is another example of the trust thing. We started as neither of us meant to go on, and yet somehow we managed to do just that.

"Morning."

I say it in the cheeriest, most enthusiastic tone I can manage. That's another tactic, to fight the apathy and the resentment with relentless, cheerful optimism. If I'm kind and nice to her, she can't possibly stay cross at me. That's the plan. She doesn't reply. She doesn't have to. Hers is the greeting, mine is the response. I slide out of bed, my head feeling like it's been cracked with an axe at some point during my sleep.

"Dogs fed?"

It is just an innocent question. I don't expect her to have sorted them out. That's my job. Still, she looks at me like I've asked her to sacrifice her first born.

"Err, no. Haven't really got the time, you know?"

Her face goes instantly red, and her eyes flash with anger. She's always like this – seconds away from exploding with suppressed rage at me. Life is a series of eggshells with us.

"Oh I know, yeah. Just checking like, in case I feed them twice!"

I say it in my nicest voice, with all manner of forelock-tugging humility. It doesn't even crack the surface of her annoyance. She turns back to the mirror, and I just about lip-read her say a single word, as the sound of her hairdryer drowns out all other noise in the room.

"Whatever."

She's gone, the usual goodbye kiss that lasts too long for her, and not long enough for me. Toast is ready. Buttered on a plate, like she taught me. The dogs look sleepy as usual, they might get a walk. I always lay the leashes out somewhere to make it look like I have, which is like anything in the relationship – the apparent messiness will piss her off, but it's my proof that I've done something, even if I haven't. There are so many unspoken white lies, which is ridiculous, as I'd never tell a proper lie to her. I tell myself that they're different; that she forces my hand with them. It isn't the dogs' fault. They deserve their little walks, it's just that it's a thing I'm supposed to do, and doing those things feels against my nature on days like this. And every day is a day like this now. Routine is everything to me, and not in a good way. If I had the nous to change things up every once in a while, it would probably kick start my motivation; but to do that takes motivation itself, ironically enough, and I don't have any.

So every day is the same series of actions, inaction, and doing nothing. The laptop comes out, the internet goes on. The manuscripts in the Documents folder sit there unopened, and the hours pass too quickly, as I write constantly; not novels or blogs or short stories. Just a series of pithy comments on the pages of people I know but have never met. My adoring public, who would happily have me not comment at all, if it meant that I finished another book for them to read and heap lavish praise on, none of which I'm ever sure is sincere, but I take, anyway. If I counted up all those keystrokes, day to day, and converted them into something productive, I'd have more books on the shelf than Stephen King and Dean Koontz combined. But then that would be the smart thing to do, and intelligent as I supposedly am, I never make clever choices.

I've overdone it on the toast. Three lots, and now my stomach's full of stodge and buttery fat. I've already smoked half a pack too, and it's barely eleven. Where the last two hours went is anyone's guess, but I've nothing to show for them. One of the dogs comes into the living room, probably looking to go for a walk, but I don't even look at her. I'm planted, there's no way I'm moving for anything or anyone, unless it's to go get some more booze. I definitely did it right the night before. No angry texts or emails since she left, and there would have been. It wasn't any sort of good work on my part; I just went into autopilot mode at the point of extreme drunkenness, and took myself off to bed. A lucky escape, again. The noises from my gut and the general feeling of being hung over are telling me that a repeat wouldn't be a good idea. But the day feels long and slow, and the sunshine in the garden is telling me that I only live once, and I should be enjoying myself. There was a rush on one of my books a few months before, so I've had a bit of a payday. That's something I kept from her, of course. My drink fund is more important than her approval. I throw half of the shite amount of tax credits I get every week into a kitty for food and groceries, with her making up the other half. It's the only contribution I make, but it isn't as if I can afford any more. I know it isn't enough for her, though. And I know that she's always thinking about how things might have been with the imaginary other husband; the one with the proper job, and enough money to chip in for the mortgage and the bills. The one who comes with her on those trips abroad which never seem to broaden her mind in the way people say. The one who doesn't have any kids, and is 100% committed to having some with her, so they can stumble idiotically into the adventure of parenthood together.

All of that's extra annoying cos this is the one relationship I've ever been in where I think that they're enough for me. Where I never wonder what I'm missing out on, or what else is out there. It might be the sex, or the chemistry, or how great she looks. I can't think of anything else it could be. Worrying, but not surprising. I can't remember what sex was like before her. Although, when we had that five months apart, I rebounded my way across London on the back of a decent internet dating profile, and had sex with a lot more women, a lot more times, than I ever let on to her afterwards. When our thing ended, I was still confident. She hadn't left me for someone else; she hadn't stopped wanting me. All the time we are apart, though we never met each other, we'd still flirt and talk about sex, and how we missed it with each other. It was one of those chats that made us have a weekend fling, for old times' sake, and we ended up back together.

My time off from her was half heart-breaking and half brilliant. I was picking and choosing women off the internet, in a way I'd never done in real life. Tiny ones, poly ones, ones who were heavy into kink, and not looking for anything serious. But the second I kissed her again, I was back to thinking 'You're enough for me'. That's how ridiculous the chemistry is. It just disappears when we're not in bed. Especially when she goes away. The holidays she takes (on her own, cos I can't afford to come, of course) are stressful, cos I know that the addiction she has to me wears off when I'm not around her, physically. She comes home distant, and I know 'a talk' is on its way. The only difference is Christmas, when she visits her parents and brother back home. She comes back from those trips nicer and more grateful, cos a week of passive-aggressive sniping and put-downs always brings home to her just how loved and looked after she is here. It's a nice feeling, but it doesn't last. Once the holidays are done, we're back in the real word, and the shit starts again.

I've finished the coffee for the day (a whole pot to myself), and moved on to cans of generic Red Bull that cost a few pence in the shop. Caffeine is like anything else – I don't understand moderation. There's no doubt it contributes to the depression, but that doesn't make it easier for me to quit it. I go to sleep at night with the best of intentions and plans, but when I wake up, I just go back to doing bad things. I tell myself the self-destructive thing comes from being artistic, like the rock star doing smack and a bottle of Jack, but I'm not a rock star. I'm barely a writer. Writers have to write. I'm not sleeping right, either. In the old days, it was easy. We'd have great sex, long chats, and I'd drift off, happy. She put the kibosh on weekday shags a while back though, cos it tires her out, and weekend sex only happens if the fights don't happen. Or if they're big enough fights that they need make-up sex after. It's shitty, cos it's the only thing we are good at together, and the less we do it, the more distant she gets. And it has to be real. Whenever I feel she's doing it out of duty or pity, I read her straight away and stop it. It's like, even in the middle of sex, I can't turn down the chance of an argument.

Now, we brush our teeth, get under the duvet, and, for about 30 minutes, everything's good again; even though there's no chance of a shag. That's fine with me. It's still my only chance to feel liked by her. I'm used to managing my expectations by now. When she's going to sleep, I pop in some earphones and listen to whatever podcast I've become addicted to that week. Unless there's a sugar craving that gets me up for a biscuit or some juice, I drift off after a few hours and have dreams that are better than my life. Then I wake up, watch her get dressed, and try not to start another fight.

MS Word isn't open yet. It's that much of a struggle to do something that's supposed to come naturally; the only thing I've ever felt comfortable having as my job. Procrastination is everything these days. I know from experience that once I start typing I'm in it for the long haul, and have to drag myself away from the keyboard around five, to start dinner. But every day, I go back to thinking I can't do it, and it's a nightmare trying to tell myself I'm good at it. I've always wanted to be a writer. Right from school, when I wanted to be a journalist, before the cynicism for just about everything set in. I can never pinpoint exactly when that was, and it's probably when I started having depression; but at some point I became a pessimist about everything. Life, working, university: all the things that normal people just do. Younger me decided it was all a crock of shit, and that he wasn't going to be any part of it. Of course, I didn't have any other plans, but that didn't matter. From the outside looking in, not working, partying hard, drink, drugs, and women, looks like a lot of fun. But I've never been anything better than miserable, save for a few times when I discovered MDMA, or met a girl to obsess about, or pretty much anything involving my kid. Those are always just spikes though, and everything else has been lows. There has never been a middle. I've become good at hiding the highs and lows, especially from her. One of the reasons I need to keep on with the cigarettes, the drugs, the secret drinking, is that I'm afraid if I ever stop for long enough to take stock of my life, I'll end up throwing myself under a train.

The internet is as boring and exciting as it always is. I'm always around 50% of everyone's newsfeed. I don't know if I thrive on the attention or hate it, but I can't live without it. It's counter-productive, I know. Most of my 'friends' are people I've never met in real life. They come and go too, often without any explanation. Sometimes it hurts, but you can't ever show it. I never chase them up and ask why; something in my stomach tells me I mightn't want to know. I go online while off my face a lot. Never a great idea. I always wake up shitting myself, and deleting posts, or comments on other people's posts, where I've been acting like a lunatic or a shithead. Sometimes I'm just being cheeky or rude, but if someone starts an argument with me while I'm pissed, the anger comes out of nowhere, and I can say some nasty shit. Usually the shame is so much I just block whoever it was, and lie low for a while, hoping no one brings it up again.

There's an email from her. That's surprising, cos work is where she gets away from me. I used to text her about nothing during the day, just to talk, but after I while I realised it made her hate me. The note is short and there's no smiley faces or kisses. That's how she is at work, I'm used to it.

"Hi. Listen, there's an off licence on the way to the station, the little red place. They're looking for staff. Why don't you pop in today, when you get a minute?"

I feel the doom. Things like this break into my bubble of bullshit. Real life things: decisions, actions, plans. I want to work. I worked in the past; it isn't that much of a nightmare. The last proper job I had was years ago now, and a bad experience. I went from knowing all the ropes in one place to being one of the new guys in another, and never got to grips with it. The longer I stayed, the less patience my bosses had with me, and I cracked under the pressure. I handed in my notice in the middle of a recession, with nothing else lined up. My confidence was shattered, and I doubted everything about myself. Now, when anything is available, my only thoughts are on how I can get out of it. The application form, the phone call back, the interview. Again, it's nonsense. I'm great at filling out forms, fine on the phone, I do fantastic in interviews. But the part of my brain that knows this stuff isn't as loud as the part that tells me 'No', or 'Run away'. One's based on facts and experience, and the other is irrational bollocks, but that doesn't make a difference.

I have to do something. I have to go down there. I'm panicking. I want a drink. I don't know what I'm afraid of, just that it's right to be afraid, and anything would be better than doing what I'm supposed to. I think about all the things that make me scared. Meeting new people, learning new skills, pressure, and responsibility. I need a fag. It'll be all right; it'll be fine. How hard can it be? People work in shops all the time. People much stupider than me. That's part of the problem, though. I didn't go to university after school. I put it off for a year.

Then one year became two, and so on. Eventually I ended up on some art course for dole people in Ireland, then a UK poly. I left after a year, cos I got someone pregnant, and I needed to get a full-time job. So, I've got a smart person's brain and a stupid person's qualifications. My jobs have all been unskilled, and around people who have that Dunning-Kruger Effect thing of thinking that they're smarter than clever people. People like me, they tell me, are very intelligent, but we have 'no common sense'. Ridiculous, obviously, but if you hear it enough, you start believing it. Doesn't matter that I've no interest in common sense, or that having it doesn't sound like something I'd want. Bit by bit, being around those people and their comments makes me think I'm a freak. A freak that can't fit in, or do simple things, in the normal world. After a few years of no job, I started writing again. Not just the blogs I'd been messing around with, an actual book. I showed bits of it to the internet friends, and the feedback was good. That novel never happened, but it set me off. What mattered was, I'd found something I could do, something that was me. And I was good at getting it done. The fact that I'd given up the booze and the fags around that time probably had a lot to do with it. But it was meeting her that gave me the push to take ideas and half-ideas, and turn them into an actual story. Though I look back at it now and see it was basically bullying from someone who was appalled that I didn't do something to make money, at the time it felt like real support. Perspective is everything.

I'm not ready. The caffeine isn't helping. Instead of spurring me on, it makes me into a ball of anxiety. My nerves are jittering, the sentences in my brain are all jumbled up and making no sense. This is probably why I drink, a way to stop all the up feelings, which aren't up feelings at all. Well, not good feelings. Alcohol is a downer, even though it doesn't feel like one. The job is there, down in that offie. She's coming home at some point, questions will be asked. Everything else is up for discussion, if the insane shit going on between all the different parts of my brain can ever be described as a discussion. It's more like an angry debate in the United Nations, on a day when all the translators call in sick. They say that when you're insane, you don't know you're insane, so thinking you are is proof that you're not. I'm not sure about that. I've thought about it all my life. *A fine line between genius and insanity*, but I'm not clever enough to get near that line. That said, I mightn't be able to see it, cos it's behind me. I used to take tablets, but I'm *better* now. It's past midday. There's hours left, unless she decides to mail me again for an update. If I have a small drink, it will calm the nerves. The gin is probably good for another few shots, and if not, I can top it up with water. No, that's stupid, she'd probably notice that. I know after a few of them I'll think differently, though. I'm not as smart when I'm drunk.

I go to the cupboard and look through the bottles. A little of everything will make enough of a drink. No one will miss a little of everything. I take a glass and pour about a shot of Gordon's. There's some Russian Standard vodka that neither of us drink, that'll do too. Another full shot. Pimm's is weak, and she drinks it in the summer time, so that's okay too. A bottle of tequila someone brought to her birthday the year before. Or was it just a random party? I can't remember. It's open, so some goes in the glass. You drink it neat, so topping it back up isn't an option. I take a sniff of the cocktail, and almost bring up the toast from my gut. It needs something to mix, or I'll vomit it straight out again. M&S Apple and Mango from the fridge. Perfect.

I try sipping it, but the taste is too bad. Down in one, immediately regretting it. My nostrils are full of the rankness. I push the glass doors to the garden open and spark up a fag. The sun is harsh on the grass. *Mad dogs and Englishmen*. There's no plan. There's never a plan, just the medicine, and the consequences. The panic hasn't gone yet. It mightn't go at all. I can go from anxiety to fake euphoria quite quickly, without so much as touching the ground in between. The drink won't hit me for at least a half hour. I need to chase it in the meantime. The dogs are inside; I can go out the side gate. The passage by the gable end of the house is in shade, so when I pull the bolt and step out into the front, it feels like being a dark room, and coming out into the light. A little wobble as I walk, or did I just imagine it? My shoulders start to feel relaxed, like invisible hands are giving them a massage, and I autopilot my way down to the shop that never closes. When we moved, I said to her that an off licence that sold booze 24 hours a day would be 'great for parties', but I was probably thinking of the parties I'd have with myself. No matter how close a relationship I have with anyone else, the one between me and getting hammered is always number one. Nothing can come between us. Inside the offie, it's shady again, save for the light from the drinks fridge, which bathes me and the other daytime alkies in an almost heavenly glow. Glancing side to side at their ruined faces, I know that most of us are in Hell. This isn't the place where the job is. I'd never apply for a job in here. They wouldn't leave me alone with the merchandise. I get a can of Union Black and another of something weaker. I kid myself that I'm being responsible. What annoys me the most is that the less alcoholic one costs twenty pence more than the proper rocket fuel. Doesn't make sense to the part of me that wants to get wrecked, but it's probably down to how poor the quality of the strong stuff is, and how less of a headache the other one gives you. The guy at the till says nothing much as usual, and I check my change as I walk out into the sun.

It occurs to me to pass by the place on the way back; not that it's on the way back. No, in a bit. That's what I tell myself. A few ciggies, a little drink. I bought two cans of the strong stuff, and two of the not so strong. Somewhere in the middle of those, the courage will come. Or the smartness to think of something good that'll get me out of it. If I go too far along though, the moment will pass, then all the ideas I have will feel smart, despite being idiotic, and I'll be on the way to a major bust-up with her.

The liquor from the bad cocktail isn't in my brain yet, so I choose the hard stuff to start with. The laptop's playing a movie; some recent download of a sequel which isn't supposed to be any good, but I'm finding it hilarious, so something must be working, liquor-wise. I'm flicking between the player and my Facebook page, banging out little updates about the film. I'll see them later or the next day and not remember writing them, or people's replies, but that's standard. The dogs are up on the leather couch with me. That isn't against her rules, surprisingly enough. She makes far more exceptions for them than she ever does for me. They give her less stress, she says. Even though I've never pissed or shit on the kitchen tiles. Not yet, anyway. Touch wood.

Still sunny outside, but I sink into the leather of the couch, with the dogs across me. I'll get up to go for a cigarette, but that's about it. I've never smoked in either of her houses. There's no way. She'd smell it, even if it was weeks later. I get brave when I'm drunk; stupid too. Never that brave or stupid, though. Sometimes I fantasise about the day I leave her. Waiting until she goes to work, then getting pissed up and smoking in every room. Stubbing out fags on the kitchen work tops, the antique chairs, the expensive duvet covers. But I'm never going to leave her; and anyway, I don't hate her. Maybe sometimes, in a moment, but never all the time. I love her, that's always my first thought about her. Not that I'm sad, or badly treated, or oppressed, or wronged. Just that I love her, and I miss her when she isn't here, and that I love it when she's happy.

An hour and three cans later, I'm high as a kite. I could probably go down now and talk to them about the job. But, balls to her. Why should I? I don't know what I'm thinking. I feel myself rising from the couch without my brain directing me to; upwards in a diagonal way. Momentum coming from somewhere. I stumble a bit, smashing my knee against the old trunk in the middle of the room that she uses as a table. She's rearranged the front room three times since we'd moved in. She isn't finished, either. If we had any blind friends, they'd have killed themselves falling over things by now. I'm outside the shut door before I remember to check if I've got the key. A minute of panic, checking pockets, before I find it in the first one I looked. Somewhere in my head, a conversation is happening; an argument. I can go down now, it'll be fine. No, it won't. I'm drunk; I'll make an idiot of myself. I'm not drunk. It doesn't matter. It does. She'll be cross. Bleh, screw her, who is she, anyway? Plenty of time. Go somewhere. Do something. One more cigarette.

Past the bins again, a little fear comes over me about how I've left the place, and I almost go back. There are empty cans on the trunk, a full one still in the crisper. She won't be back, though. She never comes back. I can't remember properly. There's a chance she will, but I can't think of why. Home, feeling sick? She wasn't ill this morning. Who knew, though? Anything is possible. I'm going in the wrong direction for the job. Down into town, well the centre of this town. I never know how to phrase it, since living in London. People who live near the capital always call it 'Town', even though they live in other towns themselves. 'I'm heading into town', means you're going to London. If you're just going down the shops, say, in Dartford, then you say 'I'm going into Dartford'. Confusing. Leytonstone is technically in London, it's a borough, not a town. But every borough is like its own town, especially if you come from outside the city. I'm rambling to myself now, cheque's in the post.

I pass the old Victorian fire station; it seems to be still going, and the police station, which doesn't. The shops on the way are all either fried chicken places or greengrocers; large ethnic population. Scattered here and there though, are some new coffee shops and bakeries, a sign of a place on the up, she says. That's her thing; buying somewhere in an up and coming area, then selling after the place gets all gentrified and the house prices go up. Hackney's become too expensive to get a two bedroom flat, in the two years we were there, so she went east, selling the one bed for a hundred grand profit. She's smart like that, and I do my best to make her think I gave a shit about it. I don't. Property, money, all that rat race malarkey doesn't mean at thing to me. Bores me at best, makes me feel sick otherwise. She hates that – me not being interested in money. Her point is that it's only cos she has the job and pays the bills and owns the house that I can afford to be like that about money. And maybe she has a point. But, as I've pointed out to her a million times, if I wasn't around, she wouldn't be paying any more or less. And no one would be cooking her dinner, looking after her bloody dogs, or any of the other things I do which save her money. I'm not costing her anything, I'm just not contributing in the way her imaginary ideal guy would, so her fight isn't with me, it's with herself, for bagging such a loser. It's a logical argument, and you can't have those with someone you love. I'm by Sainsbury's already. I wander in, for no reason in particular. Fresh food, veg, bread. Nice smells. I see some bargain stuff. I always pick up whatever's going cheap. I usually figure out something to do with it later. I used to pick up random stuff, just cos it was on offer, but she'd got me out of that habit. *We don't need it, so how is it a bargain?* Unless it's a dessert; there's always room for that. Either in the freezer or her stomach.

They have little bottles of wine. It's hot out, white wine would be better, but they aren't in the fridge, so red it is. Room temperature red on a hot day isn't refreshing, but it's 13.5%, so it'll do the trick. I can chug it in the street too, it'll only take half a minute to down. I've gone through all sorts of mini liquor in the past few months. MD 20/20, Cherry B, some weird tonic wine shit designed to give black men stronger erections. Didn't work on me, but I can't complain to the ombudsman about it. Not unless I can become black in the meantime. Outside, I open and neck it, not caring who sees. People drink on the street all the time in East London. Not decent people or anything, but enough of them that I won't be the only one. Even though it's boiling outside, I get that familiar warm feeling as it goes down. I gag a bit, cos red isn't for gulping, but it's already in the bin by the time I've get to the end of the street near the Tube. I shudder. I met *her* here, a week back. She'd gone to work and I'd gone down town. There'd been a problem with the trains, and she had to get off again. I was just wandering under the subway, smoking. I'd just stubbed one out, so she hadn't seen. But she was there, suddenly, in my face, and I panicked. I thought she was going to sniff me out, or try to hug me. But she just smiled awkwardly and said hello. I gave her a funny look, feeling my face go red, and told her I had to go. My hands were shaking for a couple of minutes after. It shouldn't be that way between us, but it is.

Some guy with dreads makes eye contact and starts towards me, some spiel at the ready, looking for spare change, or a specific amount. I can't tell, I don't listen. Beggars and charity collectors give me anxiety. If I've had a few I'm able to just charge past them, or even say something smartarsed. But straight, I don't have the balls to say anything. The phone comes out, hopefully already on silent. Nothing worse than pretending to be on a call and have it ring while they're watching you. Life is full of small panics like that, well mine is. Like when you're in the queue at the supermarket and there's no dividers. Watching my little pile of stuff like a hawk, in case the person in front of me accidentally ends up paying for something of mine. Using a hand to hold them down, just in case.

I don't know Leytonstone yet, except for this little part, and the walk from the house to there and back. There's 99p Store and a Poundland, a Sainsbury's and an Iceland, a Boots, and lots of newsagents. London's full of them, sometimes two or three on one stretch of road, never seeming to be in competition with each other to the point that one struggles. They all sell fresh fruit and veg for cheap, booze for similar, and anything else you can think of. In Hackney, our local one on the corner was where I could get pretty much anything. And if I stood in there looking confused long enough, the guy(s) would ask me what I was looking for, and refuse to let me leave until he found it for me. I miss that place. I haven't built up a rapport with any of the shop guys in the new place. There's one on the corner before you get to the big blue one, and that guy has been nice to us both from the first day we came to look around at houses in the street. But I've been in there plenty of times where I'm in the queue, and found out that he's like that with everyone. Good business sense. That shop is strange. No booze and no bacon. Normal Muslim shopkeepers never seem to be religious about their stock – most of them sell the Lottery, or porn mags. This place is all *Hal Al*, no *Haram*, and as everyone knows, that makes Jack a dull boy. Pain the arse if you just want to get pissed, or recover from being pissed, with a nice bacon sarnie. None of them sold good bread either. Just pan after pan of shitty, sugary white.

Some people are eating lunch in the park across the road. I look up and notice that it's the grounds of a big church. I never look up when I'm walking around anywhere, so I miss out on half a city. All the places where people go to live, above shop level, in their poky little flats. It was the same when I lived in Limerick – I never looked up if the point of interest – the shop front or whatever – ended at the first storey. If there's no break, like in a cathedral maybe, my eyes would follow all the way up the spire. It's a habit I picked up somewhere, maybe from being very shy when I was younger. Eyes to the floor and all that. And from visiting a new place, like Dublin, where you know that if you go around looking up at things all the time, you'll stick out like the tourist you are, and someone'll mug you. I don't know where I picked up that idea, but it's stuck, regardless. I'm still on the same stretch of road; I've gone up and down it a few times, still stalling. Still waiting for some magical sign from above that I'm ready. Ready for what, I don't know. I step into a newsagent's, to get something to drink. A can of pop, maybe. I have about a fiver. There's a normal fridge and a booze fridge. The one with the Lilts and the Cokes isn't working. With the door closed, things in there are worse than tepid. They're nearly hot. I open the other one, and touch a can of Polish beer. It's icy; another sign from above, probably. I pick the *Desperado*. Not in a beer mood, but it's colourful enough to look like an energy drink, so I can have it in the street. Waiting in line, I think about getting a scratch card. I'm not winning on those, in the grand scheme of things, but that doesn't matter. It's only the one you're scratching now that counts. I get one, and take it outside with the beer.

There's a ritual to the scratch card. I always have to use the coin with the biggest denomination in my pocket to scratch it. That adds power. And the order I scratch the boxes is important too. Sometimes, before I start, I scrape something lightly into the silver. Either some initials that spell out a phrase like 'It is my will to win this today', or my own initials. Or a symbol. The symbol can be made up of the initials too, that helps it fit. I read about Sigil Magic before. You take a phrase, and it has to start with 'It is my will', that bit is important. Then you write it down. You get rid of all the letters that repeat, until you're left with individual characters. Then you make a symbol out of them, it doesn't matter if they're the same size in the symbol, or if they're upper case or lower case. The trick is to make it look magic. Once you have your symbol, you have to charge it with energy. You can do that by thinking of something extremely happy, or sad, or by putting sexual energy in it. Have a wank, basically; or put it under a mattress where you have sex. After that, the two schools of thought are in direct opposition. One says you should keep the symbol, or reproduce it lots of times, and put them somewhere not in direct sight, but where they'll be seen subliminally; the more of them the better, for the chance of your wish coming true. The other lot say you should destroy it. It's all bullshit, regardless. But it doesn't hurt to try. Sometimes I pray too, not to God, more to people I've lost from my life. If they've died recently, that's even better, cos maybe they're still hanging around in the ether, waiting to be called to heaven or hell. Like Patrick Swayze in Ghost. Or Patrick Swayze in real life. I don't bloody win, anyway. The Desperado tastes like piss, but at least it's cold piss.

The thing is always inside me, not even that deep down. I want to be free of it, but I can't anymore. I was okay, and clean, and sober once. I didn't smoke, or drink, or eat sugary foods, or do anything. I wasn't that healthy, then. I didn't exercise. I went on a lot of walks, so that ended up losing me weight and things. I felt less bloated and out of breath, but I wouldn't have taken my shirt off in the park or anything. People have said they liked my body before, but it's just my body. I haven't done any work to achieve it. I've never been to a gym. So it's just me. Broad shoulders, small waist; genetically lucky, I know that much. For some people, they can put in all the work they want in the gym and still just end up a less fat, musclier version of themselves. It's still not pretty to look at. If I did some weights and exercise, I'd probably look amazing, although I'll never be tall. I don't, though. That time with the no drinking or smoking or junk food – that was enough effort for me. The walking wasn't deliberate either, it was just something to do instead of having a fag, and I used to think a lot too, so when I got back home, I'd write. That was when I first thought seriously about writing novels.

When I met Emma, I'd said I was a writer. I wasn't doing anything else for a job, so that's what I was. I didn't know about self-publishing, or Kindles, or any of that. So it was still a case of writing something, getting an agent, getting published. Especially in her head, cos she worked in the industry, and she told me that's how it worked. She asked to see some stuff, in those early emails, before I'd met her. That was our first falling out. Me, used to utter praise and gushing from my pretend internet friends. Her, on the spot, thinking I wanted some intelligent and constructive critique. I didn't. She doesn't write novels, or have anything to do with them in her job. She works in non-fiction. But she still gave me a review, and I took it with all the oversensitivity and hurt that was going to become the norm in our future relationship. She was immediately sorry, once she saw my reaction. I managed to smooth it over, pretending I'd just been joking, and that it was fine, and that she had some good points. She didn't. She never has good points about my writing. She hasn't a bloody clue. She's just used to telling people how to do things, and doesn't realise that she employs them to pretend that she's right. Her bookshelves are full of the original prints of books that went onto be movies, so she definitely knows what sells. But I don't think that's a professional skill. I think she's just a pleb, and plebs buy books like those ones. She's not stupid, but you don't have to be stupid to be a pleb.

I thought the other thing had gone away, when I met Emma. When I found love. The thing from before. I thought I'd kicked it as much as I'd kicked the booze and the fags. But some feelings are just inherently you, and you'll never get away from them, until you die. I always think of myself as a good person, but everyone probably does. It's harder to deal with the idea that you're bad, that you're rotten inside. Cos you have to live with you, and be alone with you, and you have to present you to the rest of the world, and act like you're normal, and that everything is okay. I'm not normal though, and I'm definitely not okay.

A pretty girl goes past on her own, looking a bit lost. She might be foreign, but then everyone's foreign in London; including me. She has a Day-Glo orange t-shirt on, they must be back in fashion. Reminds me of the 90s, and being a teenager, and those feelings I had when I saw some gorgeous girl. The hint of her bra under a tight t-shirt, full of things I'd never touched, and never thought I would, with my ugly face, and dirty acne and blackheads. They'd wear cycling shorts too, even though they weren't on bikes. It was almost painful to look at them, with their young womanly bodies under the Lycra, showing off everything to me, stuff I'd never have. I couldn't even speak to girls; it was like I was an open sore. And not just the spots. My personality was so shy and weak and almost feminine, compared to the boys around me in that estate. Even when I went to secondary school, where the boys were posher and less blokey, I was still just nothing. If they talked about girls and what they'd done, I'd feel myself going red, burning, hoping the conversation never came around to me, cos I wouldn't have been able to even fake it, or lie. I'd never had those moments with a girl, with any girl. Even though girls were all I thought about, for as long as I could remember.

When I was about five years old, I'd fantasise about girls in my class; dreaming up mad scenarios where I was an Indiana Jones type guy, saving them from snakes, and big rolling boulders. It was so elaborate, and the emotions were so strong that I can still remember them now. I wanted so much to have someone, years before it was even normal to do that. And then when it was normal, I wanted it even more, but no one seemed to want me. I'd have been too scared, anyway. Always too self-aware. How do you kiss someone for the first time, when you don't know how to kiss? They'd know, and they'd laugh, or they wouldn't laugh, but they'd tell their friends later, and then you'd be pointed at, and everyone would know what a loser you were. I couldn't bring myself to do it, to get up and dance with someone at one of those painful local discos. The kids in my estate were rampant by the time we were about eleven, but I wasn't involved in any of it. I hung around with boys who were still into throwing rocks and making lead soldiers. We'd talk about girls, but I don't think any of us had done anything yet. Me and one boy called Niall, we obsessed about particular girls. We'd have favourites, and follow them around. They probably knew too, it was too much of a coincidence for them to be constantly running into us all the time. We were creepy little stalkers, but we didn't know what else to do. I'd go to bed at night imagining impossible scenes, where the girls found it all flattering, and they'd been obsessing over us too, they just didn't know how to make the first move. In those mad moments before I drifted off, everything was clear, and we all knew what to do, and I got to kiss the girl at last. And I was good at it too, cos it wasn't real. And no one laughed at me. And everything was great.

The girl in the orange top doesn't know I'm following her. And I'm not following her. She's just in front of me, and her being on front of me is nice, so I keep walking to where she's walking. I'm not a clueless eleven-year-old now, or a spotty kissless teen. I could have her. That's what I tell myself. Cos I'm drunk. In reality, I'm still the kid at five making up Indiana Jones stories, I'm still ugly and spotty; I still can't talk to girls. I'm all those people at the same time, cos they were all me. You don't ever change; you just add new layers over the old ones. She turns down to the left, and so do I. She has great legs. Smooth and olive coloured. Great calves. I can tell she's young, or she's never been out of shape or had a kid. You can see it in how the cheeks of her arse poke out from the tiny denim shorts. The bit where the bum becomes the leg, it's springy, no fatty deposits. You could put a pencil there and it would drop straight to the ground.

There's tiny drops of moisture on the backs of her thighs, and the sun makes them look like glitter. I think about her lying on her front, while I use my thumbs to massage her, deep into the tissue. I'm good at that. She'd probably like it. This is madness; I haven't even seen her face. She has long dark hair. It's a trigger to me, this sort of look on a girl. There was one in particular, when I was eleven. She looked like Jennifer Connelly, who I was in love with at the time, and probably still am. Her name was Amanda. I'm probably still in love with her too. I never knew her. It was this one summer. We were at a thing at the same time. It wasn't a camp, we went back home every day, it was just a scheme where the kids got taken off the parents' hands during the day, from Monday to Saturday, for four weeks. I went every year. She had been new though. She was from up the road, but she might have just moved there that summer, cos I'd never seen her until then. She was perfect, that summer. I'd never seen anyone in real life that looked like that. It was like she was from another planet. My friends knew I liked her, Niall especially. There were the usual winks and nudges. With anyone else, their friends might have gone ahead and asked her did she like me, and would she like to go for a walk with me or something. I would have died on the spot. It wasn't a question of will she or won't she. I knew I was nothing, and she was perfect. I knew there were boys around her, and she didn't know I existed. I knew I'd never have Amanda, and it was okay. I didn't want her. Well, I wanted her more than anything, but I didn't want her so much that I'd have risked finding out that she didn't want me. I was okay with what I had, which was just those four weeks of being able to look at her from far away. She made me feel hot and warm and happy and sad, all at the same time.

This girl isn't her, despite what my stupid drunken head wants to believe. She's some random, in a city with eight million people, and she's safe from me. She's just walking in the sun, and so am I, and if she turns somewhere I don't fancy heading myself, I'll keep on walking. I have stuff to do. Or stuff to avoid doing. She stops now, cos she's met someone she knows. Shaved head, stocky, foreign voice. Eastern European, he sounds Polish. Looks like a real man. Her body language changes now he's there. She leans into herself, one leg straight and the other bent. I go past them now, and take a peek at her face. Beautiful, but she's not as good as my Amanda was. No one ever is. She came back into my life again, in a weird way. Twice. When I wrote my first book, I named the main character's love interest after her, made her look like her, gave her the same name. Of course, he was me, so I got to finally be in love with her and stuff. And the other time, I was in secondary school, and a guy I knew started going out with her. He was my pal, and we'd been talking about girls from where we were growing up (he was from near me, one of the only people in my posh school who was), and I'd mentioned her. A lot. I had had no idea what had happened to her or anything then, she was just this memory. Then, one September, he comes back to school with this big grin on his face, and tells me:

"Remember that Amanda Garvey girl you were going on about before? Guess who's going out with her?"

It cut me to the bone. It's ridiculous that it should have, but it did. And he went out with her for years. Until at least after we left school. I even met them once, out in a pub. I was mortified. He must have told her the story. I couldn't look at her, but I did of course. She was ten times more beautiful than I'd remembered, too. I'd have given anything to be him, even though by then I was all fixed, and getting girls of my own. But they weren't as good as her. No one was. I've swung back towards home again, thanks to orange t-shirt girl. There's another shop there. I need a drink.

Four

This year, Limerick, Orla

No matter who you go out with, the relationship is the same, sometimes. That's cos you're the one constant element. I notice that if I'm having the same problems with different girls, the problem is probably me. If I fix me, I fix everything. But I can never fix me completely. I can fix all the things no one is asking me to fix and then act like a martyr and want praise for them. But the other person doesn't care about those things. They're bonuses, at best. If they mattered, I wouldn't have to point out that I'd fixed them. No, me fixing those things is usually just over compensation for not being able to make the change that would make a real difference. And if they fixate on that difference, I take the stance that the problem isn't a problem; it's who I am, and they should love me for who I am. And that makes them feel guilty for a bit, but it never lasts. They still want it, I can't give it, and we end up drifting apart.

Every time I start something new, I think to myself that I'll do it differently this time; I'll learn from my mistakes. I'll get it right. But I'm still me, and I'm still the problem, so it doesn't matter. People don't want all the things I give them – all the little bonuses. They want simple things – to be comfortable, to have fun, to enjoy being with someone. I overcomplicate everything, and end up with nothing cos of it. Even though I always seem to have someone. I can get them, no problem. Making them stay has been the problem. I like getting a new one, though. Women are like the opposite of jobs with me. I enjoy the application process, the interview, sealing the deal. I like moving from one type to another. I enjoy the challenge, as people like to say when lying on their CVs. I only enjoy the challenge of getting the girl, though. The challenge of making the relationship work is no fun to me at all. I sometimes tell myself that I care too much, that I feel too much, that I'm too compassionate. All of that is nonsense. I don't care about them. I care about my own ego, and it being hurt, and the lack of control that comes with it. I care about being ignored, defied, and treated like a fool by someone who is clearly less intelligent than I am. I'm probably a misogynist, just like any other guy who tells you he 'loves women'. But it's hard not to be one, if you've ever been around women for any length of time. Even women would tell you that. Women hate women more than they hate men.

Ireland is already losing its sheen. I miss London. I don't miss her. I miss her dogs more than I miss her. It's unbelievable to me now that a few months ago I was wandering around Wood Green, pining for her like I wanted to die. And, the thing is, I knew at the time it was just a temporary thing. You always know it, when you've been through enough break ups. You know it, but it doesn't stop you thinking they're your one and only, and that this one's different, and that you'll never get over them. It's bullshit. You always get over them. There's always someone new. It just takes time, and that's the one thing you can't influence. There's always gonna be 24 hours in a day, and seven days in a week. You can't do anything about that. You just have to stick it out. Or get drunk a lot. I did both, and it worked out just fine.

I came here with the pretence of finishing a book. There were at least three on the go, and I could've finished any of them. I haven't opened them since I got here though. The block is strong. Or the lack of motivation. Or whatever it is that stops me. What it probably is, is that this is the one thing I'm good at. The one thing that can get me out of this mess; so, of course, my brain decides it's not going to play ball. For anyone else in my shitty situation – homeless, jobless, no CV worth looking at – it'd be suicide time. I have this gift though, apparently; a talent that can take me out of the gutter. I just refuse to use it. I have no idea why I'm like this. It's like I'm contrary against myself, and consistently so. I can't stop it, either. It's just one day after the other, and it never changes. It did change though, once before. Around the time I met Emma. When I was all clean living and healthy, and writing. I don't know what made that go away, but it must be that I started drinking again (to make things better with her), and I started smoking again (cos she'd broken my heart, in those five months we broke up, or that was my excuse anyway). So I have the convenience of being able to blame Emma for it all, which is much easier than pinpointing the real culprit, who's me.

I'm in the front room, glued to the laptop as usual. Dad's on his couch, simultaneously watching the soaps and a movie on YouTube. I *think* it's a movie. My sister is somewhere, upstairs probably. She doesn't come downstairs and sit with us. She's either talking on the phone, or locked away with her boyfriend. I've been to the offie already. It's only half eight, but they close at ten here, so I went over when I was out doing something else. No 24-hour drinking in this country, even if we're known the world over for being pissheads. I got four cans of strong cider, and a little bottle of vodka. I had some of that in some Coke at the start, so it didn't look like I was on the booze. I don't know if my dad would care, but she'll get upset about it, now she's trying to turn over a new leaf and be good. I won't get through most of it before I have to leave, but that's a good thing. I've got braver now, and am drinking the cider from a pint glass. I still take it down and put it under the table when I hear her moving about upstairs though. I feel like a naughty teenager, and not the good ones, from porn.

Orla is on my mind. She has been for days, since we met. I can talk to her, of course, through Facebook or whatever. That's the beauty of the 21st Century affair. There's less sneaking around. Less physical sneaking around, anyway. I suppose people still have to be discreet – not leaving their phones around, deleting texts, etc, but it's really come along. Even back in 2004 there was no real social media like we have now. Except maybe the MySpace/Bebo ones, but they weren't for grown-ups, like Facebook is. And back then, you'd still have to fire up the PC at whatever time, and have an excuse to be going on the internet, because you couldn't really get the internet on phones in a way that didn't make you half blind looking at it, or half murderous waiting for the pages to load. Now it's lightning fast infidelity. The modern marriage is probably doomed.

It's not really infidelity anyway; we haven't done anything at all. Not yet. We just met. It's the same amount of infidelity we got up to back then, which was none really either, but we both felt bad about it then as well. And neither of us would have been okay with people knowing about it. We'd do the most innocent things – just 'accidentally' bumping into each other at times we'd planned before, and sitting on walls, talking. We didn't even touch, really. Although I can probably remember every time we did, clear as crystal. How it made me feel, but again, that could have just been the wrongness of it. Or that buzz you get when you like someone and you haven't kissed them yet. It's hard to tell. But it's lasted this long, I can't deny that. The one that got away, yes. But maybe it's more.

She lives somewhere different now, because of course she does, she's a grown-up, like I should be. That's another thing fucking me up – the fact that I'm not just living back home, I'm living *back home*. Literally. In the house I was in as a kid. So of course it feels like a step backwards. I look at the clock on the laptop – I should get going soon. I've arranged to meet her – just for a few minutes. She's up at her mum's house, in the South Circular Road, where she used to live when I knew her back then. I remember walking to the Crescent Shopping Centre a few times just to *run into* her back then, when she'd have *just popped out* to the shops. It was just around the time phones could text, so we were able to time it fine. When she said, the other day, she'd be visiting her mother today, I'd come up with the plan. She'd laughed when I said it, cos she probably remembered the significance of the place. Then again, she mightn't have. I'm probably the only one being an obsessive lunatic over this thing – she just seems to find it… flattering. But if she wasn't interested, she wouldn't have come the other day. And she wouldn't be coming today either.

I don't say anything to my Dad when I go out the door. There's no point, he won't need the information. It's not like someone is gonna call looking for me when I'm out; I don't know anyone here anymore; and it's not like I'd want them to know where I'm going either. It's still bright out, and nice too. It's a long walk up there, so I've given it plenty of time. I have a fag, because it's something to do, and I'm – am I nervous? Nervous, excited, it's the same thing. I have chewing gums. Orla doesn't smoke. I'm not going to be kissing her – at least I don't think so; but I'm really self-conscious when people don't smoke. If you just hang around with smokers you at least get to be in that club where everyone pretends we don't stink, and no one argues about it. We do, though. How couldn't we?

I'm in town already, and I have to remember to turn off at Henry Street, because of where I'm headed. Everything's changed here now, and some things are still the same. The Franciscans is still standing, but it's not a monastery anymore. It's not an anything anymore. Across from it, the two chip shops we used to go to after clubs are called something else now. They used to be Friar Tuck's and The Lobster Pot. Now, you wouldn't recognise them. I go past the big Dunne's, that used to be Speight's, and the big Poundland/Dealz that used to be… Termights? I don't know anymore. The red church that sinks into its own foundations is offices now, even though it's still the original building on the outside. There's a Subway in Windmill Street now, I think there's three or four here altogether, and now I'm up at the church next to Clement's school. I think it's called the Redemptorist, but I'm not sure, cos there's so many churches, and I get them mixed up. I pass the bit where the girls from Laurel Hill used to come out after school, and I get a funny feeling in my stomach, about more than one girl from the past. And then I'm at Mary Immaculate, where everyone went to college back then – everyone I knew, anyway. Everyone I knew seemed to be doing an Arts Degree. Except me, obviously. I'm not far from where I'm supposed to meet her. It's gone really quickly. I'm early. I can have another fag or something. Or find a newsagent and get a drink. Not a real drink; they don't sell real drinks in corner shops over here. I'm tipsy enough already, anyway. I don't even know why I had those drinks before, but I never knew. If I knew, I might be able to figure out how to stop.

Meeting her the other day had gone like a dream. It only happened in the first place because I found her on Facebook (she'd been using her married name; I'd literally gone through every Orla in the city and just hoped she was still living here) and sent a message. I didn't add her. There are too many people from the past that are still linked to her who I don't want seeing me or finding me now. I wouldn't know where to begin if they started making small talk either. So I messaged her, and hoped she saw it, eventually, in her spam folder thing. And she did. Eventually. And we started talking – about two weeks ago, and then bit by bit, softly softly, I managed to get her to agree to meet. We only had about two hours, and it flew past like it was ten minutes. It always had with us, and apparently it still did. We got on. The conversation flowed, apart from a couple of bits where she mentioned the husband by accident, and it got awkward, but we moved on from it. He was just some guy; I didn't know him, he wasn't from the old days or anything. He was just some guy. Fuck him. I don't know him. And we haven't done anything wrong. Not yet, anyway.

I'm around the corner from the gate – it's not her mum's gate, it's a big house, by the bridge. God only knows who owns it. Mightn't even be the same owners as there were fifteen years ago, or whenever we last met there. It probably is, though – a place like that stays in a family for years, and the economy went to shit here a few years ago – it wasn't really a seller's market. Especially not for mansions. I don't even know if it's a mansion, anyway. You can't even see it through all the trees in the drive. I have 20 minutes, still. There's shops across the way – with a big Polish grocery place in the middle. It's not for Polish groceries, although they do have some in there; it's just a big shop, and the people who work in there all seem to be Polish. I go in there sometimes on my walks out to Patrickswell, when I'm trying to be good. Or when I'm trying to be bad, sometimes. They don't have a liquor licence, though. But there's an off licence in the complex too; I spot it when I cross over from the other side. I don't know this part of town. I think it's Ballinacurra, or Weston, or both of them. There's loads of Limerick I don't know, cos I never needed to know. All those shopping centres out of town, where we never went, cos we didn't have a car. The Parkway, Jetland, the Crescent, here – whenever people use them as a reference point for directions, I struggle. But we have Google Maps now, so it's cool. There's some kids with a bike outside the shops. I stare straight ahead and ignore them, cos I know in my head that Weston's probably a rough place, and whenever you see kids with bikes and there's a higher ratio of kids to bikes, it's usually a bad sign. That's true in London and Essex too. I've never been to Paris or Madrid, but it's probably the same as well there. Or maybe I'm just full of shit.

The off-licence door has a bell on it, and I hate that, cos it makes me feel I have to say hello to the guy when I come in, but it's okay today, cos I'm a little buzzed, and it's Ireland anyway, so everyone says hello to you, rather than the London thing where they just look at you and wonder is today the day they're going to be killed in an armed robbery. I feel odd about getting a can of Fanta in an off-licence, so I pick up a small can of Captain Morgan's with cola, and then I pick up another one, cos they're on offer if you buy two, and maybe Orla will want one. Fifteen minutes now. I go up towards the counter and then I feel funny just buying two cans, like a tramp. I do that thing you do when you slap your forehead – when you leave the house and you forgot something, and there's people watching, so you have to do a little act for them, so they'll know why you're about to turn around on the spot. As if they're even watching. As if they care. I go and pick up a four-pack of the same cans, cos there's plastic rings holding them together, and that seems more like I'm buying them for a social occasion – for someone other than just me. I'll ask for a bag too, make it seem like I'm a decent person, or something.

She's already there when I get to the place – even though I'm still five minutes early. I haven't opened one of the cans yet, cos there's four of them now, with plastic rings, so if I take out three of them, it'll look bad. I think so, anyway. She's got her back to me, so she can't see me. She's small – all over. She was probably the reason for my petite girl thing – that, and the fact that I'm a shortarse. Whatever it is, I love it about her. The sun's going down now. Or it went down ages ago, and the light from it is going. It's dusk, the lights are on going across the bridge, and I can see them shining through her hair. It's still the same shade of red it was the first time I met her, years ago. That, or she's found a dye the exact same colour. She was probably the cause of my redhead thing too, and my pale skin thing. She's been a big influence, clearly. She's wearing sort of yoga pants – they're black and tight, and she has a t-shirt on that's baby blue and fitted. Her arms are really thin, and pale, with no freckles. She's never had freckles. I'm about to say something, but she does first, without turning around.

"You remember this place?"

I even love the sound of her voice. I love how Irish it is to me, after all the time I've spent away, and all the time she hasn't. She's still looking out over the bridge. I don't think that bridge even existed back then. Or they've built a new one, since. I can't remember.

"How could I forget?" I'm centimetres away from her, but I don't reach out a hand to touch her. Feels like I mightn't be allowed to. Feels like I should wait for her to.

"You don't forget anything, though. You're like an expert on… well. Hello, by the way." She turns around and I feel the breath draining out of me, just looking at her. She puts her hand out to me, and I wonder if I'm supposed to shake it or something, but I just hold it for a bit too long, until she takes it back, and now I feel kind of naked, standing there.

"Yeah. Yeah, it's handy though." Now I'm feeling weird for having the bag in my hand. She makes me feel like an awkward teenager sometimes, and more comfortable than anything at other times. It's familiar. It's the one you get when you're falling for someone. But it's not like that's new. I've been falling for her forever, it seems like.

"Handy for?"

"Writing books." Being able to remember things, places, people, and feelings. I'd be lost without that. It's what makes it easy, sometimes, when it's easy. The other times, nothing makes it easy. And it's been that way for a long time now.

"You gonna write one about me, then?" She has the best smile, or smirk, or whatever it is she's doing now.

"Depends." I want to explain the bag now, cos she's looking at it. I want a fag too, but I don't as well, cos it'll smell rank, and I want her to think good things about me.

"Depends on what?" She moves closer to me, in a way. Her hips move across, so they're nearer to mine. With anyone else, it wouldn't even register, but with her it nearly feels intimate. Because I want her to be near me so much, I guess. It's all relative.

"Depends on if there's anything to write about." I don't know if I'm flirting. I never knew if I was, with her. Sometimes, if were in a pub, with people we knew, and I'd ended up sitting with her, I'd have to stop myself, because I'd feel people looking – people who knew Holly, or who knew her bloke, and I wondered if we looked too cosy. But it was never intentional – I didn't want anyone to find out how I felt about her. We just had the chemistry, though, so it looked like that even if we weren't trying.

"That sounds like a challenge." The smirk again, and a wink. She nods down at my hand. I forgot I'm holding the bag.

"Brought me a present?"

"What? Uh, yeah. Yeah, I suppose so. Captain Morgan?" I open the bag so she can look in.

"Ooh. Naughty. What are you, some sort of alko?"

"What? No! I just…" I panic, I don't know why. Probably because I am some sort of alko, though.

"Haha, I'm only messing, like. I've actually been having a few rum and Cokes round at Mum's, so you read my mind, really. You hero, you."

"Heh, you know me." I'm relieved now. I pull a can off the four pack and hand it to her. My fingers touch hers as I pass it over, and there's that feeling again that I can't really describe. My face is kind of hot, and my heart is loud, and we're literally just talking.

"Not as much as you know me, apparently. Sláinte." She's talking about the rum, but maybe she's talking about the rest of it too, I wonder. The other day I went into a fair bit of detail about how long I'd been looking for her, how much trouble I went to. I wondered did she think I was a bit mad. But she's here now, so I should probably stop wondering. The drink tastes nice – sort of chocolatey, but not really.

"We've never had a drink here, have we? How grown-up are we?" I want to sit down, but there isn't somewhere to. I'm sure there used to be. I have a picture in my head from a long time of me and her, sitting. Her flicking her hair while she's talking, me sneaking little looks down at the way her little arse would curve when she sat down. I can even see what she's wearing back then – navy cords and a Nirvana hoodie. But maybe my mind is mixing up two different times.

"Remember there was that concrete bit where you could sit here?" she asks, and I'm not even surprised that she's in my head, cos she's Orla, and she belongs in there. She's been there long enough. But now she's here in real life too.

"Hah, I was just thinking that. You still bad at squatting?" I'm remembering a time outside HMV, when it had been raining, and sills were too wet to sit on. Her legs kept going dead, and I had to hold onto her to stop her from toppling over when she stood up. God, that was a good day.

"Haha! I've got better, I think. Wanna try?" She slides her back down the iron of the gate until she's down; looking even tinier, and sort of vulnerable, even though that's not a word I'd usually use to describe her. I follow her lead and we're both nearer the ground. This feels better. Feels closer.

"So…" I say, cos we're in Limerick, and that's a whole sentence.

"Well?" she says, for the same reason. I look at her face and wonder what it is that makes it so special. Chris – probably the only friend of mine I've ever told how I feel about her – he asked me to explain it one night, when we were sloshed in some seaside pub in Dorset, and I got all nostalgic and started telling him about this girl from back home that I carried a crazy torch for. I found some photos of her on Facebook and gave him a gander. He thought she was hot and everything – most people did, I think, but he was a bit mystified as to how strong a thing I had for her. I couldn't explain it then, either. It wasn't some symmetrical perfection bullshit. It still isn't. She has flaws. They're just not flaws to me. If anything, they make me like her more. I could sit here swapping "So…"s and "Well?"s with her for the next hour and it would still be one of the best nights of my life. I wonder is it the same for her, but of course it isn't, because she's not a lunatic.

"Remember what you used to bring me? When we met here, I mean?"

"Was it 'sunshine'?" I say, but I know exactly what she means.

"Haha, no. I mean my little presents." I look at her face again. Whenever I used to meet her out on the town, I'd always think there was something really different about her, and then I'd notice that it was that she had make-up on, because most of the time she didn't – in the daytime, and the daytime was when I saw her the most. I asked her about it once, and she told me that she never went out without make-up, and that boys were silly sometimes.

"Ah yeah, the Tic-Tacs." They were her favourite. The green and orange ones, especially. I didn't know anyone else who liked Tic-Tacs, but someone must have. Someone must still, cos they're still making them.

"You remember!" A smile now, not a smirk. She has one front tooth with a tiny chip in it, and the bottom row is kind of crooked and jumbled, and I love that about her too. Little flaws. Perfection.

"I remember everything, remember?" I stand up for a second, cos my jeans have gone all weird and I need to straighten up. She stays where she is, and I think for a second she's looking at my-

"Whoa, that's some belt."

"Eh? This old thing?" I'm making a joke, but it is pretty old. There's a cheesy Jack Daniel's buckle on it, and the end of it has a metal tip.

"Yeah. Wouldn't want to be on the wrong end of that! Or would I…" The way she says it makes feel something I haven't felt in a long while. And it's not a feeling about her, either.

Five

Two Years Ago, London, Eleanor

Ellie lives in Camden, she's 39. She doesn't look it in her pictures. I've been single for a couple of weeks now. Emma decided to ditch me on New Year's Eve. Not at a party – in the afternoon, so she'd still be able to go out later with her friends and get tanked. Ever the pragmatist, that girl. I met Ellie on the dating site. None of her photos were too obvious, which is good, cos I've become suspicious of cleavage. Hers are the usual London middle class girl stuff; all stripy tops and laughing in beer gardens. She's petite - five three. I love tiny girls; I've had a thing about them ever since Orla Keane back home, but I've never gone out with one. I'm not a chooser, and all the girls who've chosen me seem to be around my height. All of my relationships start cos the girl shows an interest in me, not vice versa. And it's got to be strong and obvious interest, cos I'm very shit at picking up signals. Even on the dating site, every meeting I have comes from them making the move. On the rare occasion I drop anyone a line, I never hear back, so I stopped bothering with that.

We had a good matching percentage, normally a sign I'll click with someone, so I went through her answers, and started to see a submissive streak emerge, borderline BDSM. She didn't come across as a sexual snob though, so I messaged her back, and we got chatting. It turned out she was exactly my kind of woman, or the kind of woman I needed at the time. As well as the height, she is tiny everywhere else, except the chest. Even then, she's had reduction surgery, or so she says, which makes me wonder how crazy looking they'd been before. Doesn't matter to me, I'm not a boobs man, but they do look good in photos, I guess. She's been sending me a lot of photos. Breasts are always much more impressive to look at than they are to do anything with, I think.

It turned out her submissive side (I say *side*, all of her is submissive, there's no light and shade) included loving being told what to do. She'd later tell me a story about having a bloke make her stand on one leg for two hours, not allowing her to move from that position, and how much it made her wet. I just nodded and tried to look like it wasn't the most messed up thing I've ever heard. This little fetish extends to her loving me to tell her what underwear to put on, and what poses to do. It's the polar opposite of my relationship with Emma, who knows I love stockings and suspenders more than anything else, but has worn them for me twice in two years. Being told what to do is definitely not her thing. Not even being *asked* what to do. Nicely. Bless her.

Soon my hard drive is full of pictures of Ellie in all sorts of gear, from the elaborate, expensive stuff she loves, to the cute, simple pants that turn me on for some unknown reason. It's a match made in Heaven, even if we never have conversations that don't involve sex. That's okay too; I'm not looking for a girlfriend. Of course, I'm rebounding like nobody's business, so if someone offers to be my girlfriend, I'll bite their arm off. A petite, submissive, sex-obsessed girlfriend, who likes dressing up…well, I mightn't be able to turn that sort of thing down. We arrange to meet as soon as we both can. I'm broke, so I want to wait until I have enough for the fare, something to drink, etc.

When I meet her, it's outside Camden tube. I blank her at first; no one looks like their dating profile photos, and all the *good* ones she'd sent me were faceless, for obvious trust reasons. If she was waiting for me wearing a basque, and some Jasper Conran fishnets, I'd have spotted her straight away. She recognises me though, which is a good sign. We go to a pub on the corner, which is like every other pub in London. Picnic benches outside, lots of wood interiors, leather upholstery, and sawdust on the floor. She orders some food, and makes me have some too, or she wouldn't feel comfortable. I go along with it, and pick something small. I've no idea how the bill is going to be split, so I'm already doing damage limitation. I watch her go to the bar. She is tiny. I could probably fit her arse in one hand. Skinny black jeans, the obligatory striped top, and a leather jacket. She hasn't come whorish, but it's still daytime. And anyway, if it goes well, her flat is just around the corner, she says. That's where the whoring happens, by all accounts. It's going to go well though, I can already tell from the body language. She comes back from the bar with two Diet Cokes. Eleanor is a recovering alcoholic and drug addict. This is going to be a dry encounter, vaginas notwithstanding.

She sits close to me almost straight off; I can feel her thigh against my own. She has a quiet voice, but it's deep, and sort of sexy, and a filthy laugh. She smells good. Some of it perfume, the other part her. We aren't talking about anything, it's more of a game to see how many times we can accidentally touch before one of us lets our hand stay. Normally with me, it's the girl who does it, but I feel different now. I'm confident enough to understand when something is on the cards. I'm here, so is she. It's gonna happen.

We're sitting to one side of a low table, on a comfy leather couch. Across from us are two blokes, definitely not on a date, drinking pints of Strongbow and pretending they can't see us. Ellie leans into my face a lot while we talk, so I never catch the blokes' eyes. The bit where I kiss her is coming soon. I think I better make it happen before the food comes, in case I get onion breath. She smokes, so I don't have to worry about that part, at least. There's something odd about her teeth, but I can't work out what. They look great, much better than mine. There's just something slightly off about them. I run my fingers into the hair behind her ear while she's mid-sentence, and feel a crackle of imaginary static from all the sexual tension. Her eyes open a little wider, pupils going blacker, before she closes them again when my mouth pushes into hers. It's long, and not clumsy. She feels great, and after a few seconds, we both part our lips, and go in a little deeper. The pub goes away for a while, the two blokes and their ciders with it. I put a hand on her ribcage, and pull her little frame closer. When we break, there's that nice little pause you get after a good kiss, and I look at her and say,

'Yep.'

She does her throaty little laugh, and reaches for her Coke.

'Yuh-huh.'

I slide my hand down onto her hip, and put a thumb through the belt loop of her jeans. One of the men across the way catches my eye, and gives me an approving eyebrow raise. There's a little rushing feeling in my chest, and I wonder would it be shitty to suggest going for a fag before the food comes. I sometimes need one as a sort of punctuation between major things. And between minor things. Ellie is way ahead of me, leaning into the two guys, while giving me an eyeful of her arse.

'Hey... Can you guys keep an eye on our stuff while we nip out for a ciggie?'

They look at her in the way men do when a good looking woman asks them anything, and give her a bunch of *of courses* and *no bothers*. She's someone used to getting what she wants from men, clearly, without ever having to be bossy with it. I try not to look too smug as we pass them on the way out, my hand on her back, already feeling like it's normal.

I take the coward's way when ordering the food. Even though I finished with being a fussy eater years ago, there's something about pub grub that makes me play safe. A burger, with some chips. She has pasta, something creamy with chicken. Of course, it's London, so a plate is out of the question. A plank of wood, with the burger, onion rings, oversized gherkin, and a coffee mug full of chips, arranged from left to right. It's a big one. Too big to fit in your mouth and still come across as a sophisticated sex god. The meat is tender. I've asked for medium, but I can't remember what that's supposed to look like. There's red onion marmalade in it, which isn't disgusting.

'Nice?'

She holds her fork in the proper hand, and eats with her mouth closed.

'Am, yeah,' I say, after a little struggle to get the meat and bread down my throat. I wash it down with some of the cola. It's odd to be in a pub with a new person this long and be sober, but we both are. If I was the only one not drinking it would be different. That's what it used to be like with Emma, before I went back on the sauce.

I'd been off the drink (and the ciggies) for months before I met Em, and kept off them for about two years, before my not drinking became such an issue that I jumped off the wagon to make things right between us. She told me it was all in my head; that she was fine with socialising with me when I was sober; wasn't a problem for her. Of course it wasn't, though. If things got tense or uncomfortable, she could just drink harder, until it went away (for her). And she didn't have to be in my shoes – where I have to be straight while someone else gets tipsy and unreasonable. Terrified of getting in an argument, cos the other person would be drunk and wrong and think they're right. And you can't point out that they're drunk, cos drunk people not only think they aren't drunk, they're appalled and offended if you even suggest it. It was easier to give up two years of willpower and healthy living, than to go another evening sober with her. Of course, it wasn't enough for her, and about two weeks after I started drinking again, we broke up. Leaving me single, devastated, and no longer out of the self-destruction loop. Good times.

*****

"Any requests?"

Ellie's standing in front of a large chest of drawers. I guess it's where the underwear lives. I'm across the room, examining her Nikon DSLR with some envy. It must be what she takes the photos for me with, on a timer. They're too high res for a camera phone.

"What have we got?"

We came back straight away, after the food. When you aren't on the booze, there's no need for 'Just one more', or for anything to steady the nerves. I'm kind of liking it. I've not done sobriety with someone else before. It's a whole different thing.

"Come and see."

We aren't exactly formal, but our real life interactions are far more polite and reserved than our emails. My inbox is full of filthy discussions of the photos she sent, and I'm aware that some of those had been influenced by my having a few cheeky lemonades at the time. But this, it doesn't feel awkward. We've already kissed, and I've had a much of a grope as you can get away with in a public place. There had been two good years of completely sober sex with Emma – and she has a strange thing of not being horny when she is drunk. I'm used to it, which is handy for today.

The top drawer is all socks, stockings and hold-ups. Even the oversized football socks that I've seen models wear in magazine shoots. Drawer number two is bra and pants sets, three is lacy knickers and cute cotton short, and the last, a lot of corsets.

"Well? You approve?" she says, looking up at me with earnest eyes and false modesty. She knows full well I do.

"They'll do, I suppose."

My fingers find the small of her back, and I move the shirt up a little, so I can touch skin. I lean my face closer while we look through the untidy pile of waspies and basques. She smells good again. I kiss the skin where the side of her neck meets the shoulder, scraping my teeth over her as I pull away. She shivers. I can't decide what I want her to wear, it's all good. Dithering isn't an option. I'm not assertive in normal life, especially not in jobs. Sex is a different world, though. She needs to be instructed, told what to do, or this isn't going to work.

I pick some long socks, cute shorts, and a crop top with American football numbers on it. She doesn't question; she takes them into the bathroom and shuts the door. The flat is a studio, with a toilet by the door, and the shower off the kitchen area. Not clean or dirty. I don't know if I should take anything off. Shoes are gone already, when I came in. The socks should go too. She's taking her time. I'm feeling somewhere between anxious and ready to get on with it. No fear or nerves. We've had more than a week of build-up, but I already knew how she looked, how she dresses, what she's into. We've already had enough kissing for me to know it's going to be great. Slight penis worries, since she's older, and a bit of a nympho, but there's no point in worrying about that. She's tiny, it's going to look enormous anywhere near her. It's the first time with anyone else in a couple of years, though. It feels like cheating, and I can't have a drink to make that go away.

When she comes out, I swallow dry. Everything fits, and if it doesn't, it just makes it better. I'm a fan of less is more when it comes to women's clothes – bit of mystery, but when it's bedtime, exaggerated is fine. Not that it's bedtime. Sun's still out, and she doesn't have curtains; just shutters that she hasn't closed. We're on the first floor, and I think if someone *is* managing to watch from the flats across the street, she's probably into that. She climbs onto my lap, thighs either side of my hips. She weighs nothing. Her tits look enormous in the top, and she isn't wearing a bra. That throaty giggle again, before I grab her face and pull it toward me. She's grinding on me, and I can already smell her. I feel overdressed. Something's going to have to come off in a minute. I slip a hand up her top and brush the heel of my hand over her nipple, which makes her moan a little. I kiss her more, and tug a bit on the hair at the nape of her neck, and feel her reaction to that. It's a good one. I want to take off my top, but not hers. Her clothes are staying on for as long as I can help it. The outfit is half of the fun. I put my hands on her hips and press her against the thing that's straining to get out of these jeans. The smell again, I can feel the heat of her against me. Her crotch is soaking already. I roll her back and forth over my lap, still swapping tongues; deeper and longer, now.

I stand up and put her feet on the ground, ripping off my shirt with no real awkwardness or fiddling. She smiles at me and runs her hand through the hair on my chest. I haven't touched her between the legs yet, so I take her, lift her up, and throw her down on her back. Before any words can be said, my face is between her thighs, finding her clit through the cotton of her shorts with my tongue. I can taste her, even from here. And the smell is intoxicating enough that I've forgotten about drink already, and the neighbours who might be watching. She's squirming and moving about, in that way women do when they're trying to tell you what they want, without having to ask. I know she wants those pants pushed to the side so I can tongue her properly, but I'm going to make her wait a little. I dip my tongue into the dimples either side of her crotch, and tease her with soft circles of my tongue. I bunch up the cloth and pull it tight between her lips, giving the skin the lightest up and down licks, then letting the material go back to covering her. I press my lips against her and blow through the fabric, my breath is as hot as what's underneath. I can hear the frustration in her groans now, so I'm going to stop with the teasing. I have a real urge to taste her; I can tell from her smell that it's going to be delicious.

Knickers to the side, I skip the clit, and take a tongue full of the wet that's been building up inside her. Without a word, I come up face to face with her, and we swap her taste between our mouths. On my way back down, I slide two fingers inside her, and run them over the ridges of her g-spot. She bucks and arches, but I have her in place. She's going nowhere. Fingers still inside, to the hilt, I start on her clit with my mouth. She doesn't want it gentle, I can tell. I press hard, and move my tongue from side to side, until I feel her little button pop against the soft flesh on top of her pubic bone. Once I have it, I chase it around, adding more spit to keep it wet. I'm just finding my way, so I do everything for a little while at a time, and then try another way. Suction, tapping, flicking, licking. She seems to like it all, but that's not a surprise. We've had some long talks about it all, before. I know what she likes, in theory. This is the practice.

I've changed from stroking on her G spot now, to giving her a full three finger banging, while I go to town on her clit and everything around it. I can hear the wetness of her, loud in the room with each thrust of my hand. She's tight, and yet I'm thinking I could get another finger inside without hurting her. I don't want to stretch it too much before I get inside her though. Not even sure why I think that, but I do. I look up for a second and see her top is pulled up, gathered at her neck. She's rolling her nipples between finger and thumb, and pulling on them hard. I want her now, but my jeans and pants are still fully on, and I don't want to break up the rhythm of all of it. I have a brainwave, and come up from her, the best part of my hand still pumping away inside her. I drag her towards the edge of the bed so I can stand, and her eyes look amazing; full of filth and want. With the other hand, I pop my buttons and move the pants and trousers down my thighs. I'm hard as a rock, and it looks massive to me. It always looks big when I'm very into the sex, and the girl. I take my fingers out of her, and use the wet on them to lube myself up. Her own hand goes down to her clit, so I grab her other one and put it on me, showing her how to pump me, again without a word. She's incredibly wet now, and the room already smells like sex. I lean down and kiss her, the hardness of me moving down her stomach, and over her nicely trimmed mound. She takes her fingers away from her clit and tries to guide me into her, but I grab her wrist and hold it above her head. I can tell she likes that. I feel her feet, the long socks still on, tip-toe up my chest, until her legs are over my shoulders. Perfect. I look down at her as the head of me parts her lips with no effort at all, and I slide all the way in. She's either tight, or I'm enormous today, but either way, it's perfect. Her fingers are back on her clit again. This isn't going to take long.

*****

"Do you know how to strap someone?"

It's the second day I'm there at hers. There's no reason not to be. She doesn't work, and I'm not expected back at Andie's, who I've been crashing with since the split with Em. If anything, the more I stay away from hers the better. She could do with the break, I think.

"You mean like tie you up?"

I know she's into the real kinky shit. All that Japanese rope bondage looks like too much effort to me. And I hate the way they tie up the breasts. Looks painful. I've seen photo shoots, and it's not my cup of tea.

"Haha, no. Well that'd be nice too. I just mean like spanking."

"Oh. Yeah, I can spank, I think?"

I have spanked. It's not rocket science.

"But with a strap."

"A strap?"

"Yeah. Or a belt."

"Oh. Oh, I guess so. I've used a paddle and stuff. Before, I mean."

"Yeah? Mmmmm."

"Yeah."

It was more the back of a hairbrush, but she doesn't have to know that. I tried it years ago, in Ireland. And I did it with Emma a few times. She said it was one of those things she'd have felt ridiculous doing with anyone else, but there was something different about me. I took it as a compliment. I think it was a compliment.

"I like it."

"Yeah. I mean, takes a bit of skill, I think."

"Skill?"

"Well yeah. With the paddle. Or just with your hand. You need to kind of know what's too hard, what hurts too much, what's the limit."

I sound pretty experienced here, I'm thinking. Totally winging it.

"Hah. I don't think I have limits…"

"Eh?"

"Well… I have *limits* limits, sure. Everyone has hard limits."

"Yep."

I'm nodding like I know what she's talking about. I think I'm getting away with it too.

"Like, kids, animals, scat."

"Not even if we combined the three?"

"Haha. No thanks."

"Lightweight."

"Haha. So… do I get my strapping?"

"What, now?"

We haven't even had lunch.

"Mmm-hmmm."

She shifts around on the bed. She's wearing Brazilian-fit knickers in a nautical stripe pattern, they make her tiny arse look curvy – it's the Kylie Minogue effect. There's an off the shoulder 80s t-shirt too, that I saw her throw on this morning when she got up to have a fag at the window. I'm hard straight away.

"Don't I need to get you in the mood?"

Feels weird that I haven't even touched her. Or kissed her. I can taste my own mouth, and it's all orange juice and nicotine. Probably for the best.

"Hehe, I'm always in the mood."

She's on her knees with her arse in the air, shoulders to the mattress. I can see the outline of her lips through the cotton, peeking out from between her cheeks. Without saying anything else, I slap her; medium hard, but it still leaves a little pink mark. She gives an approving squeal. I give her another slap, but it's not as clean this time, and my palm hits bone.

"Sorry."

"Shhhhhh. Gimme more, please."

"Okay."

I use my other hand to rub where I've left the mark; tender, like I'm making amends. Her skin is warm. My fingers want to be between her legs, but I know she doesn't want it or need it. She's able to get off just from the pain. Once I've lulled her into a false sense of security with the massaging, I move out of the way and swing in with the other hand; I connect perfectly, and there's a loud slap. She makes more noises. I can already smell her getting wet.

"God… yeah."

"So… is there a strap? A whip or something?"

I know she has a box of tricks under the bed. Probably more stuff somewhere else.

"Use your belt."

"My belt?"

"Yes! Stop asking me. Just fucking do it."

She's being assertive in wanting me to be assertive. I get it. I have to make her regret it though. She'll think less of me if I don't. I yank her head up by the hair, and slap her face. Her eyes widen and water at the same time. I kiss her softly where I've marked her, and push her face back into the bed. She's not near enough the edge for me, so I take her by the hips and pull her more towards me. Another crack across the arse with my hand to keep her motor running, then I stop to take my belt out of its loops. She squirms on the bed, but stays in place. I don't know how to start, so I just do. The end of the belt, not too hard, across one cheek. She lets out a little whimper. I'm still in the mode where I have to listen to her and see what's enough and what's too much. Nothing is too much though, I have to get that into my mind. Another crack, harder, and an even more grateful noise. I feel like I should say something, but nothing sounds right in my head, so I don't. It's broad daylight outside, and the cars are honking.

I build up a rhythm, harder every time. She doesn't tell me to stop, she doesn't move out of the way. Smash after smash of leather on skin, and I find I'm enjoying it, in spite of myself. I've never been into BDSM; I've never thought I was a sadist, or someone who enjoys hurting someone. I'm enjoying how much she likes this though. It's her pleasure that's turning me on, not her pain. That's what I keep telling myself. Her arse is red now, not quite raw. She can take much more than this. She's sent me pictures of her with welts. I didn't find it sexy. I see now that it's cos I didn't make them. It's like when I see a photo of a girl with come all over her face. Doesn't make me stir in the slightest. But when the girl is real, it's in front of me, and it's my come she's licking off her own lips, that's a different story. I'm hard as a rock here, and I don't know if it's cos of her pleasure, how wet she is, or the power itself. I just know that it's cos it's real, I'm here, and it's me doing it. Controlling it. The only one who can make it stop.

My arm is tired, so I put it down for a second. I swing my other hand at her, but stop it, millimetres before it lands. She jerks with the anticipation, and then lets out a little disappointed sigh. I can't help myself, I bury my face between her thighs an inhale the smell. The cotton of her knickers is saturated in her own come. I run my tongue up and down her slit through the material, stopping at her clit, to poke at it, and swirl it around. I can feel her being torn between the vanilla stuff, and wanting me to go back to hitting her. That's okay. Teasing her is just as good as giving her what she wants. She can wait a little while. I pull the cloth to one side and lap up as much of her as I can, slipping two fingers inside, which makes her gasp more than all the pain I've been doling out. I drag over the g-spot a few times, which makes the hollow between my fingers and her fill up with fresh, hot liquid. In one smooth motion I reach around to give her a taste of herself. She cleans me with her tongue, and I thank her with another hard slap to the face, before bringing my hand back, and going inside her again, this time with three instead of two. I start to slam her with the fingers now, making sure the tips are hitting the right spot with every bash. She's brimming over, the stickiness rolling out over my skin and dripping down her thighs. I want it now, but again, I'd have to break the rhythm and get my trousers down. I decide against it, and pull out, picking up the belt again. She's gasping and disorientated now. I'm incredibly turned on by it all.

I thrash her for a little while longer, making each lash harder; partly for her, partly to stop myself getting bored. She isn't bored; I can tell she could take this all afternoon. I'm going to explode if I don't do something soon though, and it can't be all about her. That's not me being dominant at all. That's almost passive, despite everything. I suddenly have an idea. I wonder should I ask her about it, then I realise that asking her about it would be the worst thing to do. She wants to be helpless. She wants me to be in control. She wants me to make the decisions. Without another thought, I take the belt and loop it like a lasso. I can feel her curiosity already, but she doesn't look back at me. Pulling her towards me by the hair, I put the loop over her head and around her neck, pulling it tight straight away. She looks at me with a mixture of surprise and pure, animal sex. It's the type of belt that loops through a couple of rings, no pin, it just goes as tight as you pull it, so it's ideal. I pull it tight until I hear her choke a little, then let my hand go slack. Holding her there, I use my left hand to pop the buttons on my jeans, the smell of her rising up from underneath. No time to get it all off, I just push the trousers and underwear down to the knees, keeping her in place with the makeshift collar and leash.

I yank the knickers down to the back of her knees, and think about spitting in my hand to lube up, but I don't need to. I push inside her easily; the mixture of tight and wet is immediately familiar. The normal sound she makes when I slide into her is different today, cos she's struggling to breath. The more I tighten the reins, the harder she seems to squeeze me. I'm not even thrusting; just filling her up, and concentrating on the choke. There's a pulsing feeling as the muscles inside her grip me and let go, in a rhythm that can't be accidental. I pull it even tighter, still just docked in her, not moving my hips. There's something I can feel her telling me, without saying it. I can't quite figure it out. Until I do. Of course. There's somewhere else this can go, and it's better for both of us. I look down at her tiny hips and arse, and me, pushed into the hilt. I take myself out slowly, and how big and thick it looks coming out of her little frame makes me more turned on than I've been all day. It's either going to work or its not, and I'm just going to go for it. Again, no asking. I don't need to ask. She wants it. And if she doesn't; if I've misread the situation, she'll want it soon enough, after I do it. Pain is hardly a hurdle in this situation.

I push the head against the opening of her arsehole. I considering going in there with a finger or two, but there's probably no need, and this way is going to hurt her more. She likes being hurt. And I like hurting her, which is new. It's a push at first. A bit of a struggle. But I know it'll give eventually. I ease off on the choking, in case it's causing involuntary tightness. She seems to be reading my mind, cos I hear her breathe out slowly, and relax her muscles. All of them. I get it inside with one last push and once the head is through (with a little scream from her that almost makes me stop), the lube from her helps me slide all the way through, and now I tighten up the noose again, cos I know that's what she wants.

I'm in charge, I'm in control. There's no beta-male reach around going on, no need to rub off her clit while I'm doing her like this. The pain, the restriction, the powerlessness – all of it together, is making her come, without anything else. And then a feeling comes over me. A feeling of *what if?* And I don't like it. But I do, too. I'm still in that moment with her, but I'm somewhere else as well. I'm someone else as well. I look down at the sheer pornography of me sliding in and out of her, and suddenly that's not the most exciting thing. It's the power – the strap around her neck, the absolute control I have over her – over her life. Over her death. There'd be nothing she could do. The end of the belt is double-wrapped in my fist and her face is almost purple – eyes bulging, breath almost stopped. It would be the easiest thing in the world just to-

She comes hard and I feel her muscles clamp down around me, and it snaps me out of whatever that was. I feel myself letting go, and filling her up, pump after pump, twitch after twitch. The belt's dropped from my hand and I fall forward onto her, still held into her by her grip. The room smells like fucking, and I can hear her gasping while she tries to undo the strap from around her throat. I'm there, but I'm somewhere else too, and I reach over to give her a hand with the belt, and I wonder if she'll ever know how lucky she was today.

Six

Last Year, London, Emma

A week to myself. She's gone to her parents for a holiday. I'm delighted, cos shit has been bad, and I was starting to dread the evenings. It's not that good though, cos now I'm on my own, with no chance of being caught. I'm going to smoke. I'm going to drink. I'm drinking already, and it's half ten in the morning. I have no self-control. I don't even want a drink. I just can. So I am. The laptop's open, I'm being *enthusiastic* on Facebook again. I wish I could stop this now. I want to be able to stop, but I don't want to stop. Compulsions and obsessions. I can't go back to that boring life, being the only dry one at the table. But this isn't good either. I want to be the person who can have a few on a night out, and then just shut off the valve. If I could have that, without having to go through days like these, that'd be perfect. But it isn't like that with me. I either don't at all, or I do, and then this shit happens. I sink the gin and tonic, and think about a fag. A week, she said. She's not going to smell one fag, a week later. I'm not taking that risk, though. I get up and move out to the back garden.

I should've had toast. Seedy bread, purple pack. Hovis. The best kind. I love the taste of the pumpkin seeds when they've been in the toaster. I haven't got any butter though, and I've not been to the shop yet. A cafetiere to myself, then straight on the gin. She won't be back for a week; I can get another bottle and replace hers. It is sunny out. Very sunny. The dogs are loping around, I think I fed them. She went early, about the same time as she'd normally go to work. Bank Holiday today, so there won't be a lot of people heading out of London so early. Or into London, come to think of it. She's taken the whole week, to go see her family. I volunteered to stay and look after the dogs, but I wouldn't have been invited anyway. The two options were: she goes on her own, or she goes and takes the dogs with her on the train. It's me she's getting away from, so me coming with her would be kind of stupid.

There's mushrooms in the grass. Us having grass is new. It was pebbles the last time. Easier to pick up dog shit. When we came, it was overgrown, and there was a border, with mud in it, and plants. She didn't want those plants. Homebase is around the corner, so we've been there about a hundred times already. I'm not the most practical person, I always tell myself, but since I've been with her, I've made myself be. First with the cooking, then the painting, now the gardening. She seems to enjoy emasculating her men – she mentioned something before about her last boyfriend saying that about her - and I didn't want to give her the pleasure of doing it to me too. I look around at the borders, and it's been mostly my work. I've forked the earth over, put down bark. Carried the bark too, and the compost. We don't have a car anymore, so occasionally we'd borrow a Homebase trolley, and bring it back, after. When we couldn't, I just carried the bags. They were big. Like 30kg, or something. I've done a lot of shit in this house, and garden, considering I wasn't even supposed to come when she moved. I've helped build things, I mow the lawn every week, dig things, paint things. It's almost all done now, and it doesn't feel like a coincidence that she's started pushing me away again. I can't reconcile the I Love Yous with the way she uses me. But I carry on. I'm too used to being here. And I want to be here- with her, I mean. Not just in this house. A house is just a house. What I have with her, I spent ages trying to find.

They're not Magic Mushrooms. Not nipple shaped, and it's completely the wrong time of year. I'm on the grass now, foraging, on my hands and knees. I pick some, they're brown, and they smell a bit. I'll look them up on the laptop in a bit, but I know they're no good. I am properly drunk already. There's a need in me, a kind of hedonism or something. If there were any drugs in the house, I'd have taken them. I wish I was in Hackney. Our place was nice, and the little gated estate was nice, but you're cheek by jowl in London, so there were always lads about, and if it was mild out, I could find a few half-smoked joints on the ground, and light up. I don't like weed, but some days I just want to be somewhere else for a while. I always regret it. I get so messed up and crazy and paranoid, that I want it to stop very quickly after it starts. But it never stops me doing it. Anything is better than straight me, some days.

Another glass, gin over ice, clink clink, half-flat tonic, don't care. Have half of it in one go. Internet says mushrooms are duds. Same family as the Liberty Cap ones, but the best you'll get off them is mild nausea. I put some Bowie on the iPod dock, cos that's the last thing that was playing from the night before. No texts on my phone, nothing exciting going on with the internet and Facebook. I have friends from all over the world, who are awake at different times. Sometimes I don't notice that, cos Americans will talk to me or reply to my stuff when it's about lunchtime, and I forget that it's the very early morning for them. Some of them live in Australia, and I can't even do the maths for that on a sober day, let alone now. One's in the future, one's in the past. That's as much as I can handle right now. The dogs are sniffing around me. They need a walk. I wonder how many they'll get this week. It's not fair on them. I'll take them down the small park soon. In an hour or so, I'll start to feel that strange drunk social thing, where I want to talk to people, and the internet won't be enough.

Obviously, I don't know anyone around here, so if I start talking to someone it'll be a stranger. And they'll think I'm mental. I know that now, but I won't, in about an hour.

Shite all on the telly, cos it's daytime, and I don't watch TV anyway. Everything is torrents and streaming, of things I've heard were good from other people. We're watching a few things at the moment; that's our nice time, in the evenings. Dinner, then watching something after dinner. I've learned to not care that she's on her iPad, looking at antique furniture, when we're supposed to be having some us time, and she's supposed to be paying attention to the show. I don't give a shit anymore, I just like that we're not fighting. It's always there under the surface though. The only reason we don't fight is that I've learned to play her game so well, and not start her off. It's completely one-sided, I know. There isn't a fibre of her that ever thinks about how I feel, how to get on with me, or what she can do to avoid us arguing. Unless you count her not attacking me apropos of nothing for being a useless loser without a job, and telling me how great she is to keep a roof over my head and pay all the bills. That doesn't count as a good deed though, cos she still thinks all that, and it's the fuel that keeps her resentment burning. I have only got two fags left. I've just finished one, but the panic of seeing so few left makes me light up another, straight away.

Went to the shop, back now, four cans of the strongest stuff. I need that toast, but I'm fighting the urge to make it. My stomach is just liquor and fizz, and a bit of bread might balance it out a bit, make a foundation for the 8.4% shite, but another voice in me is telling me butter will make me puke. I don't know who's right now. Not that we have butter. Or maybe we do. I can't remember. The sun was scorching on the way to the offie, even more than it was out the back, it seemed like. I'm just in a t-shirt and jeans, and it seems too much. I go out the back with a cold can, and take my top off. There are no mirrors near, but I wouldn't want there to be. I'm pale all over, except the arms, which have a bit of colour, and those permanent Irish freckles. I don't like my body- not cos I'm fat, or there's anything wrong with it. It's more that I don't do anything to achieve it, so it can't be good. Andie always said I had a nice body, but if I do, it's natural, so I can't be proud of it, in my own head. I eat whatever shit I like, and drink like a wino, so I can't be proud of being thin either. I don't think Emma rates it. She's never said anything about it, which means to me that she's not impressed. Obviously, she's never going to say she doesn't like it, so, for me, the silence speaks volumes. It's like the penis thing. I don't think mine is big. She says it is, all the time. She's so good at saying it, I've started to believe her. It might be the reason I stay with her. I've never believed anyone else.

Once, in Wales, some girl raved about it, before, after, and all the way through the sex. It felt so good, drunk as I was, that it made me sad. It made me think how great it would be to really have a massive one, and hear that all the time. We're like that though, boys. We obsess about the stuff we can't change – penis size, height, baldness – and convince ourselves that if only we had that thing we lack, we'd be happy. We totally ignore the idea that there's guys out there with ten-inch penises who are unhappy cos of something else. And that's cos those guys don't exist, clearly. Emma says things about mine all the time, so I think it must be decent. She never says anything about my body, so it must be shit. It's worrying how much I take her opinions to heart. Once, when we were watching some film, a guy was on screen with big arms, and she said something throwaway like 'Phwoarr, look at those guns.' I not only got deeply hurt, I interrogated her for about a half an hour, in the neediest, most beta male way possible, about how she liked gym guys, and she must think I'm disgusting. No matter what she said, I took it as an insult and as confirmation that I was shit and ugly and not at all her type. She didn't help things with statements like 'I never go for the macho guy,' or 'I like looking at them, but I don't like the personality that goes with that sort of guy,' and similar, but then she's never been one for tact. I look down at my white, sunken chest, and feel like putting the t-shirt back on.

    I got ciggies in the shop. 20, cos bollocks to her, and bollocks to everything. She won't be back for a week. I won't even have to wash my mouth out with shower gel later. What a luxury. There's a noise from behind next door's fence. It's a big dog – some sort of Boxer/Great Dane cross. I saw it out the window the other day, terrifying thing. It riles up our dogs. They're only little shits, but they go crazy at the other one, through the fence. They probably know it's too high for him to jump, if dogs can think that way. I should write something. I should always write something, but it's hard enough trying to do it when I think someone cares, and is keeping tabs on me, or just gives any sort of shit about how it's going. She doesn't ask anymore. She hasn't cared in a long time. I need someone to care. As an incentive, or something carrot or stick-related. When no one asks, no one cares, and when no one cares, neither do I. I'm too wasted already; it would just be garbage. Or I'd look at the screen helplessly, and drool a bit, while the thoughts refused to come out and go into my fingers. I hate that feeling. It's like, years ago, in Wales; I was fairly new to the internet- well, to message boards and chat rooms. And I was on my own, on a couple of Es, happy and chatty and having the best time ever. Then I tried typing, and my fingers and the keyboard just wouldn't meet each other in the middle. No depth perception, or too much, whichever. Being pissed and trying to write is like that, but less physical. It's more like my ideas and my hands won't meet each other in the middle, and all the drunk wisdom just falls between them, onto the carpet. We don't have carpets. She hates them.

I want something. To do something, maybe. I can't think straight, but whatever I do think, I believe in it, and think it's a great idea. I can only create thoughts though, and interact with people. I can't process things that already exist – like reading a book, or doing a quiz or a crossword. There's a window for that, it lasts a small amount of time, then it's over. Quiz machines in pubs – I can be good at them at the start, cos the drink makes me more confident. But eventually it makes me more stupid, and not able to remember things I know. I think that's what happens in conversations too. They're fine when I'm just drunkenly running my mouth, or talking shite back and forth. But when someone challenges something, I can lose it. On the internet, it's usually a chat with lots of people on a public thread, and then someone new I don't know appears, and I take their sarcasm at face value, maybe, and launch into this stupid argument that lasts ages, and ends with me deleting everything when I've sobered up, and blocking people, cos I'm so embarrassed. In real life, it just happens with girlfriends. Cos they're close to me, so I get the most offended by stuff they say. Especially if they're like me. If they're like me, I get offended if they have some thought that I'd hate myself for having. Or if they say something that I'd think, but never say in front of them. It's complicated, but it's consistent. I never had those with Emma at the start, cos I didn't drink. I was calm and reasonable. She'd get drunk though, and be like that with me. It was unfair, cos what could I do? Tell her she was drunk? That's never going to work out. Drunk people never think they're drunk, especially if that's someone else's opinion of them. And we're always about half an hour drunker than we think. That's why we keep buying it when it's time to stop. Or, why I do, anyway.

I want something different though. I want a different kind of wrecked. She's gone for a week; I don't have a real job. I can do anything I want, and this is what I want – to get off my face. I wouldn't cheat on her. If I was that guy, this would be ideal; I could have women over every day. I've just never felt the need to do it while I'm with her, and I've probably cheated on everyone else I've ever been seeing. She's different. I'm crazy about her. Even though I sort of hate her, and I can't think of anything I like about her, off hand, except for that body. And that's stupid. Lots of people have good bodies. I've been with people who have great bodies before. But just one-offs, usually. I can never find someone whose brain I like as well as their belly. That's the bane of my life, probably.

I want mushrooms. Magic ones. It's not the season. I've checked on the internet. I checked even though it's obvious it isn't the season. I still want them. They might be somewhere in Hackney Downs. Or Hackney Marshes. I remember that I don't live in Hackney anymore, all of a sudden. I'm quite sozzled. I could go there though. Dogs could have a walk. Can't walk there though. Need to take a bus or a tube. Can't take the dogs with me then. Not while I'm like this. I don't think about it anymore, and just go out the door. I have my wallet; it's got money and my Oyster card. I'm in that determined drunk mood, where my body seems to point forward; head first, at a 45 degree angle. Go, don't think. Go, don't discuss. Go, go, go. My legs are stumbly; I'm in no state to be going anywhere, or to be around people. But that's just an opinion. It might be wrong. There's a bus that goes to Hackney. A number 144. Or 188. It doesn't matter, I don't want a bus. And the only place I've ever seen it is around Leyton tube station. And I get lost going to that place when I'm sober, let alone now. I'll go on the Overground. That stops in Hackney. No, wait, the one from here doesn't. I'd have to go around the houses. Leytonstone tube. Leytonstone's right next to Stratford on the Central Line, then from there on the Overground to Hackney. My phone doesn't have juice in it. Or money to use the internet. I'll get some in a minute. I pass the Overground station, and nearly walk up there. No. Get a hold of yourself. There's a shop. Could get a cider. No, I'll wait.

The tube's hot, and full of people who smell. Or maybe it's me. It's not, though. I shower a lot these days. Didn't have one today, cos she's not coming home. Mightn't have one in a week now. Depression, drink – they all stop me bothering with washing and brushing my teeth. I don't know why. Self-respect issues, probably. Meeting Emma has made my teeth relatively white and shiny, and my body smell great. Thanks, Emma. Apart from all the other stuff you do to me. There's just blokes in the carriage. Well, there's one woman, but she looks mental, scraggy haired, like she's about to stand up any minute and start talking about Jesus. They do that, sometimes. Sometimes they just stay on the stations all day, and get off one train, onto another, talking about the Lord, to anyone who won't listen. They're one sort, the buskers are another. They walk through, playing a song on the guitar, while everyone does the usual ignoring thing, and then they walk back through with a hat held out, so that everyone can ignore that too. Then you get the tissue guys. Beggars, from Romania I think, although that's probably racist. They come and leave a pocket pack of tissues on every seat, with a note saying how they're immigrants, and that this is their only income, and can you give a pound, or more, for these nice tissues. It's trickier when you're with a kid, cos they get fascinated by it, and they don't know the Code of the Tube yet; which is basically: ignore everyone, talk to no one, and if someone starts telling you about Jesus, get off at the next stop. We're in Stratford already, and it's bustling. Stratford is hardly ever not busy.

Overground is quiet to Hackney - that's rare. When Emma came home on it or went on it every morning, it was the worst part of her day, by far. She's lived in London ten years, but she goes back home to Plymouth so much she must constantly be aware that there's quieter places to live, and less stressful ways to get to work. Houses are about a quarter of the price down there too. But everyone wants to live here. They don't care how much it costs, or how packed everything always is. It's worth it for them. I just live here cos she does. But it's definitely cool. There are things you'd miss, like an infinite amount of new pubs, all the parks in the summer with things going on in them, all the famous places, all the cheap fried chicken, and the 24 hour offies. We're here already. I get this idea that I should've taken the normal to train to Hackney Downs station, but I think I'm confused. I don't think that's any closer to Hackney Marshes. I think Hackney Marshes is more up the top of town. I'd have had to go from Stratford to Liverpool Street to get the train to Hackney Downs anyway, and you have to come out through turnstiles then go back through other ones, and I can't remember if that's expensive, or if your Oyster card just knows, and settles the fare up at the end. I don't know anything right now, except that I should eat something. And I'm thirsty. I should get a chicken box meal thing, or go to that place up Mare Street where they have cheap chicken chippy prices, but the chips are real, made from potatoes. It's a waste of booze though. Or maybe it isn't. I don't know. I roll into a brown people shop. It's been a good while since I had any booze, I can have some more. They have an offer on some beers. My stomach makes a noise. Doesn't approve. The White Ace will tear me apart too though. And it's too blue to drink walking down the street. Too obviously trampy. I get four cans of some 7.5% stuff that's 'medium', it should be easier on my stomach. I only pick it cos the cans are black and it'll look vaguely like *Monster* if I sup it in the street.

 iMaps showed me Hackney Marshes as a massive green area up around here somewhere, but I'm sure I've been there before with Emma and the dogs, and I can't remember how we ended up there. We might have driven. It's not clear in my head, but neither is anything else. Hackney Downs looks like a massive green area too, but to me that was just a field across the road, when we lived here. It's technically four big full sized fields, if you walk around the edges. The Marshes is way bigger. They play Sunday League football there, but we never went to that bit. We've found a place called Wanstead Flats, in Leytonstone, that's kind of similar. It's amazing how many big green spaces there are in Central London. Hampstead Heath is basically the size of Limerick, in my head.

 I don't know which way to go in, or which part I'm looking for. I'm not looking for any part. I'm looking for… mushrooms? I should think things over before I get on tubes and go places. There's green beside me, and railings. That could be it. The iMaps is just confusing me now, I can't tell what side of the street I'm on, even. I just want to sit down and have a can, but I'm still in the street, kind of. This bit up here has to be it. It's got a country walk feel to it, like when I've gone to Ally Pally. It's green and nice; I think the sun's going down.

I'm ratarsed. I walk in a bit, everything smells like trees. It's pretty, and it's vast. I don't recognise any of this part. I'm annoyed I didn't bring the dogs, they'd have loved it. I don't think I'd have been able to let them off the leash though, there's all sorts of places they could get lost, or drown. And I'm too drunk to be able to get them back if they decide to be stubborn. I go down off the path to a little hollow. Reminds me of somewhere I was before, on a Cub Scouts trip, when I was a kid. A big long hole in the ground, shaped like the inside of a bath. There's holes at either end. It's rabbits. Or hares. That's what they told us on that trip.

  All my memories of the past get mixed up when I drink, but sometimes I don't know it. Sometimes I remember the same memories again, from when I was drunk before. A memory of having a memory. Like when you're just about to fall asleep and you remember old dreams you've had, but you never remember them in the middle of the day. It's something to do with being in an A State and a B State, I remember Paul McKenna saying some time before, in a thing I read. I have recurring dreams, and I can remember them all right now, even if I'm not about to nod off. I must be in one of those states now, A or B. I'm definitely in a state, anyway. That makes me laugh, and I look around to see did anyone hear. But there's no one there, not even rabbits or hares. I have dreams about swimming, even though I don't swim. The water I swim in is a river or the sea, and it's in Limerick and England all at the same time, cos it's a dream. I can row properly too in the dream world, and it's a lot of fun. I can remember it clearly now. Rowing and swimming, neither of which I can do properly or well when I'm awake. I can drive too. I can drive an automatic, and I drive around for what feels like hours, and it's not like it's new to me. Neither is the swimming or the rowing. It's more like I could always do these things, and I've just forgotten. That's the feeling I have when I'm dreaming, but it's not a feeling of dreaming, or I'd be aware, and I'd wake up.

  I have more stuff in dreams that I'm remembering now, as I start on the cans. I live in a house that has no middle. It's just an attic that spans four or more different houses; like someone has knocked the walls through, and a dark basement. The attic is a fun place. Every friend I've ever had in my life is there at the same time, all at the ages they were when I knew them and we liked each other and we got on. There's pool tables and video games and pinball machines; it's a bit like the flat Tom Hanks gets in Big. It's fun, all the time, and there's drinks and laughing, and I love spending time there. There's a weird end to it every time though, before I wake up, or move onto the other part of the dream. I've been having this dream since I was little, so I don't think the weird part has anything to do with real life, or that it's literal. Dreams aren't literal. In the middle of the party, I always get an odd feeling, and make my way down to the end of the attics. And there's a sofa bed there, but it's folded up. And I lift up the seat cushions and move all the sheets and bedding they store under there, and I see there's a body. Dead, decomposing, and I can't make out who it is, cos it's rotted away too much, but at the same time I know that... that it's me.

The basement isn't fun at all. It's more like a big barn, it's only dream logic that makes it a basement and makes it have anything to do with the attic, even though it would make more sense for it to be a separate thing, and not have the mystery of where the middle of the house is. But dreams aren't supposed to make sense. It's completely pitch black in there, and I have a torch. When I shine it in, it turns out that the room is full of things from my past that I'd forgotten. A bomber jacket with a puma on the back that I had when I was ten. A little yellow car that someone bought me when I was in hospital with an abscess. An X-Wing fighter from Star Wars, from before my mum gave away all my Star Wars to my little cousins. And I want them all, cos they make me feel warm inside. So, I go in, and the door shuts on its own. And there's a feeling of sheer terror, and of something in the dark, there with me. And I'm in so much danger, and I should get out. But I want my things. My torch is flickering; the battery is going, so I can't see where any of the things are. And I'm dizzy in the dark, like someone has spun me around with a blindfold on, so every time the torch comes back on, it's pointing at something else, not what I thought was there. So, I start grabbing all the things I can, but I can feel the danger getting worse and worse, the longer I'm in there. I need to get things and leave, but I don't know where the door is anymore. Every extra thing I pick up makes my legs go slower and I need them to be fast for me, so I can get away from whatever is there in the dark with me, when I find the door again. I have so much stuff now; all of it that I need to make me feel happy. But I'm getting slower and slower, and the thing is at my neck, I can feel it breathing. I can see a crack of light, it must be the door. I try running, but I'm so slow, like my legs are in glue. The thing is nearly on me, and it's so much more terrifying cos I don't know what it is. It seems to give off pure fear though, like a stench, and it's all I'm breathing now.

I figure it out, finally, every single time I have the dream. I'm going to have to drop some of the things if I want to get faster. I don't need them all. Being safe and getting out of there is more important; I'm in so much danger. I drop the little yellow car, and I'm a small bit faster. I'm sad, cos I loved that car. It was made of rubber, so you couldn't break it no matter how you tried. I'm still not fast enough and the thing is near now. The heat of him is making me sweat, and I can hear his tongue lolling, scraping against his teeth. I throw away the jacket, the one that I wanted so much and my mum had to save up to buy, cos all my friends had one, and she didn't want me to be left out. I'm a little faster, but the door is still so far away. I want to cry, it feels like I'm drowning, only in darkness instead of water. I let go of a few more little things, all of them important to me in some way, and each time I get faster for a while, and nearer the door. He's still there, my chest is so full of fear it's like someone has poured cement in my lungs. I'm not going to make it out of there. I only have the Star Wars plane left and I don't want to let it go, cos it was my favourite thing and I hated her so much for giving it away. She didn't ask me. I wasn't too old for it, like she said. I just want that, that's the only thing I need from here. Can't he just let me out with it? Can't he just feel pity for me? I'm so near the door and so far away, and he's on me now, his jaws are around my neck, and I know there's no choice anymore, cos he's going to kill me, and I have to let go of the X-Wing fighter, or my legs won't be fast enough to get me to the door, and it's okay, cos I'm too old for it anyway, and she hasn't seen me play with it for ages. And I let go, and I'm fast, and he's gone, and I'm outside. And I have nothing now, except remembering, and it's time to wake up.

  I almost drifted off. Or maybe I did drift off. It's duller, but it might just be clouds. There aren't any clouds though. There's a second can open. I don't remember doing that. There's none gone from it. Strange. Still no rabbits. Or hares. I should get up and walk somewhere. Farther in. Further in. It's farther when it's real distance. It's further when it's a metaphor, or something. Grammar, grammar, grammar. I don't know if that's grammar or spelling. I should walk, but there's an open can. It's not safe. I don't know if it's safe or not. I can go anywhere I like. It's like a park. Like a big park, with trees in it. All parks have trees in them. This one has rivers. Or lakes. Some kind of water. There's none here, right now, but I remember, from before. I'm still thinking about dreams. I get up and walk, and I forget the bag of two cans, and have to go back for it. There's no one around right here. It's nice, like a little forest. There's small buzzy things on the beams of light that come down through the holes in the tops of the trees, and the sides of the trees. Between the trees. I don't think I'm going to find mushrooms. Not the right ones, anyway. Stupid idea. I'm here now, though. It's fun. Or it's something. Where I'm going is anyone's guess.

  I have a job in my dreams. I have two, and neither of them are 'poorly paid author'. I work in a bookshop that's a mix of lots of bookshops I've been to in my life, and the library I did work experience in. I loved that place. They put me in there cos I was unemployed, to give me a chance to learn some skills. There was a promise of a job afterwards, I thought, but after the four weeks they told me there were no jobs. The back to work scheme I was on lasted eight weeks, so I just asked could I keep doing the volunteering in the library, cos it felt good having something to do, and I liked learning where everything was, and impressing people by finding stuff for them. I like jobs. I like working. I just… once I'm out of the loop and I've lost one before getting another one, I slip into the anxiety thing, and I can't face the application process, or interviews. Just the thought of them, though. If I ever have an interview, I always get the job. I have a job though. I'm a poorly paid author. It doesn't matter if Emma doesn't think it's a real job. Her job isn't a real job. She's just another middle-class graduate in a made-up position who's been given a management role cos she's been at that company too long. And when she leaves, it'll be to another management job at another company, cos she's been a manager before. It doesn't seem to dawn on anyone that she's not very good at management. That's not how life works for rich people. If you're poor, and in a normal job, you have to show some potential or skill at managing people. Then you might become a supervisor, and after that, a manager. It's different when you've been to university. It's like cadets and soldiers. It's bullshit. Or maybe that's just what I tell myself, cos I'm a fucking loser who can't do anything right.

She can't handle her job. There's always some bird there who's making her life a living hell. It's always someone else's fault. The more I talk to her, the more I find out that there was another bird in the last job, and the job before, and the job before. It's always some other woman, not the fact that she's not cut out for it. But she has a job, and she's better than me, and she pays for everything, and that's that. I give half of the pittance I get every week towards food, and she matches it. Matches it, not doubles it. Even though she's on 40 grand a year. And of course, that's fair, cos she pays the mortgage and the bills and the rest. Which she'd do anyway, if I wasn't there. I feel like I'm repeating myself now, I don't want to think about her. She's gone for a week; I should give myself a week off from her.

I'm farther into Hackney Marshes now, and further into my own drunkenness. I got the farther/further thing the right way around in my head there. I want to high five myself for it. It's so beautiful here, I wish I felt a bit less out of it. I have a look at my phone, and it's nearly dead. I try Facebook, even though I have no internet, but I do have internet, and it works. Did I top up? I can't remember some stuff. Maybe I was asleep. The time on it means nothing cos I can't remember what time I left the house, apart from it was obviously not rush hour, cos it wasn't packed on the trains. Rush hour in the afternoon is 4.30 to 7.00, so it was before that. It's getting duller and duller now. The phone says it's 5.45. That can't be right. I must have slept, sitting there. Probably wasted the drunkenness. I suddenly feel like I'm not off my face at all, and I was just thinking I was, cos I didn't realise I'd slept. There's someone up ahead. The first people I've seen since I got here. It's a bloke and his wife. Or girlfriend, or daughter. I feel dirty and guilty with my can, so I don't look at them. I'm not going anywhere, but I'm going in a direction, at least.

I miss her. I don't mean today. I miss how we used to be. I can't think of when that ever was though, so maybe it's always been like this. I think it has. There were a couple of days at the start where we just snogged and had sex and barely remembered to eat. I always remind her of them when she hates me, and it makes her go softer. We were sitting on the kitchen floor on one of the days, her legs thrown over my hips, and the kissing was so good we got lost in it. The chemistry and the pheromones; I felt like I was in love. Really in love, like they describe it in poems and movies. Not the sort of in love I'd been before, where I'd just gone out with someone long enough to say 'I love you', cos it seemed like the right thing to do, and I only felt it after they were gone. That was how it used to be. I'd only ever thought of love as something you lost. With Emma, on that kitchen floor, us barely knowing each other – that was the first time I'd ever felt in love with someone while I was still with them. And it was far too crazy a thing to have said out loud. It doesn't matter though; no one can take that weekend away from us. I'll remember it forever, no matter how things work out between us. And they probably won't work out. I lost her before, and I got her back. Cos again, I did it differently. It was easier to play the long game with it. I loved her. I could wait. And I filled in the time between with whatever and whoever. But I was calm, I think. Calmer than the person I used to be. I got her back. And it wasn't even cos I'd changed, or done anything good. I just made it possible for her to see me again, in person, after all those months. And when I kissed her, and she remembered what it was like, I had her. Even if I've never had her like that since then. And even if she gets further away from me, whenever she goes farther away from me. High five again. Like this week. I am in a different part now, like a big field, and the sky isn't getting any brighter. It's the summer. It won't be dark until nine or ten. No, wait. It isn't the summer. Is it? How drunk am I? I look at my phone, but it's dead. I don't know where I am, and it'll be dark any minute.

*****

I don't know where this is. It's been a while now since it got dark, and I've been going through the fields, the woods, the Marshes, but I don't know to where, or why, or how I'm going to get out of here. Everything is messed up in my head. I wanted something, but I've forgotten it. The swimmy head feeling came on me quickly, and I don't know if I drank the rest of the cans or just left them somewhere. But there's a place there, with lights, across this field. It's house shaped, and kind of wooden, like those weird houses where I pick the kid up in the mornings. Some mornings. When I'm back there. I don't do that anymore. She goes to school on her own. I'd forgotten that. That's not here though. There's lights, and voices. I need something. I need to be somewhere. The field is damp, or my shoes are damp. It's not the summer, it's not sunny today, it's dark, and I think it must be late now. There's cuts on my fingers where I fell into some thorns. I couldn't get out. I was trying and trying and trying, and the ground was empty, like holes, but the holes had long thorny branches across them, so I tried to stand on those, but I kept falling. And I didn't want to fall into the holes, so I grabbed on with my fingers and the palms of my hands, but there were thorns in the things, and they cut into me. They didn't hurt, they just stung. There were stinging things there too; nettles and thistles, and I didn't know which way to go when I got up – forward or back, cos I couldn't remember which way I'd come in. Bushes and trees and branches and thorns and holes that go down, down somewhere, and it felt like I'd done it before, some other time, in a different place. Or the same place, but I've never been here before. Except I have, with her, so that's not true. But it doesn't feel like the same place it was then, it feels like another place from another day, but the same thorns, and the same holes that go down.

But I'm out of it and away from it now, and I'm in the field, going to the thing that looks like a house. And maybe it's toilets, or changing rooms, or a place where there's someone at a desk. It looks like there's writing on the side – big silver letters, but all I can see is 'CKNEY' and that's from 'Hackney', so I know I'm in Hackney, but I know that already, I think. But it doesn't feel like it at all. The air smells different. Everything feels different, and I don't know how I'm here. I'm getting closer to the house thing, and there's people, cos I can hear them, and I can kind of see them. And they're talking, or singing, or something in between. And I need to sort myself out or straighten myself up, cos I'm covered in cuts and I must look a state. There's mud on my knees that I can't see in this dark, but I can feel the wet of it, through my jeans. I haven't done a bad thing. I'd remember that; I haven't done that. The house is nearer, and it has no windows, and it does say 'Hackney', but it must be a trick, cos this isn't Hackney, and reality is bullshit; we all know that. The people are fuzzy and my eyes won't let me see them. I can hear them though, talking, and singing, or something in between. It's taking forever just to get through this grass, and my feet are wet and cold, and I'm not sure if I had those last few cans, or if I just left them somewhere. I already had that thought in my head, I think, I can't remember, everything is repeating. Just like those holes and bushes and thorns and trees, cos that happened another time, years ago, and it wasn't in Hackney, so I can't be in Hackney. I know better. I know better than signs on houses that aren't really houses. The people are invisible or disappearing, cos I'm off the grass now, and I'm where the people should be, but there aren't any. Just poles and the shadows from poles. And I think maybe I just made them up with my eyes, but then where were the voices coming from? And then I listen to them talking, and singing, or something in between, but it's not there now, and I'm just on my own, on the stone path thing, with the house that isn't a house. I walk around it and look for a door, but I don't know what I'd do if I found one, and I don't find one, so that's fine. But I have nowhere to go, cos this was where I was going, so I have to go somewhere new now, but it's okay, cos I see another path, and I bet that goes somewhere. Every path goes somewhere, even if it's just into a dead end. I need to find a road, with cars and buses on it, cos I'm cold now, and I'm never cold.

I go down the path and it looks like a path that takes you to a road, cos I think I can hear cars or trucks, and trucks are usually going to the big town, or coming out of it, and I'm not sure where this is anymore, cos it smells like a different place, and I can't see anything that says I'm near home, and I know she'll be at home waiting for me, with the kid, worrying, and I have to get to work, and that's the wrong memory now and I'm confused, cos of the smell, cos it smells different and not like here at all. My head is fine and it hurts and I'm dizzy and I think I have fags cos I had fags and it's still now and I should stop and have one but if I stop I'll stop. And I don't want to stop. I should have another can, cos I'm thirsty, but there's no cans, cos they're gone, or I left them somewhere. And this path is long, but it's going to the road, and the road will take me back home, and I can ask someone or get a bus and it'll be fine. The fag is half smoked already but I don't remember lighting it so maybe I didn't, but that's stupid, cos I'm smoking it, and it tastes different cos everything smells different and I can feel the phone in my pocket but it's dead, so I can't see the maps thing, but this path is nearly over now, and there's trees, and I come out, and I think I'm out of where I was, cos there's a road, but there's no cars on it, and it feels like I'm out the country, and I can't see or look up properly. I know where I'm going now and I was just stupid.

It's just trucks now, passing me, and I'm going under bridges, and I don't know them to look at them, but I'm going the right way, cos it's up there, and I'll be there soon, so that's good. The ground is gravelly now, so it's not a real path anymore, and I shouldn't be on it, but no one is going to knock me down, cos I'm on the right part of it, where the trucks come toward me on this side, and they come behind me on the other side, so they can't knock me down, cos I'd see them. It's okay now, and it's better, cos I know those bridges. And I was being stupid, cos I know where I'm going now, I just have to get there, and it's just up here. But I'm really tired, and I'm really thirsty, and I'm really afraid, and I want to be at home. Even though it isn't really my home. And she isn't there. But it's good that she isn't there, I think. But I still want her to be.

There's lights, and I can't remember how to go in, but they'll be glad to see me, like they were that last time, and it's okay about work, cos I can just have coffee when I get there. I just need to change my clothes and stuff, I can sleep when I get home. It's all big and made of stone, and I don't recognise this way in, but I go up the steps anyway, which aren't steps, they're like a ramp, cos the steps are on the other side, and I know this now, and it's fine, and I can hear people, and there's lots of lights. And I go around the corner, and there's glass, and I don't know this bit, but it's all right, cos they'll know me when I come in, and I have to check that I'm not smoking, cos I don't think you can smoke in here. And there's the door, but it's more like glass, and it opens by itself, and the people aren't making noise anymore, and I walk into the doors that open by themselves, and they don't open, and now I'm just against the glass, looking in, and there's no one there, so I think I'm around the wrong side, so I walk around again, to the other bit, but none of this is right, and I can't think or understand properly, but it must be here somewhere, cos I'm here and I got here.

It's the wrong place, and I don't know why. And now I don't know what place I thought it was, and I've walked all this way to get here, but I don't know where here is, and I think I'm going to get in trouble for being here. It's all made of stone, and there's no one behind the glass, and they weren't waiting for me, and I just want to find the way back to go out the same way that I came in, but I walk around and around it, and I can't find it again, cos I don't know what I'm looking for. And I hear people again, but they're far away now. I'm squinting across this yard thing, with all the machines in it, and I know I'm not in the place, and the people aren't here, they're over there, in a house, where there's lights. It's like a garden, and I don't know them, and they're having fun, like it's normal, and they don't know me. And they're over a fence, and the fence is over a wall, and there's too many machines in the way, and I need to go home, and I know now why it smells different, and why I knew all those bridges, and I find the steps this time, not the ramp, but I still go on them, cos that's how you get out. And I'm on the road again now, but I have to cross it, cos I have to go back the other way, by all the bridges, and I need to walk on the right side, so cars don't come up behind me and knock me down.

It's so funny and stupid. I know now, though, so it's fine. I just need to get past all this big road, and get down to where I know where I'm going, and get home. Dad will be fine and stuff. That's where I'll go. My sister has my room now, but I can sleep on the couch or something. Doesn't matter. Everyone's gonna think it's hilarious, but they'll be glad to see me. I can't even remember going over that bridge, but I did, obviously. How else would I be here? I'll be fine once I get in, through the door, and sit down. They'll be okay. It's a nice surprise. I haven't got my passport. I must have just walked along the bridge down the side and not realised I was going over the border. I feel guilty, but that's the drink. Stupid to drink that much. I've got to sort that out. This might be the thing though; the rock bottom. It's all obvious now. I can see the green bits, and the river, and that's Sarsfield Bridge, there. I'm only about ten minutes away. I love the smell of the air now, cos I realise that's what I was smelling – home. My Mum will be surprised as well; she'll probably come down tomorrow or the next day. I dunno how long I'll stay. Might be good. A little break. I was so drunk. I was doing that thing, where I get so messed up I forget who I am or something, or I forget what time it is in my life. Back there, I was being crazy. I was going home to the kid's mum, and the kid, and the kid was a baby. I thought it was before, and that I was in Wales, where we lived when the kid was born. It's crazy dangerous to drink that much. I have to stop. This road is taking a long time to walk down; the bridge doesn't seem to be getting any nearer. I can't see it properly anyway, I can't see anything properly. When I was back in the field, and there was that big house thing, I remember now that I thought there was an ATM, but there wasn't. I'm laughing now, thinking of myself tying to use it, if it was there, and only getting out Euros instead of pounds. I don't recognise this bit I'm walking through now at all, they must have built it when I was away. The bridge doesn't even look like the bridge. There's no lights on it, it's just black, and it's the wrong shape. They're gonna be surprised when I just show up. It must be late now; I've been walking for hours. I must, cos I'm here now, and that takes a long time. I dunno why I didn't realise it before, but I don't even understand it now. I'm here though, at home, in Ireland. You can't argue with the facts. The bridge is gone now, there's nothing there at all, and I don't know this road. It's been such a strange day, and I'm so tired. There's no river next to me anymore either, I must have gone a wrong way somewhere. I turn around to check, but there's nothing behind me, no road or anything. I turn back to the front now, panicking, but there's nothing there either. I look up, but it's just a hole, not the sky, just a hole, like the ones with the thorns over them. I look down and I'm falling, fast, and I can't stop, and I'm scared, and then it keeps going and going, and I stop being scared, and it's like those dreams you have when you're drowning, and eventually you just stop fighting it and you give in. And I wake up properly now, and I'm in the stone place with the glass and the machines, and I never went anywhere, and I'm not in Ireland, cos you can't just walk to Ireland over a bridge. Someone walks past and gives me a look, like I'm some tramp. And I'm ashamed, and I need to get out of here.

The road back is the same one here, but it's completely different, cos I'm half-straight now, and not thinking I'm in different countries. This isn't the first time it's happened to me. There were a couple of others, drunk as well. Something in my brain snaps back to other times, when I lived in other places, and it tries to look for landmarks that are vaguely from there. I feel bad. I don't know what time it is. I'm not anywhere where I could find out, either. I'm just on a road, in the dark, with lots of bridges, and I don't even know if I'm going the right way to Hackney. And I don't even want to go to Hackney; I need to go home, to the new place, and the dogs. It could be three in the morning, they're probably starving. There are no bus stops. Bus stops have maps on them, sometimes. The bigger bus stops, not the poles. I wish the kid was here. She can read those upside-down maps and figure out where we need to go. And she always remembers how we got somewhere, and how to get back. Didn't get that from me. That said, she's usually sober.

This is soul-destroying. I am so tired, even though I must have slept at least twice. I'm disoriented, and I'm so sad, and I want Emma. I miss her so much. I need her now. And that's crazy, cos she's not nurturing or comforting. She's the cliché of an Ice Queen. I don't care though; my chest is hurting from how much I'm pining for her. Cars go past, every so often. They're no use. Even if they were taxis, I don't know where I am, or if I have enough money to get where I'm going. I'm lost. I must be in Hackney though. I can't have walked that far. But, when you're somewhere you don't recognise, you could be anywhere. There's a hopelessness to being lost; that's why it feels so good when you finally find the way home. And Emma's not at home; she's far away. And that's good, cos I stink of drink and fags, and she'd probably think I've gone off and killed myself. I might yet, if this road doesn't go somewhere soon. I won't, though. I'll get home, eventually. I always do.

Back at the house and it's pandemonium. The first thing I notice is the time; it's only half past nine. I have to check, and double check, and make sure the clock on the iPod dock isn't wrong. My concept of time was all over the place. I thought it was like three in the morning. Then, the dogs. They were supposed to be fed around six or seven. They're whining, but they're okay. I feel really bad though, cos I love those dogs. I'll do it in a minute. In a minute, when I get my head back together. I stick my dead phone in the dock, and it makes the little chirp noise and starts charging. The house phone is blinking a light at me, and while I try to remember what that means, it rings at me, incredibly loud and shrill. I pick it up, thinking it's telesales, cos it's a new number, but it's too late, even for them. Emma's voice comes on the line. She sounds like she's in hysterics.

"Oh, God. Oh thank God you're okay."

"Sorry?"

The dock for the phone is moving in and out of focus as I try to read what it says on the LCD thing. I can't still be drunk. I make it out eventually: *19 Missed Calls*.

"I've been ringing all day! You disappeared!"

"I did?"

I'm panicking. I don't know what to say. I need a story. A good one that makes sense.

"Yes! I've been so worried. I didn't- I didn't know where you were."

"I was here!"

My eyes are refusing to focus. The dogs are making needy whining noises behind me. It's all too much.

"You weren't!"

"I was. Well, I was earlier."

Think of something. Quickly. It won't come.

"Well I've been calling all day. All evening. No one has seen you on Facebook. I asked. I asked all your friends. I've been so worried. Where were you?"

"Hey! Hey, it's okay. I just went out."

"Where? And for how long, Tom? What about the dogs? What's happened?"

"Nothing's happened, honestly. I didn't think I-"

I stop talking cos I've got muddled, and I'm paranoid that I'm slurring. I can't be slurring. I'm not still drunk. *Christ.*

"You weren't answering your phone. You didn't pick up the house phone. Where the hell were you, Tom? I'm in bits. I've been crying for hours here."

I have no idea what's going on. I'm not used to her being concerned about me. Caring about me. She must have thought I'd done myself in. That's the only thing it could be. It's not love. It's guilt.

"I just... I took the dogs to Hackney Downs."

"Hackney Downs?"

"Hackney Marshes, sorry."

I'm still pissed, somehow. I don't know what I'm saying.

"Why the hell did you go there? We don't even live in- what were you thinking?"

"I dunno, okay? It was nice out. I wanted to take the dogs for a big walk. I'm sorry."

"The dogs? Why didn't you just go to Wanstead Flats!? It's only down the road, Tom. Hackney Marshes? What the hell is going on? I've been in bits here. I've been so worried about you."

"I know. I know, I'm really sorry. I was stupid. I didn't think to charge my phone and stuff."

Why the hell *didn't* I go to Wanstead Flats? Although it's not like I was making intelligent decisions to begin with.

"But… and you took the dogs?"

"Yeah."

"On the bus? The tube?"

"Yeah, on the train. They were very good, don't worry."

"Right, then how come when I rang Dee next door and asked her to come check on you, she could hear dogs barking? They were going mental. You can't have had them with you. Where the hell were you?"

I don't know who Dee is, or how she's managed to make friends with our new neighbours so quickly. It's not like she's… friendly, or anything.

"When was that?"

I'm thinking on my feet, even if I'm having trouble standing on them.

"When was what?"

"Dee. The neighbour. Coming round and stuff?"

"It was only a half hour ago."

Perfect.

"Oh right, I must have been at the shop."

"The shop?"

"Yeah, the corner shop. I went up to get some bread and juice."

"When was this?"

"About twenty minutes ago, I think."

"And you were back from Hackney Marshes then?"

"Yeah."

"But how long was that? With the dogs? Tom, they must be exhausted, walking around that long. What were you thinking?"

"I don't know! I just took them for a walk. And then it was nice, so I was sitting down for a while. And the time just went. I'm sorry! I didn't know you'd be freaking out."

"Of course I'm going to freak out. You disappear off the internet; you're not picking up your phone. You're not picking up here. I didn't know what had happened, Tom. I'm still in bits."

"It's okay. It's okay now, I'm sorry. I really am. Thank you for caring about me and stuff. It means a lot."

I shouldn't have said it. It's gonna put her on the back foot, I know her inside out. There's a big pause. I know it's cos she's realised she's let her guard down, and shown me how much she cares about me. And, in her screwed up head, that's a bad thing. Eventually, she speaks.

"Yeah, well. You know... I just- I was just worried. I'm sorry I made such a big deal about it. It was just- everything altogether, and the way you've been feeling recently. It just all sort of snowballed and I jumped to conclusions."

"Hehe. What sort of conclusions?"

Me hanging myself in the hall, without a shadow of a doubt.

"I don't- it doesn't matter now. You're okay. I'm so glad you're okay."

In spite of myself, that makes me feel warm and happy. I hate the hold she has over me. I really do.

"Me too."

That makes no sense. I don't care. I feel warm and happy. Thanks, Emma.

"I love you, you know? No matter what happens with us, I… I just want you to know that."

It's not lip service this time; she means it. And that makes it hurt even more. I can't explain why right now.

"I love you too. You gonna be okay?"

"Yeah. Yeah, I'll be fine. I wish you were here now."

"Me? Thanks, I wish I was too."

I genuinely do. I don't like missing out on this blue moon sentimentality. I might never see it again. Can't be helped, though.

"Thank you. How are the dogs?"

Absolutely starving, probably.

"They're good! All fed and watered now. Sleepy looking."

They're tearing around the kitchen, making wild eyes at me through the glass door.

"Good! God, they must have been starving when you got in. Were they?"

"Nah, I brought some treats with me."

Stupid thing to say. In the version of the story she's heard, I didn't know I was coming home late. I'm tripping over my own lies now, and I'm gonna screw it up.

"Did you? Oh, cool. That was lucky. Why did you bring them?"

"Oh, I thought they might play up on the tube, so…"

Genius.

"Good thinking. Okay, listen, I'm gonna go back to Mum and Dad. We're watching Doc Martin again. You sure you're okay?"

"Of course. Never been better."

"Okay, cool. Well, bye then. I'll try texting you nanight later, yeah? But Dad might turn off the Wi-Fi again, and you know the 3G down here is-"

"Shite, yeah. Well, if that happens, don't worry. I'll nanight you now. Nanight!"

"Haha. Nanight you too. I love you. I'm so relieved. I- never mind. Talk to you soon."

"Yeah. And I love you too. And I miss you. Loads."

Too much. I always take it too far, and then the ball's in her court, and she leaves me hanging. Not this time though.

"I miss you loads too. I'll see you this time next week, yeah?"

"Awesome. We'll go to the pictures."

"I'd like that. Thanks, Tom. And thanks for being okay."

"My pleasure. Nanight, you."

"Hehe. Night night. Bye."

"Bye."

The line goes dead. I untense my shoulders, and put the handset down. I want to cry now. Not cos of the day I've had either. I want to cry cos she's able to love me like that, and it takes her thinking I've killed myself for her to let me see it. I'm going to have a gin and tonic. I've earned it.

Seven

This Year, Limerick, Orla

Obsessions and compulsions. My obsessions are always much healthier than my compulsions. I go to sleep at night thinking of my obsessions, but I wake up thinking of the compulsions. And every day I can put off at least one of those compulsions is a better day for me, and every day I fail is a worse one. Smoking, drinking, eating shit that's bad for me – they're the simple ones. And some of the hardest to kick. It gives me a goal to aim for though, every night, when I'm on my own, and everything seems less complicated, and I tell myself that tomorrow will be the day. But tomorrow is almost never the day, so the day after that becomes the new tomorrow. And, before you know it, ten years have gone past.

Orla is my new obsession, even if she's always been, really. Now, more than ever, though. Because I'm in the same place as her. And I've found her again. But also because I have nothing else. No job, place of my own, no friends, no human contact outside my own family – when there's nothing else, the obsession fills the void. Really fills it. Which is okay for me now, because the alternative is unthinkable. None of that stuff has happened since the day I left England, though, so maybe I've quit that. And I have her now, kind of. So maybe she'll be the one who saves me. I'm meeting her again – in twenty minutes. That's why I'm on a bus to County Clare. She's the only thing getting me up in the morning these days. And it shouldn't be, cos I have a kid in another country I need to get back to, I have four books I need to finish, and I have a life to get back on the rails. But she's somehow jumped to the front of the queue. So maybe not all my obsessions are good.

*****

The pub is massive, and packed, even this early in the day. All tourists, on their way to or coming back from Bunratty, with the castle, and the medieval village. The Yanks eat that sort of thing up. They always seem a bit disappointed when they're in the modern cities – like they didn't pay thousands of dollars to fly over here and find out we all don't live in thatched cottages and smoke cork pipes. They all seem to like wearing powder blue leisure suits too. Maybe they sell them at the airport.

Orla is wearing a dress. I've never seen her wearing one before – not in real life situations. There was that Hunt Ball we all went to when Holly was at UL, but that was different. Everyone was formal that night – even me, although I did wear Vans with my tux, cos I was such a rebel and all that. But this is new. Just the kind of dress I like too, and I didn't even give her any hints. Sleeveless shift dress with a Peter Pan collar. No shape to it really, but they never do, that's why you have to be a bit fit to wear them – nothing gets accentuated with magic seams or push-up bits – it's all you. And it's all her, today. And she looks amazing.

"I think we're the only Irish people in here."

"Ah, I think there's a few locals," I say, looking around to make sure I'm right.

"Yeah, but they're alcoholics," she says, whispering, as if she's afraid that hearing it will make the two old fellas next to the fire realise they've wasted their lives or something. It's not lit or anything, even if they both are.

"You know what, I hate to be that guy, but when I lived in England…"

"Here we go…" She rolls her eyes. People here hate it when you do the 'England has better this that or the other' spiel, or the 'God, isn't everything expensive here?' thing, even if it is. Expensive here, I mean, not better over there.

"Fuck off. No, seriously. When I lived over there, Wetherspoon's would open at like nine in the morning or something. And if I went in there to get a coffee-"

"Sure. To get a coffee, I believe you." She gives me a wink and I think to myself that even her winks are gorgeous. I've already got it bad for her; although I always have had. This is just… more, because she's actually here.

"No, really. They did coffees for like 50p or something."

"50p? Jesus."

"Yeah, I know. I think it was just like a *loss leader* or something. To draw you in, and make you buy a sandwich." I think that's the right phrase. It doesn't matter. If you say anything with enough confidence, people won't question you. I think Hitler said that, or someone like him.

"What was your point again?" She's fiddling with a cardboard beermat and I remember how much I like her hands. That's a weird thing to like about someone when you're a boy. Girls notice hands and shoes all the time. We usually couldn't pick our girlfriends' hands out of a line-up. Not that she's my girlfriend.

"Oh. Yeah, sorry. When I went in there to get coffee."

"*Definitely* to get coffee." She smiles and it's like someone drew the blinds and let more sun in.

"Yes. Well, anyway, you'd see these guys sitting down drinking pints. And it was always Guinness."

"Guinness? Were they Irish?"

"Oh, Orla." I wish she was near enough for me to touch her hand in a patronising way, mainly because I'd be touching her hand, but she's just out of reach.

"What?"

"Irish people don't drink Guinness over there," I say. An American guy at the bar gives me a little look just now, as if he thought I was talking about him. He's got a pint of Guinness next to him, barely touched. From the colour of the head, he's had it about an hour. They buy it for the experience, but most of them can't stomach it. I suppose in my head that they're used to horse piss like Bud and Coors, and stout is a whole different ball game to them. Most of the Americans I know (on the internet) drink wine. But that's because they're all women in their 30s, I guess.

"They don't?"

"Nah. Doesn't taste the same, innit?" I do the accent without thinking. I forget sometimes how offensive it is to Irish people just to hear it. *Trigger warning: colonial oppression*. She doesn't seem fazed though.

"Oh. Why?"

"Cos they don't know how to pour it, duh." I remember working in a pub over there, when I used to work, and they had *instructions* on the back of the stout taps. The blasphemy of it. And it still didn't do any good. I couldn't pour their bitter right either though, or use the pump on the real ale, so it's swings and roundabouts, I guess.

"Oh. Bloody Protestants, am I right?"

"Spot on. They have pubs open on Good Friday, though, fair play."

"They'll pay for that in the next life." She crosses her legs and I wonder how I've gone all these years without thinking how good they must look, considering how good she always looked in jeans. She isn't wearing tights – her skin looks creamy.

"They will. Actually, they have pubs open on Christmas Day as well over there."

"Really? Who'd go to the pub on Christmas Day? I know people go to restaurants and have their Christmas dinner done for them, but… the pub?"

"Yeah, it's hard to explain, really. It isn't big chain pubs. Small, local ones open for a few hours, and people pop in to wish them happy Christmas, give them a few quid tip or whatever. It's quiet, like. Cosy."

"Were you living in an episode of Eastenders when you were over there?"

"I did make it sound like that just there, didn't I?"

"Whass gawin on??????"

"Get ou' my pub!!!!!"

*****

Later, we're in the outside smoking area. It's Ireland though, so the 'outside' part is debatable. It literally has a roof and four walls. Never fails to amuse me. I'd said I would go out by myself for a smoke, cos she doesn't, but she'd insisted on coming, and I wasn't going to argue. There's a different vibe in here. No Americans, for one thing. They're not big on smoking, I think. Or at least, the ones who can afford to fly over here for a holiday aren't. I don't really know that much about them, even if I do know lots from being virtual friends with a bunch of them, and from watching their TV shows.

"Hey, they have a jukebox," she says, nodding over by the bar.

"Do they?" I can't hear any music out here, but that means I can't hear the piped-in diddly idle-die stuff either, and that's a good thing.

"Yup."

"Think it works?"

"Only one way to find out…" She hops down from her stool like a little girl, instead of a thirty-something woman, and I remember that she's always been like that. Small and cute and ageless. It's one of the reasons this doesn't feel like fifteen years later, more like we just picked up where we left off. And we kind of have. I can't see myself though, just her. If we were sat in front of a mirror I might think a bit differently. She goes over to the jukebox without looking back to see if I'm coming too. There's a fella behind the bar in here, washing glasses, and I see him look her up and down. People always did, but she was never mine to be jealous about it back then. He says something to her and she goes over to him, but I can't hear what they're saying. She's still not mine, of course, but now I do feel the jealousy. A little ouch in the middle of my chest. The heart, I suppose, and then I wonder how we came to think of the big pump in our body as some sort of centre for emotions, and I think it was probably cos of moments like this.

"What did he want, then?" I hear the words come out of my mouth when she comes back to the table, even though I know I didn't plan on saying them.

"The barman? Oh, nothing."

I want to say something like "It didn't look like nothing," or "He clearly wanted something, he was talking to you," but that would be completely batshit insane, even for me, so I don't.

"What did you put on?"

"Hmmm. A surprise," she says, but I can already hear it's The Smiths. *That Joke Isn't Funny Anymore.*"

"Great taste."

"Hah. That's like the worst compliment ever, you know." She looks at me with what a bad writer would describe as a flash of mischief in her eyes. I'm not sure what she means.

"Eh?"

"Well, it's not the worst compliment ever, like. 'You've lovely eyes' is the worst compliment ever, cos that's like the only part of you that you can't be fat in, your eyes, so it's like saying to someone 'At least your eyes aren't fat'.

"Haha, I think you're overthinking that, like." Although she sort of has a point. I'd never thought of it like that before.

"I'm not. Any time I get a compliment on my eyes I'm straight on the fucking weighing scales, soon as I get home."

"Pffft, there's nothing there of you. I'd say you don't even own weighing scales."

"Oh, I do. Do you know nothing about women at all?"

"I know they don't have fat eyes, now, thanks to you."

"Yep. Or hair. 'Your hair is *gorgeous*, like,' is another one. Might as well just say 'So how long have you known cake, then? You two seem pretty close.'"

"Hahahaha. You can't say stuff like that anymore, you know. It's the 21st Century."

"Apparently you can. Cos I just did. Your hair is lovely, btw. And those eyes…" She does a wit-woo whistle and I kick her foot under the table.

"Oi, that's abuse, that is."

"Is it?"

"Yeah, in the 21st Century it is. I'm pretty sure that's actually *rape*, now. I read that in a blog the other day."

"What a time to be alive. Want another one?"

"Another kick? No, you're grand." She's rubbing her toes all dramatic, but I barely touched her.

"Another drink, you spa. I've to have a word with that barman anyway, like. Let him know the score."

"Oh yeah? What is the score, then?" She gives me a look and I'm not sure what it means yet.

"Between you and me?" I feel anxious, but in a niceish way. Heart is a bit in my mouth, but it's kind of okay that it.

"Maybe."

"We're just a couple of old friends, out for a drink. Nothing dodgy. All above board." I put a tone in my voice so she's doubly sure that I don't mean that literally.

"Oh. Fair enough."

"Unless that cunt over there asks, obviously. Then you're my wife," I say, hopping down of my chair to go get the drinks, and she laughs, and then she doesn't laugh, when we both remember that she's someone else's wife.

*****

"Hang on, why was it the worst compliment ever, anyway?" It's an hour later at least, and now the smoking area is getting busier. We've moved over to some soft seats. I haven't as much as grazed her knee with my fingertips yet, and it's still the most exciting afternoon I've had with anyone in years.

"The taste thing?"

"Yeah!" I'd forgotten she said it, then I remember, in one of those drunk brainwave moments, even though we aren't really that drunk.

"Oh, it's cos it's not a compliment. Not to the other person."

"Yeah it is."

"No, it's not. It's you basically agreeing with their taste in whatever – films, albums, books, yeah? It's you saying 'I like that too, and I've brilliant taste, so you're basically as great as me."

Again, I'd never thought of it that way.

"Jesus. You're not just a pretty face, are you, Orla?" It's a cliché, but I mean it.

"Nope. And I've lovely eyes too, everyone says."

"Yep. And really chubby hair."

*****

There's about twenty minutes left before we have to head back, but I don't feel like I'm in a hurry to do anything. I think maybe I don't want to do anything at all, because if I don't – if we don't, then we *are* just a couple of old friends, catching up, and we don't risk fucking everything up. But then we'll never know, and that was the old state of affairs – never knowing. What's the point in this unless we're doing something new?

"Remember that time on my birthday?" There's a tipsy sound to her voice and I'm surprised I notice it, since I'm half-cut myself.

"Yeah, of course." There's only one time she means, because I didn't really know her for that long back then, and I only remember knowing it was her birthday the one time.

"You said to me the other night that when you gave me my present, in my house, remember? And I kissed you on your cheek. You said that was like the best day of your life, or something? Did you mean that?" The look she's giving me now is a different one to all the others, but I recognise it from a long time ago. It's a look that leads somewhere. A dangerous one. I take a breath.

"Well, yeah. I suppose. Bear in mind I'd had a shit life up until then, so I wouldn't get a swelled head about it or anything." I don't really feel embarrassed about all this – cos it's her – but I still make the joke, because old habits and all that.

"Haha, well, yeah. But anyway, I dunno. When you said that, it made me feel all…"

"Scared?"

"Haha, no. Special, I guess."

"You are special." I love saying things like this to her, cos I mean them, and that's really rare. Sort of like when you're on ecstasy and you're with someone you actually love and you tell them you love them. The truth makes stuff like that feel amazing, I think.

"Jesus, stop, I'm gone scarlet." She hides her face in her hands for a second, and I already miss it.

"No, like, seriously. It was like… I never wanted to wash that cheek again."

"Haha, you fucking lunatic. Here, close your eyes."

"What?"

"Just close them."

"Okay." I close my eyes and feel my heart starting to rush, cos I think I know what's coming. It feels like ages before I feel her lips on the side of my face, and she leaves them there for a little longer than you could get away with and still call it a peck.

"Whoa."

"Bad whoa or good whoa?" she says, her face still close to mine.

"The best whoa."

"Yay! Want another?"

"Yes please!" I say, and she does it again, but this time I keep my eyes open. The smell of her is so good I can sort of feel my mouth watering.

"Just a couple of friends, right?"

"Yeah," I sort of mumble, my head feeling light because of how close her mouth is to mine now. I wish she wasn't saying anything, cos I don't want guilt to get in the way. She hasn't moved away though; guilt or no guilt. I push her fringe away from her face with my two fingers and she does that nice sort of shudder girls do. My lips are half an inch away from hers now, and there's fifteen years of anticipation behind me, nudging me to bridge the gap.

"Friends do this, right?" she says, and before I can reply she's pressing her lips against mine – not too soft, not too hard – it's not a real kiss, but it's definitely more than friends do. When she breaks off from me I feel like I need to take ten deep breaths just to recover, but I don't want to recover from this just yet.

"Yeah. Close friends." I don't wait for permission, I just kiss her back – the same way, no tongues, maybe a little firmer than she had done to me. So firm that hers come apart a little, probably not on purpose, but I can feel her teeth for a second. I'm really slow in pulling away from her, because I can feel she doesn't want me to. It feels like we're a million miles away from everyone else in the place. Like we're not even breathing the same air as them – just recycling our own, back and forth.

"We're pretty close, to be fair," she says, and now she's kissing me again, and it's firmer from her, and my lips are the ones that break apart, and now all thinking goes out the window, and instinct takes over, and we kiss each other properly, for the first time ever, after fifteen years, and it's everything I ever imagined it would be, except it's ten times better than that, and I can feel she's feeling exactly the same, and I hope she can stay a little longer than she said, because if this is what the first kiss is like, I can't even imagine how it'll be when we've had a little practice at it.

Eight

Last Year, London, Emma

It's the middle of the day, she's at work, I'm writing. I'm not writing at all, obviously. I'm smoking, and drinking cheap knock-off Red Bull, and watching torrented movies from the 80s, and trying not to get drunk. Or trying not to try to get drunk, more specifically. The later I leave it, the less likely I am to start. Weird Science is on. Kelly LeBrock. Great body. Strange film. So many of these give me a special feeling, and it's all down to them having a bit of nudity, and me having seen them when I was a little too young to be allowed to see it. It's like how porn magazines on a shelf give me a feeling. Stuff on the internet isn't the same. It's an old feeling, about being in a shop, and wanting to buy one, but you're too young and it's never going to happen. So you have to wait until you accidently find one in a field, or in your friend's house, or hidden away in the house by your dad. My dad kept lots of old mags and newspapers in the house, in stacks and piles, everywhere. My mum hated it. One day I was just nosing through them when I found some soft porn in between a bunch of normal magazines like *Sun Day*, or *Ireland's Own*. It gave me a warm feeling in my chest, looking at those naked women, and knowing I shouldn't have been. I knew it was rude and naughty, and I'd be killed if someone caught me, but I thought they were all beautiful. I loved their boobs, and the thrill of seeing a nipple. The hairy bits down below weren't as nice though, they made me a little ill.

It's the bit where she has the shower with them, and they keep their jeans on. She still gives me a fair old nostalgia horn, looking at her now. The clothes are a bit dated, and I never liked a perm, but every guy of a certain age knows the shot of her standing in the doorway in her little blue knickers and a cut off t-shirt. That was what we had, instead of PornHub. Robert Downey Jr is in this. I'd forgotten that. He's very young. Probably the same height as he is now, though. *Iron Manlet*. Dogs are on the couch again. Haven't taken them for a walk. They suffer cos she's such a twat to me, it's not fair. I like them, they're no trouble. Apart from all the worming and de-fleaing that they need, which is something only posh people do. My dad has dogs at home and they've never been near a vet. Still alive, no fleas, no worms. It's amazing there aren't any conspiracy videos on YouTube about it. Although there probably are. It's only half past one. I can't imagine getting to seven without something happening. And 'something happening', is liquor.

It's been nearly a year since we got back together. I don't think things have changed. They've maybe got worse. They're bad now, anyway. And a year ago, they were great, but only cos we'd just re-met and rebooted, obviously. It's not a fair comparison. It's just strange now. Every day is me, on my own, in this new house that doesn't feel familiar yet. Doesn't feel like I'll be here long, but I can't imagine being somewhere else. Not for good. We've had lots of almost overs. They don't turn into genuine overs, cos I manage to calm things by taking the lead and talking about us breaking up. Accepting it, cos it seems to break the bad spell of tension. If I'm there in front of her and I'm saying "Well, I guess it's over then. Can you give me a few days to figure something out, so I have somewhere to go?", it's better than crying, or telling her I can't live without her, or reminding her that she's my only safety net. That only makes it worse. It's when I say that I'm leaving, and that it's fine, and it's not her fault, and not to worry, and I'll survive. When I act like that, she suddenly stops wanting to break up, cos no one is fighting her anymore. If no one is fighting, there's no fight to be hand, and it's hard to keep on fighting. It's not on purpose, my little game; I think I genuinely think those things and feel them and mean them, every time I'm saying them. It's not an act. And cos I'm being sincere, it shows, and she thinks I'm brave, and almost someone who can stand on his own two feet. And she respects that, so she respects me, and she lets me stay. I can't stand on my own two feet though, and I'd be screwed without her. I can't keep going on like that. It's not healthy for anyone, and I don't have many lives left.

I used to read books, but I stopped a few years ago. I remember someone buying me a Stephen King one a few years ago, and it was shit. No one has the balls to edit him, he has too much power. People said my first book was just like early King, and I took that as a compliment. It was also inevitable, cos I grew up reading everything he wrote. And James Herbert, and Dean Koontz. I was into horror, and stuff what wasn't horror, but written by horror writers. I don't know why, I was just dark as a kid. Some things never change. I don't read anymore, it's too hard to take the writer out of me while I do it. I'm too critical of everything; the way their dialogue is unrealistic, and things like that. I don't care about structure, or sympathetic characters, or show don't tell, or any of that other shit that you see hack reviewers talk about. Those people are idiots, just trying to sound clever. They like books less than I do, probably. When I get a bad review, it's usually cos people couldn't stomach the content or the subject matter. People who couldn't get past the first chapter, but still feel the need to give me one star out of five, and leave a shitty comment. Bollocks to those people. If they have a go at the writing though, I get personally offended. My writing is good. I don't care if they don't like how graphic it is, or they hate the main character. I write graphic things, and I write characters you're not necessarily supposed to love. Maybe you might grow to love them, but they're not going to know that if they give up after one chapter.

If they call the writing 'poor' or 'pedestrian' though, or say the story 'dragged', or the ending was 'rushed', then it hurts me right in my soul. 'Pedestrian' is just one of those words people use when they're talking about a book they don't like, though. Anything is going to seem pedestrian if you're not interested. And the amount of detail, scene setting, and soul searching that's in my books, well that's bound to be the case for some people. I like Irvine Welsh, and the Chuck guy with the hard to spell last name. The guy who did Fight Club. They write characters who aren't sympathetic. Almost all the time. And then they are, if you stick with it. I have their books on my e-Reader. The ones I've read before, and ones I haven't yet. I have an e-Reader, even though I don't read. It's a tablet, it just doubles as a reader thing. And all the books are pirated. I never read a full one on it, though. Most of them I read when they were real books, years ago. I just like them being on the shelf thing. They look nice. When I'm on a bus to go see the kid, or a train, I take the thing out and start on something, but I never keep going, or finish. It's easier to read the non-fiction ones, like Bill Bryson, cos there's no story, and I'm just learning interesting things. I should read more of those, cos I like being smart, and knowing stuff. I always have. It makes me good at quizzes and stuff, and I think it makes me a great person to talk to. But I talk too much, and people just want peace and quiet. It's okay when you're on a date, and you think you're being sparkling company, but even that's bullshit. People don't want to listen to random facts, apropos of nothing. That's just you, filling in the silence, cos you love the sound of your own voice. People on dates want to talk about themselves, and the only thing for you to do is to give them the opportunity to do it. And, when you're in a relationship with someone, people want to talk about themselves too. Not you, or your interesting trivia about the Big Bang, or the Hundred Years War. They want to talk about what happened that day in their boring job, with their boring work people. Or about where they're going on holiday, or something else just as boring. They don't want to talk about politics, or what's going on in the world. The nearest you'll get to an actual conversation with them about something that matters to you both, is if you both like the same TV show, or reality karaoke thing, or if you're having an argument. If you're having a fight, that's something you both care about, but it's not like it's enjoyable.

There's something about the summer in London. It comes early. I get the feeling it's a pollution thing, or smog, or the fumes from all the cars, but I don't think that makes sense. Whatever it is, the sun is splitting the rocks outside, and it's only May. Irish summer is May, June, July, on the calendar. That's what I grew up thinking, even though you'd be lucky to see the sun by July. Here, like everywhere else in the civilised world, it's June, July August. But someone should tell that to the weather today. It's not my thing, the sun. I used to get sunburned a lot as a kid. Used to hide from it. I'm freckly too, and I always thought freckles were ugly, so I hid out of it for years. They're still there on my arms, but my face lost them, after years of spots and ripping off my own skin from the spots. Emma loves the sun. She's constantly chasing it around the globe, or sitting out in it when she has the day off. She tans though, and she's one of those people who are happy just to sit and be cooked in it. I always think it's a sign that someone's stupid, if that's what they look for in a holiday. It's just a bit of fire in the sky. And it gives you cancer. Go see a museum or something.

I'm feeling bad feelings. Old ones. They're not that old. But they've always been around. I'm itching to go out and do something again. I ignore it though, like it's a pang. I got good at that, a few years ago – ignoring pangs. When I wasn't smoking or drinking. It got easier and easier with the smoking. The drink is different, cos social occasions are built around it, and they don't stop being that way just cos you've given up. These are different pangs though, and I've never been able to ignore them for long, once they come along. I haven't had them in years, but now they're here again. It's a feeling that's hard to describe. Something niggling. Something reminding you, like a thought about some skirting boards you meant to clean, or the attic that needs clearing. And you can put it off all you like, it's still going to have to happen at some point. It's not like anything else though; there's nothing you can start doing to replace it. Addiction is like that. They say there's no point in replacing the fags with sweets, cos you'll get fat for one thing, and you're trying to fill a certain shaped hole with a thing that doesn't fit. So you can eat and eat and eat, but if it's a cigarette you want, you'll still want one after all the things have been eaten. That's what this is like, but there's no sweets for it. Unless everything is sweets, cos I literally try doing everything to make this go away. But after I'm finished, I still want it, and I know what I have to do.

It's not something that needs drink or drugs; I learned that a long time ago. But, when it's happening, I might as well be off my face, cos I don't have any control of myself, and I can't stop, and I don't feel guilty or bad, or anything like that, while it's still happening. It's its own medicine and its own cure. And it's the only thing that makes me feel whole. I'm not me unless I do it, and there's nothing else that feels as right. It's not a luxury or an indulgence though, it's a necessity. I need a drink. There's open white wine in the fridge, I can get more to replace it. I have money.

Weird Science is over now, and so is most of the wine. No word from her, no chance she's coming home soon. I check my FetLife – Steve's FetLife. It's been a long time since I've done this, but I know the log in and a password without thinking. Nothing much going on, no messages. Steve has a Facebook, a Twitter, a FetLife, his own email address, etc. He hasn't been a part of my life since I lived at Jim's, before I met Emma. He was around before Jim's too. Before there was even an internet. He did some very bad things, and he got away with it. I got away with it. When I look back at my life, even before all of that started, I always got away with it, whatever it was. A façade of being 'a good boy' meant I could steal from my mum's purse, or take the sponsorship money I'd raised for handicapped kids, or shoplift whatever I wanted, and there was never even one case of anyone suspecting me, let alone me having to face the music. A charmed life, definitely. An exalted birth, as those websites I looked up about a particular mental illness had put it. I don't have that illness though. Cos it's just fake and made up, like the rest of the world, and those are just labels they put on people who understand that. Crazy is just an opinion, a point of view. It's not a diagnosis. Just cos you say or think something that other people haven't got the capacity to understand, it doesn't mean there's something wrong with you. If Einstein or Newton or Hawking had no scientific fields, with peers in them, what they said would be laughed at as insanity. That's what a so-called crazy person is – a genius who just hasn't got the right people around him. I'm not crazy. I'm me, and that's not like anything else in the world. I'm thinking like him again. It's usually okay if I catch myself. It makes it go away. I don't think it's going away today. It's been a long time, but it feels like yesterday, for some reason.

    I'm down the park now, with the dogs. It's the smaller park, so I have to keep them on the leash. That's better though. Makes people come over. I've never had dogs in this way before. There was always one in Ireland, but they were different. Mongrels, never taken to the vet, or given expensive medicines. When their time was up, my mother would have them put down, and there'd be a little talk about it when I got home from school or from playing. There were tears of course. From us, not her. Death was matter of fact to her, it felt like. These ones are different though. Pedigrees, and handsome looking. Strangers on benches outside pubs smile at them when you go past, and other owners come talk to you in the park, and you have to pretend that you care. They're just animals; but then, we all are. I'm pretending to enjoy my walk, but I'm scanning the place. Someone on their own. That's all I need. And a bit of seclusion. The feeling is strong. Sometimes I have weird dreams about pressure. Sometimes I'm awake and aware in the dreams, but they're still dreamlike. Things happen in them that couldn't happen in life, but none of it seems strange or weird, of course. The pressure is in my head. Like someone has the air hose for car tyres and is pumping it into me. And there's only one outlet, every time: my teeth. The pressure builds and builds behind my gums, and my temples feel like I'm concentrating hard. And it isn't painful, per se. It's just something that needs to happen before I can move on.

Before I can wake up. And it never does. The teeth start to move in their settings, and the pressure build up behind them, like the teeth are bullets and the gums are the chamber. And I can picture it; visualise them coming out and hitting the wall. But they don't. I forget, and I wake up later feeling that a whole other scenario happened in the meantime. But it drops out of my brain so quickly that I can never remember what it was. But I remember the pressure. This is like that, only different. Different, and the same. I see an old guy with a can. He might be in his 50s, or he could've just had a hard life. I give him a grin. Or Steve does. It doesn't matter right now. Distinctions like that are pointless. He makes a nice face, and looks down at the dogs. I'm in.

*****

"… and then she went. Me own fault, pal. All me own fault."

We've been talking a while, if you could call it that. We're down by the water, behind the trees. No one passing would see us. I told him the dogs wanted a drink.

"Ah, that's too bad, man."

He smells of piss and vomit. It isn't even a life. He's still sad about his wife walking out on him twenty odd years ago. It's a pathetic existence, not one worth preserving.

"Yep. Yep, that's it, mate. You got a girl?"

"Er, yeah."

"She nice?"

She's an absolute bitch, mainly.

"Yeah. Yeah, she's very nice."

"That's good, mate. Nice ones are hard to find."

"Yeah. Yeah, they are."

I'm looking at his shoes, all full of holes, and probably got from a clothing bank. His big toe is poking out, the nail is yellow-brown. He's barely human by now. He's rotting while still alive.

"She a nice looking bird?"

"Er, yeah. Yeah, I'd say so."

"Nice tits?"

"Haha, yeah."

"What about the arse? Nice bit of arse on her?"

"Oh yeah. Best bit."

Beats her personality, anyway.

"Nice one, geeze. Got an photos of her? On your phone, like? Nice ones? Good ones?"

The cheeky tramp prick.

"Nah, mate. She's a bit shy, you know?"

I have lots, but not for you, you human toilet.

"Oh. Pity. Could've done with a nice little gander, yeah? Hahahaha."

He drinks down the dregs of the shitty cider he's been nursing. I look at the can, and it's a brand I pick up myself sometimes. That gives me a sicker feeling in my gut than the smell of him does.

"Yeah, mate. What's your name, then?"

"Alfie. Alfred, that's a king's name, you know? I'm practically royalty, me."

There's a smell all of a sudden, a worse one than there already was, and my nose wrinkles automatically. He's passed gas in front of me, without making a noise. He probably thinks he's being polite.

"Alfred the Great, yeah."

"Yep. That's me. That's what they call me. Alfred the Great. Or Alfie. Or just Alf, really. I don't mind, mate."

"Who's they?"

I give him a smile and have a fiddle in my back pocket. The dogs are going to be a problem here.

"The lads. You know, me mates. Want one of these?"

He reaches into the bush and pulls out a blue plastic bag, with a few more cans in it. I wonder what his mates look like. Or smell like, for that matter.

"Ah, I'm alright."

I do want one, but later will do.

"Oh, come on. Not going to break bread with me, mate?"

I wonder how long ago it was that he ate bread. Or any solids at all.

"Okay, then. You've twisted my arm."

There's a hooked branch on the tree a few feet from us. I chuck both the dogs' leash handles over it. They pull and tug a bit for a second, and I give them a look. They sit down straight away, and go into quiet mode.

"Fucking hell, that's a skill."

He hands me over a can; they're lukewarm. It doesn't matter to me.

"What? Oh, right. Years of practice."

It isn't. They're just terrified of this me. They know better than to cause a fuss. They live on their instincts. Alfred the Great could do with some of that right now, but he's not to know that. I take a swig of the tepid apple piss, and try not to gag too much.

"Nice, ain't it? Well, it's not nice. It's fucking rank. But it does the job."

"Yeah. I've had it before."

Cold though, from a fridge. And without so much urine and puke in the air.

"Nice one. What do you do then… sorry mate, I didn't catch your name."

"Steve."

No going back now. Or maybe there is. I remember back years ago, to that one time when I was Steve to lots of people, and all of them survived it. Maybe that had just been luck, though. Cos it's never been that way again, since.

"Steve, yeah. Nice to meet you, mate. What's it you do then, for a job?"

"Me?"

"Yeah, you. Who else would I mean, you daft bugger?"

"Hehe, yeah. Sorry. I'm in engineering."

Why not?

"Engineering, is it? La-dee-fucking da, Steve! An engineer. That's something all right. How long you been driving trains then, mate?"

"No, that's not what it-"

"Aaaaaaaaah, I got ya there. You fucking nob end. Your fucking face, mate. It's a picture."

You know I think this guy is probably going to regret taking the piss in a little while. Just a hunch. I do a pretend smile and laugh along with him.

"Hehe, yeah. Good one."

I sink some more of the can. The dogs aren't making a sound, they're already snoozing, I think. Good pooches.

"Yep. Got you right and proper, I did. Back of the fucking net."

All right, calm down there, Ashton Kutcher. It wasn't that good.

"Classic, mate. Naw, I work out in Stevenage. Aerospace. We make shuttle parts, actually. Pretty cool stuff."

It's someone else's backstory; a girl I met once. This twat's never gonna know that though.

"Shuttles? Like for space and that?"

"Yeah. Space shuttles. For going-"

"- to space?"

"Exactly."

Well deduced, Poirot. I'm restless now.

"Jesus. I didn't even think they went to space no more, mate."

"No, they do. Americans, and there's a European Space Agency too."

I think there is. I'm just making this up now.

"European? The Frogs and that?"

"Well, yeah. And us. We're part of Europe too."

"Pfffft. Wish we weren't. All them immigrants, coming over. Stealing our jobs, mate. Fucking ridiculous it is."

I want to point out that I'm an immigrant, and that neither of us are in any danger of having a job that someone could steal, but it's not Educate a Tramp Day. I feel around in my pocket again, and when I touch what I'm looking for, a little ice comes over my chest.

"Yeah, true. But like, there's an International Space Station up there right now. So they're always sending people up there. It's a big thing."

"Yeah? You never see it on the news though, do ya? Not like in the old days."

I don't think he's in a position to comment on what's in the news or not, considering he probably doesn't have a telly. Or, if he did, he probably sold it to buy White Lightning.

"Nah. I guess it's not that newsworthy anymore. It's all about the terrorism now, isn't it?"

I give him a smile, and feel my fingers tighten on the thing.

"Fucking too right, mate. Fucking nothing on now except them Muslims. And they ain't just blowing stuff up, neither. Some of 'em is in big gangs, going around finding little girls, taking 'em back to their-"

He never gets to finish his Daily Express ramblings, poor old Alfred the Great. I take the knife out of my pocket so quickly that he probably never sees it. I slam it so hard into his throat that it goes all the way through and gets stuck in the bones of his neck, or his spine, I can't figure which. Before he even has time to gurgle out a scream, I grab him by his collar and belt and launch his skinny little frame face-first into the water near our feet. There's no real sound as the bubbles come up, the water going bright red around him. It only takes a half a minute of my full weight on the back of his head, before his body stops struggling and I can turn him over to get my blade back. His eyes look like they're still alive, and it creeps me out a little. I take the dogs and the rest of the cans, and head back home. Wasn't much of a walk for them, but you can't have everything.

Back at the house, I throw some ice cubes in a glass, and pour out a toast to poor Alfie. He was a solid geezer, him. A filthy homeless alcoholic racist arsehole, obviously; but we don't speak ill of the dead. People never do, no matter what. Whenever some parent is on TV talking about their dead teenage kid, it's always 'She was so full of joy', and 'Everyone had a good word for her'. No one ever just goes "Well, she was a moody bitch, to be honest. Cracking tits though." That's just the way people are, though. I feel very calm and invigorated at the same time. It was always this way. They'll find him soon, and it'll barely make the news. Same as the space shuttles. No one cares if a homeless guy dies. Even if they're murdered. Police will just reckon it was another tramp. A fight over some booze, or money. Or the romantic love of a tramp-lady. You don't see a lot of tramp ladies. I think it's cos they get into shelters, for their own safety. Whenever I think about being homeless, being raped is always the biggest fear. I'm stronger than I look, but I doubt I could hold off more than one of them if they were trying to lovingly copulate with my arsehole. That's why prison's out too. I'm never going there though, so it's irrelevant. I think I'll watch Pretty in Pink next. I like that one.

Nine

This Year, Limerick, Orla

I picked the Woodfield House Hotel. She asked me where we could go and I chose that. Not particularly off the top of my head, mainly because it's not in the town centre, where she might run into people she knows; it's out by the Ennis Road and Caherdavin, and she's not from around there originally. That was as deep as my reasoning got. She asked me, and I made a quick decision, because that's what you're supposed to do. That was what I was supposed to do when Emma asked me to choose things, so I assume that's the same with all women. Maybe it isn't. It doesn't matter now. It's done.

I've never actually been to the Woodfield, I've just heard of it. I've never stayed in a hotel in Limerick, obviously. What would be the point of that? It was touch and go whether it still existed really, but it does, cos I'm outside it now. I have a weird excitement in me. Weird cos it's sort of subdued, when you consider what's about to happen today, and how long I've waited for it. Maybe I already know something I don't, if that makes any sense, which it definitely doesn't. There's a restaurant on the right-hand side of the doors. I know because they have an outside seating area, and people are there, having lunch in the sunshine. I check my phone to see if she's messaged me. I'll ask them for the WiFi password once I've checked in. I assume they have WiFi. Hopefully it's free.

It's been a week since that day in the pub in Clare. We haven't stopped talking since. Well, whenever we get the opportunity. Which for me is always, but her life's a little more complicated than mine. This hotel thing wasn't spur of the moment. We were basically talking about it when we left each other that day. We'd stayed another hour and a half after that first kiss. She'd made all sorts of flimsy excuses – she didn't care, she wanted to stay, and I wanted her to too. Every waking hour since then has been amazing for me. I'm not down, I haven't had a drink on my own, I haven't even thought about the other thing. It's like a big cloud has lifted, and I'm able to cope with everything now – cos of her. I'd almost say I'm happy, if I knew what that felt like, and how to spot the signs. Maybe I am, though. Stranger things have happened. Gotta stop thinking in clichés, I tell myself, as I walk up to reception to check in.

*****

"No, I love it. It's a great song – especially now, cos, well, we're grown-ups, and,"

"Speak for yourself, there." It's a joke, but I also mean it. I don't think I'll ever be a real grown-up. I think it's cos I'm not tall enough.

"Well, yes, but you know what I mean. It's like… they wrote that when they were pretty much the same age as us."

"Did they?" I hadn't ever really thought about the ages of the 90s band Ash. Hadn't ever come up.

"Yeah, well, your age, really. I'm a bit younger."

"You are that. Still haven't caught up with me, have you?" We're in the bar, in the afternoon, not the restaurant part, but we're eating food anyway, cos it's a hotel bar, and hotel bars always serve food.

"Haha, no. Anyway, what I'm saying is, when he's singing about her still being in her school skirt and her summer blouse, it's not nostalgia. That song came out in like, 1994, I think, and he was about 17 then, so he's literally just remembering like… last summer?"

"Hmmm. Why does he mention driving her home then, after midnight?"

"What do you mean?"

"How was he driving her home, if he was like, sixteen?" I don't drive, and I never have, but that still sounds young to me.

"Yeah. Good point. Maybe cos they're from Northern Ireland?" She's drinking Bulmer's Light, which is really Magner's Light, in my head, cos I'm a traitor who went to take the King's shilling a long time ago. I think about starting a conversation about how the Bulmer's name changed hands so many times over the years, and how Magner's is actually the correct name, but I think – even I'm not that boring. Yet, anyway. Give it a couple of hours.

"Probably. But yeah, it's a great song. Except for the name."

"Exactly! I say that all the time! Are you inside my head?"

"I er, never mind." I had a really filthy answer cocked and ready there, but I decide against it. Not because I don't want to offend her, more because littering the conversation with sexual terms is one of those

PUA techniques you read about on the internet, and I really don't need to subliminally introduce the idea of potential sex here. She's married, we're booked into a hotel under false names. If anything is in doubt right now, us fucking isn't it.

"Either way, it's just a silly name. Like, *Oh Yeah*. Could they not have thought about it for like two more minutes?"

"I know! It's like the first words of the chorus. What are they?"

"Bon Jovi?"

"I sort of love you," I say, because it's funny, and I get to say I love you without any risk. I still scan her face for a reaction like I'm Hercule Poirot, though.

"Haha. Yeah. Oh Yeah, even. Oooooooooooh Yeah-"

"It was the start of the summeeeeeeer."

"Seriously, like. The Vengaboys could have come up with a better name."

"Don't be slagging off the Vengaboys, mate. *Boom Boom, Boom Boom* is a brilliant name for a song. Leaves you in no doubt about what you're in for. You can't improve on perfection. Another one?"

"Ahhhhhh. Yes, please. Isn't it my round?"

"Nope."

"Okay. Something different this time though, yeah?"

"Oh right. What's your poison?"

"Vodka and lime."

"Double?"

"Do I have a choice?"

"Nope."

"Where have you been all my life?"

"England, for a lot of it. Back in a tick." I walk off to the bar thinking about that time a friend of mine shat all over one of my books for various reasons, one of which was '200 pages of you describing what people were drinking, how much of it they drank, and the effect it had on them", and I was really offended at the time, because hey, that's just how I write, and also, he was someone I based a character in that book on, and I don't think he liked how I portrayed him, even though I thought I was quite affectionate. And, most importantly, alcohol is an enormous part of social interaction – I was sober for two years, so I definitely know that's true, looking in from the outside. Everything comes with drinks, and everything goes with a drink. She's getting a double. I like that she picked lime cordial too, because getting a mixer in this country is a second mortgage affair most of the time. No splash of Coke from the hose for 20p. They've had a Marriage Equality referendum, and they're pushing for an Abortion one, but what they really need to tackle is the over-pricing of 250ml bottles of pop in pubs. It's called *priorities*. The barman tots up the price and I remember that shots here are 35ml not 25ml and this isn't Wetherspoon's.

*****

"Are you still doing your league?"

"Huh?" We're still in the bar, we haven't even been up to the room yet. No real need, since we don't have suitcases or anything, but a part of me feels like we're wasting money sitting here in public, when we could be upstairs, well…

"Your league. The one where you made up all these soccer teams and wrote them down, and all the players had the names of kids you grew up with or went to school with or whatever, and you used… was it playing cards?"

"Playing cards, yeah. Or sometimes I'd flip a coin; to decide the scores, like. I can't believe you remember this." I can't believe I told her about it, either. Such a private thing, such a glimpse into how much of a secret loser I was back then; staying up until four in the morning, watching the chart show thing on Sky One and doing my little leagues, like some sort of psychopath.

"Course I do. I remember a lot. I probably forgot most of it, but I remember it now you're… since you've, well, you know what I mean."

"Yeah. Yeah, I get you." It's different for me, cos I pretty much remember everything about everything, but when it's stuff to do with her, I remember it even more. It's impossible to describe the effect she's had on my life, and if I ever try to, they'll lock me up in a padded cell. Even now I can remember a bunch of times when I was on my own in bed, feeling down, like I'd wasted my life or ruined it, and I'd close my eyes and imagine her face, laughing at something, from about ten years before, and everything would be okay again. That's some top notch crazy, even for me.

"I thought it was sweet. Like, you were secretly into role-playing, like a little geek." She laughs when she says it, but I love when she laughs, and how she looks when she does it. It's almost a carbon copy of that mental snapshot I used to rock myself to sleep with back then. She's sitting across from me, not beside me. We've sort of reset back to zero today; from the heights of last week. I'm not sure why, but I'm going with her flow on this. She's got to be in charge of this part, because she's the one with something to lose. That's what I tell myself, but I still wish she was closer.

"Role-playing? I wasn't role-playing, you spa."

"Well, you were. It's just it wasn't orcs and goblins. It was little boys in shorts running around an imaginary field."

"Now you're making me sound like a pervert."

"Well… if the cap fits."

"Haha. So, what's the plan, anyway?" That comes out of nowhere, but it's out now.

"The plan?" She looks a little nervous, and she's running her finger over the rim of her glass, like when people try to make wine glasses play music.

"Well, yeah. What's the story? Today, like?"

"Oh. Oh, am, can we – will we just have another drink or two here?" I don't know what the look is that just crossed her face, but I know it's not a good one, and I want it to go away.

"Yeah, of course, no probs." I hadn't thought that things could go bad or sour now, considering we're here, we've paid for the room, and she's told people she's somewhere else for the night. And cos it's her, and nothing is ever bad when I'm with her. But she's the one taking a big risk here, and she's the one who might still get cold feet, so I know not to push it here. Take my time. There's plenty of the day left.

*****

By the time we're on the way to the room it's after six and everyone's a little tipsy. I didn't push it, I'm still not pushing it. I just let her be, and let the day go on, and didn't ask again about plans. And eventually, she necked her drink, picked up her bag, and off we went.

"This the right floor?" She's a bit unsteady on her feet, and I'm annoyed that we had so many drinks, because I really don't need Dutch courage for this, and I want it to be amazing, and to remember it all. We've had a couple of bowls of chips each though, and some other snacks, so maybe that's enough soakage.

"Er, I think they only have the one floor." I glance at the keycard for effect, but I know the room number off by heart. It's at the end of this hall.

"I know, silly. T'was a joke. Listen, when we get in, can I use the bathroom?"

"An bhfuil cead agam dul amach go dtí an leithreas, máis é do thoil é?"

"Haha, no, really. I need to freshen up." I never know what they mean by that.

"Powder your nose, yeah." Or by that.

"Something like that. I just, I mean, I – can we…"

"Shhhh, shhhh, whatever you like, honey." We're at the door and I swipe the card. It works the second time around. I let us in, and the room is clean, but a bit 80s looking. There's a folded up thing on the wall, and I figure out it's a trouser press after a few seconds. There's a phone on the desk thing that's a rotary one. I feel like we've gone in a time machine, except the TV is a flat screen.

"Okay, I won't be long." She moves her head towards me and then away, like there might have been a kiss on offer in the middle of it, then there wasn't. I don't know what's up with her, but I hope it's going to pass. She takes her shoulder bag with her and goes into the loo.

I'm sitting on the bed, and I kick off my shoes. Feet smell okay, had a very thorough shower before I came out, and they're brand new socks. I wonder if I should take them off too, because there's nothing sexy about socks, but then I think that might be a bit presumptuous. But can you be presumptuous if you've already booked a hotel room for the night with a married woman, and you're sitting on the bed, waiting for her? I take them off, roll them up, and put them inside the shoes; one in each. Now I want a drink. I'm sort of humming, because the bathroom is kind of close, and I want to give her some privacy, in case she's going. Not sure how me humming so low that only I can hear it gives her privacy, but it sort of does, so I keep going. I'm nervous, or anxious, or excited. I can't decide which, or if they are all the same thing. I'm waiting, though. I'm definitely waiting for something. I wonder if you can smoke in this room. It doesn't matter if you can or can't; there's always the window. I want a ciggie now too, but I'm definitely not going to have one. That will really spoil the atmosphere. That can wait.

I wonder if I should say some clichéd thing like "Everything okay in there?" but I don't, because whatever answer that came back wouldn't be much use to me. She'll be out in a second. Probably just doing her make-up. She was wearing a fair bit (for her) earlier, so she might just be touching it up. I've got slim fit jeans on today – not skinny, so there won't be that really emasculating bit of awkwardness later when they get stuck around my calves, and I might even need some help rolling them off. Never a romantic moment, that. I close my eyes and picture myself with no clothes on, and I'm glad I've been keeping relatively fit and doing weights (when I can be arsed), compared to the skinny-fat lump that came over on the plane a few months ago. For all she knows, I always look this good, and that's probably the way I'll keep it. I hear the door open and snap out of my little daydream.

"Are the heels a bit much?"

I look at her, standing in the doorway. She definitely did her make-up again – she's all smoky eyes and light pink lips. And what she's wearing… I've probably imagined this moment in my head a thousand times, and even my imagination wasn't as good as what's in front of me now. I look her up and down, slowly, because I can't even think of what to say. Strappy high heeled shoes, flesh coloured stockings with suspenders, black knickers that dip really low under her bellybutton, a gorgeous, fancy looking bra that makes the absolute most of her small breasts. I swallow but there's nothing to swallow. I'm dry.

"I, ah, Jesus Christ…"

"Good Jesus Christ or Bad Jesus Christ?" She's joking, obviously. No one could look this good and not know it.

"The best Jesus Christ." I want to tell her to come over here, but she's already on her way.

"Glad you approve." She sits herself onto my knee and thigh and I barely feel it – weight-wise, anyway. I feel it all over in all the other possible ways. It's too much. We haven't even kissed yet, today.

"I more than – I, like, - have you been taking notes or something?"

"Haha. What do you mean?" She puts her perfect, pale arm around me and rests her hand on my other shoulder. The smell of her is like drugs. Her hair falls down a little and touches me, and even through the t-shirt it feels amazing.

"Like, you're basically dressed like all of my -" Brain is pushing towards *wildest fantasies* here, but I really don't want to say something that cheesy. The other choice was *best wanks* though, and that'd probably kill the mood. Even with her.

"Uh-huh? Mmmm, yeah. Well, I do listen, sometimes."

"You really do. I…"

"Shhhh," she puts her finger against my lips, and then replaces it with her own mouth. I close my eyes and open my mouth a little for her, even though I was really enjoying that view. We sink back into the bed without any awkwardness or fumbling, and my fingers find the skin on her back, and the little lumps and bumps of spine that are always so prominent on girls as tiny as her. I feel like I'm going to explode with happiness, and good feelings, and warmth, and everything else. My brain stops thinking in words and thoughts and everything just melts into colours and lights and perfection.

*****

"Will I get us a drink or something?" I don't know why that's my first thought. Well, I do know, but it still doesn't make it right. Drink doesn't solve stuff like this. Not after the fact anyway.

"I… don't know. Just carry on with the… just keep holding me, yeah?" She's nestled into me on the bed. I've plumped up some pillows so I can sit up a bit. We're still boiling, I can feel it off her, and she's not shivering, even though she's wearing next to nothing. I wonder if there's a mini-bar. Even for some cold water, if we're not having more drink.

"That, I can do." I feel odd. Not in a particularly bad way. It's just different; everything is different now. I'm glad she's tucked into me like this though, rather than sat on the end of the bed, away from me. She's not looking at me. She can't really, with the angle, but maybe that's deliberate.

"I'm sorry."

"Shhhh, don't be stu- don't be silly. You have nothing to apologise for." I'm telling the truth. That's the way I feel, even if my body isn't really agreeing with me now, but that's always the way. That's just me thinking with my cock, and that little guy has the worst ideas a lot of the time.

"I do. I just… I wanted to. I was so, so sure that I wanted to. And, you saw me, coming out of that bathroom. Did I look like I was gonna chicken out?"

"No. No, you looked amazing. You still look amazing. You're wonderful." I want her to feel better. I want her to know that it's okay.

"Heh, not so amazing now, I bet. My mascara's a state, for one thing."

"Nah, you look perfect. You always look perfect."

"Even when I'm bawling crying, like?" She pinches me on the arm in a jokey way, and it feels nice. Everything she does feels nice. I wish I could make her see that.

"Absolutely." I push her hair away from her fringe, to get a better look at her face, but she's still dodging any sort of eye contact.

"Pervert." She gives my thigh a squeeze, and leaves her hand there, which makes me happy.

"Always."

"Look, I really am sorry. I feel terrible. I feel like I… like I led you on, or something."

"No. No it's not like that at all, Orla. We're both grown-ups, we both knew what we were doing here. It's not a big deal that you-" I'm not sure how to word this, which is a new thing for me, not knowing what to say to her. I've always known what to say to her, even all those years when she wasn't even there, and I was just imagining the conversations in my head.

"I choked. I don't know what happened to me. I just – everything we were doing felt so nice – everything you were doing felt so nice. So perfect, and amazing, and like, you're really good at *stuff*."

"I'm all right, I suppose." I'm playing it cool, but hearing her say that makes me incredibly happy. And it makes me want to do it again, but I'm not sure if that would be a great idea, so I carry on listening to her.

"I mean, all the times – all those times in the past, when we used to talk, and we'd flirt a bit or whatever, and we couldn't have ever done anything, cos I was with someone or you were with someone – whatever it was that was stopping us. I used to think about how it would be. With you, like…"

"You did?" I don't know why I'm surprised by that, but I am. Surprised and happy.

"Of course! Are you kidding me? I thought about it. A lot. And I always pictured it to be pretty great. Cos we had that chemistry, and you were older, so you'd been with more people, I suppose, and you were very… sexy."

"I was?"

"Oh, yeah. I mean, not that you're not now."

"Good save there." I love hearing all this. I wish I'd heard it a long time ago, obviously, but that's neither here nor there now.

"Haha, but no, really. And, what I'm saying is, no matter how good I imagined it was gonna be – back then – no matter how good I imagined it was gonna be just this week, for Christ's sake, after those kisses the other day – well, this was better. It couldn't have been better. Real life was actually better than me imagining."

"I know. I know, I feel exactly the same."

"You feel exactly the same as me about most things, I think."

"Yeah. I think I do."

"And that's why I – well, anyway. Even though this was so, so good and I was enjoying it so, so much. The things you did to me, the things you made me feel just then – what you were doing with your hands, your mouth, that's literally the best I've ever had it. Not even exaggerating to make you feel good or anything. It's never, ever felt that good. With anyone."

"Yeah, ditto." I thought things had been great with Emma. I was sure that that was the best that sex could ever be, which is probably why I stayed so long, and why I'd just resigned myself to the fact that it was never going to be that good with anyone again. And then this had come along.

"See, I believe you. It's like, there's no doubt in my mind that you're not just telling me what I want to hear. I trust you, you know? And anyway, you were there, I was with you. There's no way it was that good for me and you were just like 'meh', right?" She's giggling now, which is a much better noise than crying.

"Not a chance, no. It was perfect."

"Perfect until I ruined it, yeah." I can't see her face, but I know she frowned after saying that.

"Shhhh, you didn't ruin it." I'm stroking her hair now, and it's probably doing me just as much good as it's doing her. It's sort of therapeutic, I don't know why.

"That's nice of you to say so and everything, but I did. And now the moment's sort of gone, I guess."

"Is it?" I don't want it to be, but I don't want to piss her off or push her away. It's taking all of my self-control not to have a stonking great erection during this little heart to heart, because I'm only human, and she's lying on top of me dressed like that, and looking like that, and being Orla Keane, who I'm ridiculously in love with now, even if neither of us have said it out loud.

"Yeah. I mean, I just froze. And I know that's awful. For you, like. I mean, why didn't I freeze during all that time you were making me come with your hands, or when you were going down on me, right?"

"Ah, don't be silly," I say again, but there's some truth in what she said, obviously. She could have at least waited until I had a blow-job, and I mightn't be sitting here all blue-balled and frustrated. But that's the sort of logic I'd have about it happening with someone else. She's different. I don't really know how to make her see that, though.

"You're very nice, but it's true. Anyway, I did freeze. Got the guilts, or whatever. And now, well… I'm kind of stuck there? I'm really sorry."

"It's okay. You're still here, aren't you?" It doesn't feel like the wrong thing for me to say, but I feel her tense up when I say it.

"Yeah. Yeah, maybe I shouldn't be."

"What?" My heart jumps into panic mode. Did I just fuck up? I wasn't trying to. I don't want her to go now. I don't want her to go, ever.

"Maybe I'm being even worse of a hypocrite, you know? I'm cheating on my husband here. I didn't stop before it became cheating, just cos I didn't stick your dick in my mouth. I've already cheated. I cheated last week, in that pub, and those... amazing kisses. I cheated all this week when we were planning this. I-"

"Hey, hey, hey... stop beating yourself up, Orl. It takes two to tango, you know. It's not just you. You're here because I wanted you too, you know? This is my fault as much as it's yours." I'm trying to save this, but she's sat up from me now, and I feel like every second that passes is me losing her a bit more. I really don't want her to go. She's saving me, as much as anything else. I don't want to go back to being without her in my life. She's been keeping the bad things at bay. I'm not strong without this.

"Yeah, but you're single. You're single, and you're not really doing anything wrong, and I'm... I'm doing everything wrong. I need to go."

"Please..." I don't want her to go. I don't know what to do to keep her here, though. Once again, I don't know the right thing to say to her, and I don't like it.

"I'm sorry. Look, I am absolutely – I can't think of the right word to use without sounding like a mental case, but I have feelings for you. Really serious ones – whether they were always there and you brought them back up, or it's just a new thing, it doesn't matter. They're there, and I shouldn't be having them."

"But I thought you felt good?" I'm grasping, and she's already moved herself away so we're not touching skin anymore. I feel like my heart has been wrenched out of me.

"I do! That's the problem! I do feel good with you, and you make me feel good, and today you made me feel things I've never felt before – emotionally and physically, and the way I feel about you, well, it's dangerous."

"You can't help – we can't help how we feel, though." I don't want her to go, but I know she's going to now. I have to think of something quickly, but there's nothing left to try, outside emotional blackmail or other shit I can't – I just won't, with her.

"I can. Or I can try. I sort of have to, you know? I know you don't want to hear it, but-"

"Well don't say it, then!" I hate when people warn me about what I'm not going to like hearing and then say it anyway.

"... but I made vows, you know? To someone I loved. Someone I still love, I think. And it's not fair on him. Even if... even if this thing is better than that thing. I made a choice, you know? It's not fair." She's up off the bed and she still looks amazing, even if she's tearing my heart out. I want to tell her I love her, even if that would be the absolute worst thing to say right now, and the craziest. I want to tell her, but I won't.

"Well I wasn't an option when you made that choice!" It's the first thing that comes into my head, and it's true, but it's not fair either.

"Well I can't change that! You just... you disappeared. You came out of absolutely nowhere when you started going out with Holly. I'd never seen you before. None of us had. International man of mystery, like. Then, when you guys broke up, and she went to live in France, you disappeared as well. Just as I was actually single. I didn't even know you'd been in England all that time, not until you told me. You weren't here. I couldn't choose you. I had to get on with my life. And now you're back – you just show up again, and I meet you, and I have all these feelings, and it's not fair, cos you weren't here. I had my life. I had James. And now it's all..."

"I'm sorry." I don't know why I say that. I'm not sorry. It was true. I'd met Holly in a pub one night, hadn't exactly been planning on a relationship. Then I kind of decided I liked her, and we started being a thing. I'd met her friends, including Orla, obviously. When we split up, it was like I split up with all of them too, cos they'd never been my friends to begin with. Not really. So I cut them all out of my life too, and I was gone from the country a few weeks later, so it didn't matter. It was a strange time in my life, for lots of reasons.

"You don't have anything to apologise for. It's me. I never should have agreed to do this. Sorry, that's wrong again of me. I never should have suggested this. It was my idea, in fairness. You're the one who agreed to it. But I shouldn't have. I'm the one who needs to be sorry here." She looks miserable, defeated, and beautiful. I'm full of conflicting feelings now, but the most pressing one is to do whatever it takes to make her happy again. Cos I miss that smile.

"No, it's down to me as well. I should have said no. I can't act like I'm not doing anything wrong here, Orla. I am. If I was him, and you were my wife, this would kill me. I'd want to kill whoever was doing it." Wrong thing to say, I realise it the second it's out of my mouth.

"Thanks."

"No! No, that's not what I meant. I'm sorry, I just-"

"Look, I need to get dressed. We'll talk again in a second, okay?"

"I don't want you to go." I don't know if I sound really pathetic, but I've stopped caring. About that, at least.

"I don't want to go either. Look, it would be the easiest thing in the world to just climb into that bed again with you, open a bottle of wine or two from the fridge, and just let things happen. But I'd still feel like this later, or tomorrow, and we'd be right back to the start. I want to have sex with you. I really, really can't think of anything I want more than to pick up where we left off, and have you do amazing things to me, and me do them back. To feel what it feels like to actually have you inside me. To have you look into my eyes while we're doing that – to kiss me the way you kiss me, to make me come really fucking hard and to hold me when it's over, and say all the perfect things you always say, and for me to fall asleep next to you and your lovely smell, and wake up with you in the morning and do it all over again. But I can't. So the only other thing I can do is go. I'm so sorry."

"Hey. So am I. It's okay. Let's get you out of here, yeah?" All I want to do now is limit the damage. Today is fucked, but I want there to be another day. I need to be the big person. I need to be the best version of me right now. And this is the way.

"Uh, are you sure? I mean, of course you – thank you. I really mean that." She gives me a look that makes it all worth it. No one else could ever manage to do that to me with one look. I'm going to do whatever I can to hold on to her, even if it means sending her home tonight.

"No probs. You're not going home-home, are you?"

"What? Jesus, no. I'll go to Joanne's."

"Joanne's?" I don't know a Joanne belonging to her. Not from the old days anyway.

"Yeah. Joanne from work. It's where I said I was – she'll be grand. She'll understand."

She goes into the toilet and closes the door behind her, and I don't know if I want to cry, or get drunk, or murder someone. For some reason I start thinking about Millie, the Scottish girl, from after I broke up with Emma for good.

Ten

Last Year, London, Millie

I open the door of Celia's place, and Millie's there on the step. She's gorgeous, even though the heat outside has already made her make-up look a bit see-through. No one looks as good as their Instagram pics, me especially. The hair is dyed black, with a Bettie Page fringe. I love that look, but I've never been with someone who has it. I've never even talked to someone who has it. Most of them seem like shitheads. But what do I know?

"Hello!"

Her voice is soft and Scottish. We spoke on the phone last night, but it's even sexier in person.

"Hey. Come in."

Her body language is a little distant. I don't feel like I can touch her arm or her back as I let her pass. Baby steps. It'll come. She has a bottle with her; Prosecco, I know from us talking earlier. I've got one too; I bought it in the shop. Two might be enough. Two is never enough.

"Here, I'll stick that in the fridge…"

"Oh, I think it's cold, actually."

"Yeah, I've had some chilling already though, should be well frosty by now."

"Oh right, so. Okay."

She's wearing a flowy looking thing, I can't tell what shape she is, but it's not hiding a multitude of sins or anything. She's lean looking; I can see it in her face.

"Do you smoke?"

I can't remember if she's said, or if it says it on her okcupid. I smoke, and it says on mine that I don't, so –

"Only when I'm drinkin', really."

I'm already in love with the voice.

"I'll get you a drink then."

I move between where she's standing at the breakfast bar, and the big fridge door. I get a little wedged between, my knee is between her thighs, and our faces are kind of close.

"Can't say no to that."

"You ever say no to anything?" I say, reaching in for the bottle.

"Yeah. Cheeky fucking Irishmen, usually. When they're trying to get the ride."

"We'll see."

There's a raised eyebrow at that, but she doesn't move from where we've been pushed together. I reach past her to grab two flutes from the rack, and the smell of her is nice. Our legs are still touching. I might kiss her now. Her phone starts buzzing inside her handbag and the moment's gone.

*****

I'm cooking. She's standing with a glass of fizz; the second of the night. It's still warm outside; balmy even. I dunno if we're getting on, I'm just doing my usual shit of talking a mile a minute. When she called me on the phone the night before I did the same, but I was pissed then, by myself. It's like that now; I'm not able to function sober anymore since splitting with Emma. I don't want to be alone with my own brain. Too much ouch. The peppers are frying in the wok and they smell great. I can do this cooking thing; it's turned into my party trick, and a good thing to get them to come to the house, instead of going on some date that I can't afford. And, once they've agreed to that, it's obvious we're going to do it. And doing it's what I need. I can keep the thoughts of her out of my brain as long as I'm drunk all the time, scouring okcupid for new women, or having sex with the ones I've already found. It's not an exact science, but it's all I have at the moment.

"Is it going to be spicy?"

She's good looking. Not sure if it's a type of mine, or she's just generically hot, but she's definitely an eight or a nine. Might be a ten if she's a good kisser. Still haven't got there yet. Yapping too much, as usual.

"Yeah. Kind of. Why, do you not like?"

"Oh no, hotter the better."

She pronounces everything gorgeously. I've always had a thing for that accent. Trainspotting didn't do anything to put me off.

"That's my girl."

I pull another chilli out and chop it to add to the stir-fry. A green one this time, fiery stuff. She'd better be telling the truth, or she's screwed. I remind myself to scrub those fingernails again, or her vagina will get a surprise later. If we get there. We'll get there though. She's here, and I can see she's got suspenders on.

"Aye, I'm definitely up for the hot stuff."

"Baby, this evening?"

"What?"

"Never mind."

"You're weird."

I dunno why it pangs me in the chest when she says it. I think I'm just sensitive in general. Mustn't look like I give a shit though. Can't manage a smile at it. Change the subject.

"Prosecco okay?"

"Aye. It's not bad, no."

"Marvellous."

I finish the rest of mine, the fizz burning the back of my throat, as the pieces of chilli hit the oil, smoking up almost straight away. I turn my head to keep from coughing. She's not near me. The body language is still a bit stand-offish.

"If you want a fag, there's chairs outside, and a table."

"Aye, I know. I'm fine though."

"Rice just needs to sit in its own steam for about ten minutes, then we'll eat, yeah?"

"Aye. Good, I'm starvin'."

She looks like she eats half a salad a day, no wonder she's starving. I keep that one in my head though. Skinny girls are funny about stuff like that. Even more than bigger girls sometimes.

Outside at the table, I'm trying my best to remember how to use chopsticks. She likes the food. Well, she's eating it anyway. Hasn't said anything about it. I'm the width of the table away from her, and everyone has food in their mouths. Not ideal for trying to slip her the tongue. First bottle's almost finished. I should've had water with this; spicy food makes me gulpy, and gulping down booze like it's pop isn't very clever. She's doing the same though. I dunno if she's noticing we haven't kissed yet as well, and is just trying to get pissed, to move things along. Even if she isn't, it's going to work. I look her up and down when her eyes are somewhere else. I definitely want to do her. Emma's just a memory, until I think about her, and I don't want to think about her now.

I talk a lot. Not just now, in general. And the more booze involved, the more I talk. I talk to fill in the gaps, to have something to say, to impress. Doesn't ever occur to me to let someone else have their say, sometimes anyway. But I think I'm a good listener too, for some reason. Everyone thinks they're a good listener, but we're usually just waiting for our chance to say our thing, which is way more important. I have met some good listeners – the type who don't interrupt you, and give you the impression that they heard everything you said, when it's their turn to speak. Those people are what they call 'active listeners', in books about how to succeed in business. I know this cos I tried to read one of those once; I didn't get very far, cos I don't care how you succeed in business, or in anything. I don't know what kind of listener Millie is, cos I'm drunk, and I'm just filling in the spaces, before we end up in bed. I'm not a good listener when I'm talking, or when I'm the dominant personality. But I am when someone else needs to bitch, and I give good advice. Which is funny, cos I never bitch about my problems to anyone, mainly cos I wouldn't take their advice. Other people's advice always seems like soundbites and trite, worthless platitudes to me. I'm probably an egomaniac, even though I'm ridiculously insecure. Maybe all egomaniacs are like that though. More than likely.

We are talking about absolutely nothing. This is a booty call. A sex date. I don't know if I'm ever going to see her again. But maybe she has other ideas. She knows I've just broken up with someone. She knows what's on the table. Maybe she'll be on the table in a bit. Once I've cleared the plates. Doesn't look sturdy enough. I tune back into what she was saying and try to look like I was listening. At least it sounds nice. She's getting better looking too, with each glass of wine. She's intelligent enough. They usually are, if they can get through my okcupid profile and still want to message me. Both in its length, and the sense of humour. So much of it is me basically slagging off the type of women who use okcupid, even the type I want to meet. So if they have a sense of humour about that, I probably want to have sex with them. If I'm browsing drunk, I kind of want to have sex with all of them though. It's like interactive porn. Except there's no nudity until I meet them. Or maybe if they send me some. I love technology.

"So, you write books?"

Dinner's been cleared away, not quite to the dishwasher, but it's a start. We're still outside. We've still done nothing. Getting anxious about it now.

"Yeah, well I try to. I've a couple already published. Well, self-published, but still. And I'm writing about four more."

"Yeah, you said."

"Did I?"

"Yeah, in your profile. And last night."

"Last night?"

"Yeah, the phone call? You talked about yourself for about an hour. Didn't get a word in edgeways, to be honest."

She doesn't say it with a smile or a scowl, but it still feels like a dig. I feel embarrassed. Maybe I'm not just being too sensitive. Maybe she's just a bitch. She reminds me of…

"Oh, sorry. I didn't mean – what do you do then?" I sink the rest of my Prosecco.

"I told you."

"Oh right, yeah. Racing cars, wasn't it?"

"Hah. Something like that."

"No, go on. Tell me. Tell me again, it sounds interesting."

"No it doesn't, you twat. I mean, it is interesting, just not as interesting as you are. To you, like."

I'm way too prickly for this, for her. I need to be less drunk. Or more drunk.

"Haha, sorry." I don't know what else to say.

"Ach, you're all right. It actually is kind of interesting. I could never do that."

"Write a book?"

"Yeah. Or talk about how great I am for an hour." She's smiling now. Maybe it's fine.

"Hehe. Go on, though. Tell me about racing cars and stuff. Have you been to Silverstone? So you know Lewis Hamilton? Is he really small? Do you have a helmet?"

"Fuck off, ya prick."

"Haha. More wine?"

"Finally, you're useful. Cheers, yeah."

"I'm useful! I make nice dinners!"

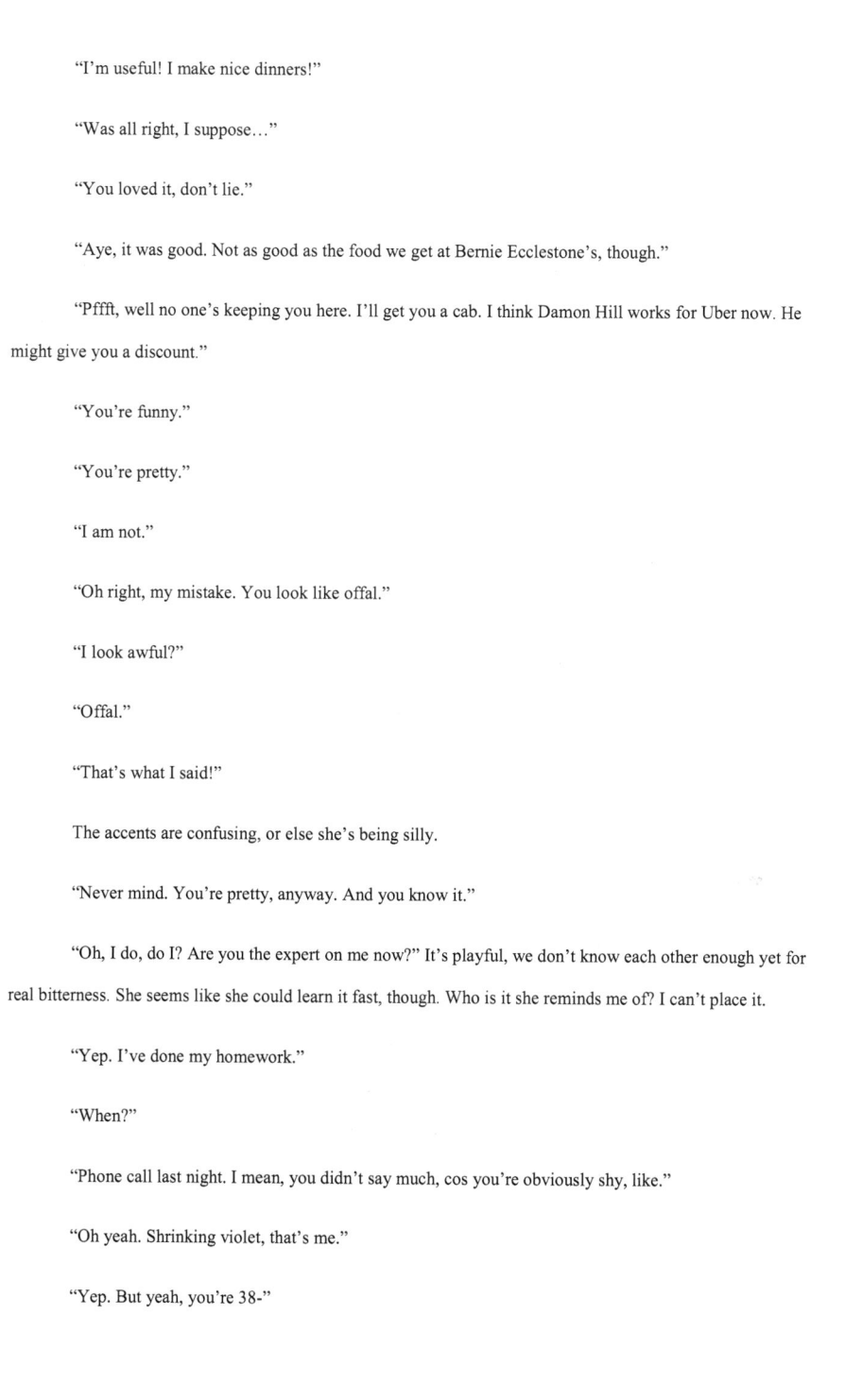

"Was all right, I suppose…"

"You loved it, don't lie."

"Aye, it was good. Not as good as the food we get at Bernie Ecclestone's, though."

"Pffft, well no one's keeping you here. I'll get you a cab. I think Damon Hill works for Uber now. He might give you a discount."

"You're funny."

"You're pretty."

"I am not."

"Oh right, my mistake. You look like offal."

"I look awful?"

"Offal."

"That's what I said!"

The accents are confusing, or else she's being silly.

"Never mind. You're pretty, anyway. And you know it."

"Oh, I do, do I? Are you the expert on me now?" It's playful, we don't know each other enough yet for real bitterness. She seems like she could learn it fast, though. Who is it she reminds me of? I can't place it.

"Yep. I've done my homework."

"When?"

"Phone call last night. I mean, you didn't say much, cos you're obviously shy, like."

"Oh yeah. Shrinking violet, that's me."

"Yep. But yeah, you're 38-"

"37…"

"Close enough. You like Formula One, casual sex, and listening to Irish guys go on about themselves for ages."

"That's me in a nutshell."

"I'm very intuitive."

"That's one word for you, yeah."

"Any others? I prefer compliments, if that helps."

"I dunno, really. I haven't had a chance to find out what else you can do, except talk, cook, and be a prick."

"I'm good at all of those, though. And cunnilingus." That word got into the sentence like a shy kid whose friends nudge him forward when someone asks for a volunteer. It was not smooth.

"Oh aye. Who told you you're good at that?"

"Literally everyone."

"Aye, well maybe they were being nice. We're like that, girls."

"You're really not."

"Well yeah, that's true. But well done on being good at the cunnilingus. Must be great, and stuff."

"What about you?"

"Me? No, I'm terrible at cunnilingus."

"Haha."

"Good at blowjobs though."

"Pfft. Every girl says that."

"Do they?"

"Yeah. It's cos like, blowjobs are great. And if you have a girlfriend and she's giving you a blowjob, and it's shit, you're not really going to tell her."

"Why not?"

"Cos then you get no blowjobs."

"I see…"

"And if you like blowjobs, the best way to get lots of them is?"

"Tell her you love them?"

"Well, yeah. But tell her you love her ones, specifically. Tell her she's the best at it."

"Haha, yeah."

"Ergo, every girl who's ever had a dick in her mouth thinks she's the queen of blowjobs."

"Aye. Yeah, I know what you mean. I'm still good at them though."

"Of course you are, dear."

"Fuck you."

"Promises, promises."

"What you mean? I can't fuck you if you're over there, can I? You haven't even kissed me yet, you daft twat."

"Oh, I've to kiss you, is it? What kind of feminist are you, anyway?"

"I'm not a feminist!"

"What, with that fringe?"

"Fuck off. You're a prick, you know that?" Scottish people can say the harshest things to you in good humour. They're basically the Irish, with more heroin.

"I'm lovely."

"A lovely prick."

"Cheers. Didn't think you'd noticed."

"In those jeans? I can practically see what you had for dinner."

"That's cos you had the same, in fairness."

"Touché"

"En guarde!"

"What?"

"I dunno. Are you still over there?"

"I am."

"Coming over here at any point?"

"For what? Cunnilingus?"

"Baby steps, Millie."

"Aye. Is there any wine left?"

Damn it. Thought we were getting somewhere finally.

"Some in the fridge, I think."

"No, I think we've had that. Are you drunk or something?"

"No!" Yes. Almost maybe definitely.

"Hmmm. Well I've some cash. Is there a shop?"

"End of the road there."

"Right then. Wine. Then maybe cunnilingus."

"And blowjobs."

"No blowjobs. I'm shite at them."

"It's fine. I like you. I'll take one for the team."

"Prick."

"Yeah, preferably. Unless there's some other way you know."

"I know ALL the ways. I'm the queen of blowjobs." She gets up and takes her handbag off the chair. I start to get up too, and when I'm standing, she's face to face with me, though a little shorter. Her eyes are telling me to go ahead.

"Well, I-"

I kiss her and stop the words. It's a soft one to start, and she breathes in hard. My hand is on the hot skin between her shoulder and her neck. She kisses me back, and it's good. We keep it up for half a minute, then I let her go. She gives me a smile that makes her look ten times prettier, even if it still looks derisory for some reason. I feel like slapping her arse, but I just give it a squeeze, and let her walk ahead of me, like the gent that I am.

I let her go into the shop for us; she asks why, but I just tell her I hate shops, and she accepts it with a sigh. She doesn't like me as a person – I'm getting that vibe, but that's fine; I don't need her to. I just need her to fancy me for a little while. I don't hate shops, I hate ringing takeaways. Or ringing anyone. People I don't know, and people I do. If I ever have to move out of the country, my kid is going to suffer, unless she's the one who rings me first. Millie comes back out with fags for me, and two more bottles.

"Prosecco?"

"Nah, just white. Good white, though." She's not defensive. She's not the type. She doesn't need my approval for anything. She's either going to be a fantastic shag, or a terrible one (but oblivious to it). Doesn't matter to me. I don't need her to be good at it. She's hot, she's in great shape, she's got good tattoos. She looks like a Suicide Girl. I don't need her to be anything else, except submissive and dirty, and I already know she's both. We've talked.

"Marvellous. You not cold?"

She hasn't got her jacket on. I'm fine myself.

"Ach, no. It's fucking boiling for Glasgow weather, like."

"Yeah. You ethnics are good at weather."

"Ethnics?" She raises an eyebrow at me. The bottles make a clinking sound as she makes her way across the little road bit and into the alley.

"Yeah. Bloody Porridge Wogs."

"Aye, I do actually like porridge, mind. It's healthy, like. Gotta watch the figure, yeah? Not getting any younger."

That's extra funny to me, obviously, cos she's middle class, and my people look like dog shit by the time they're her age; especially the women. She looks about ten years younger than she is, especially below the neck.

"S'okay. I like potatoes too. Some stereotypes are true."

"Oh right. Which other ones?"

"Er, Greeks and Turks, all rapists. Italians, sexist."

"Well, that's just science."

"Black people…"

"Lazy?"

"No, they'd have made terrible slaves if that was true."

We're almost at the door. I like how we're eyeing each other carefully during this, to make sure neither of us is being serious.

"Haha. Good point. They can't swim though."

"Definitely not. Otherwise they'd have just jumped over the side of the boats and buggered off home."

"I remember that from the Discovery Channel, actually."

"Black Week?"

"Aye. Just when you thought it was safe to go back in the water…"

"You suddenly remember you're from Zaire…"

We go through the door, and I realise I've not locked the Chubb, and I don't have the key for it either. I need to start being more careful with Celia's house. Apart from bringing women back and shagging them in it, obviously. I watch Millie wander through, past the living room and into the kitchen. We'll probably go out the back again, so we can smoke, so no chance of jumping her on the couch just yet.

*****

It's about a week and a half later and I'm sat on the floor of her flat in Finsbury Park, taking off her fingers with some bolt cutters, and I wonder what went wrong, if anything. Sometimes nothing goes wrong. Sometimes I've just introduced myself as Steve instead of Tom from the start, and I have to commit. But usually, if I've done that, I know what's coming. Even if I pretend to myself that I don't. There's only been one exception, and that was a long time ago now.

The sex was great. Different great. She was submissive, like she'd said, but she was really fit and athletic too, so there was a very active feel to her submission. Like she'd be pushing herself back against me so hard sometimes it almost felt like a fight. Lots of stuff felt like a fight with her; that was probably the problem. She didn't look anything like Emma, but God if she didn't think like her. Whatever it is about Emma's personality that makes us not be able to gel properly – that makes being in a room with her unbearable, Millie had that too. Might have been the middle-class thing, might have been the thing where she thought her job was really important, or whatever. It only took a few meetings for her to show her true colours and they were really not my cup of tea. Must stop thinking in clichés. I throw the last of the fingers into a Waitrose bag. The floor is manky from blood, but she showed me a thing the other day where there are grates on either side of the stone floor in the kitchen and you can just basically put a shower hose on the hot tap and blitz it, and all the run-off goes into drains. She had no idea what a help she was being.

She really was a bit of an arsehole. I can be pretty over-sensitive, especially around the wrong sort of people for me, but she was consciously trying to be a cunt. She said sorry for it a few times. Tried to explain it. I reminded her of someone else. She didn't say who, but it was probably an ex, all things considered. She didn't like me doing nothing. As in, if I had my laptop out to write, but I was on Facebook, she'd sit there, asking me what I was doing, in a sort of condescending tone. Like it mattered. Like I mattered. It was weird. I barely knew her, but she was already acting like all the worst parts of having a girlfriend. Of having Emma as a girlfriend. No great sex and gorgeous body is worth that. I'd learned that the hard way with the other one. I'm trying to take the leg apart at the knee with one of her expensive knives from the block on the counter, but it's harder than it looks. Or I'm weaker than I thought. The Kooks are on her iPod in the dock. Fucking Kooks. What's next, Razorlight?

    I just couldn't get on with her, but the sex was great. I'm starting to think it's me. Maybe the sex is always great, cos I'm great at sex, and I can't get on with anyone, cos I'm me? It's a worrying thought. I wonder if I'll run out of bags, but she seems the type to keep a few and re-use them. Typical middle-class. We working class keep even more bags, and never re-use any of them. Probably because we don't think Climate Change is real. I'm saying 'we', but I never really include myself in the working class, cos I've always been trying to get out of it. Not in the sensible way, by getting qualified in a job that pays, or anything. Just by shagging my way out of it, usually. It hasn't worked yet, but it nearly did, last time. And, the sex, well, I've always thought I was good at that. And everyone's always told me I am. But every time I get better at it, with a new person, I wonder if all the people in the past were just humouring me. It's hard to tell. With Emma, it was beyond good. But then, when we broke up for those few months, it was almost just as good with other people, so I dunno. Maybe I learned something with her. Not from her, she didn't have anything to teach me. It wasn't that sort of vibe between us. But I did get better at holding out for longer, and I stopped worrying about my size or how long I could last, so there less of the desperation to try and please the other person first that had been a sort of hallmark before. I've been lucky with my insecurities. When I was much younger I thought I had a small knob. Dunno why, no one ever said it or anything, I just got it into my head. So I learned all these tricks to do with my hands and mouth, and then I'd worry that the actual sex bit wasn't good enough for them or long enough, so I learned even more stuff, til I could make someone come really easily. And then, by the time I was in the middle of the Emma thing, I had no worries about any of those things, but I still had all the tricks, and the new confidence, so I suppose yeah, maybe I am good. But it's all down to the other person, really. If they give you one star out of five, it doesn't matter how good you think you are. On a practical level, though, it can't hurt to know your shit. There's about four bags around me now, full of bits of her. I did the head first, and double wrapped it and tied it. Not having that thing looking at me all day while I'm trying to do this. It was bad enough her doing that before I killed her.

There was nothing spectacular or dramatic about it. That's often the way. It wasn't like she got on my last nerve or she drove me to distraction. She was going to die eventually, regardless of whether or not she was an arsehole. I don't decide these things. They're already decided, at the start. That's how it works. Then I just pick my moment. It's a good system. If you're passionate, if it's the heat of the moment, well it might go wrong. If you're calm, and detached, and clinical, you never have a problem. She was talking about going for a run in the park. Asking if I wanted to cook later, or would she. She was bending to tie up her trainer in the living room; I was coming in from the bedroom with a massive crystal ashtray. I hit her on the back of the head, right where you have to hit them, to put them out. Then I dragged her over to the stone floor in the kitchen bit, took the grey plastic basin out of the sink from where I'd washed the plates earlier, put it under her neck, and sliced open the carotid artery. I think that's what it's called, anyway. I'm not a doctor. It's the one you squeeze when you're doing the choking out thing during kinky sex. So many men make that stupid mistake of thinking that choking a woman during sex involves crushing her windpipe or something. That's not how you do it. You push your thumbs in on either side of the neck, sort of behind the ears. That puts them out like a light. Or, if you're good at it, you can stop just before they pass out, give them a few seconds to come to, then do it again. Doesn't do anything for me – I'm not a sadist. But they seem to like it.

I can't listen to her shite music anymore, so I switch on XFM. I like that one. It's basically a radio station for people in their 30s to feel like they're still young and cool. Story of my life, really. It's dark outside, but it's not quiet enough yet. There's an industrial wheelie bin downstairs that gets emptied into a massive truck in the morning. No separation, no recycling, no one will spot anything if I put enough small bags in and scatter them around. I'll wait until about 3am. Maybe the bones might jam up the machinery, but I'll be long gone by then, and this place will be spotless. I don't normally care about things like that, because I live a charmed life, and no one has ever even come close to catching me, but that's how Steve thinks, and that's how I get through a day like today. In the morning, it won't be Steve who wakes up worrying, because he's not real, even if he thinks he is. I'm real, and I'll worry, and then it'll pass. It's the weekend, so it'll be Monday before someone at work misses her. And if they come here, they won't see anything wrong. She'll just be gone. And people will try to track her down, and there'll be a whole other narrative there about some Scottish girl who just upped and disappeared one day, and no one will ever find her, because she'll be all scrunched up in between a load of bin bags from Starbucks and Pret a Manger, and I'll be drunk somewhere, forgetting about it, and trying not to do it again. And I do try. But it never lasts long. Because Steve gets what he wants in the end. Even if he isn't real, and I am. One last bag, one last foot, and then I can have one of her posh ciders from the fridge, I think. I've earned it.

Eleven

Last year, London, Emma

"How about… would you maybe think about going back to the original – the first time you showed it to me; with them all talking about sex, in the camp?"

I hate it when she gives me advice about my writing. Especially since I never ask. I dunno where she thinks she's getting the authority to 'help' me. She doesn't write books. She reads them. It's not the same.

"What, change the whole start?"

It's a ludicrous idea. The book has been out for about two years. I don't know why she's suddenly started suggesting that I whore it around to agents again. It didn't work the first time, it won't work now. She's middle class, so it really confuses her that writing a novel doesn't instantly mean you get a book deal or an agent. You need connections, and I don't have any. Middle class people do things like leave their jobs as bankers and take up watercolour painting, and somehow magically make a living from it. I'm not bitter about it, I'd love to be middle class. I'm not though, and she is, and it's impossible to explain to her that privilege is invisible to those who have it.

"Well, yeah. Cos I mean, it's actually good; the whole thing, I mean…"

She says it like I don't know, but it's still something approaching praise from her, so I feel good, in spite of myself. I won't thank her, though.

"Right…"

"But… I mean, if you sent it to all those agents, and none of them were interested, maybe you need to grab them more in the first few pages? It's just an idea…"

"You were the one who told me to change the start! You liked the new start, it's exciting and stuff! What are you talking about?"

I feel like throwing her out a window.

"I don't… I don't know. Maybe I was wrong. Or maybe it's just… I don't know."

She was wrong, she is wrong, and she doesn't bloody know. Never lets it stop her though. I could do with a ciggie, but it's a Saturday, and she's in my face all day.

"I'm not bloody changing it now. The book's finished. It was finished two years ago. I've written another one since then. I might have mentioned."

She hasn't read my second novel. She doesn't like it. She had a 50-page sample of it off me once, when we were split up for a while, and she started off saying she liked it. Then she told me it was too graphic; that she was embarrassed reading it on the tube, in case someone looked over her shoulder and saw what I'd written. Which is a load of shite, cos she's read all those Fifty Shades of Grey books, even though she claims she hated them. She's such a pleb, and I hate remembering that. It's just easier to gloss over it, and appreciate the shagging.

"Right… There's no need for that now, is there really?"

"No need for what? My own girlfriend not reading the book I wrote?"

"I did read – I did try reading it."

"You tried reading something that didn't even end up being it; you read a first draft. I've changed it. It's different. You'd know that if you could be bothered bloody reading it."

"I'm not having this conversation again…"

"Clearly you are. Why didn't you just read it? What was so hard about it? About doing it, for me?"

She does bugger all in her life that could be described as 'for me'. Apart from all the bullshit with the house and bills, and that's for her, in reality. Whenever I need a bit of support or whichever, even her suggestions to cheer me up or fix me are basically stuff she wants to do, dressed up as favours to me. Like 'Why don't we have some nice lunch?', when it's her who's hungry. Or 'Why don't we go to the pub?' when I didn't drink.

"I've told you before."

"Tell me again."

She has told me before, but I ask her, anyway. Maybe I'll get a different answer, or she'll trip up or something.

"I... Jesus Christ. I just... I think it's not going to be that different, and I'm afraid that I won't like it. And I don't want to lie to you."

"I just... I can't empathise, honestly. Whenever there's anything to do with your work, I listen. And if you've made something, I look at it, even if it's of no bloody interest to me, I do. Cos you're my girlfriend."

"Okay, okay. Here we go again. Yeah, okay Tom. You're better than me, you're right. You're a better person, and a better boyfriend, and I'm crap, and I'm horrible. Heard it all before."

"Doesn't make you actually fucking change, does it?"

I shouldn't swear at her. It brings down the red mist quicker. Here it comes.

"Maybe I don't have TIME to change, Tom! Maybe I'm too busy going out to work, and spending three hours on a fucking train every day, making sure you have a roof over your head, and we can eat."

It always comes back to this shit.

"It's your roof, over your head. I'm just... here."

"Yeah? Yeah, well maybe you need to think about being somewhere else."

She loves it. She loves sticking the knife in like that, once she's crossed over into that bit where she's all anger and no love. It comes so easily to her, so quickly. And it suits her. Being nice doesn't. Being a nice person, for her, is like juggling or something. She can manage it, but it's easy to put her off. Even being hungry snaps her out of it. I can't relate. I don't wake up in the morning an absolute prick, and then have to remind myself to act like a decent person.

"Okay. Do that."

"Do fucking what? What are you fucking whining about now?"

"Break up with me, kick me out, whatever."

"Don't be stupid. I'm not going to leave you on the street."

It's the least caring thing anyone can ever say to you. It's like, "I *would* leave you on the street, but that would make me seem like a terrible person. So I won't. I hope you're grateful."

"I won't be on the street."

"Where would you go? You don't have anywhere. You don't have a job, you don't have money. You don't even have friends you can stay with."

"Ouch."

"Yeah, well… I'm sorry for saying it, but it's the truth. What the hell are you gonna do with yourself?"

"I dunno, stay here, with my girlfriend?"

I hate that one of her turn-offs with me is that I don't have a nest egg stashed away somewhere for the purposes of getting my own place when she kicks me out. That's romance, right there.

"Well… I mean, that's not looking good, is it? And I'm not trying to be a bitch, so don't tell me I am, yeah?"

"Like you have to try…"

"Oh, fuck off."

"Yeah."

"Yeah, what? Are you gonna fuck off? Go on, then."

She's in full rage mode now, I have to act fast to bring her back.

"You want me to go?"

"Yeah. Fuck off and leave me alone. I'm fucking done with this."

Her voice is hard, no wobbles, no tears coming. This is going to be harder than usual. I try my calmest, softest voice. And a little smile. The type of smile that looks like you're smiling through the pain.

"Okay. I'm sorry, Em. Look, just give me a half hour, I'll see if Celia can have me. For a couple of nights at least. I'm sorry, okay? This is my fault. You're right, I should go."

Her face is somewhere between still angry, and a little confused. I've thrown her by taking the sting out. She doesn't do well when she's the only one raging.

"Thank you. Look, you don't have to-"

"No. I do. You're right. I'm a mess, and I'm probably always going to be one. Thank you for everything you've done for me. I mean that sincerely, Em."

I don't.

"But… thanks. Look, I don't know, okay?"

"You don't know what, babe?"

'Babe' always gets her. I don't have to worry about putting my shoes on anytime soon.

"I just… this. It's so exhausting, Tom."

"I know, babe. I'm sorry."

I'm not.

"I know you are. I'm sorry I'm such a witch."

"Heheh. You're not."

She's much worse than that.

"I am. It's just I… I want to do things, you know?"

"I know, babe."

Can never have too many babes, I've learned.

"I want us to do things. Together. I want to go travelling, to have a social life. I want to have babies and get married. And I really love you. I want you to be able to do all those things with me. Do you understand?"

"I do. I'm sorry. I'm sorry so bad at stuff."

"You're good at so much stuff, though. You really are. You can do stuff I wouldn't ever be able to figure out – your writing is amazing. The blogs, and the articles and stuff. And it's great that you've changed so much, and I know I haven't, but I mean I do all this stuff – I go to work, I pay the bills. And I know you don't think that's anything, but it is. It's real life. It's the real world."

Amazing she knows all this stuff about me and she still treats me like I'm a piece of shit.

"I know, Em. I do."

"I don't know if you do, Tom… I think you have – I think you have the luxury of thinking that money means nothing, cos you don't have to worry about it. You know?"

"Yeah. Well. I do worry, sometimes."

"But you don't act! You worry, but you don't do anything, cos at the end of the day, it's me who has to pay for everything. I'm really, really not trying to be nasty here."

Clearly just a talent then.

"I know. I know."

"But you have to do something. I can't live like this anymore. I just can't. It's making me miserable, and I'm making you miserable cos of it."

"Nah, you're all right."

She's not.

"Thank you, but I'm not. I'm just gonna keep on treating you like shit, Tom, until something changes – until you change. That's how it's going to be, and it doesn't matter how much you help me around here, or all the kind things you do for me, or any of that. At the end of the day, you need to stand on your own two feet. Financially, I mean. Cos I think I've lost all respect for you."

"Oh."

"I'm sorry to say it; I wish it wasn't true, really I do, Tom. I love you. And where we're together in bed, or on the weekend, and we're just wrapped up in our little bubble…"

"With the Time Thing."

When we're together like that we manage to make hours fly by, all gooey-eyed for each other. It's usually only the dogs going mental that snap us back into the real world and remind us it's seven in the evening and they should've been fed an hour ago.

"Yeah! With the Time Thing. You know I love you, and I've never had that with someone – that intense stuff. And the sex is amazing. It gets better and better, and I love it when we're not fighting and we get to have some of it. It's the best thing ever, yeah?"

"It is."

"It is, but we don't get to do it as much as we should. Cos we'll waste a whole weekend, fighting. I can't stand that. I don't like it. I hate being so… uncomfortable with you."

"But we've always been like that. Right from the start. Even when Kitchen Floors were happening."

"That's cos you're so sensitive."

Oh, bugger off.

"You're the bloody same. Come on, like."

I know I'm gonna lose this one. I shouldn't have bothered starting it.

"Pfffft. I'm not as sensitive as you! You're so… everything I say. Everything I say to you, you take it personally. It's exhausting."

There's that word again. Her favourite one.

"I'm just sensitive cos you're so…"

"What!? What am I so… Tom? A bitch?"

"I didn't say that…"

"Yeah, well maybe I am. Maybe I'm a bitch cos you won't get a fucking job, yeah? Walk a mile in my shoes. See how it feels."

"Bit cramped, probably."

I throw in a grin, might as well.

"Very good. Look… what were we talking about again? I don't even… for fuck's sake, my whole night's gone again."

"What do you mean?"

"This! This… bullshit. Every fucking night, it's the same. That's my spare time, you know? I work really hard, I'm out of the house all day."

Yeah? You never mention it.

"I know, babe."

"Don't 'babe' me, okay? I'm serious. This is the only time I get to relax, and you're filling it up with this bullshit."

"You did start it…"

I know straight away it was the wrong thing to say. She's not even in the mood for 'babe'. She's never gonna take this, even if it is true.

"I started it??? When!?"

"It doesn't matter."

"It matters to me. I'll tell you who fucking started it, Tom. You started it, by being in the same fucking situation that you were yesterday. And for the past three years. I'm sick of it."

Obviously I've changed. I know that; she knows that. Facts and rebuttals are useless here. I need to play the damage limitation game if I want a bed tonight. Might even manage some make-up sex. The thought occurs right there that I might be a sociopath, but I don't think that's news.

"I know, ba- I know, Em. I know. I'm sorry."

"Sorry's not going to cut it anymore, Tom. Something has to be done."

"It does."

"So, what are you gonna do?"

Anything I say at this point is going to sound like bullshit, so I might as well think big.

"I'll sit down and re-jig my CV tomorrow. See if I can make it look at bit more impressive. Be hard, mind; considering what I have to work with. I'm a good liar though. I done acting in college."

"Okay. Okay, that's good. And will you apply for some jobs?"

She's untensed now. Probably still full of knots though. I can knead them out for her in bed, later. Might end up being something more. It usually does, although not so much lately. Lately, I've not expected the shag at all. Made a point of giving her the massage, feeling her wait for me to try it on, and then not tried it on at all. She appreciates that as much as she does the massage. And she's such a control freak that she'll turn over five minutes later and suddenly have enough energy for a good old fashioned rogering. She's not that hard to figure out at all.

"Yeah. Definitely. I promise."

Might even change the phone number on the CV back to my real one, if you play your cards right, love. Although I doubt it.

"Thank you, that's all I want."

"Hug?"

"Yes please."

She slides into me so easily, and the smell of her reminds me how much I can't bear to walk away from this. I'm running out of time where it gets to be my decision though. I have to fix this soon. She's not going to wait for me.

Twelve

This Year, Limerick, Orla

Killing someone is easy. I'm sure it's hard for some people, like if they have no choice, if they have to do it to save their own life, if they're not used to it. But those people aren't me. They think differently. They think wrong. It's just a matter of changing someone's state. Turning them from one thing into another. They used to be alive, and now they're not. It's a simple transition, if you don't overthink it. That's how some people can commit suicide, and some people just threaten it a lot, but never go through with it. Those people, the second group, they overthink it. They remember their whole lives, all their experiences, and they think about what they're not going to get to do, who will miss them, what it'll mean. They think about whether there's something afterwards, a God, Heaven, if it won't be the end. And it scares them too much, so they don't. The others just feel that life is pain, and that ending it will end that pain, and they do it. Ending someone else's life is ending their pain too though, and we are all in pain, whether we admit it or not. Killing someone is the biggest favour you can ever do them, cos their whole existence after that was going to be pain of some sort, with some good times in between, to heal the bruises. That's the way it is, and not the other way around. The stupid thing is, I've always been part of the second group. I've always been too scared to end my own life, but I know that's stupid, cos when it comes for me, it'll just come. And there'll be nothing afterwards. At least, that's how I think today. Tomorrow it'll be different. Orla hasn't talked to me since the day in the Woodfield. I can't contact her, just in case the wrong person sees the message, so I'm relying on her to make the first move. And she isn't. And she has no idea what it's doing to me.

I'm by the river, about a mile from my house, or my Dad's house, if you want to look at it that way. I don't, not now, not when I feel pure. When I've done the thing that needs to be done, I'm in a kind of nirvana where thinking like a normal person isn't an option anymore. If I ever take my own life, it'll be in a time like this, cos right now, I'm not scared of anything. The body beside me is still warm, I can feel it off her neck while I'm playing with her hair. I'll get rid of her soon, but there's no hurry. No one is coming to get me, I never get caught. No one finds me, even if they're looking for me, and they are looking for me, somewhere. In England after that happened last year. What happened years before that. They're looking for me, they just don't know it's me they're looking for. Not yet, anyway.

By the river is good, but it's not like I planned it. When I left the house this morning, I had the feeling in me, the thing, so I knew it was going to happen, maybe. If I got the right opportunity. I didn't want it to happen. I never have. If I got the choice, I'd always choose not to. But it's not me who chooses. Or it doesn't always feel like me. And Orla's not said anything. She just left, in a taxi. Didn't even kiss me goodbye. I thought she'd text me or message me later, but she didn't. Or the next day, but she didn't either. It's been days and days now, and I haven't heard a word. I was doing so well too. It's a shame. But it's not like I can explain it to her. Not this. I can't explain this to anyone.

She came out of nowhere, today's one, a gift to me from whoever or whatever controls the universe. I never get too emotional about it, or excited, or nervous. I just know when I know, and then it's just a matter of time. It has to be done, and I do it. I'm the only one who gets to do it. She was young, pretty, I didn't ask her age; why would you? It's not something that comes up. I'd taken some money with me over to the off-licence and bought some booze. I had the big jacket on, with the deep pockets. Good enough for four cans, even if it looks a little bulky. I went down by the old salmon weir first, and had a look out over the river. Tide was in, so you couldn't see the rocks and the moss. I love the river, reminds me of being young and slipping and sliding down there, looking for eel fry. We'd take them home and let them swim in a big Tupperware thing, until they got tired and died. I used to fish too, but there was nothing to be caught down there. It was more about the experience.

I had a can there, at the wall. First one's always the dodgiest, cos there are people around, and living in the houses opposite, so they'd see you, and... and I don't know what I worry about. It's not like they're going to call the police on me. It's illegal, technically, but no one gives a shit. Especially not around these parts. And it's a can of cider. I'm not shooting heroin. When I finished the can, I dropped it on the grass and moved down the road, down to the Barrack Lane, which is all fenced off now, it looks like someone bought it, and then did nothing with it. There's an aluminium factory after that, then a part of the river you can get to, and after that, a little country walk thing, where you can get out to the Metal Bridge. I had no plan, just a few drinks, a think, and whatever happened after that wasn't up to me. The more drink, the less responsibility for whatever might go on. I know what I'm doing even when I don't know what I'm doing, sometimes. I went and stood by the river for a bit, near the outflow pipe that smells rotten. There was a girl there with a buggy. Cute kid in it. I gave them both a smile, but she looked funny at me, cos of the can. I moved on, and went along the little walk, deeper into the undergrowth, for a bit of privacy. Once I got in there I felt a little unsafe, and I was glad I didn't have my laptop bag with me, cos you never know who is in there. Gangs of boys and stuff. Once you see them and they see you, there's not much you can do. You're just screwed, if they happen to be dodgy. I didn't meet anyone like that though, so it was fine. The whole walk was peaceful, just a few rustles from where there were rats running about, and I got through there without meeting a soul.

I met her by the Metal Bridge, next to the dump. I used to come to the dump when I was about twelve, it was fascinating, going through other people's junk. We didn't care about it being dirty, or catching diseases. It was just part of a big walk, and we were usually out looking for fork shaped bits of young trees, that we could snap off and make into catapults. I got to the bridge, and thought about going across. I can't do heights though, and it's very high up. I couldn't get across it as a kid unless I did hands and knees, and I'm a bit old for that now. I never know if it still has trains going across it either. In my head there's a bit where I saw one going across it once, but that's memories mixed up with bits from films and books, I think. I didn't see her at first, I just wandered down to where the tide had come half way up, and there was still sand to sit on. Or mud; I'm not sure what it is, just that it's dry today. I took my jacket off, sat on it, and cracked open the third can. It was only once I'd lit up a fag and had a little stretch that I saw her, standing under the star of the bridge, looking over at me.

"Oh, hello."

I gave her a little smile. She was wearing shorts and a t-shirt, no shoes or socks. Her feet were in the water, just up to the ankles.

"Hi."

"What you up to, then? Having a swim?"

The feeling started to come over me like hot rain. It's not an arousal in the normal way. It doesn't give me the horn or anything. There's never anything sexual in it.

"Haha. No. Paddlin'."

Her voice was odd. She might've been a gypsy. She was pretty. The gypsies are always gorgeous when they're young. I couldn't tell what age she was. Not pre-pubescent, anyway. There was the usual lumps and bumps in places. Not that it mattered.

"Wicked. I used to love doing that."

I did, too. I can't swim, so it was the most I could do at the seaside.

"Haha. Me too."

She was shy, gypsy or no gypsy.

"You here on your own?"

I couldn't see another soul.

"Yeah."

She was talking to me, but she didn't seem interested. Like she could turn around any minute and ignore me to go do something else.

"Where's everyone else?"

"Gone home."

She said it like she was sad. Must have been with friends. Parents wouldn't just leave their kid there, even if she wasn't that young.

"Awww. They're not coming back then?"

I regretted it immediately, but I was probably just being paranoid. It was a normal question to ask. She didn't know that I was making sure, or why.

"Nope."

She squatted down as she said it, not looking over at me anymore.

"Have a fight or something?" I thought about getting up and walking over, but I didn't want to scare her off. If it got messy I'd probably be okay, but if I can do it the simple way, there's never any point in making it more complicated for myself.

"Yeah. No. Well… I didn't – sorry."

"Why you sorry, hun?" I didn't get up, but I shifted around on the coat, so my knees pointed at her. Body language thing, trying to seem a bit more friendly, welcoming.

"Mama says not to talk to a stranger." Definitely a gypsy. She couldn't have been too educated then, I thought. Might be an advantage.

"Mama's right. I'm not a stranger though, love. My name's Steve." There it is. No going back now. Or is there? Cos that one time…

"Steve?"

"Yeah, Steve. Has your Mam never talked about me?"

"I dunno. Where's you from, like?" She was standing up again, swaying her hips a little. Felt like she was being coquettish, but I was probably imagining that.

"Ah, all round, like. Same as you. What's your name again, love? I've forgot it." Nothing ventured, nothing gained. She heisted a little, as if she was sussing me out. Then she said:

"Sarah-Jane."

"Of course it is, sorry Sarah-Jane. How could I forget a lovely name like that? How's your Mam anyway? I haven't seen her in ages, like." I was in. Just had to secure the trust, then it was only a matter of time. The black feeling was all over me now, in my pores and my veins. In the follicles on my scalp. Filling up my lungs and stomach.

"She's grand. The baby's coming next week."

"Oh yeah, it is, isn't it? That's exciting. Do you know if it's a boy or a girl?"

"Nah. It's a surprise."

"You looking forward to it anyway? New brother or sister?"

"Nah. Boring, like. Got too many of them." She started walking towards me. I was calm, blood like ice. It's always how it is.

"Yep, how many will that be now? Of you, all together?"

"Well... with me, and the new baby, and all the rest of them, that's... ten. No, eleven."

"Wow. That's a lot. Must be great to have a big family," I said, even though I was probably thinking something different. No one needs to have that many children. I was going to be doing the world a favour, even if it was like throwing a deckchair off the Titanic. She was very sweet though. It wasn't her fault.

"Nah, bit too squashy." She was almost a foot away from me now. I could smell her, it was familiar. Couldn't tell if it was perfume or deodorant, but it was clean.

"Have ye to share a bed?"

"Nah, I've my own bed now. Too old for that." She scooched in next to me on the coat, bold as brass. It was too easy.

"Oh, hello. Want a drink?"

"Yeah, what's that?"

"Cider. Here, have a full one if you want."

"Ah no, I'm not allowed."

"Not allowed? G'way, will you. You telling me you've never had a bit of booze?"

"No." She giggled with it, and rubbed her head on my shoulder. She was very cute.

"Liar."

"I'm NOT!" She gave me a playful little punch on the shoulder. I liked her. It was a shame.

"Okay, okay. You're not a liar. Try some of mine here, and if you don't like it, don't worry about it. Yeah?"

"Er, okay..."

"Go on, get that down you, you gowl." That made her snort laugh, and she almost spilled the can.

"Shaddup! You're the gowl." Such a cutie pie.

"I'll give you gowl in a minute. Well? What you think anyway? Nice, is it?

"S'all right, like."

"Yeah. Yeah, I don't think that's your first drink ever, Sarah-Jane. I think you're not as innocent as you look."

"Ah now, I'm lovely."

"You really, really are."

The look in her eyes when the knife went through her chest and into her heart will stay with me for a while. Not haunting me, or anything like that. It was beautiful, it always is. No one is ever that beautiful in life. It feels good to give them it, for that half a second. After that, the light starts to go out, and they just become nothing. A shadow of themselves, already losing its warmth and softness. I'd forgotten this. Or maybe I made myself forget. I played with her hair one last time, kissed her forehead, and then pushed her down the bank, into the river. There's some bricks and rocks to throw in after her, but that's not going to keep her under for long. She'll be floating in a couple of days; bloated and black, looking nothing like she did when I said goodbye. Doesn't matter now. Dead is dead, whether it's pretty or ugly. I finish off the cans and take them with me in my coat pockets. No point in being stupid, even if I do live a charmed life. It could be a few days before she comes up from under the rocks. And then she'll float downstream with the current. Or upstream. I don't know for sure, I'm just guessing. Hopefully Orla will have got in touch by then. This isn't London. I can't get away with as much here as I did over there.

Thirteen

Last Year, London, Emma

There's nothing more frustrating than being in a situation where you try everything within your power to make things right, but the only thing that can fix it is beyond your control. It's bad enough in a practical situation; but, when that situation is tied to your actual heart and emotions, it's the worst of the worst. She thinks it's within my control. That's what makes her so angry. It's right there in front of me, in her mind, and I'm just refusing to take it. But she doesn't know. She doesn't know the half of how shit I am at these things, and she doesn't live in my head when I'm thinking about jobs and new places or people, or any of the anxiety shit. I don't think she realises that sometimes I'd rather be dead than have to do something other people would just find mildly intimidating. And there's no use telling her, cos everyone can recognise emotional blackmail when they see it, and no one with any self-respect goes along with it.

I've never been good at relationships. It's too uncontrolled, and I like control. I'm not a control freak, and I don't need to be in charge, but I like to control what happens to me, and my emotions. A relationship is handing over the reins to someone else. And there's no logic to it. When things go bad, like an argument or whatever, you can't just shut it down with the truth or facts or logic. Once they are angry with you, they're like cornered rats. They flail and they bite and they spit. And I can't handle the stuff that gets said, or respect the person who's saying them. I can't forget it afterwards and not hold it against them. I'm in that moment too, and I manage to control myself and not fling out personal remarks just to make the other person hurt. It's barbaric, and I'm not like that. Not in those contexts. The other thing doesn't count. I don't know how to describe that. Is it a dichotomy? Or cognitive dissidence? I don't know what either of those means, really. What I mean, is that one can exist while the other does, and they don't interfere with each other. They never have. I've been lucky like that.

Today feels like a day for something. Celia is away again, she's given me so much work this summer; this year. I don't make much money from it, on aggregate, cos I have the overdraft that Emma thinks I've cleared, and the small matter of having to get off my face every day. I got here about eleven this morning, cos she was leaving at nine, which means ten, with all the kids and bags and getting ready in her scatty, disorganised way. I like a chat with her, but I didn't want a chat with anyone today. I've pinched a few finger fulls of MDMA crystals from the little baggie in Emma's dressing table, and a little coke from the other baggie. She never seems to notice. The only reason there's any there at all is that we have to order at least a hundred quid's worth from Jay, the dealer who delivers, and when we're at a party she's still ridiculously sensible and tight, so some comes home with us in her purse. If it was up to me, it'd all be gone on the night. I can only have so much Molly before it stops working, any more is a waste, it's not like pills, where you just keep going until the bag is empty, and you've started seeing elves in the corner of your eye, or spirals drilling down at you like stalactites from the artexed ceiling. But, with coke, you can have a dab of one, then a dab of the other, and the coke keeps you awake while the MDMA does the business. I'd never had a use for cocaine until we figured that one out. Now I get it.

Celia's place is a nice old Victorian house in a nice, tree lined street in Haringey, but cos it's London, she's a minute's walk away from all sorts of depravity. They call it Wood Green Shopping City, and that's a good description. From one tube to the other, it's just lines of shops, banks, and takeaways. So it's always humming, and there's a nasty vibe in the air. I hate it after dark, if I'm any way sober. It's like Limerick, but more ethnically diverse. I'm not afraid of people cos they're brown – I've lived in Hackney, and now in Leytonstone; and I'm not a racist. No, I'm just afraid of people cos they're scum. And that's a reasonable prejudice to have, in my mind. I'm in the front room; Celia's left the dog here this time, and he's going apeshit, as usual. He always wants attention, or for you to throw a ball and stuff. The opposite of our dogs. Our dogs wouldn't chase a ball if it was made out of Pedigree Chum. Probably cos they're posh dogs, and they prefer Cesar.

I took a dab of Molly when I got in. I'm amazed I didn't have some on the train. I'm not a big waiter when it comes to getting wasted. I've done it on a train before though, and it's a bit dangerous, having a crazy heart rate and smiling at random strangers like you love them. I suppose if I started talking about Jesus though, people would just shrug and think nothing of it. I don't know when it's going to kick in, so much of it is in your mind. Music helps speed the whole thing up, or looking at some crazy fractal videos on YouTube, or both together. There's a TV here, with a Freeview box. We usually watch torrents at home, so I hardly ever see real TV, with adverts, unless Em is watching her property porn. Middle class conservative people watch shows about property and renovation the most, I read somewhere. It makes sense, cos it's all about spending money to make money, which is them all over. And her. She doesn't vote, but if she did, I know it would be for the Tories. She has that deluded, messed up mentality that they all do – that the problems of society are all caused by the scrounging poor, rather than the people at the top creaming off stuff for themselves. Living with me is hardly helping her to shake off that stereotype, I suppose. I picture her face, and I get a warm feeling. Drugs are working now, definitely. I take out the coke, and my Halifax card. Time to go to Happy-Happy Land.

Doing drugs on my own is my favourite way of doing them. Doing them with other people is great too – social in a way that doesn't make me gag at the word. Talking to strangers like you love them, hearing big sincere confessions from people you already know; hugs and kisses and the constant feeling that this is what you should do all the time, cos to hell with alcohol, and this should be legal, and we never ever want to come down. I love MDMA for that. I used to love pills back in the old days, before we knew you could get it purer. Those had their bad side, with the nasty comedowns and the Tuesday blues. But they were honest. You knew you were tapping the keg of good feelings at a rate that it didn't normally pour, and that there'd be none left for a few days afterward. But you took that, cos what you got on the night was well worth it. It could change your whole outlook on everything; change your life, if you were in any way a thinker. Of course, if you weren't, it changed bugger all, and just made you dance like a spastic for ten hours. Each to their own.

Doing it on my own is definitely a thinking thing, but I dance as well. Dance like no one's watching, is what they always say. That's literally the only time I do dance, though. So, my saying is more 'Dance when you're absolutely sure that no one's watching. And be on a lot of drugs'. I've never understood dancing, in a social way. When we were young, it was this thing you were told you had to do, or girls wouldn't fancy you. I passed. When we were a bit older, in proper pubs and clubs, they told you that a bird can tell a lot about how a bloke is in the bedroom by how he is on the dancefloor. I still passed. I'd make a joke of it to girls, something along the lines of 'Yeah, you can tell he likes it up the arse!', or 'Yeah, too tired to shag you.' Sometimes it even worked. I couldn't ever do it, though, too self-conscious. And then E came along, and it was all different. It made you want to dance, if only for the science of it, where you knew that it would get the drug booting around your bloodstream, and give you a better buzz. That might have been bullshit, but we believed it, so it worked. You could meet people all night, go back to parties, talk to beautiful people who were not beautiful at all, but the drug made them all seem like Cindy Crawford, and then end the night not getting a shag, cos your dick didn't work anymore. That's another great thing about the crystals: they don't banjax your cock. There's no one to put it in today, but having a wank is almost as good, and porn seems like poetry when you're on this shit. I love it. I wish my whole life could be like it, but then you can't appreciate the sweet without the sour. I don't know how true that is. If everything was perfect, I think you'd just enjoy it. Or maybe you'd go out of your way to make things bad for yourself. Feeling philosophical already, clearly. Breathe in a big deep one, teeth are clenched. I have chewing gum somewhere. The line's chopped, I roll up one of the twenties Celia left on the table for me and horse the powder up my nose. It burns a bit, but that just makes me feel more Rock n' Roll.

I love me like this. I love me now. I put on some tunes, the Prodigy, from YouTube. Gotta find a full album, or a playlist. Playlist won't do, too random. I don't want to hear new things. I want old skool. I want old memories. I come up much better if it's Experience, or Music for the Jilted Generation, or Fat of the Land. Some of Fat of the Land. Smack My Bitch Up. I want to hear that one now. I want to see the video too, with the naked woman. I want to experience everything fully. I'm already completely horny, but I'm not going to have a wank. Not a full one. Not gonna waste my mojo so early, in case it ruins everything. Better to be fully charged. I could have a little tug though, get the heart rate up. Dangerous later on though; when I've had one or two already, and I'm just willing it, half-soft, to do another one. You can get to heart attack levels of too many beats then. I could die. It wouldn't be a bad way to go. But a bad way to be found. Celia's not back for a week. The dog would probably eat me. And the cats. I find the full, uncensored version. My crotch feels like there's warm bath water all over it. The bird in the video is some Page 3 girl or porn star. She looks so beautiful, like someone out of my Dad's magazines when I was a kid. I remember getting the blood up one day, when I was about twelve, and ripping out one of the pages. A real old fashioned Russ Meyer film type girl. Small waist and massive tits, all covered in baby oil. I wanted to show it to my friend, Niall. I snuck it out under my t-shirt, shitting myself, looking like someone in a customs queue who has a back of heroin up his arse. I got to Niall, took him somewhere quiet and away from everyone. Showed him it. Straight away I felt stupid. It was only a few seconds' worth of fun, for all that risk. I couldn't put it back in the mag, either, all ripped like that. I couldn't do anything with it, except leave it there in the secluded place, on some waste ground. That's probably how a lot of porn got in those places, whenever we used to find it ourselves. Maybe. She's so gorgeous now, the girl in the video. And the music is no longer coming from the speakers – it's inside my chest, beating along with my too-fast heart. Amazing. I think I'm in love. The video finishes and the playlists moves onto Satisfaction. The one with the models and the power tools, and the dance beat. Someone up there loves me. Or someone down here, who makes YouTube playlists.

I'm in heaven now; strange, tits and drugs heaven. It's ecstasy, quite literally. No drug has ever been better named. They discovered it long before the 90s, I know that, I read it somewhere. It was around a long time ago. Maybe even in Victorian times. It just came back in the 90s. Like the Wonderbra. I think it actually came back in the late 80s. The Summer of Love. Acid House, although no one was doing acid. I wasn't old enough then. I think I took my first pill when I was eighteen, but I could be remembering it wrong. The video's finished and another dance one comes on, but I don't know it. And there's no tits in it. Someone up there has stopped liking me, temporarily. I feel good. I need chewing gum though, and for once, I don't have any. I always have it, for Emma and smoking reasons, but I can't find any on me now. I've searched all the pockets, and my bag. I'm rolling in absolute joy, but I'm not destroyed yet. It's not like that. The gum isn't just there and I can't find it. I don't think so. I can go to the shop. I'm not tripping. It'll be fine. I can get some nice water there too. Although that'll look dodgy. Me, buying chewing gum and water. Eyes like saucers. Does that rhyme? I look at myself in the hall mirror and I'm beautiful. She's an idiot. She isn't though; she knows I'm beautiful. And she loves the sex. Oh God, the sex. I love the sex with her so much. I love it so much that I don't want it with anyone else. I've had it with other people, like in that time we were split up, and some of it was good. That Ellie girl. Don't think of it. Don't think of it. Don't think of it. But sex with Emma is the best. Emma is the best. I think of her all the time when I'm wanking. I haven't done that before, with the girl I'm with. That's new. She's new. She's not new, but this feeling is new. Not the Molly; the feeling I feel for her. Kitchen floors. All that.

    I'm outside now and I hope I locked the door and I hope I brought my key, but I couldn't have locked the door without the key, so I must have it, I'm being stupid. I don't check, either way. I'm not having good luck with pockets today. I pass a few people on the way down to the alley that goes to the shop. I can't help smiling, cos everything is positive to me now. I pass a couple and they look very in love, and I love them too. A bird pushing her baby, and I look down at him (or her) and he looks perfect, cos he's life, and life is amazing, and babies are amazing, and I want to have babies with Emma, but I'm always afraid she'll ruin her body, and that's selfish of me, I realise that. I'll just love her anyway, she's so beautiful and hot and sexy. She is so hot, and perfect looking. Even her face. I'm such an arsehole about her. And to her. She's right, you know. I'm just not cutting it. I need to get a job, and fix everything, and fix us, and everything will be all right. And she can have a baby, or two babies, like she wants. And we'll have babies, and we'll be happy, and it doesn't matter if she gets fat, or gets old, cos I'll just love her. It's all so clear now. Everything is going to be fine.

    I'm standing in the shop. Or moving around it. Both. It's a small shop. They know me here, to see me and salute me. They must think I'm a complete alcoholic, so thinking I'm a druggie isn't going to make a difference. Drinking isn't against the law though. It's okay, I'm not paranoid. I remember one time, years ago, in England. We'd been up all night on pills, and I was at the spastic phase of chewing your own face off and talking gobbledygook. I had to pop across the road to the Spar, at six in the morning. I spent at least an hour staring at the chewing gum display, trying to remember how words worked, or how to do a transaction where you give someone money and they give you goods. I eventually managed it, but I was in a complete paranoid other universe, and it felt like the woman behind the counter was deeply ashamed for me. I was probably only staring at the gum for a couple of minutes, I know that now. But at the time, it was horrible. I'm okay now though. I can speak and everything. I'll probably speak too much, but I can do words and sentences. I pick up a triple pack of Wrigley's Extra, so I don't have to come back later, when I'm full Cerebral Palsy. The bloke at the counter is the handsome guy, looks like Thierry Henry. His smile makes me feel warm. I love this drug.

Back at the door to the house I fish out the keys first time and open both locks like poetry. I'm in flow now, this is the good bit. I can't remember when I took the first dose, but it must be more than a half hour ago, if I'm up this much already. Maybe 45 minutes. I can wait until it's an hour, or go again now. They call that Double Dropping, I think. Taking another hit as soon as you come up off the first one. I don't know how up I am though, cos the coke hits you straight away, so some of the feeling might be coming from that. I'm walking sexy; my hips are rolling, and my stomach feels tight. It's immense, feeling this good. I want it all the time. I am a depressive. I'm aware that my depression might be caused or made worse by doing this stuff, but I'd never give these times back. If someone came along right now and told me they had a magic time machine that could take me back to every time I'd done pills or powder, make them not have happened, and in return, I'd get to be normal, like everyone else, I'd tell them no thanks. I don't think it would be worth it. I am who I am today cos of some of those times. It makes me sad and angry that not everyone in the world has done this. Even worse that most of them think it's bad; that it'll kill you; that it's dirty. I was so happy when I did the usual subtle suss out on Em, and she turned out to be someone who takes drugs all the time. I can't do the non-drugs people. Especially Andie, who's never taken a drug in her life, but has all these opinions on them. I love Andie though. She saves my life a lot, and she's gorgeous. They were all gorgeous. Now, anyway. I am too loved up, if that's possible. No, that's stupid. Loved up is good. No harm can come from loving people too much. Well, it probably can. I should stay away from the internet today; or at least the parts that let me say things in public, or in private messages. This isn't a state that goes down too well if people aren't clued into what you're on. It's fine when you're all there together, ballsed off your faces. Everyone understands then, and they take your mad love both seriously and with a pinch of salt at the same time. That's the best thing about MDMA. You're in an altered state, but you know you are. No bad trips. Even in the old days when pills had all sorts of shit in them that made you hallucinate if you overdid it – there was no panic to it. You just thought 'Oh. That's trippy. I'm okay though. I'll just enjoy the show.' The amount of times I've been naked with a girl in the early hours of the morning; both of us pointing at little piles of angel hair on skin, that the other one can't see, cos it just exists in our own eyes, not theirs. It's not freaky though, and no one gets weird about it. It's just another thing, and it's great, and you're both on the same page. I love this drug.

My YouTube is still playing, and cos someone up there loves me again, this video has hot girls in it. I slink down into the couch cushions and suddenly remember I smoke. Can't smoke in the house though, Celia would flip. Even if the Celia I picture in my head now is a totally cool Celia, looking all hot and MILFy, and off her face on gear, same as me. She does do a bit, she's not very 50 at all. I was in the toilets with her, at her 50th, doing blow off the cistern, with her best friend from when she was growing up. Her CD rack is full of the bands I listened to when I was a teenager, and she's so slim and sporty looking, she can't be 50. But she must be, cos she was about 46 when I first got to know her, on the internet. That's a very long game to be playing if you're just trying to blag a fake 50th party. I make myself giggle with that. I like Celia. She's nice, and she's hot. I didn't realise quite how hot she was until that party. She came over to say hi in a little black dress, all made-up and done-up, and she was much less tall than I always thought, and much prettier. I think I touched her arse in a flirty way when we were in the bogs that time. I know I did, cos she said out loud: "Did Tom Carroll just touch my arse in a flirty way?" It was a great night. I remember now that I was there representing me and Emma. She didn't want to go. She'd found me passed out from drink on the couch the day before, one of those days where we'd pretty much agreed to split up. She told me to go to the party though, and have a good time. She looked nice when she said it as well, not like she was still hating me or wanting me to suffer. I hate her being like that. I like her being nice. She's away now, another trip back home. She's taken the dogs, cos I can't mind them. I wish she was here. Sort of. It's okay, she doesn't have to be here. I can just think about her and stuff. It's time for more MDMA. And a fag then, now that I've remembered I smoke.

It's absolutely beautiful in the garden, with the wind on my skin and the heat on my face. I take my top off and laugh at how pale I am, and how I'm somehow not a fat beast yet, with my shitty lifestyle. I've never had that body where you can take your shirt off in public. Things like exercise and weights just seem a little too much like hard work. Not now though. If there were weights here now, I'd do them. Piece of piss. Probably give myself a heart attack though; whatever it is about this stuff, it definitely makes your reach longer than your grasp. Or however that goes. I might do some press-ups later. And squat thrusts. Gets the blood going around. Like dancing, or running up and down the stairs. I found that out years ago, when I took Speed for the first time, and it did nothing for me. I ended up doing hill sprints on the stairs. Didn't make that much of a difference, but it worked. I feel horny, but not like normal. It's all over me. All over my skin. Feels great just touching myself, along my chest and stomach. This is a bloody amazing day so far. The sun is splitting the pavement, I should be careful. Don't want to overheat that way. Stupid way to die. Wanking and being eaten by the pets would be much better. I horse down the fag like it's made of air. I don't know what nicotine does when you're buzzing on Molly, but there's something about having a fag that just needs to be done. We used to go through so many of them in the old days that you'd have to ring a taxi to pick you up some more from the 24-hour garage. They were good days and nice times. I can't remember anything bad about them right now. I miss them.

I feel so nice, all over my skin, and down through the flesh, into my bones. It feels great when I walk around and feel the air on me. Or when I sit down on the comfy cushions. And when I stand up again. Every change of position is good, and feels like something I'd forgotten I could do, until I do it again, and I remember. I'm not making much sense now. I've been taking lots, and I don't know if it's in a long period of time, or a short one. I keep forgetting when I started. I should've written it down. I'm good, though. I'm very good. Even smiling feels like half an orgasm. Breathing in is great too, although the coke has burned my nostrils a bit. The back of my throat is numb from it as well. I like that feeling too, the feeling like you've swallowed some Bonjela. I associate it with drugs. With cool drugs, like they do in the movies. Drugs you snort up a twenty. Rock n' Roll drugs.

I'm not a rock star. I'm a writer, but even then, my excesses are beyond my means. Haven't been successful enough and made enough money to be this self-destructive. It doesn't feel self-destructive today though. Drink feels more like that than this does. This just feels good. MDMA is more like a little holiday from myself, to somewhere nice. Drink might start off euphoric, but it always ends in a mess, unless I luck out, and end up turning it into a good day or night. If I ever thought for even a moment about the end result every time I looked at a row of cans in an off licence, I'd never pick one up. But I compartmentalise that – the feeling of 'Oh, this is a good idea', and the fact of 'No it bloody isn't'. It's probably the same for most people. Well, not most people. Most people can just drink and have a good time. With other people, for social reasons. Not like I do it. I drink like an alcoholic. Maybe I am one. I'm not drinking today. I'm happy today. Cos of chemicals. The TV isn't on. There's some whole rigmarole that you have to go through to get the box working, and some kind of switch business at the back; three or four different remotes. I can't figure it out when I'm straight, let alone now. I think about watching comedy, but I need a beat. I have the soundtrack to Human Traffic on the laptop somewhere. That's perfect. I don't even like the film. I thought I did, but I bought it as a present for Emma a while back, and we watched it together. She said:

"This is very much… of its time."

And she was right. It was all Late 90s and cringey and breaking the fourth wall. I feel more empathy watching Trainspotting, even if I was never a smackhead. Closest I came to that was when some lunatic I knew in Limerick brought back some opium from Burma, and I had a go on it. It was a sticky brown stuff, and you burnt it on a piece of tin foil, while sucking in the fumes with the tube from a biro. It wasn't like anything the films or books said heroin would be like. It was just like getting stoned, with a thousand times the intensity. So, for me, who hates getting stoned, it was the worst experience possible. I remember walking down the street afterwards, with two much cooler people. Both of them mellowed out of their skulls, and me having the most paranoid inner conversation of all time. I felt like my heart was going to burst with the anxiety. I managed to snap myself out of it by looking at a traffic light, and saying to my brain:

"Okay, if this drug is so powerful and scary, make that traffic light into a dragon."

The few seconds I waited for a response were the scariest of my entire life, but the opium failed to come up with the goods, and I came down (up?) with a bang; exhausted, and dragonless. The *Café del Mar* tune is on now, it's gorgeously familiar, even though I didn't know the name of it for years. It resurfaces every time there's a House and Trance revival. I think it's been remixed in Dubstep now. But then, everything has. I couldn't listen to Dubstep and be comfortable on this buzz. I want to feel good and nostalgic. Not old and pointless. Emma says she likes Dubstep. She's an idiot though. She likes shit books, and you can't take her to a movie with too many explosions. Great body though. I get another all over sex feeling that isn't quite a sex feeling. I think I have some photos of her in her pants on this thing. That might be nice.

There's a new review on Amazon of one of my books. I'm tentative, cos I could go up or down quickly on this stuff. It's from the first book though; the one everyone liked, so it's probably safe. And, even if it's bad, I'll probably see the good in it. I'm invincible today. The other book isn't as safe. Apparently, the subject matter is 'too dark'; which is ridiculous, cos the first draft was ten times more graphic. I only toned it down so Emma might read it, and that was a waste of time. I look at her amazing arse in the lemon coloured knickers on my screen and I instantly forgive her. It's rare I get a bad review on that one where they've finished the book. It's all 'I put this down after the second chapter', or 'I couldn't get past 10% on this one'. Which is good publicity, cos people with strong stomachs who read reviews like that will probably give it a punt, just to see how much they can take. Those people would probably be disappointed, though. It's not that scary or sickening. It's just that it deals with subjects that are usually sensationalised in the media, but does in a way that comes across as matter of fact. I think that's what offends these people; the sort of people who get offended at things on a regular basis. They're just plebs, but as Emma's bookshelf tells me, plebs is where the money's at. I like to tell myself that I don't want the pleb money, that I'm all about integrity. But I don't love that book or stand by it. It's a bit dumbed down. Another thing I did to please her, ironically enough. The first one though, that's safe. It's about some dark things too, but it's mostly a coming of age thing, and full of nostalgia. People keep comparing it to *Stand By Me*, which is a compliment, I think. And not a coincidence either, cos I must have read the book version of that about 20 times when I was a kid.

"It took me a few pages to get used to the Irish childhood slang in this book, but I'm glad I stuck at it. The author has an incredible talent for scene-setting and detail, much like early Stephen King. I felt transported to another place and time, and the characters were so beautifully drawn, and the relationships between them so real and relateable, that I finished this book in almost one sitting. Although hilarious in parts, and deeply touching, this isn't a light read, and I found myself sickened, saddened, and moved as much as I laughed out loud with the proceedings. Definitely a five star read, from a writer who needs to be discovered by more readers. I'm looking forward to more from him. Recommended."

Can't ask for more than that. I might be on drugs, but I think that would have pleased me just as much if I was on nothing but a cup of tea and a fag. I love it when they get me. Scene setting and detail. I love when the stuff Emma would warn me against, like not enough action, too much introspection, not enough dialogue, too much describing – I love it when people say they liked those things. Cos I like those things. All this shit about action beats and things having to happen for the sake of something happening, I don't want to do that. Show, don't tell – all of that seems like guidelines for people who can't write, and want to sell books, regardless. I don't read those books. I don't want to write something I wouldn't read. I grew up on King and Koontz. I like detail, and characters, and inner thoughts, and rambling, and dark things, and dream sequences, and the occasional bit of tastefully rendered gore. I want people to love the writing, not the story. The first book was about the writing, even though I did it in the first person, through the eyes of a pre-teen boy as he lived it;

so I couldn't use any words that anyone over twelve would know. But that *is* good writing. Good writing isn't big words and fancy sentence structure. It's being able to tell what you want to tell in plain English, or in slang, like I did in that one. People don't get that. People who don't write books usually think someone is a great writer if they use words that have to be looked up in a dictionary. The same people don't read the books by those writers, cos they're a bit thick. But they think that they must be good writers, in a weird forelock-tugging way that makes no sense. I don't think you need to be a good writer to write a good book; Dan Brown writes them all the time, and he's terrible. But if someone hands me a book and tells me it's great, the writing and editing part of my brain can't settle and relax, and I end up hating it, cos it appals me that people can get a publishing deal when they clearly have no idea how real humans speak to each other. Or that no one else seems to be noticing this except me. I don't care about stories, I let them tell themselves. I care about writing, and I'm my own editor, so I'm my own worst critic. And, if I'd written 'I'm my own worst critic' in a book of mine, I'd have deleted it in the second draft. I can't seem to write anything these days, so that's not likely.

Every movement is its own buzz now. If I sit down too long and get up, whoosh! Same if I just walk quickly from one room to another. I've turned on the stereo in the kitchen, found an all-day dance station on the DAB. I don't understand dance music in any other context than this. I couldn't just sit down and listen to an album, like it was real music. I've met people who don't do drugs and like dance music. Even ones who don't drink either, and just like going clubbing, and dancing all night. That's just monkey behaviour. They can't be fully formed humans. The music was made for drugs. They were probably making music in Peru thousands of years ago, when they were smoking the bark of that crazy tree that has DMT in it. Although whenever I see Peruvians playing music it's those bands in the high street playing pan pipes. I don't think I could get my DMT on to an instrumental of *The Heart Must Go On*. I'd love to do DMT. Even though the descriptions of it are always insane – you get a ten-minute high that feels like a week, and you touch the edges of the universe, and reality. It sounds scary, but at least it's doing what it says on the tin. I smoke half a joint and I'm lying on a bed, questioning my sanity and my existence. That's not what's supposed to happen. But I keep doing it, cos it's better than going down the shops for bacon. Anything for a break from the routine. Story of my life. I don't even have a routine. It's routine nothingness. It's prison, without the rape or bad food. It's shite. But sometimes I have day like this. And that makes it easier.

I wish I could have more days like this. I wish drugs were legal and alcohol wasn't. Getting pissed is nothing compared to this. It's nonsense. It's liquid sadness, and this is powdered joy. I'd do it all the time if I had the money and I wasn't sure that it would kill me. The booze is going to kill me though. Either from liver failure, or some stupid thing I do while I'm drunk that makes me end up dead. I don't want to die. Not today. Or ever, if I can only keep feeling like I do today. But I won't. I won't even feel like this in a few hours, when the stuff wears off, and real world comes back. I pass a cupboard in Celia's kitchen and pick up a bottle of Smirnoff. I twist off the cap and take a glug without thinking. It makes me wince. I don't drink when I'm doing this. It brings you down. Emma can't do MDMA without booze. It's too intense for her, otherwise, she says. I don't understand that. But it's her all over. She doesn't like deep, hippy thinking. She's not even stupid. She just likes living her life on the surface, I think. That's why she hates our relationship, or why she tells herself she does. She just wants a life where she makes enough money to do things like go for dinner and a movie, or have a holiday. Travelling never broadens her mind, as far as I can see. It just justifies her going out to work to make a living. I've never had that wage slave mentality. I prefer to spend my money on constructive things. Like ciggies and drink.

Fourteen

This Year, Limerick, Orla

It's a special kind of Hell, being back home. I'm not hard to get on with, and I'm usually okay in any situation, unless it's the first half hour of a social one, or any other kind of Organised Fun. That's something I'll never get used to but I'm all right after a half hour. And a drink. When I didn't drink, it was different. When you don't drink, the company has to be good for you to have a good time. Here though, it's not a social situation, it's a living situation, and it's just… odd. I'm at my Dad's house. I call it that, but it used to be my house. I never lived with my Mum, apart from when they were still together. She buggered off when I was about fifteen, not her fault, more his. Being shit at keeping a woman runs in my family.

It's a different house now, my house. My sister's still living here, and she's taken what used to be my bedroom. There's three bedrooms altogether, so I should have my own now, but she's thrown out the bed and turned it into a walk-in wardrobe; fair enough, I wasn't here. She has a lot of clothes. And she's constantly washing them. My Dad is middle class, originally, but he ended up poor cos his family didn't approve of him marrying my Mum. So, having been brought up around intelligent, well-off people, and had every opportunity, he's now been left on his own, in a council estate, with no friends, and just the internet for company, apart from me and my sister. It's a sad situation, but it's down to him. He may not have thrown himself on the scrapheap, but he's stayed there by choice. He could've met someone else, it's been twenty years now. He could've kept friends, or made new ones, but he didn't. He enjoys being martyred, and that's sad too. I look at him sometimes and think 'I hope I don't turn out like that,' but at the moment, I'm not far off it. Right this minute, I'm living in a council house, I don't have any friends, and the internet is my only company. I thought I had someone, but she hasn't said a word to me in two weeks. I've managed not to contact her, but that's been down to luck more than self-control. I'm living my life in review these days – waking up every morning with a hangover, frantically checking all my outboxes to see if I drunk-texted her. I haven't, so far. But I don't know how long that's going to last. As I said, it's just luck.

The house is tense, all the time. My sister's been in rehab. While I was in London. I remember my Mum emailing me about it, in the middle of me emailing her about how miserable I was. It was like, "Look, I know you're a bit sad and want to kill yourself and stuff, but your sister's got a *real* condition, cos we're paying money for someone to fix her. Get in the queue for sympathy. At the back, please." I should probably be in rehab, I've just never thought about it. She was getting drunk a lot, and taking drugs. Apparently, when she does that, it's time for the family to intervene, pull together, and get things sorted. When I do it, it's just a Saturday. Or a Tuesday. She's in the program now and going to meetings, and she's managing it, but she's not happy. She's still at that stage where she feels like she's depriving herself of fun, of a life. Rather than feeling like she's finally free. And that's a road to ruin, in my experience. I feel for her. I try talking to her about it sometimes, when we get some time alone, and she listens, she gets me, and she appreciates it. But she's miserable, and she can't understand how well she's done or how far she's come, so I worry about her. Because it's in our genes, I think.

She's not much like me. It's strange. I was (I think) brought up by my mum, even though I can always remember her working. You'd think, to know me, that I was brought up by Dad, cos I'm nothing like my mother. But my sister was essentially brought up by him, and she's nothing like him. Although she is, in a lot of ways. And so am I. I definitely get my bitterness and sense of martyrdom from his side of the family tree. Actually, that's unfair. Even if he is bitter, you don't ever get it off him. He's like me, anything for a quiet life, doesn't like to make other people uncomfortable. He used to like to, but I think all the fight is gone from him now. He's just an old man who lives in a house now, with two dogs who are his best friends. Except he spoils them, so they have no respect for him. He sits there, eating a sandwich dinner, while they stare at him, waiting for scraps. And he gives them the scraps, off his plate, before he's even finished. When I look at that, I realise how my sister turned out to have so many problems. And maybe how I did too.

The dogs have a walk every day, at one in the afternoon. The routine is always the same. Five minutes before one, he goes up to the toilet, and then they get restless, and follow him up. Couple of minutes later, he comes back down to get the choker leashes, which are overly complicated, and always tangled up. The dogs scream bloody murder while he's trying to get the chains unknotted and around their necks, knocking each other over, and trying to knock him over too. He's not strong enough to handle them, and any chance of disciplining them he had has gone years ago. So, he struggles with them, and shouts at them, and they bark at him, and it's a cacophony, until he finally gets them out the door. All the while, I can feel the tension from upstairs, where my sister is seething away; only a matter of seconds before she comes stomping down the stairs to scream at him about the noise. It doesn't occur to her that her shouting is adding to the clamour and distress. Or to Dad, who shouts "Shut up!" at them, in the way he shouts it at the smoke alarm when someone uses the grill, and with equal amount of success.

The sister is obsessed with cleaning things. She's lived here since she was born, and it's always been one of those houses that's never clean or tidy; but, instead of getting used to it, she's made it the centre of her life now. She's convinced everything would be better if she just had a new kitchen floor, or cupboards, or if the back garden was tidied and dug and replanted with grass. She's living with a 74-year-old fella who's set in his ways, and she thinks the secret to happiness is trying to make him change. And me too, now. I've slipped into old habits of untidiness and not giving a shit, since I came back here. Three years of Emma's OCD made me think I deserved a break. It's been all frying pans and fires for me, for longer than I can remember it not being. The house could be as clean as Buckingham Palace tomorrow, it's not gonna solve her problems, or mine, or Dad's. But it's something for her to aim for, I guess. I wish she'd see sense and get the hell out of here, while there's still time for her to have a life and be happy. But I don't think she could take the guilt of leaving Dad on his own. Cos he will be on his own, as I don't plan on sticking around, as soon as I can help it.

I'm in the front room, which has become my room. At least until late afternoon, when my Dad comes in and puts on the TV, the multiple speakers, and his computer. He's able to watch one thing on telly while watching another on YouTube. It's a skill.

I need to see Orla again. I need her to speak to me. The bad thing has come back, and it's only going to get worse. While things were good (relatively speaking) with Emma, it never happened. When we went to shit, it came knocking again; like it had never been away. And it got worse, the worse we got. I got to be Tom for three years, almost. Just Tom. No Steve. Even in the five months we split up, when he could have come back easily. I was still in love with her through all of that, so maybe that was why. I don't know how it all works, really. She was still in love with me too, though. I knew that, from the way she was in our little email chats. And when we got back together, it was even more obvious. It didn't feel like anyone had fallen out of love and fallen back into it. It just felt like we'd pressed pause for a bit. Even if I had been shagging everything that moved at the time. And she hadn't. Well, she said she hadn't. and I believed her. I used to trust her back then. I didn't, by the end. My stomach is rumbling, which is weird. I don't get hungry in the day. I don't eat until about six or eight, here anyway. When I lived with Em I had breakfast, even if it was just toast. I spark up a ciggie, to stave off the non-existent hunger. I can smoke in this house, so at least there's that.

*****

I've wandered into Limerick, thinking I'm going to get some shopping, but there's a weird nagging feeling that I'm going to do something else. It's weird, me and drink. There doesn't need to be an incident to set me off. Sometimes, the incident is just me having spare money. When I'm completely broke, I don't sit around having withdrawals, thinking I'd do anything for a fix. That's how I've convinced myself I'm not an alcoholic. But the reality is, whenever there's cash in my pocket, it's a struggle to get to closing time without going over to the offie to get myself some booze. And that should be a red flag in itself.

I'm at the big Tesco. I think it's the only Tesco, at least in the town centre. Going in here is no guarantee that I'm going to spend my cash on beef mince and tinned tomatoes, though. They obviously sell booze too; and cheaper than the offie. The drink prices in Ireland are insane, even with the exchange rate taken into account. You can't just buy a three litre of White Ace for four quid. It'd be six euro, for one thing, and they just don't sell it here. You'd think there'd be a market for it, but maybe there's some sort of ban on cider being that strong here. Getting pissed in a pub is out of the question. Just my own tab would be about 50 Euro, which is still 40 quid, and that's just ludicrous, to me.

Town is full of strangers. The usual Limerick sorts – hard looking blokes and gorgeous women/girls who have too much make up on, and are too tall for me. I feel very alone and alien, and that's what drives me to the booze sometimes. There's no rhyme or reason to it – I'm very aware that getting sloshed isn't going to make me know anyone, or make them want to talk to me. There's no excuse for drinking that I couldn't pick apart in five seconds if someone else was to suggest it about themselves. But I don't pick it apart when it's me. It's like the way I'm able to watch stupid blockbuster films without analysing them. I leave my brain at the door with them. It's the same with drinking. I'm a pal of drink. I let his bullshit slide. I let him get away with all sorts of nonsense, cos I love him. I'm already in the liquor section. This one's got away from me. It's just a question of what's my poison now; there'll be no more debate. The brandy looks cheap, even though it's basically 35cl for what I'd pay for twice that in England. My brain has already adjusted to the shit prices. My idea of a bargain has changed.

I need something to drink it with, and that shit's expensive too. I want to neck it while I'm out and about, so a share size bottle of Diet Coke would be good. I could get a 2 litre of value shite, but I'd look ridiculous swigging from that in the street. Especially if I'm going to be chatting up imaginary ladies who I won't chat up at all. I don't want to chat anyone up. I want Orla. But that's me now. Me in a little bit will be making different sorts of decisions. He still won't be pulling women though. Cos he'll be a fucking mess. I ignore the price of the Coke and pick one up. Should be all right if I pour some out in the toilets and chuck in the half bottle of brandy. I say that, but it won't be all right, it'll be ridiculously strong. And it's only early afternoon. There's no planning to this. I know very well in my heart and my mind that I have nowhere to go but home after this, and that it'll be way too early to be visibly slaughtered walking in the door, trying to pretend I'm straight. I also know that by the time I'm finished this, I won't be able to just buy some chips and wait to sober up again, I'll be in Fine Wine wines buying single cans of cider, and carrying on until I pass out. It's only a road to ruin, and I know it, but I block all that out, cos I have my booze, and my fags, and it's nice enough outside today, and I'm not changing my mind now. I'd look like an idiot in front of all these strangers who aren't even aware I exist. I get to the checkouts and already feel a bit tipsy. That's the power of it. Same happens at home, when I'm on the internet. I can have a few cans in the fridge, one opened, and I'm already in the mind set that's somewhere between incredibly witty and completely obnoxious. There's no middle to it, and you can't have one without the other. A successful evening's internet drinking to me is one where I pass out before I upset too many people. Lofty standards, that's me.

I come down from the toilets (which cost 20c to go in, for some reason) with my bottle, and a sense of anticipation and fun. Whenever I get cans or a bottle of wine, the first half hour in town is stressful, cos I realise I have to find somewhere a bit secluded to pull out the drink and have a swig, but the Coke bottle gives me freedom. When it's cans, you have to commit, cos you've opened one and now you can't close it. You need a solid three minutes of no one else around to sink it. Of course, the more cans you have, the less you care about anyone seeing you. That was my London experience too. With a bottle of wine, you can just glug it down and close it up again. It's not like I'm going for the stuff that comes with a cork. Some young girl passes me in shorts. She has some arse on her, and legs. I don't know if she's legal, but I don't think it's illegal for me to look at her. Not yet, anyway.

Arthur's Quay Park is in the centre of town, by the river. Although most things are by the river here; the river is huge. It used to be somewhere we'd go sit in the summer after school, but you didn't go in there after a certain time. You heard stories about muggings and queerbashings and rapes, and it had a tall fence around it, so no one passing would see you get done in. Since I've come back, they've taken away the fence completely, which is good, and bad. Cos I remember taking my Holly in there when I was about 20 or 21, and having crazy, drunk sex on the grass, after the clubs had closed. You couldn't get away with that now, unless you want an audience. I don't know if I'd like an audience when I'm having sex. Might do if I was very drunk, but it'd have to be an invited audience, from Fetlife or something. A bunch of random Limerick knackers with shaved heads and Adidas trackie bottoms isn't quite the same thing. Especially if they're going to kill you to death afterwards. I think about going into the park, and I still don't know. There's some heads in there all right, but some normal people too. A bunch of girls who look like they're from the University. I can tell by their hairstyles, don't ask me how. I take a swig of the drink and try not to look like I'm chugging booze, not that anyone's looking.

Since the fences are gone, there's no need to come through either of the gates to get into the park, as they don't exist. In the old days, that would have meant that everyone sitting in there would look up as you came in, or it did in my head. Now I can just linger on the edge, at the corner of the park, the little jetty, and the tax office. Lean against the river rail, and just edge my way in. I don't know why I'm putting so much thought into this; literally no one in the park is looking at me or caring, but I do, cos that's who I am. The river smells okay, cos it's winter now. The tide's up, and there's a few people in a launch, mowing up and down between here and King John's Castle. I did rowing for a little while when I was younger, that's why I'm calling the speedboat a 'launch' in my head. I spark up a fag, to put some distance between me and the next drink.

I've moved a little into the park, but I'm still not quite there in my head. If someone comes along the path towards me now, I know I won't stand my ground. I'll turn around quickly and make my way out, looking nervous and embarrassed. When I used to live here, a long time ago, I was always awkward. I never fitted in where I lived, I wasn't like any of them. I have so many memories of feeling like an outcast, especially when they wanted to play sports, and I was no good at them. So much embarrassment and shyness, even now, when I think back on it. When I was about thirteen, and hanging around with the middle-class kids from my school a bit more, I got into Indie music, and started dressing the part. It was a stupid move for someone who already felt so uncomfortable in his own skin, but it gave me a sense of belonging. Of course, now whenever I had to make my way through the estate, and it wasn't a school day, I'd get the sneers and shouts from the people who were planning on staying in their situation forever, and felt threatened by anyone who had ambition to get out of that place. That's the way I put it to myself; really it was just that I looked different to them, and they didn't like that. But it gave me a funny walk. Like the walk you do if you're not good at football, and you're walking past a game in the park. The walk that says "Please don't let the ball come over here, I'll make a spastic of myself trying to kick it back." I'd walk like that all the time, if I thought any of the locals were looking at me, sitting on their walls and laughing. I didn't shake it off until I left the country, and went to a place where I could re-invent myself. Whenever I came back here, I'd still manage the confident, 'I'm a grown-up who's been places' walk.

For a while. But then the old awkwardness would come back. And I'm not on holiday now. I live here, so the confidence has completely worn off, until I notice it, and make myself walk like a human again. And anyway, that ambition to get out of there didn't really pay off, considering where I am in my life right now. The thought depresses me, and I try to shake it off, and have some more drink.

I'm finally feeling light headed, which is no surprise; I haven't eaten a thing today, it's bound to go straight into the blood. I don't know what I'm doing, I have no plan. Apart from the plan to get out of my skull. I'm not even sad about anything. I'm probably just sad overall. That's what depression is like for me, though. There are rarely any lows. Until there are, of course, and then I realise I'm unable to deal with anything bad, or critical of me, and that telling people I 'just feel numb' is utter bullshit. Numb people don't feel anything. I do. I feel everything when I'm down, and when I do, I make sure I run away from those feelings, with liquor as my starting pistol. It's amazing I'm so healthy, the damage I've done to myself. But maybe I'm not, and it's just the sort of damage that shows later in life; like the way my Mum is falling to pieces now, in her early sixties. I can't imagine making it to my early fifties at the moment, even if I do feel fit as the proverbial. I don't have a long-term plan. It used to outrage Emma, when she was deciding to take her pay rise and redistribute it into her pension fund. She had no frame of reference for working class people, and how we're bred not to care about our old age, since so few of us reach it without dying some horrible death. I can't imagine putting money into a pension, or life insurance, for that matter. Thinking that far ahead in my life seems mental, considering I've basically felt like I wanted to die since I was about fourteen. Seems ludicrous to care about stuff like that, when you're me.

Two girls, about fourteen or fifteen, come along the path toward me now, and I don't feel like moving away. We're onto Level 2, clearly. I look them up and down with a drunk smile, and one of them smiles back. I'm old, but I dress so young and London, with my trendy haircut, that it confuses teenage girls into fancying me. That's what I'm telling myself now, but she might have just been laughing at me. I can think both thoughts at once, that's called a dichotomy. Or cognitive dissidence. One of those. I can't remember at the moment, and it doesn't matter. No one is here to correct me. I look out over the river. It's not too cold today, but being near the water is chilly. I can see Thomond Bridge, and the castle, and the shitty interpretive centre poking out ever the battlements. They're not battlements. It's just a wall. I'm full of weird memories. Not full, exactly, but filling up. I wrote a book about living here, once. Not like a non-fiction thing, a novel. *Write about what you know*, and all that. It's weird that I'm now living in the same city again; in the same housing estate, where the thing is set.

And around all the people who inspired the characters in it. And none of them know, cos they don't read. I mean, I'm assuming they don't. No one has pulled me in the street to talk about my sentence structure, or why I portrayed their dad as a mad alcoholic. Which is good. The park is practically empty, which isn't surprising. It's not summer, and it's the middle of the day. Limerick is ugly in the daytime; the people, I mean. When you go out on a Friday or Saturday night, after about ten or eleven (cos the drinking starts late here, post-recession), you see the most gorgeous women you've ever come across in your life – like supermodels, all of them. Not that they're any use to me. They're usually knackers, and if they're not, they wouldn't dream of going near someone my age, my brother keeps saying. He's years older than me, so he's including himself in that too. I think he's wrong, cos I've been around the pubs here a few times, and had all the smiles while walking through the crowds, although that might have just been my own pissedness. I didn't ask anyone. It's not just smiles. I've been chatted up a few times too, which never happened before I went away. I look different now. Freakishly different to the people on the estate, the same ones who sneered at me when I was an Indie kid (realistically, it's probably the kids of those people doing the sneering now; it's been about twenty years). But, in a going out situation, there's that Peacock Effect thing. And, much as I hate the Pick Up Artist culture and all the retards who buy into it, they're right about that thing. Women do come over and talk to you if you look a bit outrageous. I'm usually too pissed to take advantage of it though. Story of my life.

Anyway, daytime Limerick is nothing like that. All the people with jobs are in work, so it's usually just the scum pounding the streets. Everything is tracksuits and trainers, and people coming in and out of Poundland, which is called 'Dealz' here, cos they don't have pounds anymore. Even those same, supermodel-looking girls are dressed down and unrecognisable, although they're still rocking about three inches of foundation, which is five shades darker than their actual skin.

I'm sick of the park, I want to go somewhere else. I don't want to walk through town, I have a sudden fear that I'll run into someone I don't want to, like my sister or my Mum, while I'm obviously off my tits. And brandy smells, too. That's the only thing bad about it that I can think. I want to go to the river. I'm already at the river, but I mean the other river. Which is the same river, just a different part of it. Up past St. Michael's Boat Club, where I used to row. There's a park bit there, where we used to go on runs, out along the bank. There'll be no one out there now, it'll be good to sit down, get pissed, and think of stuff. I need to think of stuff, sometimes. Whether it's dredging up old memories so I can write about them, or just dredging them up so I can hate myself.

Either way, it's productive. And, if you're going to dredge, you might as well do it in the river. Not that I'll be in the river. Well, never say never. You don't know how your day is going to go, sometimes.

The walk down the bank, from Sarsfield Bridge, is nice. They shoved a lot of money into the city before the wheels came off the economy in 2008. All of this is unrecognisable from when I was young. Poorman's Kilkee even looks smart; it's more concrete than grass now, and there's benches. All the way up the strand, they've built over, and put new rails. In the distance, you can see the Clarion, a massive hotel that U2 own, someone said. I'm heading to the Shannon Bridge. People still call it the New Bridge, but it must be nearly 30 years old now. I want to get over it, to the nice country walk place. There's boats on the river though. Yellow and blue. St. Michael's. I get almost across the bridge and stop to look down at the crews. The whole club seems to be there. It's cos today is mild, and the tide is in. They take it when they can get it. There'll be no one there now from when I was a member. That must be twenty years ago now, thinking about it. Not even the coaches, probably. It's relaxing, watching them go past, so I stay a while. It's bringing back nice feelings as well, even if I hated the actual rowing. I liked the sense of being part of something. Even though a few of them were tossers, remembering it now.

When I was there, there were two buildings. One big shed, just for housing boats, and another clubhouse, which had boats in it too, but space for doing exercises. Oarsmen train every day of the week; they're tough as nails. They'd still get called faggots at school, by the rugby boys and the GAA lads, but they'd get their own back whenever the PE teacher did that Beep Test thing. They've expanded since, clearly, over at Saint Mike's. There's two extra boat sheds out the back, and another two makeshift ones, which are just lorry containers. They have two slipways now too, instead of just the one. I stand for ages looking down at the boys and girls getting their boats ready and taking them down. I was never any good at it, but I love watching people who are. There's a skill and a grace to it that you can't be unimpressed by. I gave up rowing when I decided I was shit at it and never going to be any good. It didn't matter. I'd made the friends, so they just stayed my going out drinking friends. I just didn't have to break my back training every day like they did. So I took up smoking, the alternative weight control method. Recommended by billions. Most of them dead now.

Eventually I'm done watching, cos it's windy up on the bridge. I'd like to come back some day and watch for longer. I could go down and say hello, or join the club. Now that I'm fit. I don't know what I'm talking about. I look better on the outside now than I ever have, but I'm not fit. I still smoke 20 a day, and I drink like a tramp. And I can't join a rowing club when I'm 30-odd years old. This brandy is some good shit. I head down the steps and under the bit of the bridge with all the graffiti on it. They have that on every bridge. It's the law. It's leafy beyond that bit, but obviously more wintery than green now. I love it. I love any place new, or an old place I've not been to in a while.

There's no path anymore. It goes a few hundred yards, then someone has put a fence, saying don't go farther than this point. Jesus, it must be some health and safety thing. Someone must have fallen in, and they've blocked the entire thing to protect people from their own stupidity. You can't do that. It's a river. It's not supposed to have safety rails on every bank. It's the longest river in the British Isles (I know that from school), that would be mental expensive. Jesus, why is my life always being ruined by stupid people? I have to take a right, which loops me around a bit, and back out onto the North Circular. Gutted. If the tide had been out, there would have been somewhere to sit, before you get to the gate, but the way it is, there's nothing. Unless I fancy a swim. I can't swim. I realise I don't need the riverbank or the walk. I'm drinking a bottle of Diet Coke as far as anyone else is concerned. I can go anywhere. But this would have been nice. Then I see the two girls.

It's not the same two as earlier, I don't think. A bit younger, I reckon. They're drinking cans. I saw lots of empty booze tins and bottles when I was walking through, people must come down here a lot with the same idea. When I was young we'd go to Poorman's, but that's too out in the open, I suppose. When you're seventeen or eighteen, you can be a bit calm there. If the Gards come along, they'll only tell you to shift, if they're in a good mood. If you're this age, like these two, they might pick you up. Girls as well, you hear stories. I've heard a few where the Gards picked up underage girls drinking, took them into the van, and basically said 'We're taking you home to your Mam and Dad, unless you do us a favour.' Or boys, where they did the same thing, but instead of sex, they just beat the shit out of them. You hear stories. One of the youngones sees me, and nudges her friend. I freeze a second, but then I give them a smile. One of them looks like she's shitting herself, probably cos I'm a grown man, I suppose. The other once smiles back though. She's a nice looking thing, even if she's a bit too young. Too young for what, though? There's no harm talking to them. It's not against the law. What they're doing is, though. I walk over, feeling like a big man, suddenly. There's a thought in my head about something, but the drink makes it go away.

"Well?"

"How'rya?"

She sounds like she's from a nice area, from the accent. I can see now they're both wearing Laurel Hill uniforms. They must be on the mitch from school. Or it's over. I dunno what time it is.

"How are ye?" I squat down next the one who spoke to me. The prettier one, who smiled at me. The other one's all right looking too. They're both nice looking. Petite as well. Or just not finished growing yet, maybe. My mouth feels dry.

"Grand. What you drinking?" The same one again. The other one's shy, I think.

"Me? Diet Coke."

"You are in your arse. What is it? Vodka?"

"Who are you, like? My mum?"

"Haha. Give us a sup." She's cheeky. Nice teeth as well. She's sitting on her jacket, so is the other one.

"It's not vodka."

"It's something, though. You're langered. Go on, give us a sup."

I immediately want to act soberer, but I wouldn't know how.

"Does she not talk, then?"

The other one looks a bit shocked that I'm talking about her. She doesn't say anything though.

"Ah, she's shy. Never been kissed, wha?" I like this one. She's feisty. Most kids that age are, though, if they're not shy, like I was.

"Yeah? Ah now, leave her alone. I didn't kiss anyone til I was sixteen."

"Sixteen? What are you now? 40 is it?"

"You cheeky little... I'm 34." Dunno why I knocked off two years, it'll still be ancient to her.

"34? Jesus, you must have had a hard life. Didn't kiss anyone til you were sixteen, either? Were you ugly?"

"Probably, yeah. Gorgeous now, though. So no worries."

The other one opens her mouth for the first time:

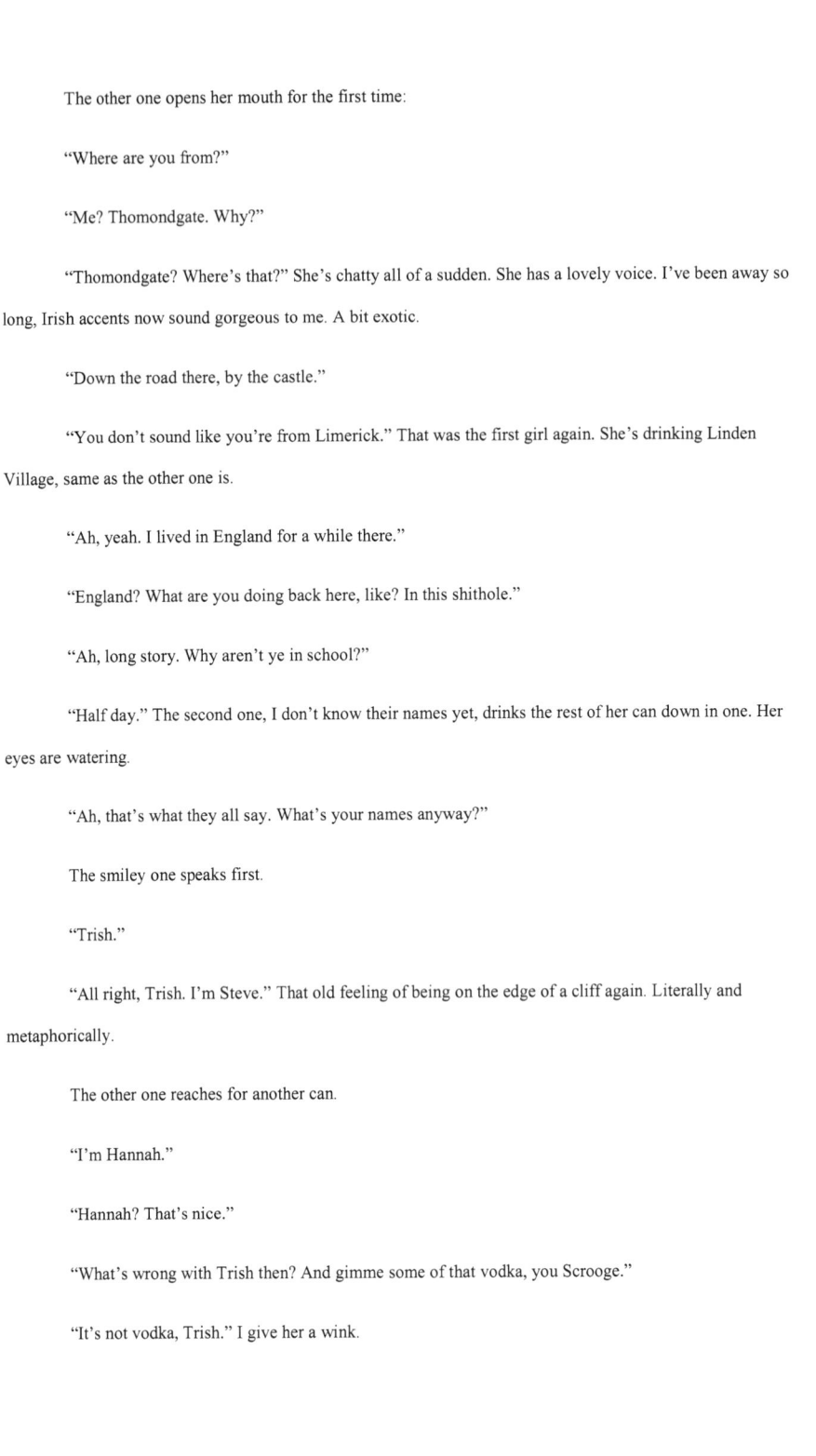

"Where are you from?"

"Me? Thomondgate. Why?"

"Thomondgate? Where's that?" She's chatty all of a sudden. She has a lovely voice. I've been away so long, Irish accents now sound gorgeous to me. A bit exotic.

"Down the road there, by the castle."

"You don't sound like you're from Limerick." That was the first girl again. She's drinking Linden Village, same as the other one is.

"Ah, yeah. I lived in England for a while there."

"England? What are you doing back here, like? In this shithole."

"Ah, long story. Why aren't ye in school?"

"Half day." The second one, I don't know their names yet, drinks the rest of her can down in one. Her eyes are watering.

"Ah, that's what they all say. What's your names anyway?"

The smiley one speaks first.

"Trish."

"All right, Trish. I'm Steve." That old feeling of being on the edge of a cliff again. Literally and metaphorically.

The other one reaches for another can.

"I'm Hannah."

"Hannah? That's nice."

"What's wrong with Trish then? And gimme some of that vodka, you Scrooge."

"It's not vodka, Trish." I give her a wink.

"Gimme some of that Not Vodka then, *Steve*." She says it like she knows it's not my real name, but that's just me being paranoid. I hand her over the bottle, there's about half of it left. Her fingers touch my hand as we pass it over, and they're soft, and it gives me a shiver. I have so little human contact these days, except for Orla, and she's deserted me now.

"Go on then. You're pure cheeky, you know that?"

"Yep!" She gives me a little wink, and tips the bottle. The coughing fit that happens straight after makes me burst out laughing. Hannah snorts a bit too. The Trish girl wasn't expecting brandy. I should've warned her, but it was worth a bit of spilled booze not to.

"You fucking spa! What's that? What *is* that? Whiskey, or something?"

"Haha. Brandy. It's brandy and Diet Coke. Nice, isn't it?"

"Bleh. Brandy? What are you, an old man?"

Hannah's still sniggering into her hand. She's the dark haired one; blue eyes. Trish has fair hair with highlights, and hers are brown.

"I'm 36!"

Shit.

"You were 34 a minute ago," says Hannah, but she's smiling, not cross. She's much prettier when she smiles, I notice, just in an observational way, more than anything else. They're kids. They're not women. You can make all the mistakes you want from far away, but once you talk to people, there's no mistaking how old they are.

"Yeah, well you two'd put years on anyone, like."

"I bet his name isn't even Steve," says Trish, handing the brandy to the other one, without asking me if it's all right first, cheeky little pup.

"Yeah. Bet you're a mad killer, on the run from England. Can I?"

Hannah nods at the bottle in her hand. Good girl.

"You still want to? After that?"

"Sure. I'm pure hard, me."

*****

We've been drinking and shooting the breeze for about three quarters of an hour now, and the liquor has made everyone get on famously. They're nice kids. They can't hold a drink, though, and they have no idea how strong the brandy is. Both of them are well on it, with the cans too, which I've been having some of. I don't need to keep straight here; I'm always going to be more sober than they are. They're just children.

"How about Truth or Dare?"

It's Trish who suggests it, of course.

"Oh right, yeah. What's next? Spin the Bottle?"

"Well, we have a bottle…" She gives me a wink. Hannah looks a little out of it. She's not looking at either of us.

"What are you trying to do, get me arrested?"

"Haha. Why would you be arrested?" She says it in an innocent voice, and tries to look coquettish, but she just looks like a drunk child with too much make-up on.

"Pffffft. I'll tell you when you're older." I have to get on with this. It's going places I'm not trying to bring it, and I don't have time. I don't think I have. It's hard to tell. I've managed to bring them deeper into the bushes, so no one can see us while passing.

"Ah, tell me now instead, like. Go on, Steve, will ya?"

She sits a little differently now, like she's making a really bad, childish attempt at being flirty, but it just comes across as messy drunkenness. I look at Hannah instead.

"You okay, love?"

She doesn't look it.

"Huh? Yeah. Yeaaaaaaah. I'm fiiiiiiiiine, like." She's sitting on the floor but she still looks like she's going to fall over. She's definitely the shyer, less experienced one. It's all the same to me though.

"Haha! She's langerfied."

"Feck off, I am not." Hannah stumbles forward into her own lap, and makes a little noise, like the beginnings of vomiting.

"Don't mind her, Hannah. You okay?"

She looks up at me with her big blue eyes, and they're watering.

"I. Am. *Grand*, says you. Top of the- I'm fine."

"Do you want some water or something?" I don't have any water. Dunno why I said that. Instinct, maybe. Force of habit.

"No! No, I'm fine."

"Okay, love."

I turn back to the other one, then Hannah pipes up again:

"Do you *have* any water, like?"

"Er. No, actually. Sorry."

"S'all right. S'aaaaaaaall…"

"Right?"

"Yup. Have you a fag?"

"She's langered, Steve. I better take her home, like…"

I wasn't expecting that. Can't let that happen. Need more time.

"Ah now, you can't do that."

"Why not?" Trish gives me a look. Hannah's trying to focus on me from her spot on the floor.

"Yeah, shoosh. Listen to Steve. Listen to Steve. He's. A. Adult."

"I am a adult, in fairness. She knows."

"I do! I do know. I know… I knows it all, Trish!"

She's spasticated. This is either going to make everything harder, or much easier.

"Steve. Steve, or whatever your name is. Cop on, like. Look at her. She's ossified. Lemme take her home, or she'll be killed."

Unfortunate choice of words.

"Hang on now, two seconds."

"Hang on for what?"

She's annoyed at me. She's not as drunk as the other one, but she's still drunker than I am.

"Hang on and listen here. Where do you want to take her?"

"Home!"

"Home to who, like?"

"I dunno."

She hasn't thought it through, like I knew she wouldn't. I'm staring right into her eyes now, trying to read her. I don't know if she's scared of me. She should be.

"Her ma and da?"

"I don't know!!! Just… just let me take her, yeah? Please."

She's going. She's going now, the fun's over. And she's taking the other one with her too. I look down on the ground and see Hannah is passing out. Now or never.

"Okay, Trish. Okay. Hang on one second here, will you?"

She looks at me funny as I reach down for one of the full cans.

"Hang on for what? What are you doing with my cans?"

I give her a little faux confused look, then I look at the thing in my hand, and back at her.

"This, I guess."

I swing my hand with such force and weight that the can smashes the cartilage of her nose to a pulp, at the first time of asking. There's a look of confusion and horror in her eyes as she falls backwards on the grass, no screams or gasps. In half a second I'm on her, my knees crushing the breath out of her chest now. The claret's streaming out of the hole in her face, so she has to open her mouth to breathe, but I slam the tin against her right jaw, and it send her head swinging to the other side. She's bitten her tongue as well, and the blood from that is spilling over her chin and down her neck. The white school blouse and burgundy blazer are starting to look the same colour. I move her face back to the centre by holding her chin, then bring the beer down on the left jaw, with the same hammer movement. She's still breathing, but there's nothing in her eyes now.

Behind me, Hannah's snoring. Cute. One last round of blows to Trish's face, and the skull falls in on itself like Papier Mache. She's done. The other one won't be as much trouble, and I can get out of here. My t-shirt is soaking hot with blood, but it's black, like the jeans. No one's going to notice.

Fifteen

Four Years Ago, Essex, Jim's House

It's a bad situation. I've never been in a bad situation before, not since coming over to the UK around eight years ago, or before that, when I lived at home. The situation I just left was bad, of course – splitting with the mother of my kid, but sleeping on the living room floor cos I didn't have anywhere to go – but that just feels like part of this thing that's happening now. It's been one long bad situation.

Having a job doesn't seem to help. Well, this job. The last one was good, and I left it. It wasn't perfect. It was a coffee shop. And so is this one. But it wasn't hell on earth. I was with a small family company. They have three places, I only ever had to work in one of them. The staff were fine, the owner was okay (for an owner), and boss was Bob. Bob's a nice racist. He's totally a racist, but he's nice too. And you can't reason with his racism or anything. Not just cos he's your boss and you don't want to get sacked, either. Cos he's decided that his views on the immigrants and the blacks are right, and that's that. But I made my peace with it, and if there was someone else around for me to throw a look at when he came out with one of his crazy, bigoted statements, it made it easier. That was usually Dave the sandwich chef. He's my kind of people.

I'm living in a room, around the corner from the ex and the kid. I was lucky to get the place, I thought, at first. Close, I can afford the rent, and still no need to get a bus to work. The first phone call should've rang a few alarm bells, but I was desperate. So, when Jim the landlord mentioned that a lot of the people who phoned about the room were 'black people or Asians', I probably should've realised that he wasn't just a fan of social geography. Nope, he was a racist. A mad, alcoholic racist. And I'm stuck in his house. I spend as little time here as possible, and when I am here, as little time in the rest of the house, but sometimes it's unavoidable. Sometimes, it's like he's waiting for the click of my door, and then he's on me, smelling of Stella Artois and pipe tobacco, ranting about Polish people.

Jim's kind of foreign himself, and a bit brown. He was born in India, but that was when it was still part of the Empire, so he considers himself English. Him travelling all the way across the sea from Asia to come live here doesn't seem to be classed as immigration by him. He even has a Swedish surname, but that's all right. Swedish people are white. I don't want to talk to Jim, ever. The first night I came here, he stood out in the garden with me, and made hints about how great it would be to have some company around the place, apart from his cat, Bertie. I remember looking at that cat, and thinking he looked like he wanted me to kill him. I was probably right.

I go to work early, which means I have the excuse to rush out without chatting, and anyway, he's not drunk at seven in the morning, so he's not as dangerous. It's the evening, when he's been down Wetherspoon's all day, probably annoying the hell out of other people, when he's the most chatty and aggressive. He's a messy, shitty drunk. Most drunks are like that. Real alcoholics sometimes are able to chug a whole bottle of whiskey and still seem like they're stone cold sober. Messy drunks are tipsy after the first couple of beers, and then it's all downhill. I don't think they get any fun out of it, just a kind of shitty confidence that makes them think it's okay to force their opinions on you. I'm not that sort of drunk. I'll argue, but only if someone else starts it. I don't even see it coming. I'm just fine and jolly and happy, and then someone makes a remark that's personal (it only takes them saying my name in the sentence) and I explode. I'm not confrontational at all, so I guess that's in there always, and it finds a way to come out.

I'm trying to nick some internet. From next door, who are unsecured, but weak. He has his internet locked down, of course. I even asked him could I shove a fiver a week onto the rent so I could have the password, but he gave me this big spiel about some guy who'd had the room before me and had been torrenting movies all day and night, when the internet was capped, and had cost him hundreds of quid. Same guy got out loans, catalogues, etc, at the address, and left a trail of warning letters and bailiffs. And he used to stub out his ciggies on the furniture. Why any of this is my fault, I have no idea. Either way, he won't let me have internet. I'm using this half phone, half computer thing that I bought off him. It's snazzy. It has Windows on it, and the screen is touchable, with a stylus. There's a pull out keyboard as well. It's basically a mobile phone that you can use like a laptop, which is mental.

The social life is non-existent now. We'd go out every so often after work in the old job, and me and Dave still have the odd one, but I'm not friends with anyone in the new place. They don't like me. Or they do, but they think I'm a freak and a weirdo. I'm so uncomfortable there, it's like nothing I've ever felt before. It's like all of them either have no respect for me as a supervisor, or they're supervisors and managers themselves, and they think I'm shit too. I was thrown into it at the start, not knowing how to do anything. They put the baristas and supervisors in together, all bloody clueless, and it took away all the confidence I had from the last job. The whole set up is different. Different ways of making the coffee, different food, different prices, etc.

Everything was new, and no one was explaining it to me like I was intelligent. It was like being in remedial class, but one where the teachers aren't qualified, and they don't have any patience with you. And I was starting with a handful of baristas, all on the same level of ignorance as me, and then a few more who'd been there a couple of weeks longer. So they knew more than me. And I was supposed to be training to be their boss. It's the stupidest bloody system ever. I got off on the wrong foot there, and I've never righted it. It's only a matter of time before I walk out.

And before I walk out of this place too. I can't handle it. And it's not like I can explain it to anyone. I tried, with Dave, and his reaction was basically that it sounded like a nightmare, and why didn't I just get out of there. But I can't, cos I can't face Jim. I can't give him four weeks' notice, and have to then spend those four weeks with him hating me, or trying to talk to me, or being passive aggressive at me. I'm so fragile. I'm drinking a lot too, which is bad. What's worse is, it's losing me quality sleep time, so when I go to work in the morning, everything feels like a slog. I can't handle the simplest shit. I keep making excuses to go out for a fag. The day just turns into one long series of fag breaks, and none of them do any work while I'm out, cos they have no respect for me, so nothing gets done, and I have to keep everyone on longer at the end. And they hate me for that, cos they're young and they have better things to be doing. And the bosses hate me, cos I'm supposed to get everything finished by seven, and they have to pay everyone extra wages. I might be pushed before I jump.

I'm trying to get Facebook to work. It's a new thing, like Myspace, but with more normal people on it, like your relatives and stuff. Grown-ups. Your boss. It's all white too, and there's no music. Anna from the last job told me about it. She's young, so she knows about this stuff. The signal is too weak though, so it keeps cutting out after I've posted something, and I lose all the text. I don't have work in the morning, so obviously I have some booze. I've bought some food at Tesco. Cold stuff. I never cook here, cos it means going into the rest of the house. I've never used the oven, or even the microwave. I have some Mediterranean salad in a plastic bowl, and some skinless black pepper chicken breasts. I don't know when I should eat them. After would be better, if it was work tomorrow. Salad isn't good if I'm boozing though. I've puked it back up a few times, never something you want to be cleaning off a hardwood floor at five in the morning, when you have to get up at six. I'll probably end up having it for breakfast. Or lunch. I never eat breakfast, and I won't be awake until noon.

I've never cared about being lonely, but it's starting to dawn on me that I'm very alone now. Whenever it's time to go home from work, even though I hate work, I stall and hang around town. Not in the hope of meeting anyone; I don't know anyone. Just anything instead of coming back to this place. If I leave it late enough, Jim is usually snoozing in his chair, and I can sneak in. Too late, and he's woken up again, and had another drink, and he'll get me before I open my room door. I've become good at walking without a sound, but he always hears my key in the front door. I don't even think he likes me; I'm just a flesh and blood thing for him to aim his rants at, instead of the people on the internet. He's not usually ranting about me, but I think he must do, to other people, when I'm not around. Whenever I'm in my room and he doesn't know I'm there, if he has visitors, I put on earphones and listen to loud music, in case I accidentally hear him badmouthing me. I'm a mess at home and at work. So fragile, unable to take even the slightest criticism.

  I don't know if I've always been the same. I can remember almost everything that's ever happened in my life, but I can't remember how I used to be, if it was different. And I only think I can remember it all, cos I obviously don't know the bits I've forgotten, or I'd remember them. It's like when you're in school, doing maths. You don't see you're making mistakes until the problem doesn't work out at the end. I'm getting maudlin now, already. I haven't even got past the neck of the bottle yet. Internet's not working. I can put on a DVD. I buy a lot of DVDs now, for something to do when I'm in here. HMV has usually got a sale on them. I love movies. To me, they're like music is to other people. I love music too, but probably for the same reason as films. Takes me away. And I appreciate it more when I'm pissed. I go to the library a lot on my time off, to use the internet. Myspace has a thing you can attach to your profile that plays music. You can load it up with mp3s from their list. I've made a playlist of songs that used to be on the jukebox in the pub I went to when I was eighteen. I'm not homesick. I went home this summer just gone. It smelled like Limerick, and I saw some places I used to go to, but it wasn't the same as being alive at the age I'm homesick for. Everyone I knew back then is long gone. And the pub is gone now too. Well, it closed down, last year. There was a lot of fuss on the internet about it; made me feel sad. Like I'd lost a part of me. People have moved on, gone off to work in Dublin and England and whatever, same as I have, but you'd still meet someone there from the old days. I think you would, anyway. I'll never know now.

  Work is hell, life is lonely, drink and DVDs are the only things that get me through. And music, sometimes. I don't like new music, but I've recently got into Amy Winehouse, it's good stuff to get drunk to. And My Chemical Romance, for some unknown reason; I love those guys, even though I'm not a fourteen-year-old girl. And the Arctic Monkeys. Everyone likes *I Bet You Look Good on the Dancefloor*, but my favourite is *A Certain Romance*, because I like the intro, and I like the irony of the title, and it reminds me of where I grew up, even if I didn't grow up in Sheffield. Class is the same no matter where you live, though, I think. Class, or the complete lack of it. I have a CD Walkman, which is an anachronism, but it's all I can use, cos an iPod would be no use without a computer. There are no women, even if I do seem to fall in love with anyone female in my new job, or the last one. Andie was my girlfriend for a while after I broke up with the kid's mum, but that didn't work out either. There's been no one since. I've had a few internet romances, but I've not slept with anyone since her. A lifetime. And the more it goes on, the more desperate I get. The more desperate I am, the less that women want me. It's not a rut I can see myself getting out of. So, I have a drink, and I feel all right for a bit. And, if next door's WiFi is working, I can use the little pocket PC/Palm Pilot thing to go on Facebook and embarrass myself.

The room is depressing. There's a bed, a couch, an armchair. The chair does the lazyboy thing of leaning back and turning into a lounger, the kid loves it. She doesn't love it here though. She told her mum that, and her mum told me. They're only in the next street over, like I said. I can see her whenever I want, and take her to school on days off and late starts. I miss her, but she's there, so it's not too bad. I don't miss being part of all of us together though, I'm not crazy. It wasn't a happy relationship. Every so often I get sentimental about it, when I'm pissed, but that's not real. I've already been replaced. There's no going back now. That's over. I don't have a life outside work, so it's just here or the library when I'm off. And drink. I hit the drink hard when we split, but I was off it when I was with Andie. That was a shit relationship too, I just pretend it wasn't, cos she's attractive, and I want to be with her again, cos I don't have anyone now. I can't talk to her or go see her though, I've never been back. It hurts too much. She's always been one of those girls who stays friends with her exes and still sees them, but I can't be like that. I'm childish and possessive and jealous. I was when I was with her too, and she'd go see an ex for dinner or drinks. I'm just not that cosmopolitan or grown-up. I need to possess someone, and I hate myself for it. Cos Andie is six years younger than me, but she's always been more mature. And smarter.

It's not good for me to be alone. I've never cared about being lonely, but when I'm alone, my mind goes to bad places. Sometimes, in the night, I creep out of the room, and try to use his computer. He thinks he's so savvy and up on security and stuff, but his password for Windows is the name of his bloody cat. I got into his PC in a few seconds. Once I was in there, I used the internet, and looked at a bunch of stuff. Porn mainly, cos it was three in the morning and I was pissed and horny. Afterwards, I panicked, of course. I couldn't just delete the whole History, cos he'd know. I had to individually remove stuff, all the while thinking he was going to come down and catch me. The fear felt like excitement though, and I got away with it, I think. He's never said anything about it. I hate him a lot. I fantasise about getting rid of him. It wouldn't take much. Old guys fall down the stairs and break their necks all the time. But then I'd have nowhere to live. I don't even have enough for a deposit. I'd have to get it back from him, somehow. I like thinking about it though, it makes me calmer.

I'm not as complicated as I should be. I'm mad, probably. But you're not supposed to know you're crazy if you're crazy. That's the rule. The idea of insanity having rules is insane in itself though. There are no rules to this. This world isn't even real. The more I read about imagined realities and the idea of a real life Matrix, via people like David Icke, the more it seems to make sense. It makes more easy reading than things like religion, and morality. Those don't sit well with me, cos if they're true, I'm going to have to pay for all this. I don't want to pay. I want to think that none of it was real, and that my dreams are just as valid as the things I think are real life. Every so often something strange will happen, and I'll think it's a glitch in the fake reality, and that makes me feel better. I feel like I'm special, definitely. I know there are seven billion or eight billion people in the world, but it's not too crazy to think that I'm completely different. That my life experience is unique. No one else is living what I'm living. And every time I do something, and take some control, and add something new, that becomes more and more so. I think I might be making the world better, but then I don't think there is a world. There can't be. This can't be it. That wouldn't be fair. Why would that be deliberate, the life that they've given me? These thoughts, these urges, these feelings that won't go away. And why does it all just work for me? Why does no one ever catch me? It's not like I'm careful. I'm not. I don't plan, I don't cover my tracks. I do what I do and I move on and I forget it. Until I remember it, and then the only thing that makes me forget it again is doing more. There's no way this is some mathematical coincidence or Divine Plan. I'm in the system and I'm self-aware, and I'm messing with it, and they're doing nothing about it. I'm the master of my own destiny and I can shape my own reality. The sigil magic people, the Satanists, the people who everyone called mad: they knew about it. There have always been prophets and visionaries, and they've always been demonised as much as worshipped. Some of us think differently, and it disturbs the rest. Some of us are greater than anyone else. I have to be one of them; otherwise, what is all this for, or about?

I put on a DVD of The Commitments. I'm not from Dublin, but it still feels nice and warm and like home. I have some stand-up stuff from Ed Byrne and Seán Hughes for the same reason. I've nicked enough money from the till at work to make today comfortable, with drink and food. I don't care about stealing. Money isn't real, nothing is real. It's my money as much as anyone else's. I'm good at it now too. There are no cameras. I just pretend to put it in the till, then I open it with my keys. I'm a supervisor, so they give me the responsibility. It was easier in the last place, the safe was easier too. In the new job, it's time locked and computerised and audited every three months. There's no point in messing around with that. In my last job I was practically the manager, and it was just one count at the end of each day, with usually me being the only one upstairs. My old manager was a dirty dog; had a bird on the side to his wife, and she'd come see him for a coffee at the end of the day, so he'd let me count up. Of course I'd been cooking the tills all day, so I'd come out with at least 40 quid for myself, and never got caught. Never even came close, cos I just don't. Rules don't apply to me in this world, cos I know none of it is real. I used to not know about any of this. I used to be a drone, like everyone else, until I stopped the stupid pills that did nothing anyway. That was a while back, and I don't miss them. I don't miss the way they made me be… whatever it was that I was when I took them. I can't even remember now. Sometimes memories and dreams get mixed up, and I don't know what's real and what's not. If anything's real. And I don't think it is.

I have gin, the supermarket stuff, and some tonic, and some bitter lemon, cos there was an offer on. I have all the fags I need, and I don't care if Jim is outside, cos I have some empty cider bottles to piss in. Getting the piss out is hard, cos I have to do it on my day off, like this, but when he's down in the pub. He's probably not down in the pub now, I can hear someone moving about in the kitchen. There's cooking stuff for me if I want to use it, and a washing machine, and a shower. It all involves being in the rest of the house though, so I avoid it as much as I can. It's not even like I can hop in the shower before work, while no one is around, cos he gets up every morning at half six, to give his cat its medicine. The cat has epilepsy and a whole bunch of other stuff wrong with him. I know, cos I had to look after it when he went on holiday. I thought about killing it – to put it out of its misery - but I was in charge of it, so he'd have gone mental. He loves the cat. He hates his own family, he tells me, and all his ex-wives, but he loves the cat. It's ancient; maybe fourteen in human years. It'll probably die by itself soon, even if I leave it live. He might too. I think he has cancer, but it might just be one of his drunk stories. He doesn't even live in the fake reality. His reality is a fake on top of that fake. He wouldn't be a loss to anything or anyone if I got rid of him. But I need this place, so he's safe.

The gin's good and the film is funny. I think I've read the books of these, or I might just have imagined it. I think I did. I remember hearing the actor's voices in my head while I went along, like you do with books where you've seen the film of them first. I remember it coming out in the cinema and there being a craze about it in my school. People playing *Mustang Sally* on their ghettoblasters, and taking guitar lessons. I have some chicken and bacon pastry things. I should eat them before the fridge cold wears off. I have enough booze to counteract them. That's such an alcoholic thing to think. Normal people worry if they have enough food in their bellies to soak up the drink. We worry about eating too much and spoiling the buzz.

The street is quiet. That was Jim's big selling point. No big rush of cars in the morning, you can sleep in. He gets up at half six. I don't know what he's talking about. I don't care, either. He's an idiot. Nothing worse than an idiot who thinks he's clever. Especially a drunk one. I'm clever; I just get drunk and talk like an idiot, while thinking I'm clever. There's a difference, I think. I need a piss. I'm not going upstairs. I get an empty two litre out of the bin, and start to fill it up. I get paranoid about the sound, and start humming loudly, cos I can't turn up the TV now, as my hands are full. The smell isn't too bad, even though it's my first of the day. It's when you open up an old one that the stench hits you. The wardrobe is only about a third full now. No need to go emptying for a while. Sometimes the kitchen sink is possible, even though I shit myself going back and forth from my room, in case he comes in the front door unexpectedly. Sometimes I just bag up a load of them and head out at five in the morning, to dump them down by the flyover. I'm sure some tramps have had a few nasty surprises, opening them up and thinking they've struck gold. Whenever I go back, they're usually gone, cos the Council are good around here for picking up rubbish.

Today could be one of those days. It feels like it. I get a strange film over my eyes, the night before, when I'm trying to sleep. Like looking up at the world from inside a puddle on the road; one that's had engine oil dripped into it, or whatever it is that causes those rainbows. It's not rainbow coloured though, more like a purple wash over the normal dark. That happens, sleep won't come for ages, and when it does, the dreams are weird. Not frightening, just vivid. Whether I've had a drink or not. I usually have, though. Sometimes even when I'm up early for work the next day. Work usually stops me from buggering up like that, but if I'm on an early, I get to go home by about two, so there's a whole day of temptation, and reasoning with my own brain that I can manage a session and still be all right the next day. Sometimes I can. Some other times, though, I get it wrong, and I'm still wide awake and crazy when the drink runs out, with still time left to go buy more. If that happens, everything is out of my control. I forget myself, I go mad, I usually pass out and piss the bed. Pissing the bed as an adult is new, but I've read about it before, in some sports guy's autobiography. Tony Adams, maybe. I can't remember now, I'm already stupid with the drink.

I don't know how many I've done since I came to live here, but it's been a few. More than a couple. Less than a lot. It started when the rest of my life ended. I had a family, a kid, a life; and then one day I lost everything. I still see the kid of course, she's my world, but the family I tried so hard to keep together finally fell apart two years ago. Then I met Andie, and that kept me okay for half a year. When I lost her, I found something else. Something that hadn't been around since I was a eight years old. And when it came back, it was like it had never been away. Like that old friend you haven't seen in years, but you meet them again and it's like no time has passed in between. I thought I'd buried that thing, that feeling, a long time ago. But it turns out I'd only pushed it down somewhere. Or maybe the tablets, well, it doesn't matter about the tablets, cos they were a lie. They'd been giving those to me since I was a kid, trying to blind me to what was really going on, and I stopped their little game. Whatever the reason is, the thing is back now.

The first time was an accident, really. I'd been drinking on my own, like most days. No idea of the time, but it was dark. I had a weird urge to go outside, so I did; sneaking through the hall so Jim wouldn't hear me and try to start a conversation. The house was pitch black anyway, so he mightn't have been home. I find it hard to figure out what time it is in the winter, but looking back, I think it was pretty late. I took a walk, not really noticing or caring where I was going. Eventually I went over a bridge, and kind of got my bearings. I knew there was a petrol station on the other side, with a shop in it. I'd been in there before. I got a sudden urge to buy some porn. Not having proper internet or a laptop had sent me back into the dark ages, so things like buying CDs, DVDs and porn mags was something I did again. Like it was 1996 or something. Crossing over the bridge I looked down at the little wooded area and heard voices in the dark. I didn't know what it was, but I decided to go down.

Under the bridge, I was that drunk sort of fearless that's always dangerous, because I might have been walking into a situation I couldn't walk out of alive. I didn't care. I had a weird excited feeling as I got closer to the voices. I wondered who it might be. Teenagers drinking, maybe. There wasn't any music, but I still felt like I was about to walk into a party. The noise of the traffic above got quieter as the noises from inside the trees got louder. It was voices, but something else too. Moaning? I suddenly felt a different kind of excited, but I wasn't sure why.

The first thing I saw was a man sucking another man off. Against a tree. One of them was standing up, the other guy on his knees. The standing guy got a bit startled when he saw me, then he nodded, I nodded back, and he went back to enjoying his blow-job. The guy on his knees didn't open his eyes once. I was so drunk that none of it even fazed me.

A little bit away from them were two more guys. One with his trousers around his ankles, the other one had stepped out of his entirely and was naked from the waist down. He was half standing, half bending against the tree, while the first guy fucked him in the arse. I felt sort of dizzy. I was in a clearing now – circular, surrounded by trees, with the canopy above hiding everything from the bridge. More couples were dotted around – some blowing, some fucking, even a couple of 69s going on. I wasn't disgusted, but I wasn't turned on either. It just isn't my thing. Never been even slightly bi. Just does nothing for me. I was wondering if I should get out of there when someone touched my shoulder.

"All right?" It was a guy. In his early twenties, maybe. Normal looking. Wouldn't have clocked him for gay. But maybe he wasn't. I'd heard things before. Straight men going on gay websites cos they were just horny and alone. Getting blown by some gay guy and then probably regretting it immediately, once they'd come. I understood, sort of. I'd felt the same after some desperation shags with women. I look at the guy and nod, but I don't say anything.

"You looking for something?" There was nothing ambiguous about what he was asking. My head had a million things in it at once, but I couldn't pick one to say.

"Quiet, are you? That's okay, mate. I like 'em quiet sometimes. What's your name?"

"Ah, Steve." When I said it I felt like I stepped out of myself and was looking at the scene from a different angle. I hadn't used that name in a long time. I thought I'd left it behind me, in another place. But here I was, saying it now. My heart started racing, and I took a deep breath that felt like it would go on forever without filling up my lungs. Last time I'd been Steve to people, things had worked out okay. For me. For everyone else, too. I let out the breath and I know that things aren't going to work out for this guy tonight.

"Okay, Steve. I'm Alan. Wanna go for a walk?" He put his hand on the top of my hip and I tried not to react. I had to play along.

"Sure. Where to?" I smiled the fakest smile. Like it wasn't me smiling at all; like someone else was wearing my face as a mask. My cheeks were hot and there was spit welling in my mouth.

"Just somewhere a little more private, yeah mate?" Alan put his arm around my shoulder in a matey way, and I suppressed the flinching feeling just in time, looking at where he was pointed. Further into the woods, farther away from the bridge. And much, much darker. Perfect.

Fifteen minutes later and I came out of that darkness on my own. I walked out a different way, cos I didn't want to pass the others. The less chance I gave them of getting a good look at me the better, for when the police eventually rounded people up to ask them questions about that night. If they did at all. It had been terrifyingly easy in the end. Alan's attempts at getting me hard in his mouth were never going to work. I think I knew for sure now I wasn't that way inclined. He'd looked up at me apologetically from down on his knees, still trying to wank my floppy, spit covered cock with his hand. I slammed him in the temple with my knee, knocking him over, and before he had a chance to recover, my full weight was on his chest, hands around his windpipe, and then it was over. Even in the dark I could see his lips were blue. The vein in his temple was still strained, and his eyes were still open and bulging. But there was no pulse, and no breath, and I felt good. I dragged him over to some bushes and made sure he couldn't be seen.

    No one found him for another two weeks. I read about it in the newspaper. By then I'd already done someone else. A woman I met on the street. Just some old drunk who was flattered by my attentions. By Steve's attentions, technically. She lived on her own. We brought some cans back to her flat. She had a dog called Harry. I stabbed her in the neck with a penknife while Coronation Street was on. No one had seen us go in together, but later on I worried about the CCTV in the off licence. I shouldn't have. I was fine. I don't even think it made the news. Lots of bad things happen in the world. Not all of them make the papers. I didn't go again for another month, but it wasn't cos I'd stopped, or was trying to stop. There just hadn't been an opportunity. The second there was, though, I took it. I don't know how many I've done since then. More than a couple, less than a lot. I look at my pocket PC thing, because it's made a noise. Next door's internet must be working again. Two emails. One from okcupid, saying a few people liked me. I've only joined it for a laugh, but you never know. True love might be just around the corner. The other is from my mother, sending me the check-in details for my flight to Ireland next week. Two weeks away from all this. It'll be good for me, I think.

Sixteen

Last Year, London, Emma

"What are we going to do?"

It feels like she's asked it a thousand times. I'm as numb to it as I am to her saying 'sorry'.

"What *can* we do? We've done everything."

"We haven't."

She hasn't tried to love me for who I am, for one.

"Well, yeah. You haven't tried to get a job."

"I have a job!"

"Tom, you haven't tried."

"I've tried to… you don't know what it's like."

She doesn't have the anxiety, the stupid terror. She doesn't know how to be me, she's her.

"I do know! I've applied for loads of jobs, and I haven't got some, and it's hard. I know that, you know? But you can't just give up. You have to keep going. You can't just…"

"I do try, and I do keep going, but no one even gets back to me. It's so soul destroying, being told over and over again that you're no good."

That's a bit of a lie, though. That implies that I've been sending out applications. I can't even get to that point. Sometimes I do, and I put the wrong phone number on it, cos I'm so terrified of someone ringing me back. So terrified of all of it. Of everything.

"I know… But, Tom – it's your own fault. And I'm sorry to have to say it, and I know it hurts. But it's true." She's not sorry, and she does know it hurts. That's her thing, using fake apologies as an excuse to kick me in the heart. I'm used to it.

"I know it is. But I can't go back in time, I only have what I have."

"Which is… be realistic, now." She's so businesslike.

"Well, nothing."

"Nothing. And how am I supposed to deal with that?"

"You don't have to deal with it. It's my life."

"It's not just your life though. It's mine too. I'm 33, Tom. I want to have a baby, I want to get married. And I'm running out of time."

"You're not running out of time. People have babies much older than you are. Celia had Alice when she was 41, and she-"

"I'M NOT CELIA."

"All right. Okay. Okay, I'm sorry." I'm not sorry, and if I was, I wouldn't know what for. Maybe I'm not the only one who uses fake apologies. Her face has the anger thing on it now. When she goes like that, it's about ten minutes before you can have a sensible conversation with her. It's all emotion and no logic. I'm trying damage limitation, that's what the sorry was about.

"You should be sorry. I'm going out to work every day, spending three hours on a fucking tube, and I hate it. I'm paying all the bills-"

"I pay for things."

"You pay 25 fucking quid a week, if that at all."

"That's half of what I get! And you only put in the same, and you make-" Wrong move. Wrong move completely. Her face goes red and her eyes are wild.

"I fucking put in everything! I pay the mortgage, this is my house. I pay the council tax, the bills, I pay for the dogs' medicines. I pay it all."

"But you'd be paying all that if I wasn't here anyway! And you'd be paying someone to mind the dogs, or you'd have to give them up."

"That's not the point!"

"What is the point then?"

"This is… this is exhausting, you know that?" She suddenly looks defeated, although not by me or anything I've said. She just looks like she's given up.

"I know, babe. I'm sorry." I try to touch her, but she flinches, and it gets me right in the gut.

"It's just… it's not good enough. I want to do things. I want to go places, and I want to travel, and I do want you to do all of those things with me. And get married, and have a baby. But we can't afford it when you're contributing nothing. And I know you think we can. But I'm not paying your way. I'll end up resenting you for it, and it'll be hell." I like how she thinks her resenting me is some future event, rather than the basis of our entire relationship.

"But it's not like you're in a shit job, on minimum wage. People manage."

"I don't want to manage! I've worked hard for what I have, I don't want to-"

Worked hard, my arse.

"You don't want to share it?"

"Share it? Why should I share anything?"

"I dunno. Kindness, love, stuff like that?"

"I do love you. And I am kind. I've let you fucking live here rent free for three years, when you have no intention of changing, I-"

I haven't lived with her for three years, I'd been in Essex, crashing at Andies's Monday to Friday (to take the kid to school in the mornings, and pick her up after) for most of those three years. And we were split up for five months too. I've only been here with her full time for about six months – before and after the move. But I let that go, cos it's logic and facts, and we're having a *relationship* argument, and facts and logic don't belong here.

"And what have you changed?"

"Me? ME? I don't need to change, Tom. There's nothing wrong with me. It's not me who needs to fucking change."

"You could be… you could be bloody nicer to me." I put a fake wobble in at the end of the sentence, for effect.

"I'm tired of being nice to you, Tom. I've had enough."

"What? When? When were you nice to me? When have you ever just thought, he's a good guy, he takes care of me, he listens to me, he does pretty much everything for me."

"Except what I want you to."

"What?"

"You know."

"That's just it, though. I do everything you bloody want, but you fixate on the one thing I can't."

"Or won't." She has a look of contempt now, I've lost her for the day, or at least until this conversation is over.

"That's not fair."

It is fair.

"Well, I think it is. It's not nice, no. But it's fair."

"If you say so."

"I do say so. And I'm the one who pays for everything here, so I think I get a say."

"You get the only say, in fairness."

"What, you don't say anything? Why am I fucking sick of listening to you then? Your whining, and your excuses – it's too much. I've had enough." Her face is completely closed off now. She's gone.

"Thanks."

"Well, someone had to say it."

"And strangely, that someone is usually you."

"What's that supposed to mean?"

"You're a horrible person, Em. Sorry, but-"

"Oh, right. This one again. Well yeah, maybe I am. Maybe I can't be like you, and be nice all the time, and live in a fucking dream world where everyone else pays for me, and I get to live in the lap of luxury, and-"

"The lap of luxury? I get to eat food every day, and there's a roof over my head."

"And where do you think those things come from?"

"Well, the food comes from when I cook it. Every day."

"Right. And the house?"

"Estate agents?"

"Tom, just… just fuck off, okay? Leave me alone." She gets up and walks into the big kitchen that she pays for, followed by the dogs that I look after, and puts on the kettle that she bought, to make herself some of the coffee I got for us when I did the shopping. I want a fag, but I've stopped for the day. I can go to the shop, and eat some spicy crisps afterwards. She's hardly going to be hugging me when I get in.

"I'm gonna pop out. You want anything at the shop?" I say it in the most cheerful voice I can. But only cos I'm being passive-aggressive.

"No. I'm fine. Thank you." The anger drops out of her voice as she says the last two words. She puts the iPod on, and turns the volume down straight away, to Emma Level. It's Adele, singing the song we listened to together in her car, the first time she drove me home from staying at hers. The opening bars of the piano make me feel things as I shut the door behind me.

I'm on auto pilot again. I made sure to nick a fag out of my jacket as I went out the door, and light it up as soon as I'm away from the front room window. I'll regret it after two or three pulls, same as always. I walk down to the shop, paranoid for no reason. I should've brought a can of deodorant but it's not a day I could get away with wearing a jacket to hide it, and anyway, I'd have had to go get some from upstairs first, and I wanted to storm out. I need a pack of cheap crisps. The beef ones do the trick the best, though I don't know that for sure. I've never done a test where I find out which snacks fool her into thinking I haven't smoked a fag. She never thinks I have. I'm either very good at it, she's oblivious, or she knows, and she can't be bothered arguing with me about it. It could be any of them.

The guy in the shop never recognises me, which is good, cos he'd probably think I'm an alcoholic if he did. I thought about buying some lemon juice, but I'd have to throw it away, and that's an expensive fag to have. I wish I could just smoke around her, but she doesn't approve. Not even a thing where she doesn't like them. She smokes herself when she's out having a drink. It's a money thing. I can't afford them, she says. I can't even do what I want with my own money, I'm so beholden to her. I don't know how I got myself into this position, but I'm stuck in it. I love her, whatever that means. I'm still on that kitchen floor with her in my head, feeling all those crazy feeling, before I knew her properly. She's in the present though, where she hates me. I don't want to be in the present. I want the kitchen floor again, all the time. And I can't be there on my own. I get a can of fizzy lemon stuff. I'll just avoid her when I go back, until I can get in for a spray of deodorant and a bit of Listerine. I hate this shit, but it's my life now. Someone with a dodgy headlight on their car almost knocks me over when I'm crossing the road, and I half wish they'd managed to.

Seventeen

Twenty-eight years ago, Ireland, Fiona

"Why wouldn't you go over and play with some of them kids, Thomas?" Mam says. She's always saying things like that. She doesn't know I'm pure shy. She doesn't know the way other kids be to me. New kids. She doesn't know nothing.

"Don't want to." I'm wearing the stupid green cords pants she bought me to wear at Christmas. I like them cos they don't have no zip or buttons on them, but I don't like them cos they're green and they're cords. No one wears cords. Boys in school gave me an awful slagging that time I wore them on the day when you can come in with no uniform, if you bring in a 50p for the black babies in Africa. I hate them today more cos it's hot and I feel too hot. But I don't like shorts, cos I've milk bottle legs, and all the boys slag me over them, so she gave me them to wear and now I'm wearing them, on the beach. On holiday.

"Ah shur leave him alone if he doesn't want to," says Dad. He's not really sticking up for me properly though. Him and Mam are just always fighting.

"Shut up, you," Mam says, and she looks at him in the fight way.

"Oh, here we go," Dad says, and I don't want them to have a fight, so I say:

"Stop it," and they both look at me funny, and then they look at each other, and Mam closes her eyes and makes a noise, and Dad takes out his cigarettes; the ones in the green and white box, that smell even worse than Mam's ones.

"See what you did now, for God's sake?" Mam says, and I think she's saying it to Dad, even though she's not looking at him.

"I didn't – listen, don't blame – Thomas, will you go 'way over and play with them kids? There's a good lad." He puts his hand up like he's gonna pat me like he pats the dog at home, but then he doesn't pat me, he puts his hand down again and scratches his belly under his t-shirt. A girl goes past us with one of them windmill things in her hand that you get off the man up on top of the hill, and I wish I had one, but when I asked her, Mam said they were too dear, and she'd have no money for chicken and chips later. I said I didn't want no chicken and chips if I can have one of them windmills, but she said don't be stupid and I have to have a dinner, and then she stopped talking about it, cos we'd to go into the shop to get her fags.

Mam's belly is fat now, and she told me it's cos I'm getting a new brother or sister when I go back to school. She said we're getting it from the hospital, cos that's where you get new babies from, but I don't know why her belly is fat as well. Alan O'Shea in school said it's cos the baby is inside her belly, growing, but he's weird and he smells like milk all the time, so he's probably just codding me, or being stupid, cos a baby couldn't live inside your belly. There'd be no room after you had your dinner. You'd be putting a load of dinner down on top of the baby, and that'd be pure lousy. You get them in the hospital, Mam says. I don't want a brother or sister anyway. Everyone is always fighting with their brothers and sisters, all the ones I know, and I don't like fighting. I walk over to where the other kids are playing, but I walk slow, cos I don't really want to go over to them. Mam or Dad says something to me behind my shoulder when I walks over, but I dunno what they say, cos it's windy in my ears and the seagulls are going mad in the sky over my head.

*****

"Why you wearing them, though? Is it cos you're a steamer?" The biggest kid is called Derek, and he's horrible. He's slagging off my green cords. I don't know what a steamer is so I dunno what to say to him. There's four of them altogether. Derek, Matthew, a girl called Fiona, and a redhead fella called Sam. I like the way Fiona looks. She's like a beautiful girl off the telly. They're not being nice to me though. I knew they wouldn't be. That's what Mam and Dad don't understand. That's why I don't like going over to new kids. That's why I didn't want to go to school when it was the first day of school. New kids are never nice to me. I'm always right about that. I wish people would believe me about it when I say it. Especially Mam.

"Ah God help us, leave him alone, Derek. They're nice pants," Fiona says, and I feel good, cos she's sticking up for me, but I feel bad as well, cos she has to. I don't want to be a boy that girls have to stick up for. I want to be a boy like Derek, who does the slagging. I never am, though. The redhead fella, Sam, sniggers, and the one called Matthew smiles, but he doesn't say anything good or anything bad.

"Pah! Nice if you want to look like a steamer. Where you from anyway?" says Derek. I don't know if Fiona likes him. She probably does. It's like that in the films. Sometimes. The pretty girl likes the big bully. At the end of the film, though, the girl ends up with the nice guy. Like me. This isn't a film though. We've gone really far away from where Mam and Dad were. Right up onto the cliffs, where's it's grassy. I didn't want to go, but they were all going, and I was supposed to be playing with them, so I went too. And they were being nice to me then, not slagging my pants and calling me a steamer.

"From Balla," I say, even though we're moving to Thomondgate soon. Thomondgate's nicer than Ballynanty, Mam says. No gluesniffers in Thomondgate. But Derek is a bully and he's strong, so I say Balla cos I want to sound like I come from somewhere good like that. Where there's gluesniffers and people getting stabbed, not somewhere nicer like Thomondgate, cos he'll think I'm a steamer, even though he already thinks I'm a steamer, and I still don't know what that is, but it's something bad.

"Pffft, you are in your balls from Balla," Derek says, and then he does a hock and snotty spit, and he doesn't spit it at me, he spits it at the ground, but I feel like it was kind of at me.

"I am," I say, cos I am.

"What part of Balla?" Matthew says. He's got really dark black hair and really bright blue eyes, and it makes him look weird, like someone from another country, cos his arms and legs and face are really brown, like he's from Italy or Spain, I think.

"Shanabooly Road," I say, cos that's true.

"That's not a place in Balla," Derek says, and he's laughing, and I feel like crying, cos he's the one lying, not me.

"It is, sham," says the Matthew fella, and he nods, cos it is.

"G'way you spa," says Derek to him, and he does another hock noise with his nose but he doesn't do a spit this time.

"It is, like. My cousin's from Balla. Shanabooly is up by the banana block," says Matthew, and the redhead fella Sam starts nodding and I feel better now, cos it's three of us nearly against one of him. Fiona isn't saying nothing so she mustn't know nothing about Balla, she's probably from somewhere else anyway, she sounds posh, a bit. She's lovely looking. Like a angel, or a girl off a movie.

"Yeah, Der. Shanabooly's in Balla. He's from Balla, I'd say," Sam says, and I look at Derek and I smile, cos I was right and I wasn't telling lies.

"Yeah, well. So what?" he says, cos that's what bullies always say when you catch them out. Cos they've nothing else to say, bullies don't. Bullies aren't ever clever kids, they're only big and they hit you, and they're always horrible to people, but they still have loads of friends.

"Well, leave him alone then, Derek. Are you here on your holidays?" Fiona says, to me.

"Yeah, for a week, in a caravan," I say to her, even though the week is over, nearly. I want to look at her cos she's nice but I don't as well cos I'm shy and when she looks at me it makes my face go all red.

"Pffft, in a caravan, haha. Like a tinker," Derek says, and I feel bad again. It's a nice caravan, we got a loan of it off my auntie that lives in Pineview. My auntie Margaret, the one that wears sunglasses on top of her head, in her hair. Even when it's not a sunny day.

"You're staying in a caravan too, Derek," says Fiona, cos she's the only one that stands up to him. She's more braver than the two boys, I think.

"No. It's a *mobile home*, you gowl. And we're staying for two weeks," he says, and I hate him now, cos a mobile home is just a caravan anyway, and who cares if he's staying for two weeks?

"You're a fool. A mobile home's the same as a caravan," she says, and I wanna look at her, or smile at her, but I can't, so I look down. I can see Sam has a soccer ball and I wonder if they'll want to play a game in a while, cos I'm not good at soccer and I'll feel like an eejit in front of everyone if I've to play.

"You're the fool, cos it isn't the same. A mobile home doesn't have no wheels," Derek says, even though some of them do, I think, but I'm not sure, so I don't say nothing, and I wouldn't say nothing even if I was sure, cos I think he might try to hit me if I get too cheeky with him.

"You know what? You're some eejit altogether, Derek." Fiona says, and Matthew kind of laughs, but then he stops laughing, cos Derek looks at him, and you never knows if a bully is just gonna hit you for doing hardly nothing.

*****

Later on, it's only me and Fiona left. We'd tried playing a game of headers and volleys with the soccer ball, and I wasn't very good, and Fiona was in goals, and Derek kept slagging me, and she kept telling him to stop, and he got all angry and he pushed her, and you shouldn't ever hit a girl or push a girl. And I wanted to back in and stop him, so she'd think I was great, but I was too scared to, and I thinked about it for too long, and then Matthew and Sam backed in and then Derek got pure cross and he hit Sam, sort of, and everyone said that wasn't on, and then Derek called us all a curse word, and went away raging. And Sam's nose was pumping bleeding so he'd to go off to his mam and dad, and Matthew'd to go with him, cos he was his brother, even though they didn't look nothing like each other, so now it was just me and her. Me and the girl. Just by accident. But I like it. Cos she's nice. We're right on the edge of the big cliff, looking down to the bit of the beach where hardly no one is, cos the sun is sunnier over on the other side. I can see all of the big sea, and sometimes you see big things jumping out there, and my dad says yesterday that's dolphins, like Flipper, but Mam tells him to shut up and stop being silly, there's no dolphins in Kerry, and Dad says there is, cos Dingle is in Kerry, and that's where the famous dolphin lives, and Mam says well we're not in Dingle, and Dad says "for God's sake", and they stop talking about it.

"Have you brothers and sisters?" Fiona says, and I have to think about the answer, cos of Mam's belly and the hospital.

"Kind of."

"Kind of? How can you have kind of brothers and sisters?" She's very pretty, I think. Like one of them girls that do be in the ads for girls' toys on telly sometimes. Fashion Wheel or one of them things girls like. I like He-Man and the Transformers.

"Well cos I've one brother and no sisters, but I might be getting a sister, or a brother, so then I'll have a brother and a sister, or a brother and a brother, like." I don't know if I said it right, but I don't know how to say it a different way. It's a bit windy up here, but it's still warm too.

"Your mother is *pregnant*, is she?" She touches me a lot when she talks to me. On the arm or on the shoulder or on the knee. Sometimes it's a rubbing touch as well. Or a squeezing touch, but it's soft, not hard like a pinch. I don't know no one who does that, but maybe girls do it, cos I don't know lots of girls as my friends.

"Yeah," I say, cos I think that's right. I think that's what they said to me. The word sounds like the word they said when they were saying about it.

"Cool. Are you excited?" The way she smiles at you would make you feel pure funny. I don't know if it's a good feeling or a bad feeling. It's a different feeling, anyway.

"Excited?" I don't know what she means, but I don't want her thinking I'm an eejit as well.

"Yeah. About the baby."

"We didn't get the baby yet. We've to get it from the hospital."

"Ah, yeah, but it's gonna come out soon, is it?"

"Out where?" I think she means out of the hospital. I'm not sure. The seagulls are squawking over my head and her head, but far away, up in the sky. They're pure noisy.

"Out of your mam's belly, stupid." She's laughing, and I dunno how to feel, cos I don't like it when people says I'm stupid, cos I'm not stupid, I'm really good at school, and when people call me stupid them people are always more stupid than me, like that Derek. I looks at her, but I don't know what to say to her.

"They said… they said the hospital."

"Ah, yeah. Yeah, shur she's to go into the hospital like, and the nurses and the doctors will help her get it out of her belly, wont they? Cos they know how to do it," Fiona says, and I'm listening really good, cos I didn't know none of this stuff.

"How do they do that?" I'm afraid now, cos how could you get a baby out of a belly, and I don't want no one hurting my mam, even if they're nurses or doctors.

"I don't really know," says Fiona, so I don't really know either, and that's that, as Dad says. There's no one around at all now, except me and Fiona and the seagulls, and I think about Mam, and is she all right, and will I go back now, in case the baby is coming and they've to bring her to the hospital, and I dunno if they've hospitals here at the seaside or anything, and then Fiona does something and I get a fright.

"What are ye doing?!" I says to her. She's put her hand onto me again, onto my green cords pants, but it's not on my leg or anything like that, or my knee. She's put her hand on my privates.

"Eh? Just being nice," Fiona says, and she doesn't take her hand away from there. I'm all hot in my face and my neck is cold, and I don't like this, even though she's pure pretty and her face is pure near my face, like she'd gonna kiss me, like they do in the films.

"I don't – what are you – how is that being nice?" Her hand's still there, and now she's rubbing me. I feel funny, like I need to go to the toilet, sort of, but not really like that. Something is bad.

"I dunno. That's what boys like. Don't you like it?" Her breaths are all hot and near me and her hand is moving still.

"I don't know. I don't – who told you boys like that?" My head is full of pictures of stuff from movies that'd be on late at night that you're not supposed to be watching, or dirty magazines bigger boys'd be looking at sometimes, and they'd try to make you look, for the sneer, to make you feel sick and stuff, and then tell you to go away off out of it, cos you're too young to be looking at stuff like that, and they'll tell your Mam on you. All things like that, but that's all grown-up things and I'm only eight and a half and Fiona's only nine, so I don't know.

"Everyone. Do you want to give me a kiss?" She is really close to my face. Her hair smells nice. My heart going too fast, and I feel nearly dizzy, like you get when you roll down a hill and get up again.

"Who's everyone?"

"Boys. Derek says it. And Matthew. All the boys. And my brothers. And my Dad. All boys like that. Will you give me a kiss?" She's closed her eyes and she's put out her lips to me, and I don't know what to do, cos I don't know what she's saying or what she's doing. I want to go away, but I want to stay too.

"Your brothers? Your Dad?"

"Yeah. But that's a secret." She looks weird when she says that, and she stops being at me with her fingers, and I'm glad. But the thing she said doesn't feel good. At all.

"A secret?"

"Yeah, like. But you won't tell anyone, will you?" Her eyes are open again and she's not doing the kissy thing with her mouth. I would probably like to give her a kiss. I just…

"Tell anyone what?"

"About that. Now, where's my kiss?" She laughs, and her hand is on me again. In the same place. She's doing something different now, and I don't know what it is until she tells me herself.

"Why's there no buttons or zipper on these pants?"

"What?" I feel very weird. I look around for people – in case they catch us – and I dunno if I want them to or I don't. I feel bad, sort of. I don't know why.

"Ah, there's none on these pants. Why?"

"Why?" She's still fiddling with my pants and now I really need a wee, and I have to go and find the toilets here if I want to do that, but that might be good, cos I'd get away from this.

"Why do you want to know?"

"Cos I want to get my hand inside, silly. That's what boys like. Wait. Hang on." She takes her hand off me for a second and I think thank God, but then she puts it right down the front of my pants and inside my jocks and I can feel her fingers on my privates and the fingers are kind of cold, and I dunno why she's doing it at all and I don't know what to do to make her not do it or what to say.

"What are you doing?!" I nearly shout it at her, nearly as loud as the noise of the seagulls up over my head and over her head and she looks like me weird, like an afraid look, kind of, but her hand is still inside my jocks, and I feel my thing start moving by itself and I don't want to be here anymore, and I don't want her doing what she's doing, cos it doesn't feel good, but it does as well, and maybe I'm supposed to like it, cos she says it's what boys like, so maybe if I don't like it I'm not a real boy, or a proper boy, and that makes me feel bad.

"Come on, just relax. I'll do it good. I'm good at it. Everyone says I am," Fiona says, and her hand is right around my thing now, and she's sort of pulling it as well as rubbing it, and I really need a wee, and I'm afraid cos what if I wee in my pants and on top of her and I dunno why she's doing this, and I'm thinking about her Dad, and does she do this to him, does he make her do it, cos I saw on TV that that's not right at all. And that you should never ever keep a secret if a grown-up asks you to. I remember that bit. On *That's Life*, that Mam watches, on Sunday nights, on the BBC, since we got the channels, and the woman on it saying if a grown-up touches your privates it's bad and you should tell your mam or dad, or if it's your mam or dad doing it, tell a teacher. And Fiona's not a grown-up, so that's not the same, but she says... I think she's saying she touches her dad's thing, and her brothers' things, and I don't think that's right either, and my thing is getting bigger in her hand, and I like it, but I don't like it and then all of the thinking stops inside my head and everything is really, really quiet for a second, even the seagulls aren't making noise. And Fiona looks at me – pure different – and I know what I have to do.

I take her hand out of my jocks with my own hand, and she looks at me again, like she's confused. And I look at her too. And I give her a small kiss, on the cheek, like your mam would give you, and her cheek feels pure soft. And then I push her. Hard as I can. Off the big cliff. And there's still no noise. Not even the seagulls. Not even Fiona when she's falling. She doesn't scream, like they would in the movies. And I wait a few seconds, and I look over the edge, even though I don't want to. And there she is. Lying pure still. On the big rocks. There's red stuff everywhere and I don't know it's blood for a little bit and then I do know it's blood. And all I can think is that she's safe now. From her dad, and her brothers, and fellas like Derek. And I get a little scared about Derek, and Matthew, and Sam, cos they know I was with her, and maybe they'll tell the police, or her mam and dad, or their mam and dads. But we're going home tomorrow from these holidays. And anyway, they all think my name is Stephen, not Thomas. That's what I told them when they asked me today. Cos I don't like being called Thomas. I always wanted to be called Stephen. So I told them I was called Stephen. Cos what's the harm in that, as Mam says.

Eighteen

This Year, Limerick, Orla

I'm in the library, trying to do the writer thing. There's this really beautiful girl working here who's just started. For the past few weeks they've had to close for an hour in the middle of the day, so people can have lunch, because of staff shortages, they said. There was an ad on the jobs website. Like manna from Heaven. Because of all the things I've ever done for a job, the two months I spent doing enforced work experience in Romford City Library were my favourite. Even if that was more than five years ago now. I loved it. When I went to see the boss guy about working there, he was almost trying to make me turn it down, it felt like. He kept going on about how repetitive it was, and how you needed to be a certain type of person to do it, and maybe I mightn't be that sort of person. I had to assure him that I was exactly that sort of person. That the idea of being given a trolley full of books, which all needed to go in the right place, either alphabetically in Fiction or by the numbers in Non-Fiction, was my idea of bliss. I am not a leader. I keep ending up in supervisor positions because bosses mistake my being clever for some sort of competence or organisational skills, and that really is a mistake, because I crack under the slightest amount of pressure, and I don't see the value in getting a quid an hour more to be responsible for other people's mistakes and shitty attitudes, when most of them are just students trying to make a few quid to go out drinking, or young mums looking for something to do in the middle of the day. They never give a shit, and I tend to agree with them. Worst supervisor ever.

This girl though, she has *my* job now. The job I never even bothered to apply for, of course, because my anxiety always stops me from doing even the things that would be the most helpful to me. The things that might save me. The things I can actually do. I look at her perfect blondeness and perfect everything else, and she's so out of place here. I remember, when I was a supervisor, and was vaguely responsibly for the hiring and firing, a girl came in looking for a job in our coffee shop, when we were actually looking for someone. Her name was Veronica. She looked like the sort of girl every drunk guy in the world told she 'looked like Liv Tyler' when they ran into her at the bar on a Saturday night. But even that was almost an insult, cos she was much better looking than Liv Tyler. I was the one who talked to her first, and I remember walking back into the kitchen area, where my boss was on sandwich making/food prep duties that day and saying "Someone's here looking for a job, and she's so gorgeous that if you don't hire her, I'm quitting, mate." He just chuckled and told me to give her a form. And he did hire her. And she was useless, really. But I got to look at her every day, so it didn't matter if the customers had to suffer badly made lattes. Priorities are priorities.

No one here has hired this girl for that reason. She must have been the only one who applied, because everyone else who works here is a woman, and none of them are in danger of troubling the Miss Universe selectors. Most of them are the 40-something version of that weird kid in school who said really Asperger's things too loud all the time, before we even knew what Asperger's was. There was an Iceland in Hornchurch, back when I lived in England, where literally every person working there was a girl from eighteen to 21 who looked like a porn star. One time I was in there and saw what the manager looked like – pervy looking fat old fuck - and realised that this was no coincidence. Here though, in this library, that's not what's going on. She catches me looking at her and I don't look away. She gives me a smile, which could mean anything, but at least it doesn't mean *eff off*. Then my phone rings, and she gives me the librarian look, and our romance is over as soon as it begins.

Outside, in the hall, I put the phone to my ear, not sure if I've swiped the right way to answer, cos I'm still getting used to Android since the iPhone finally gave up last month. I don't know the number, but it's 061, so it's Limerick, a landline, or maybe a phone box. I wonder if they have phone boxes here anymore. I can't picture one.

"Hello?"

"Hey." I know the voice straight away, even on the phone. It's Orla.

"H-hi." There's only one syllable, but I still manage to stutter it. Nerves, maybe. Or just relief. I'm so happy to hear her voice.

"I'm so sorry."

"No, don't be sorry, it's okay…" It's really not okay. She has no idea how much it's really not okay; what's happened, what I've done, what I've become again. And that's all her fault. Except it isn't, really. And, anyway, it's not like I can tell her.

"Thanks, but no. I am sorry. And I do need to say it. I just-"

"Orla, it's fine. It's so great to hear your voice." It almost is fine, already. That's the effect she has on me. I already forgive her, cos she's here. Even if she's not.

"You're so nice."

"I'm not, really." She has no idea the depth of that statement, but how could she?"

"You are. You're the nicest – you... I'm so sorry."

"You keep saying that. Stop saying that, okay? I command you!"

"Yes, boss."

"That's better. So…" I start like I'm gonna ask her how's she's been, or what she's been up to. Like it's a normal conversation. Like we're normal people, who do normal things. But we're not. Me, especially not. Still though.

"I wanted to call you. I wanted to call you every single day for the last few weeks. Or text you, or Facebook you. You have no idea what it took to stop myself. You really don't."

"I, eh…" I don't know how to respond to that, because what am I supposed to be? Impressed? It's tricky.

"That day we had – I handled everything so badly, and I've gone over it in my head a thousand times, believe me I have. What I could have done differently; what I could have said. But that's, well…"

"Exactly, Orl. You can't change the past. Don't beat yourself up." I don't want her to feel bad. Even though she's completely right about it – she could have done things differently. She could have said things differently. She could have said anything, these past few weeks. Anything to reach out to me, make me feel okay, make things right. I agree with all of that, but that's not what I want to say to her now. I don't want to tell her off. She's here now, that's all that matters. She called me. I just want her to feel okay again.

"You're too kind. I fucked up. And I should have said something after. I should have let you know. I just – this is a really big thing. For me, I mean. It's serious. I felt things that day that I haven't felt about anyone in a long, long time. The last time I felt anything like that was probably about you. I know that sounds really fucking stupid, but-"

"It doesn't. It doesn't at all. I know exactly what you mean. Trust me, I do. I feel the same."

"You do?"

"Yeah. Of course I do. I… you know how I feel about you, Orla." I say it, but I wonder if she does. If she even could. Cos it's fucking mental, to be fair. Anyone else would think I was completely mad. But then, I sort of am, and people generally do, so I don't really know what my point is.

"I think I do. And that's what makes this so hard."

"What?" I panic, suddenly, because those words are really familiar to me, and definitely not in a good way. Those words happen in break-up speeches, not get-back-together speeches. Has she only broken her silence to break my fucking heart? I try to keep it together.

"Jesus, that came out all wrong, I'm sorry."

"Stop saying it, Orla…"

"Oh. Yeah, sor- I mean, hmmm. What I'm trying to say is… that's what makes how I feel so hard, even if it makes it good too. You know? And it's what made not talking to you for all that time such a bloody nightmare. But I had to try."

"To try what?" I don't know if there's relief in my voice, but there definitely is in my head and my heart, cos it's not going the way I thought – the bad way. It's going somewhere else, even if I don't know where that is. I wish we were doing this face to face.

"To give things with – to give my marriage a chance." She exhales loudly after that sentence, and I think to myself again how weird it is to hear her say that word, cos it makes her sound so grown-up; makes us sound so grown-up, cos in my head we aren't at all. In my head it's still fifteen years ago with her, and nothing's happened in between. Well, between that and all this, anyway.

"Oh."

"Sor- I mean – I didn't mean to bring that up like that, but I can't help it, really."

"I know. I know. It's okay."

"I just. I had to cut you out for a bit. And give the life I've made here a chance. To *compete*, I mean… Does that make sense?"

"Yeah. Yeah, of course it does." All I want to know now is if it did compete. If she's phoning me to say goodbye, or to say… something else.

"Well, yeah. I tried. I really did. But all I thought about was you. About us. This new us, whatever that is. Who can compete with that? I mean, when we were just messing around, sure. I could tell myself that it was bit of a fun. A fantasy. That the real thing would never live up to what we wondered about. And then…"

"It did?" Relief again, cos now it's going somewhere much better. At least I hope so. Hope is dangerous, though. Life has a habit of coming along and drop-kicking you in the balls when you're busy hoping, I've found.

"It more than did. You know that. You were there too. I mean, it's like… I can't even describe it. This is just – you are just – whatever I thought was good, was happy, was… being in love with someone, before. It's all nothing. It's all just bullshit and settling, and all those other things, and then you – you come out of thin air after nearly fifteen years and you knock my fucking socks off. Sorry, I'm babbling."

"It's grand. It's good babbling. I *like* this kind of babbling." I don't tell her off for saying sorry, cos I think she just said she's in love with me, and it dawns on me that I've been waiting years and years to hear her say that, I just didn't know I was waiting for it until just now, when she did.

"Haha, yeah. You would, wouldn't you. Listen, anyway, I'm in a phone box and I'm running out of money, cos who fucking uses phone boxes anymore?"

"Tramps, I think." And me, when I'm acting like a fucking tramp. Makes a nice discreet drinking shelter if the windows are tinted.

"Yeah. Tramps, and auld ones that're scared of the iPhones."

"True. Anyway, what?" I'm sure she was saying something a second ago, before we got into all this.

"Am, I'm gonna run out of money, I said. But I have lots more I want to say to you. So much more." Literally every word she's saying already is like a symphony inside my soul, making me soar, but she's welcome to add some more, definitely.

"Text me later, or something?"

"No."

"No?" The symphony in my soul does a bit of a record scratch, and now I'm falling again.

"I'm gonna be more careful now, but if you can last 24 hours, I can meet you tomorrow. You don't have plans, do you?"

"Plans? Nope." I can't remember what having plans even feels like, unless they were plans with her. I'm gonna meet her tomorrow. It's like a thousand birthdays, multiplied by Christmas.

"Okay. I'll book somewhere."

"Book somewhere?" I've sort of lost the ability to decipher simple sentences now. I look back through the glass library doors to make sure no one's nicked my laptop off the table. It's fine.

"Yeah. A hotel. Let's give it another go. I promise I'll stay this time. And I'm so-"

"Uh-uh-uh – don't say it!"

"Haha, yeah, no. You know what I mean."

"I do. I always do."

*****

Walking down town afterwards feels amazing. Like having no shoes on and padding around on a big springy mattress. Or, this one time, when we were out taking Es, and we went to the Dublin Road Park at about three or four in the morning, and we went to the kiddie playground bit, with the rubber floor so the kids don't crack their skulls falling off stuff, and we ran around barefoot on it. It feels like that, only about a hundred times better. Cos she's back. And she's more than back. She's tried to do the other thing instead of the me thing, and the other thing lost, big time. And she said she was in love with me, I think. And even if she didn't, it doesn't matter. Cos I know she feels it. I know that now. And I feel it too. But I've always felt it, about Orla Keane. It's just that, all the other times I felt it, it just seemed mental. Whereas now, it's different. Now it has actual context. Now there's someone feeling it back at me. I go to Fine Wines on Catherine Street and get a small bottle of vodka and some Diet Coke, cos it feels like a celebration.

Later, down town, I'm sitting in Arthur's Quay Park, cos the weather's nice, reading one of the books I got out. I'm nicely buzzed, and everyone around looks like they're in a good mood. Parents with little kids, girls from secondary schools, people just chilling. It's sunny and bright – so bright it's almost hard to read the pages without having shades on. I got all non-fiction things. It's rare I ever read fiction now – not since I started writing it. My inner editor keeps bumping me out of narratives with suggestions on how I'd have written something differently, and I find most of the dialogue really hard to believe in. It's irrelevant, because someone clearly okayed those books – those writing styles were considered saleable by some agent or editor or publisher – usually all three, so there's no point in me getting myself worked up about them. That's not the point. The point is for me to write more, and have more books out, and then worry about it after that – after it's actually making me some money. But, the words – I don't use big words in my books. At all. And other people do. Even people who write pulpy horror. Especially people who write pulpy horror. For me, when I scan back over something even on the second draft, and I spot something that just looks like I'm showing off, out it goes. George Orwell said never to use a big word when a small word would have done, and he was no slouch. He knew what he was doing. I wonder to myself if Donald Trump is a big fan of Orwell, considering how he ran his campaign. I hope not, considering the job he was campaigning for.

"What're you reading?" Someone has sat down on the grass next to me without me noticing them coming over. It's a girl. Well, a woman. Well, she's about 20, so a girl, maybe.

"Uh, this." I turn the book over, show her the cover, and read the title out loud. It's some re-tread of the Whitechapel murders. I dunno why I always read those, it's not like they ever tell you at the end who Jack the Ripper actually was. There's something about that whole business I find strangely comfy, though. I always have.

"You did that thing," she says. She's got dyed black hair and a fringe. Pale skin, very thin and bird-like. Really intense eyes. One of those snout rings that make me feel like an old fogey when I see them, cos they put me into *disapproving dad* mode, the same way those stupid ear gauges do.

"What with the what now?" I have to squint at her, cos of the sun. She's on her own. Dunno why she's decided to come over to me and start a conversation. Especially when I was clearly reading a book. If the roles were reversed I'd have felt a right prick for doing it. Different rules for them though, I suppose.

"I asked you what book you were reading, and instead of telling me, you turned it over and read it out to me. Did you not already know what you were reading?" She's giggling, and it softens the initial *resting bitch face* she'd brought over with her. (And, yes, initial was the smallest word I could have used there.)

"Ah, yeah. But it's not like I'm reading *Catcher in the Rye*, or something. It's not like it's a novel. It's different when it's not fiction. If you'd asked me what I was reading about, I'd have told you straight off. But I don't necessarily memorise the names of non-fiction books while I'm reading them. It's-"

"Wow. I bet you're a hit at parties," she says, rolling her eyes. Two minutes ago, I didn't even know this girl existed; now she's critiquing my entire existence, for Christ's sake.

"I'm not the one using Michael McIntyre routines as a conversation starter, honey." I'm delighted with myself for recognising where her shtick is from. And also ashamed, because I hate that cunt.

"Touché. Anyway, what are you doing sitting in a park, reading about old murders, on a nice day like this?" she asks, like it's in any way her business.

"Ah, it's *research*," I say, opening my half-full bottle of half-vodka/half-Coke, that's half-cold and half-warm by now. Half-fizzy, half-flat too.

"Ooh. Research for what?" She has big eyes when she's interested or excited. Like a Manga character. Or a little child.

"New murders, obviously." I laugh after I say it, and then she laughs, and I take out a fag, and offer her one, and she takes it, and I wonder how the rest of my day is gonna go.

*****

It must be an hour later, maybe even two, and we're still talking. It's becoming clearer and clearer that she's a bit mental. I should have known, from the fringe, and the nose ring. All she's missing is the blue hair. Pretty lunatics and me; forever destined to be drawn to each other. It's written in the stars, clearly. Story of my life.

"And then he raped me."

"Raped you? Jesus." I take another slug of the Coke and Vodka, and wonder if she knows there's booze in it. Or if she cares. Or if it matters.

"Yeah. Well, kind of."

"Kind of?"

"Yeah. I mean, at the time, it was, well. I didn't say no. So it wasn't, well, it was, but." She looks at me with her big eyes, like what she just said made all the sense in the world.

"Oh. So… what happened?"

"Well, he was my boyfriend. And we were having a sexual relationship." She says the last two words in a whisper, as if someone else is listening, and as if that would warrant discretion. Maybe it still does in Limerick, though. It did when I was 20.

"I see." Do I see? Does it matter? Probably not. It's still sunny out, just not as warm as it was. The hairs on my arm are standing up, adding a bit of drama to her storytelling, even if she doesn't actually notice them.

"Well, yeah. It's just that… I wasn't in my right mind, you know?"

Oh, I know. Trust me.

"Hmmm."

"I only… it was only after we broke up." She's smoking another one of my fags, but I have plenty today, so it's grand.

"He raped you after you broke up?"

"No! No, what I mean is, after we broke up, I started thinking differently, you see. About him. About the whole relationship. My friend, Marie, she told me I'd been repressing stuff. Bottling it up. She's good at that sort of stuff, Marie. She reads lots of books on psychology and healing and that sort of thing. She sort of encouraged me to explore it, with her, in a safe space, if you know what I mean."

"I do." Literally the greatest phrase of the 21st century. The safe space. Jesus wept.

"And, I mean, it took a lot of soul searching, and finding out who I was, and just, well, eventually I realised that I'd never had consensual sex with David."

"What?" I do that thing drunks do in the movies where they look at the person talking to them, then at the drink in their hand, and then back at the person again. It's lost on her though, cos she probably thinks I'm just drinking Diet Coke. And that I'm particularly thirsty today, probably.

"Yeah. I realised that I never really wanted to have sex with him. And that it was a controlling relationship, and he'd be intimidating me into doing something I didn't want to, so... all the times we had sex, all the times we had consensual sex, it really wasn't. I mean, I didn't say no out loud, but I think somewhere inside me I was saying no. I just didn't know I was saying it. Cos I didn't feel it at the time. But I was, though. Somewhere inside. And he, well, he should've heard me, you know? That was his responsibility."

"Sure, yeah," I say with my mouth, and say something else completely with my brain.

"So it was sort of rape. All of it. I was devastated. I just felt so... *violated*."

"Of course. And was it just the one time?"

"Was what?"

"The rape."

"Oh. Oh, no. There wasn't really one time. There wasn't like, and incident or something. It was nothing like that. That's what makes it so confusing, I guess. We were together for a couple of years, and we were having sex right from the beginning. So it was basically all of those times, over the two years. About 400 times, at least, by my count. That's crazy, isn't it?"

"It sure is. And you didn't want to – you hated every minute of it? Of all of it?"

"What? No. No, I really enjoyed it, at the time. It was really good. It's just I – I didn't know what I was doing. I didn't – I wasn't able to give consent, you know? Because I didn't know I was in an abusive relationship. I didn't – I mean, he didn't hit me or anything. Not really. I mean, once, we were in Sails, up there in Arthur's Quay, and he kicked me on the shin because I threw Fanta in his face, and really, that was when the red flags should've gone up, but I was blinded, I think. Marie says I was. Blinded cos I loved him, cos he was good to me, cos I loved having sex with him. So, I mean, it's tragic isn't it? The way things turned out. Like I said, I feel violated. And betrayed. Really fucking betrayed, like."

"Jaysus." I say it because all I can think is "Jaysus", but when it comes out of my mouth it sounds supportive, for some reason. So I go with it.

"Yeah. I know."

"Did you go to the police?" I can't believe I just asked that, but when in Crazy-Rome.

"Oh. Oh, no. There was no point."

"How so?" *Please say something relatively sane. Please say something relatively sane.*

"Ugh. You know the way they are. Fucking Patriarchy. Victim-blaming, sexist pigs. They'd have laughed at me, you know? They'd have made me feel like I was the one in the wrong. That's just how it is. We think we've progressed, women, but we really haven't. It's still the same old story for us in this world. You men don't know how good you have it, trust me."

"Yeah, I suppose." I do that face people do when we're trying to look like we're agreeing, but also that we're slightly wise. The Hmmmm face.

"So, no. I couldn't go to them." She raises her eyes to ask can she have another fag out of my box. At least she's asking, I guess. Just taking one would have been a bit rude. It's not like I was going to refuse anyway. God knows that that refusal will turn into, six months down the line. Me hitting her over the head with a sweeping brush, for all I know, if she talks to Marie about it.

"So, what did you do?"

"Well, I thought about confronting him. And Marie said I probably should, but I just… I felt stupid. I felt like I'd got some power back in my life, and if I went to him – to that bastard – and I laid it out, what he'd done to me – there was a chance that it would go wrong, you know? That he'd make me feel like a fool, or a liar. I mean, he might have even beaten me up. Or killed me!"

"Hmmm," I say, and do the face again, because whole sentences are escaping me now.

"So, I just told other people."

"Oh. Like who?" I wonder if I should have said 'whom' there, but I don't think people say 'whom' in real life. Someone goes past with a dachshund. We used to have one of those, me and Emma. Or is it 'Emma and I'?

"Just friends. Like, my friends, his friends, everyone on my Facebook. He's blocked from seeing me though, so I was being discreet."

"Of course." I'm nearly out of vodka. I'm not even sure if I'm drunk. I think she's insta-sobered me.

"And like, loads of people were on my side, I think. Cos it's serious, you know?"

"I do. Listen, do you fancy going for a walk?"

"A walk? Where?"

"Ah, it's a surprise," I say, starting to get up already.

"Oh, all right."

We stroll up O'Connell Street for a bit, not saying anything. I'm leading the way, cos it's my surprise. I go past one, two, three blocks, looking for the right bit to turn up. There it is.

"Up here," I say, nodding at her to follow me.

"Where are we going?"

"Told you, it's a surprise."

"I dunno if I like surprises. Marie says I-"

"You'll like this one, trust me," I say, knowing she probably shouldn't trust me. We're in Dominic Street now, where the dole office is. Not far now. I take a right.

"Okay." She shrugs, and I take a longer look at her. She's very attractive, really. Kind of reminds of me Millie. But more alive. And in fewer sections. Last turn now, a left, and into a very deserted alley.

"Am, where are we going again?" She sounds nervous now. Scared.

"Shhhh, you'll know in a minute," I say, and put my hand on her arm. There isn't a soul around, and it's kind of dark in here, even though it's still really bright out.

"I'm… I don't wanna-"

I put my hand over her eyes all of a sudden, so she can't see. She starts to struggle in my grip, but I'm too strong for her. She isn't saying anything, or making any noise, maybe from the shock. It'll all be over in a second anyway. I'm almost lifting her off the ground now; she's so light and petite, it's no bother at all. I get her around the last corner, and take my hand off her eyes.

"Ta-dah!" We're standing outside Luigi's chipper, where they do the best battered sausage and chips in Limerick. She looks at the window with all the specials written up, and at me, and back at the window again.

"Oh my God. I'm starving, like. How did you know?"

"Eh, men's intuition or something. So you wanna get something? My treat." I can't particularly afford it, but it feels like a day for topping up the karma meter.

"Oh. Thanks, but no, I'll get my own. What are the battered sausages like here?"

"The best, mate. You're not a veggie, then?" She looks like a veggie. She looks like a vegan, if I'm being totally honest.

"God, no."

"Good answer, cos you know, if you'd said you were one, I might've had to kill you."

"Haha, very good. Listen, this is so rude, but I can't remember what you said your name was. I'm so sorry. Mortified, like. I'm Jill, by the way. But I think I said that, didn't I?"

"You did yeah," I say, holding the door for her like the patriarchy fascist I am.

"Oh. So… what's yours?"

"It's Tom," I say, and root around in my pocket to see if I have the four Euros in change.

Nineteen

Last Year, Stansted/Shannon/Leytonstone

Early morning airports are usually great for me; I didn't fly for the first time until I was 30, so it's always new and fresh to me – a bit like how I don't commute every day, so the tube is still a novelty. Today's different though. It doesn't feel like a holiday or a break, even though it's exactly that. A holiday from all the shit, and a break from her, even though I didn't choose it. I don't want to be away from her. These three years, I haven't gone back home once. Haven't seen my family. Haven't brought the kid over to see them. Emma became more important than all of that. Became my whole world. It's over, probably. I've lost the ability to know when it is and when it isn't. There's been so many close calls and near misses. Or definite bust-ups that turned into getting back together when it turned out she needed something from me. It only goes one way, obviously. When I need something only she can give me, I can go swivel.

I'm here because she suggested it. Like a lot of things, she tried to sell it to me as something that was good for me, when it's really for her benefit. Like those times I talked about before, where she'd give me love and support for my personal problems by going:

'Why don't we go get something nice to eat? That'll cheer you up!" Literal translation of that is: "Tom! I'm fucking sick of listening to your whining, and I'm also hungry. Let's go do something that makes me not hungry anymore, and maybe I'll be better able to put up with your shite, eh? There's a good boy."

This situation is like that. She can't stand the sight of me anymore, and wants me to fuck off out of her face, so she suggested I go back to Ireland to see my family, and have a nice relaxing time, and catch up with people, and then we'll see how it goes after that. I don't know if that means we're over now, or we're still together, but I guess it will be okay, cos I do still live with her, so I do have to come back. So maybe it will be a good thing for me? If it is, though, it'll be purely a coincidence, because this whole thing is really for her, and I'm super-aware of that. I might be the one on the plane, going somewhere for a couple of weeks, but this is definitely her holiday.

Just a small bag, no checked luggage, but I'm here early, anyway. Still new to airports; still paranoid about missing flights. It's half-busy. I'm trying to get back into the swing of it. There's no airport smell, like there's a hospital smell or a church smell. Too many different people passing in and out every day for there to be any lingering scent. The Starbucks in the Departure Lounge is usually the first familiar whiff I get here, but that's probably cos I used to work for them, and all their shops smell the same.

Two and a half weeks. That's as long as I've ever been back since I left for the UK fourteen years ago. The last time I was back nearly this long was the last time I was here at all – two weeks, three years back, when I met Emma. Met her on the internet, that is. I remember her messaging me on okcupid the day I arrived at my brother's. And her being pissed off that she couldn't go for a drink with me until I got back. She was one of those who go for the early date, get it out of the way, so you're not wasting time getting to know someone you have no real-life chemistry with, she said. Absolutely no evidence that this worked or anything, but that's Emma. Pragmatic. Headstrong. Not a fan of logic or sense when it comes to matters of the heart. But I love her. I think.

Obviously, she waited, and the rest is history. It feels a bit too much like history now, as I get in the queue for security. I hate this bit. Not sure if I should be taking my shoes off. Don't have a belt. Laptop out now, or when I get to the rolly things? Check pockets for change or a lighter. I think the lighter goes through without a beep, but I can't remember. I've flown since I was back – there was a wedding in Belfast a couple of years before. I was the Best Man, she came with me. It was an absolute nightmare of course – me, not drinking – back when I didn't drink, of course – when I was a good boy; her, not giving a shit. I had one of the worst weekends of my life, and she had a ball. Completely oblivious to how hard it was for me to get through all that social stuff when I was the only one sober. This was not an isolated incident. She never really understood. That's why I started drinking again, to take away that problem – the one of having to socialise sober with her while she drank, and the tension it caused. Of course, taking away that problem brought with it another problem – me, drinking, and having no safety catch. That was why I'd given up in the first place, before we met. I can't just drink socially. I can't drink responsibly. It's either don't drink at all, or drink all the time, with me. But I'd forgotten that, maybe. Maybe it's like when someone has a baby, and they think 'Never again!', and then a couple of years later, when their vagina's stopped hurting, they start to think it might be a good idea; that it wasn't that painful, that it might be easier next time. That's what drinking is with me. A healed vagina. I'll have to remember that for the autobiography.

I'm through to the other side and there's still more than an hour to the flight. The place looks fairly the same. Still a bunch of shops I'll never buy anything from, and the odd supercar being raffled for some reason. No one tries to spray me with perfume when I walk through the bit with the glittery marble floor; maybe I look like I don't have any money. Hour and a half and I can't have a fag. I don't think I can, anyway. Gatwick is different from this place. They have a sly little door/staircase combo that takes you into the open air, if I remember right. Although, do they? It seems a bit lax. What if I checked in, put a bomb in my luggage, snuck out for a fag, then just buggered off? I think I'm probably imagining it all now, come to think of it. Been a long time since I was in Gatwick. Either way, no nicotine until after we touch down in Shannon. I didn't smoke last time I was home, or drink. They won't be disappointed though; they all still smoke, except my brother, and he's just generally disappointed in me anyway, bless him. And it's Ireland, so everyone drinks, unless they're on antibiotics.

It doesn't feel like a holiday, no matter how much I've been in an airport, gone through security, got on the actual plane. It feels like a wake. I know I'll feel different when I get there, and smell the air, but right now it just doesn't feel real. It's cos I'm on my own. The kid is usually with me when I go home. It feels like I'm very far away from her now, and I don't know what's going to happen with that either. She's such a good kid; so grown up. She seems like she can handle anything, but I think it's a front. She's had to be the adult a fair few times with me, and it makes me ashamed. I don't want to think about it now, but there's nothing else to think about. I'm not looking forward to seeing anyone, but that might change once I get there too. Hopefully it'll be two weeks of people feeding me and giving me booze. It'll go easier with some booze. I'm in the brother's place, so I'll get my own room. The World Cup is on too, so there'll be trips to the pub or cans at home, if I can afford them. My card works over here, I think. Not that I have any money.

It's clear outside, I can see clouds, from the window seat. It looks like snow. If I stare into it enough, it's calming. Something about it being so big and me being so small. Like looking at the stars. It's not a cure for anything though, it's just a sticking plaster. Everyone around me is doing normal life plane things, I'm probably the only one on here whose life is in the toilet. That's just a guess though. There's probably a few suicidal people here. Hopefully none of them have backpacks with ticking noises coming out of them. The trolley's here already, and I want something, but I don't want that thing where I have to ask for it, when I usually spend the whole flight avoiding eye contact with flight attendants trying to flog me stuff. I want one of their coffees, but I'm on the inside seat, and I think about it being handed over to me, and trying to have the right change in the right money, and them having to come back to me with the order, and it's all too much. So I just say I'm all right, and let them pass. But the guy on the outside seat wants something, so now they're just there, taking his order and his money, and the cart is staring at me, and I'm suddenly thirsty.

*****

The flight back to England is a night-time one, and the eighteen days have gone so quickly I hardly noticed them. Probably because they were good, and stress-free, and nothing like living with her. But I still missed her. Or the idea of her – the version of her in my head that keeps me hanging on, as opposed to how it really is, which is awful. She's not been in touch much. Said that was missing the point. That we should be giving ourselves time to think, or to miss each other. But I know how that goes, because I've been home when she's the one on her travels, and I know she doesn't miss me. It's more like she weans herself off me – kicks the habit of me, and when she gets back, it's easier to start talking about the future, and always in a bad way. The airport is tiny, and there's hardly anyone here. Mine is the last flight of the evening, so there's only me and the rest of the people on their way to Stansted. Everyone looks tired, and no one is talking loudly. It's stormy outside. One of those new not-quite-hurricanes that's they're giving names to anyway. Really strange, dull names, like Storm Gerald, or Storm Craig. Lots of flights have been grounded today in Ireland and England. We're lucky ours is just delayed, they tell us. I'm going back to London, so there'll be night buses if I miss the last train. I hope so, anyway.

On the plane, even the Ryanair staff seem too tired to annoy us that much with all their perfume and scratch card shilling. There's an atmosphere I can't quite put my finger on. Maybe it's nerves. The plane's not that full, but not that empty either. A few spaces still left by the time they tell us to put our belts on. The take-off is a bit hairy – lights going on and off, everyone holding their breath as the nose goes up. People suddenly remembering they're Catholic in time to do the sign of the cross as we get off the tarmac.

The storm seems to have chased off all the clouds, because from my window seat I can see all the pretty lights on the ground, although not as many of them as there would be leaving Stansted. I try to figure out what I'm looking at, and it's kind of trippy, because from up here there's no way to tell scale, especially in the dark, so I don't know if one patch of criss-cross colours is really big farm, or a whole town. I have one of my own books on the Kindle App on my phone. Always feels funny reading my own book, but I don't really read other people's these days, and it's always good (and annoying) to find a typo in chapter seven, a year after publishing the thing. Part of me is always hoping some stranger will ask me what I'm reading, so I can either pretend to not be myself and recommend this great new author, or admit to being me, and have them be a little star-struck at having met a real writer. But that never happens, so it's irrelevant.

The storm is bad. I can hear the wind over the sound of the plane engines themselves, which I'm fairly certain is a new thing. People around me look tense, and the flight attendants are forgetting to engage their painted-on smiles as they go up and down the aisle, whispering to each other, or communicating in silent, worried looks. I'm trying to concentrate on the book, but every time there's a bit of turbulence I feel a little more like this might be it. Like we're all gonna die. It's a peculiar feeling. I want to die, often. But I don't know if I want to now. There's the kid to think about, and I think about her, thinking about dead me, and it's all quite morbid. And Emma; I think about her, wailing and gnashing her teeth at my imaginary funeral, and crying out that she was wrong, and she should have loved me more, or helped me more, or been less of a bitch to me, and that one feels sort of good and warm, but still bad. Cos I don't wanna go, really. Not yet. I want to be a fly on the wall at my own funeral a lot more than I actually want to die. I look around the cabin and wonder how many other people are thinking the same thing. The plane takes a particularly hard knock from Storm Gary, or whatever this one's called, the lights go down for a bit, and now I can actual hear people mumbling prayers, and someone's baby screeching, and someone else opening a can of something, cos maybe they've decided we're all gonna die, so they might as well have a really expensive Heineken, cos you can't take it with you. At least my last couple of weeks were fun, though. In a meaningless, not very memorable way.

The book is actually good. I haven't read it properly in a couple of years. Maybe it's just the fact that I'm going to die in a fireball somewhere over the Bristol Channel that's making it seem more impressive in an ironic way, but whatever it is, I'm enjoying the story, and the writing. It's one of the ones I write in slang, not in proper English, but even the ones I write properly are kind of sparse, I think to myself now. I tried reading a James Herbert book recently. And listening to an audiobook of my favourite novel ever – Lightning, by Dean Koontz, and with both of them, I kept noticing how many big words the writers used. Maybe it's because they were written in the 80s and 90s, and that's how people wrote back then, but maybe it isn't either, cos when I've tried to read modern books, or did some proofing for other wannabe writers, everyone still seems to be showing off how fancy their thesaurus skills are, and I'm just not like that. I don't think it's a conscious dumbing down on my part. I'm just very self-aware when I'm putting words down. It's like I'm simultaneously writing as the writer and reading as the reader, and whenever the writer in me uses a ridiculously flowery bit of prose, the reader in me does a face and thinks "Who's this prick think he is?". And that's how it's always been. Well, since I've been in my thirties, anyway. When I was nineteen and scribbling away at that first bestseller, when I still had dreams and goals, I definitely was this prick. But I didn't know it at the time. Reading over those faded, handwritten pages nearly 20 years on, I realise that the wisdom of knowing you're shit only really comes with time and hindsight. And I guess some people never get that wisdom. Especially if they have a book deal and millions of quid in the bank from it, because why would they? The captain, or whomever, comes over the PA to say something mumbled and staticky, and the Ryanair people make one last trip down the aisle to make sure everyone is strapped in, and no one's using a laptop that might fly across the cabin and behead someone. I check my seatbelt even though I haven't opened it since I sat down. The plane starts to dip, and there are whispered Our Fathers from pockets of holiness and desperation all around me. This is it. I switch off the screen on my phone just as the book is getting to another good bit, and promise myself that, if I survive this, I'm going to start writing properly again, cos I'm actually good at this, and I'm gonna finish some books, and make some money, and make Emma proud of me. And everything is gonna be okay, cos this is just a wake up call from God, and I

–

"JESUS!" The woman two seats over from me grabs onto the armrest as a flash of lightning goes past my window, and I try to figure out if I'm just ahead of the engine or behind it, or if that even matters. The lights go off completely in the cabin and the baby screams again. Everything is shaking, everyone is gasping and hold onto things. The lockers above our heads are rattling like crazy, then one of them pops open and sends an over-packed mini suitcase into the space between the seats. We're going down really fast, and I don't know if that's how fast you go down anyway, or if something's wrong. I can still hear the engines though, so we still have engines. Or we still have one engine. I look at my phone to see what time it is, for some reason, as if that's relevant. The lights outside the window on the ground are getting bigger and bigger, so we're close. The captain says something no one can hear or understand, and I wonder if he's said "Brace for impact!" and should I put my head between my knees, and if I don't do it, just cos I didn't hear him, will I die, and I look around at everyone else, and none of them are doing it, so I might have imagined it. But what if I didn't? Or what if I did, but I do it anyway, and it makes everyone else panic and think they have to do it? I wonder why now, when I'm literally about to die, I'm worrying about shit like that, but I guess I'll never change. And then the wheels hit the floor, the tyres screech, it feels like we skid across the tarmac for a full minute or two, and then we've stopped. And there's silence for a few seconds. And then it's like everyone on the whole plane, the cabin crew, and the two guys in the cockpit, all let out our breaths at the same time. And someone starts clapping, then we all start clapping, and fuck me, we're okay, we're safe, and we're home.

*****

The storm didn't just affect stuff in the sky, it seems. Once I'm through the departure lounge I find out that the motorway is closed due to falling trees, and almost all of the National Express coaches out of Stansted have been cancelled. I'm already about 45 minutes late, and I was going to be getting home at a late hour as it stands. I get panicky, cos I've obviously not got enough for the train out of here, and I'm not sure if that's even running anyway, considering it's five to midnight. I ask someone and they say there's a limited service out on the coaches to Stratford and Liverpool street, but only for people who pre-bought their tickets, which is usually not me, but tonight I've actually got one, cos I was worried if the ticket office would be open at night. I take my crumpled printout down to the coach bays, and they let me on, last but one to get a seat, and the driver says it's gonna take an hour and a half to get out of there (as opposed to the normal 50 minutes) cos he has to take some back roads and a different route, but I'm just so happy to be on the bus and heading somewhere, I couldn't give a shit. I have no credit so I can't call Emma, and there was no working WiFi either, so I couldn't even Facebook her. I'll call her from a payphone as soon as I get to Stratford, I think. There definitely won't be any tubes, but I think I can get the 34 bus from the station to Leytonstone. Or that might only go to Hackney/Clapton. And it might be the 38, not the 34. But either or, I'll get home tonight. Hopefully she'll have a left a key out somewhere for me. I want to see her more than anything, but I know how much she needs her sleep, and the last thing I want to do is piss her off, if I can help it.

It's really easy to piss Emma off. Or, maybe, it's really easy to upset the balance between us. It's insane, sometimes. We're so bad together, compared to other couples, in that way. The ease at which I can say the wrong thing and make her fucked off with me for a whole two or three days is more like the sort of thing you'd expect from a couple who've been together for 20 years and are just staying together out of habit than love, than a couple who've had barely three years, love each other ridiculously, and have the best sex ever. But that's how it is. That's how we are, and I hate it, even though I love her. And she hates it, even though she loves me. And I think it's her fault, she thinks it's my fault, and we never agree or compromise, we just grind each other down in a war of attrition until someone breaks, and we make peace, and we have great sex, and wonder what it was we were even upset about. Until next time, when it all happens again, and we make the same mistakes, and go around in circles, and no one ever learns, and it's all very sad, and my boundless optimism for our future is matched only by her relentless pessimism for it. A match made in hell and heaven, but what can you do?

The coach doesn't get into Stratford until well after one, and I can't find a phone to call the house. I need to find out which bus to take anyway, so there's no time for faffing around. I wish I had credit on my phone, or money in my bank to top it up from my card, but that's the story of my life. I drift, I subsist, I get along for the most part, and then every so often I get fucked by the little things that wouldn't be a problem to anyone with an actual income and savings; anyone who hadn't thrown their life away for whatever reason, not that I needed reasons. The bus I get on will take me three quarters of the way, and maybe I'll luck out and find a phone box there, and maybe the couple of quid I have in change will be enough to call her mobile, cos I realise I don't know our landline number, as the house is so new. Her house, the one she was going to move to without me, a few months ago. When she decided it was over, and then decided she wouldn't be able to do the move alone, so she let me back into her life on a sort of probationary basis, with no promises. The reason there were no promises this time was probably because of the last time, a year or so ago, before we broke up for those five months. She'd pretty much drawn a line under us, and then her dog got very sick, and needed round the clock care, and she couldn't take the time off work, so I stayed, and I helped, and she was grateful, and we were sort of back together. But, when the dog had recovered, and the dust had settled, she started getting itchy feet again, and I was out the door by New Year's day. She probably remembers the shittiness of that, and that's why she tacked on the 'no promises' clause. Sitting on this freezing London bus, trying desperately to get home to her, I think about how all the moving is done now. How we built the shed, tore up the carpets, sanded the floors; how I dug the garden, painted things, lugged things over from Homebase, etc. How she can pretty much do the rest by herself, and how there were no promises, and how she sent me away to Ireland so easily. And how, when I was there, her texts got colder and colder, and she got to the point of asking me flat out where I was planning on staying when I got back. That cut me in two. I told her I was planning on staying with my girlfriend (after the two weeks looking after Celia's that starts in the morning, I mean, and before the next house-sitting job, a week after that), and she told me it wasn't fair of me to 'use her house as a base between house-sittings', cos how was she supposed to move on with her life? I told her I didn't know her moving on was a thing that was happening, that I thought we were still together, and she told me she didn't want to have this conversation right now, and that was a week ago, and I haven't talked to her since, apart from the Facebook message I sent earlier, reminding her I was back tonight. That was seen, but there was no reply.

I think all these things about Emma the bitch, and how she's fucked me over, and used me, and whatnot, and it all makes for a great narrative, but I know as well that the reason she was kicking me out before the move was that she'd twice come home to find me passed out on the couch, surrounded by empty booze tins. And the reason she'd sent me to Ireland was that it had happened again, in the new house, and she couldn't take it anymore. But those things contradict my wallowing in self-pity, so I dismiss them as the bus pulls into the stop, and I see a payphone on the wall, and I wonder is it too late to call, but that doesn't matter, because I have to call, otherwise I can't go home.

She's nice when she comes on the line. I don't know if nice is the right word, but considering how cross I thought she'd be, getting woken at two in the morning on a work night, whatever she is sounds like music and poetry to me. And it's amazing to hear her voice again, anyway. Like two bare wires coming together to complete an electrical circuit. My heart swells, and I want to cry, but in that happy wedding cry way, not the sad one.

"Hello?"

"Hey. It's Tom. I'm really sorry about how late it is. There was crazy storms, the plane nearly crashed, then the motorway was closed, the coach took ages, I had to get the night bus, and I'm still not-"

"Hey. Hey, shhhh. It's okay. It's… just, it's late, and I'm sleepy, and I don't wanna wake up too much, in case I can't get back to-"

"Nononononononono, that's grand, I know, I understand. I'll be there in a half an hour. Is there a-"

"The key is under the recycling bin. I already did it. You can let yourself in."

"Oh. Okay, thank you so much. I'll get on this bus then, and I'll see you soon." I'm so excited. It feels like everything I was worrying about was nonsense. I think she missed me. Or, she didn't realise that she missed me, but now she does. She sounds so lovely. I can't wait to get to her.

"Okay. I might be asleep, but okay."

"That's fine. I'll see you then. Okay, bye. Love you." I say it before I realise I'm saying it, and I hate myself for it, cos I was on top there, and now I've handed the power over. If she doesn't say it back – if she hesitates, or dodges it, or does anything other than–

"Love you too. Bye bye."

That's good enough for me. I get the change from the little drawer in the phone and hop on the bus to Leytonstone, and the Oyster machine beeps after I swipe my card, to tell me that's the last time I can use it before topping up.

*****

In the front garden, I'm staring at the three wheelie bins next to the side gate and wondering which one is the recycling one, and if it was the recycling one she said the key was under, and I've sort of forgotten, cos I'm panicky and nervous and excited. I pull the brown one forward, without really thinking about it, and it catches on something and falls over with a massive bang. Fuck. No key under it either. Above me, the window of Emma's room slides open – she hates those windows, cos they're UPVC sash windows and she prefers wooden ones, to go with the faux-Victorian build, in a street full of genuine Victorian builds, but I like them, cos they're double glazed and they're easier to clean than wood – and I already wince before I look up, cos I can feel the tension. This isn't going to be Romeo and Juliet.

"For fuck's sake, I said under the recycling bin, Tom." Her voice is immediately at the pitch and tone of when she's having a genuine fight with me. It's a skill of hers – going from 0-60 in 2.5 seconds. She's like the Lamborghini of anger. My heart drops immediately, everything is already fucked, and I'm not even in the door yet. I don't say anything to her, cos I'm putting the brown bin back, and by the time I reach under the green one and find the key, she's already slammed the window shut. The street's even quieter than it normally is, but it's London Quiet, so there's still a hum of something – people not too far away, living 24-hour lives. I missed that noise over the last couple of weeks. I missed everything, even though I'm only realising it properly right this minute.

Upstairs, I come into the room without touching the light; I'm not crazy. I try to make as little noise as possible, like I can rewind how angry she seems with me by doing good deeds. I don't think it'll work. I just want to get into bed – with her, next to her, to smell her, and maybe feel her. I've missed that so much. And it's bed, so everything's always okay between us in bed. In our little bubble where the time flies past and nothing outside matters. I wonder if I should leave a t-shirt on; if that'll be less intrusive, and then I wonder why I'm thinking stuff like that at all. How can I be intrusive? She's my Emma. This is our bed. How can I be intruding here? Sure, in the rest of her life it sometimes feel like that. But not here. Here's the only place it always feels okay. No matter what's happened in the day; no matter how much we've fought, or argued. No matter what's been said. Once we go to bed, and I spoon in behind her and rest my hand on her hip – or lie side by side with her and put her head on my chest – everything gets okay again. Even if it's only until the morning, when she comes to her senses about me. I slide under the covers really quietly and without letting a draught in. I don't need to wake her up. I don't need to have sex with her, even though I would in half a second were she to initiate it. I just need to be here. With my girl. With the love of my life. I need to be here, in this bed, with Emma, and for her to want me to be here.

She smells just like she always does, and it's like inhaling the best drugs anyone's ever invented. I hesitate for a second, not knowing what to do with my hand, and I think to myself that that's silly, cos I always know what to do with my hand; there's never any awkwardness here. Never any doubt. She makes a noise next to me, but it sounds like a sleeping noise, cos she hasn't said anything to me since I came in, and I know she's well able to go straight back to sleep when she's tired, or she's had a few drinks. It's okay. It's fine. I'm here, that's what matters. My hand is still by my side. I'm almost spooning her, but I'm not. The natural thing where her bum moves into my crotch and my knees slip into the backs of hers hasn't happened yet. I take a deep breath, like I'm about to do something scary, and I put my hand on the flesh of her hip, a couple of my fingers dropping into the dip of her tiny waist. And she flinches. She's not asleep at all. I don't know how to process it. I've had the flinch from her before, plenty of times, but that was always outside, in the other rooms of the house; in the real world, not the bubble. I wonder if it was just some involuntary sleep reaction, something she didn't mean, and of course it was, of course it must be, cos why would she flinch from me touching her here?

Touching her now? I put my hand back where it was, and this time she doesn't just flinch, she shakes me off, and moves herself a few inches towards her edge of the bed. She says a single word:

"Don't."

And I roll over to my own side, so we're back to back, and put my index finger into my mouth, and bite down hard. Cos I can do physical pain, just not emotional pain. So, if my brain is distracted enough by the teeth breaking my skin, there's a good chance it will forget that I need to cry as hard as I do right now about the person breaking my heart.

Twenty

This Year, Thurles, Orla

Being comfortable; that's the thing with Orla. Of all the things I love about her, or I thought I loved about her, all those years when she was just a memory or an idea in my head, being comfortable is the thing that I like the most. And that's a new thing. That isn't something I've always appreciated or wanted. I wasn't looking at videos of Belinda Carlisle or Susanna Hoffs from the Bangles when I was a horny, confused twelve-year-old with funny twitchings in my underwear, thinking "Phwoar, I bet that bitch would make me really *comfortable*." It's an Emma thing. Cos I was never comfortable with her, when I wasn't in bed with her. Every single day with her, and especially weekends or holidays, where she'd be around for more of the time, it was always a ticking time-bomb waiting to go off. No nice silences. Just silences where it might turn into an argument; and if we got to bed that night before it did, that was a success. She made me into a low-expectation-having motherfucker, as Chris Rock would say.

And Chris Rock is a good reference point to have, cos I remember a routine of his where he says something about: do you ever catch your woman just staring at you, and how she's staring because she's thinking you weren't her first choice. There was a lot of truth to that with Emma, even though with her, it wasn't that there was someone in her past she would have chosen over me, given her time again. I was definitely her second choice, but her first choice was either an imaginary me who had a proper job, or that imaginary future other guy who'd her as much as I did, in all the ways I did – care about her like I cared about her, would look after her how I looked after her - but he hasn't fucked up his own life, financially speaking, and she can have a life with where she gets to spend all her own money, plus even more of it, cos future other guy is sharing half the bills. That guy was always way better than me, in her head. Even though he's probably a dick, because you can't have everything. But you can *want* everything, and in the end, Emma did. All I wanted was her, and I had her, but not the her I wanted either. The difference between our dilemmas was that, for her to have the version of me she wanted, I'd have to change a hell of a lot about my personality, and most of my past. A lot of which was impossible – I'd already changed so much. For me to have the her I wanted, all she'd have to do is accept me for who I am. A lot of which was possible, and she'd already changed so little, and even then, she resented me for having to do that.

But I couldn't do it. And she couldn't do it. And I understand that more, now. And I don't blame her for it anymore. Which I think is a step forward. But I haven't done it by myself. It's only meeting Orla and seeing how it can be better, and that me and Em were just a bad fit, no matter how well we fitted in some ways, that's meant I can let go, and feel okay, and wish Emma well. And that's progress, I guess. Where there used to be this pain in me, like a hot coal under my ribcage, every time I thought about her, and me, and the past, now there's just a sort of peace. Cos I realise I wasn't so hard done by, and she tried her best, but life isn't a romance movie, and it doesn't always have happy endings, and it's not always one person's fault. I'm more than half-way through my thirties, for God's sake, and I'm still growing as a person. I wonder when it is exactly that will stop. Or if I want it to stop; cos maybe it's a good thing that it keeps going.

I'm thinking all these things while I wait for Orla in a hotel room, not a hotel bar. In Tipperary, of all places. As far away as we could go, reasonably speaking, to make sure we didn't run into anyone we knew. To be safe. To relax. She kind of insisted I check in for us early in the day, and that she meet me up in the room. She didn't say why, but hopefully it's for a good reason. Of course it's for a good reason. She'll be here in a little bit. There's a bottle of Moet on the side, that I bought earlier; in a bucket with no ice yet. I wonder if *Moet y Chandon* is really tacky and chavvy, but that's the sort of thing I'd have worried about before, with Emma, cos I'd be trying to second-guess her upper middle class opinions on stuff. Looking back, that was just me; cos, in reality, she was always really grateful for the thought, when I bought something for her. She wasn't that snobby at all, relatively speaking. Well, unless it was clothes, cos I apparently didn't understand her style. So she'd just sort of grimace at them, and try to feign gratitude, and I'd get all tense and offended and take it to heart, and we'd have another horrible evening/few days.

Again, looking back now, I can see that was my fault. She had warned me. She was honest with me about it – instead of doing that thing where people expect you to read their minds - and it can't have been easy to bring up – not to me, and my little victim-mentality, girlfriends-are-bitches, it's never my fault, persecution complex attitude. But she did. And I still didn't listen, and kept *surprising* her with things she'd never wear in a thousand years. Cos I'd been told before I was great at picking out clothes, by girlfriends who weren't her, and I assumed that would apply to all future girlfriends. But it didn't apply to Emma, cos she dressed in a very particular way, in very particular fabrics, and she had enough clothes already, and even if she didn't, I couldn't afford the sort of things she'd have gone "Ooh!" over. I was still good at buying underwear for her, though. She did say that. She never grimaced at those presents; partly because my taste in them suited hers, partly because I made her feel beautiful and sexy, and she was going to enjoy wearing them with me later. I bought Orla some underwear the other day. Left them in a box at her work, addressed to her, no note. Inside, between the pretty baby blue boyshorts and the fancy matching bra, was a box of green and orange Tic-Tacs, though. So she got the message all right.

There's a knock on the door and my heart races, like I'm about to go on stage. I get up and open it, and she looks like the most beautiful thing I've ever seen. More beautiful than the last time I was with her; more beautiful than the first day I met her. I go to say something but she's already kissing me, and I close my eyes and it's like fireworks all over again – even without seeing her it feels like I've got more than the four senses left over – like God or the universe is giving me some more of them, just to appreciate this moment; to appreciate her. She's moving me back into the room towards the bed behind us, and I don't open my eyes, cos everything feels perfect, and I'm not afraid of falling. It's like a dance, where we both know where each of us is in that space, and no one can make the wrong move. The backs of my thighs are against the mattress now and I can feel her fingers opening the top button of my jeans, and I don't mind, cos even though I'm always the dominant one, always the initiator of things, in the rest of my sexual life, it's Orla, and there are no wrong answers when it comes to her. The skin of her hands is cold and warm against mine and our breathing gets louder and more frantic. She comes away from my mouth with one last nip of my bottom lip, dragging her teeth along it just hard enough to mean something and soft enough not to bite. In one smooth motion, she moves down onto her knees and I feel her fingers drag the jeans down off my hips and over my thighs. I haven't even had a chance to open my eyes before I feel myself inside her mouth – perfect, first time. No awkwardness, no clumsy scraping of teeth, just warm and wet and ridiculously nice. She steadies me with her hands on the backs of my thighs, and goes to work, totally in charge. But I don't mind. Cos it's Orla Keane, for Christ's sake, and I don't know what I've done to deserve her, but I'm not gonna jinx it now.

*****

"Cheers."

"Sláinte."

It's a bit after and we're sitting cross-legged on the bed, drinking the champagne that she went down the hall to get some ice for. I'm still reeling from what just happened, and my legs are still like jelly.

"So. Do I get the thumbs up, then?" she says, her nose twitching in a hopelessly cute way from the fizz in the bubbly.

"Huh?" *Brain no understand. Brain no work. Brain all broken from orgasm.*

"The blow-job, idiot. Worth the wait?" She gives me a wink. She's dressed in skinny jeans and a light, long-sleeved summer top, and she's doing that very Orla thing of pulling the ends of the sleeves over her fingers, like a kid in a school jumper that her mother bought too-big and told her she'd grow into it.

"Oh. Oh, Jesus, I – I mean, yes. Yes! Worth fifteen years of waiting, definitely." It's not exactly fifteen years, but no one's counting.

"Haha! I meant the wait from a few weeks ago, you fool. But I'll take that. Cheers again. My pleasure."

"Oh, I think it was definitely *my* pleasure," I say, a little wave rolling over me, just thinking about it again.

"Hey! I enjoyed it too, you know."

"You did?"

I'm not used to girls in Ireland being candid about sex. England, sure; I'd feel weird if one of them *didn't* say stuff like that. But when I'm back here, I sort of reset my expectations of women. When I'm chatting someone up in a pub I'm never thinking "I'm getting a shag tonight." I'm thinking 'Well, I might at least get a snog and a fumble, and a phone number. Then I can work at it for a while, and eventually something might happen, I guess. If I'm lucky.' But that's probably my own prejudices. For all I know, the modern Limerick girl is totally *DTF*, but like I said, I reset. It's the same as how the second I touch down in Shannon Airport, I immediately forget how to use my knife and fork in the right hands, cos when I lived here, I used them in the wrong hands. Or how I eat my veg first, potatoes next, and meat last, cos that's how my mum told me to do it when I was a kid.

"Of course. I – it's hard to explain. It's just – it feels good, making someone – making you – feel good. D'you get me? I liked it. I loved it."

"Well you did say 'Om nom nom' when you swallowed at the end, to be fair."

"Well that was just to add romance, like. I'm a classy bird."

"So classy." I want to immediately add something after that – something reassuring, so she knows how much I like her, I fancy her, I'm into her, but there's no need. That was one of the most infuriating things with Emma and me. We got the wrong end of the stick from each other a lot. It was a lack of trust. When you don't trust someone, they can't say funny, ambiguous things to you, cos you don't assume they are always gonna mean something benign and playful. With us, it was the opposite of that. We always assumed it was a barb or a slight, especially if we were around other people at the time. When you trust someone, that's never an issue. The best couples I've been around are the ones who can slag each other off for hours, and no one cringes around them, or feels awkward, cos we know they're mad about each other – we know they're going to leave holding hands and go back home to shag each other's brains out. Those are the couples I envy the most. And that's what it feels like with Orla, as if it wasn't already perfect enough. I look at her in the comfortable silence, and think how I want to tell her I love her, and feel how it feels to say it. And not just once; lots of times, for a long time. Forever. Then she says:

"I'm just gonna go into the bathroom and change into that stuff you got me. Get ready for Round 2, buddy. Tell your little friend for me, yeah?" nodding not so subtly at my crotch.

"Less of the *little*, eh?" I say, but it's a joke. I'm not insecure around her. She can say anything she likes, and there isn't even a wobble. It's totally different with her.

"Yeah, I don't think you have anything to worry about in that department, like," she says, hopping down from the bed in a way that's as cute as that shit she does with her sleeves, and she's gone, with her bag, into the little shower/toilet part of the room. I breathe out like I've been holding it in for an hour, but in a good way, like I'm on the best sort of drugs, and my little friend lets me know that there's no need to give him a wake-up call.

*****

Later, we're in the hotel bar, which isn't really a hotel bar, it's more like a proper pub, cos this isn't really a hotel, it's more like a fancy inn. When I walked in the door with her it was like something out of an Eric Clapton song – everyone *did* turn to see. And I loved it, cos when I'm caught up with all the feelings I have for her and my specific obsessions about her, I sometimes forget that she's so stunning, in conventional ways as well as all the nuanced ways that I think only I notice, and she's really made the effort, considering what she was wearing when she arrived. This sort of Midnight Blue coloured strappy, backless dress, that skims without clinging, and I wonder is there some top-secret dossier on all the things I love somewhere, and has someone let her have a peek at it.

"Nice here, isn't it? For out in the sticks, anyway." She's sat on a high stool opposite me, across a small round table a bit away from the bar. I'm drinking a Bulmer's Light from a longneck bottle, cos recently I've felt an actual purpose to trying to keep in shape. Mainly the prospect being naked around her. I hit the long walks and the weights pretty hard when I first came back, cos I'd bloated up over my last few months with Emma, and the weeks after that when I was drinking my feelings every day. I'd let it go for a while, before all this started up, but I'm one of those jammy bastards whose body remembers its muscle tone quickly, and who can drop half a stone of flab in a week if I just cut down on food and take out the booze. She just looks the same as she did when she was a teenager. Better, really. Cos girls are cute and women are sexy. That said, she's still cute, as well as sexy. I don't know if she does something specifically to keep herself in such good nick, or if she was just born perfect. If it's the latter, I'm not surprised at all.

"It's, ah, got its charm," I say, subtly motioning towards the fella in the corner who seems to be drinking his Guinness out of a jam jar.

"Haha, yeah. Lots of character. How are you?"

"How am I?" Feels like an odd question at this point of the evening.

"How do you feel, I mean. About… everything. Are you okay?" She's asking me this like I'm the one cheating on my husband, or something. I'm fine. I'm more than fine.

"I feel great, Orla. Better than great. I can't even – this is amazing, all of this. And all of that, upstairs? Jesus, I – I don't even know how to-"

"All right, all right. I didn't ask for your fucking life story," she says, and pokes out her tongue at me, and I laugh, and think again how that might have gone very badly if it was Emma I was sitting here with. We were so wrong for each other. How did I not know?

"You're not too old to go over my knee, you know…" I say, and it sounds familiar to me, like I've said it before. I probably have.

"Ooh. Can we do that for Round 3 then?" she says, raising her eyebrow in a way that makes me want to finish up my drink right now and drag her up the stairs by her hair like a caveman in a cartoon.

"I'm still recovering from Round 2, to be honest."

"Yeah. Right, your next drink is a Lucozade. With a Red Bull chaser. Mama wants a new pair of shoes. And by 'Mama', I mean 'me'."

"And by 'a new pair of shoes'?" I'm enjoying this so much. I'm enjoying her so much. I never want this to end.

"I mean, 'sexual intercourse', baby."

"In the missionary position for the sole purpose of procreation?"

"I love it when you talk filth." She sucks some of her vodka and lime up through the straw, and it makes a noise that says there's no vodka or lime left, and it's time for a refill.

The sex had been mind-blowing. I wasn't expecting it to be rubbish, or anything. But someone once told me that you had to 'have at least three dances before you know your partner's moves', and I always sort of believed that in the past. But it hadn't been like that with Emma (although it did get progressively better, so I suppose there's some truth to it), and it definitely wasn't like that with Orla. It helped that we'd already sort of done it a few weeks ago, I suppose. I could tell back then that we were totally compatible. But there was still a lot that could have gone wrong. It didn't, though. Round 2, as she called it, wasn't complicated or show-offy, or anything that felt like a one-night stand, or Stranger Sex. She came in from the bathroom wearing the things I'd bought her, and we didn't say a word. She sat on my lap, facing me, put her thighs around my waist, and kissed me. My hands were on her arms, then her shoulders, then fingertips trailing down her spine, firm hold on her hips, the two of us grinding against each other like teenagers who hadn't gone all the way yet, and weren't going to tonight either. And we kept that up for ages, because there was something fitting about it – something that felt like it belonged back then – in a different reality, where we'd actually got together.

Every time she touched me it was perfect. No annoyed mumbling from me to hint she was doing something wrong, or no her frustrated guiding of me to the right place with her words or her hands. We just did it. There was no real foreplay; we'd done that bit weeks ago, and earlier tonight, and in our heads for more than a decade. We went from sitting like that, to lying down, always kissing, never stopping, hands always landing where the other one's mind wanted them to land next. I didn't even take off her bra, partly cos I loved how great it looked on her – how much it fitted her (especially since I'd just guessed the size, not asked her, high fives all round), partly cos there's something just inherently *naughtier* about taking off someone's knickers first – doing it in the wrong order – I don't know why that is, but it works for me. And, from the tone of her little gasp when I did it, it worked for her too. I slipped a couple of fingers gently in to check what I already knew was a certainty, using it to lube myself up, and pushing inside her for the first time ever. What happened after that, the details are unimportant, really. The fact that it happened is the main thing, and as I watch her come back from the bar, I can't wait for it to happen again. But I can wait, too, and that feels important. Cos I'm just as happy sat here trading jokes and winks as I will be in a couple of hours, upstairs, trading God knows what else with her, and that makes me feel good, and I want to tell her, but I don't need to, cos she already knows, cos she feels that way too.

*****

"Well?" some bloke at the bar says to me, in that Irish way that I grew out of over fourteen years of assimilating into British culture, but picked up again within a few weeks of coming back.

"How'rya?" I say back, not caring how he actually is – but, *when in Tipperary.*

"That your missus over there, is it?" he asks, not looking at Orla, but obviously talking about her, unless there's been an atrocious misunderstanding. I wonder what I should say back, for a second, then:

"It is, yeah." It feels even better than I'd imagined it would. I could get used to this. Very easily. The barman puts the drinks down in front of me and I give him a nod, handing over the funny looking note of a currency I'm still not used to thinking is real money.

"Jaysus. You're a lucky man, d'you know that? *Cailín áilinn ar fad, a tá sí,*" he says, mixing English with some primary school level Gaeilge that even I can understand.

"*Ar fad, ar fad, is ea. Cailín go hAn-mhaith,*" I say, not sure if I made any sense, but knowing the message will get through anyway, from the tone, like I'm some sort of linguistics horse whisperer.

"Haha, *is ea, is ea*. Look after her now, yeah? She's one you'd want to look after, shur. Not a lot of ones like that around, there isn't. Cheers," he says with a big toothy smile that's bigger on smiles than it is on actual, countable teeth.

"I will of course," I reassure this fella who I've never seen before in my life, or probably will again, cos I don't want him losing any sleep. Back at the table, Orla's playing with her phone; first time I've seen her even take it out all day. She puts it back in her handbag when I sit down with the drinks.

"Making friends, are we? Cheers."

"Cheers. Ah, yeah. I think so. It's either that, or I've pulled."

"Oh? Well I don't think I want him coming upstairs with us. So, you're gonna have to choose. Me or him? What's it gonna be?"

"Hmmm. Don't rush me. How long have I got?" In the corner, someone starts playing a fiddle, because of course they do.

"Pfffffft, I'm not sure. What is it you need to debate, exactly? What's that *bastard* got that I don't, eh?"

"You'd be surprised. I mean, do *you* have any arable land? Road frontage? Didn't think so. Don't be dissing Worzel Gummidge over there, love. Beauty's more than skin deep. I like a man with substance."

"I like a man with teeth."

"Women in their thirties, eh? Choosy bitches. Always pricing themselves out of the market."

"Really, though; I don't do threesomes. Well, not with men anyway," she says. Her shoe is off and she's curled the arch of her foot around the back of my calf. It feels nice.

"Yeah?" If it was at all possible to pique my interest in her any more, that would probably have been the peak of the piquing. But the piquing already peaked ages ago, so now it's just some words she's saying.

"Well, I don't do threesomes with women either, don't get me wrong," she says, and again, it doesn't matter. I don't care.

"Just animals then, yeah?"

"*You're* an animal." The rubbing on the back of my calf turns into a little kick to the shin.

"I know, right? Raaaaaaaaaawr," I say, doing a tiger claw at her with my hand.

"You fucking eejit, you. Anyway, yes. Threesomes. Never done one. Open to the possibility though," she gives me a look but I can't tell what it means and it doesn't matter.

"You are?"

"Well, yeah. In theory. When we're in our forties, like, and we're bored of just shagging each other."

"Nah, I'll never be bored of shagging you," I say, without planning it, and the sincerity of it crosses over, cos she blushes, and then tries to compose herself again.

"Awwww! I bet you kind of sort of even meant that, bless you."

"I did. You know that, though." I don't have to reassure her. She does know it. She's just pretending not to, cos she can, and she knows I won't ever misread her, or her jokes.

"Hmmm, yeah, I pretty much do. That's great, isn't it?"

"All of it's great. You're great. We're great-"

"Like Kellog's Frosties are great?" she says, and now it's her doing the tiger claw at me.

"Just like that. I love you, by the way." I say it and it's like someone sucked all the wind and noise out of the airlock on a spaceship, and I'm terrified, like I'm standing on the edge of an abyss, and the whole room seems to have disappeared around us, along with all the people. And I look at her, and her eyes are wet.

"I love you too. So much. How fucking crazy is that?"

"My mama always said, crazy is as crazy does," I say, doing possibly the worst Gump impression anyone's ever done in history.

"You literally ruin everything," she says, smiling, and reaching for both my hands with hers.

"Make it up to you?" I say, pointing at the exit with a nod, because all I want to do now is get her alone, and out of those clothes, and into our bed.

"I thought you'd never ask."

*****

The next morning isn't like anything I've experienced before, or anything I expected to happen on this occasion. It's definitely not like anything I was afraid of happening – guilt, second thoughts, sadness. We wake up, we find each other's arms straight away, and mouths shortly after. We stay locked together for ages, we have amazing sex again, even though we must have had so much of it the night before that we can't have had more than three hours' sleep. And it feels so good, and perfect, and natural, and right, that there's no room for bad feelings. No space for doubt, or guilt, or any of that. And we've said 'I love you' so many times throughout the night that, if it was any other phrase, it'd be boring by now. But every time I say it to her or she says it to me, it actually gets more exciting. I guess that's how you know it's real.

We don't have any deep discussions, even though we know there's deep discussions to be had – about the future, about our future, about what to do next. But we only have this room until Midday, so we make an unspoken pact to spend every minute of that time no more than an inch away from each other, whether we're just talking, or doing other stuff. The smell of her is everywhere on me, and I think to myself that I have to meet her again soon, cos that'll be gone after my next shower, and I've spent too long with it around me, like a second oxygen, and I need it just as much as the regular stuff. But I don't need to say any of that to her, or have her say it to me, cos we know. We know without speaking a word, and I'm in heaven as I wave her off in her taxi, even though it's already hell to be without her.

Twenty-one

Last Year, London, The Last Day

I have to go. This isn't a dress rehearsal. This is it. I've been at Celia's for two weeks – looking after the house and the animals - then couch-surfing until the day of the flight home – calling in old favours, hooking up with new women from the dating sites – playing it by ear, flying by the seat of my pants, all those clichés. But now today's the day, which I suppose is another cliché. I'll add it to the list. The flight isn't until nine in the evening, so I have plenty of time to kill.

I'm back at Celia's for one last cleaning and dog walking job, same as any other Wednesday – my little Housewife Pin Money job, as Em called it. I do that defence mechanism thing of physically shaking my head to get out the bad thoughts when I think about her just then. I'm still so raw. I haven't seen Celia today, she was still at work when I left. I needed to leave before she went because I've already had a skin full, the day that's in it. She's a bit pissed off with me anyway. Something to do with me shagging people in her house while she was away. I did explain that me shagging them somewhere else would have meant I wouldn't be there, looking after the pets, but she wasn't having any of it. It was more the shagging them in her bed thing that pissed her off, really, and that's understandable. It was really only Millie anyway, and she's not going to be coming back any time soon. Hard to explain that, though. I didn't say sorry properly in the end, just brazened it out and pretended I'd done nothing wrong. That never actually goes well for me, I should stop doing it, really. Either way, she's annoyed with me, and it's my fault, so it's probably for the best I didn't see her today. She's been very, very good to me. I'm a fucking cunt sometimes. Something else I need to work on. Another day, maybe. I'm busy today.

I haven't eaten anything, and I need to, if I'm going to be sober later and not miss my flight. And if I want to keep on drinking. I'm in the corner shop now, looking at some big bags of corn snacks and crisps, but I don't feel like I can stomach them. Or maybe I can, and it's just that usual battle between my drunk brain and my sensible brain, where one wants to do the right thing and the other doesn't want anything to get in the way of doing the wrong thing. The drunk brain is winning, cos when I get to the counter I just have some cans of pre-mixed Gordon's and tonic, and nothing resembling actual food. I can get some chips in one of the chippies up the road, I think. That'll be real food, kind of. Better for me than crisps, maybe. The guy behind the counter here knows my face. He knows I drink a lot too, but he's like all of them, he never judges. Or, at least, he doesn't to my face. I get some fags as well, even though I have some, because I'll be in Stansted later, with who knows how much time left doing nothing, and I'm not paying those airport prices for ten ciggies.

I'm starting to realise that I can't stop anything. Or if I can stop some things, I can't stop everything. Most of all, I can't stop myself. Every night when I've got fucked off my brain, after I pass out, and wake up again about four hours later with that weird clear head thing (the eye of the storm before the craziness and the headaches kick in and you're half awake, half asleep until noon, thinking a thousand thoughts a second) I've told myself tomorrow will be different and tomorrow will be the day I fix everything, make myself perfect, get it all back on track. That never changes (or works). I put on some 8-hour white noise track from YouTube and black out the world until I'm okay and sane again, or at least until the pounding in my skull stops. And when I come to, it all seems possible for a few minutes. It's a new day, so I haven't smoked. And I haven't had a drink yet, of course. And I've not eaten anything, so I'm not wrecking my body with shite. And, well, I haven't done a lot of things, cos I haven't done anything. And then, slowly but surely, things happen, one by one. First, the demons come – the self-doubt, the self-loathing – anything for Nick O'Tine to get his oar in and convince me that we'll give up that tomorrow instead. Once that's fucked, I need a coffee to go with it, so giving up caffeine is out the window too. And, of course, once I've done the usual four cans of cheap energy drink and three big mugs of strong coffee, I'm too wired to function, so I need a drink to bring me down. After that, I'm too drunk, so I need to eat something, and what I eat is usually shit. At least when I was still with Emma, dinner would be something healthy. I'd still have some shitty carbs before she got home anyway though, so that's a moot point.

You've got to drink fast. There's no slow build-up to getting fucked. Even if you're slamming cans of 8.4% tramp fuel, it's still not fast enough – you have to neck the first couple (I have the gag reflex bypassing skills of a veteran porn actress at this stage), cos that means the balance of water and alcohol in your body gets upset quicker – or booze in your bloodstream – I'm not a doctor. But I know it works. And I'm an expert on the results, not the science behind them. It's always a mistake. Cos I don't stop drinking for a while after those. I just slow down slightly, if constantly drinking whatever is in front of me until I have to go out to buy more, or I pass out, can be counted as slowing down. There's no real slowing down for me. The nearest I come to it is gulping down stodgy food as a sort of de facto Hoover dam for the oncoming obliteration, and I must be pissed now, cos I'm thinking like the sentences from bad pulp fiction, or a YA novel.

Sometimes I manage to be good. To give up things. But never everything. And when you don't give up all the things, it's like you leave Hansel and Gretel style breadcrumbs for the other ones to find their way back out of the forest – although, in my analogy, those crumbs lead straight back to the witch's house. If I haven't had a drink all day, I'll smoke more, half as a compensation, half as a reward. If I haven't smoked, I'll buy all the junk food in the world, and binge on it, like it fills the square hole when all I want is triangular pegs. I rewind my own thoughts with a sort of 1980s movie sound effect of a Dictaphone, and realise I sometimes think entirely in tortured metaphors. Maybe I should have been an erotica writer.

That last morning with Emma, three weeks ago, was the worst. And yet, it was practically unremarkable. I hardly slept. Spent most of the night awake, sad, feeling like I was being tortured, because the only thing I wanted; the only person I wanted, was inches away, but I couldn't even touch her. I suppose I deliberately stayed awake, wallowing in my sadness, to make it worse for myself. I've always been one for melodrama, so if you're gonna go, I guess you should go big. I must have dozed off eventually, cos she wasn't in the bed when I opened my eyes. I pulled on some clothes and rushed downstairs, panicking, and saw that she was still there, and instantly didn't know if that was good or bad, cos I was still panicking. She hardly said a thing; she just went about her morning routine – the one that's always perfectly timed, with nothing in it that's surplus to requirements, not even breakfast, but she still always leaves slightly late. I make the mistake of offering to make her breakfast, cos I dunno why, really, since I know she never has it, and I know she never breaks her routine – probably a thing I get from my mother, who's always trying to feed you to cheer you up. But Emma didn't need cheering up. She didn't want to be cheered up; not by me. It was her choice to stay angry at me.

When she was leaving, I gave her a pathetic, doe-eyed look, and I saw something in her crack for a second, and she came back across the massive, spacious kitchen that she'd coveted so much when we were viewing places in the Spring. The one that she had now, or that we had, up until a short while ago, even if I didn't pay for it. I helped make it a home, though. You can't buy that. She came close to me and gave me a hug, and then a kiss on the lips that I felt her pull away from involuntarily after a few long seconds, as if she was afraid the drug of me was going to get in her system again, and scupper her plans to – her plans to do whatever it was she was planning. It hurt almost as much as the flinching the night before, but at the same time I was pathetically grateful for the kiss itself, and the hug, and just the nearness of her. She stood back, looked at me for a minute, then said:

"Are you still drinking and smoking? I saw pictures of you on Facebook, at Dave's house, with Valerie. You looked drunk. What's the story? I don't know what's going on with you anymore. Weren't you supposed to be giving up? Turning over a new leaf? You say one thing to me and... Is there a-"

"I was – you told me to go over and enjoy my-" The words come out all squeaky and adolescent, with no conviction or confidence in them. I'm broken.

"Never mind. I'm late. I'll see you... I'll see you whenever." She knows I'm starting my two weeks minding Celia's today, so it's not that dramatic or harsh a statement, but it still feels like one.

"Okay. I... I *love* you." I know straight away that it's a mistake to say it. You should never say 'I love you' like you're saying a silent 'but' before it, any more than you should say it with an audible 'but' after it. Those are my own rules. I should know them by now. She turns away and walks to the front door, throwing me another single word as she leaves.

"Bye."

I didn't cry after she'd gone. I wanted to, but it just wouldn't come, cos I was angry as well as heartbroken, and the anger was winning. I went and poured myself a gin and tonic, and sat down to write her a text. I can't remember the exact words, cos I deleted it since then, and I spent the next 48 hours straight drunk out of my brain; but the long and the short of it was that I'd had enough, and she didn't have to worry any more about being 'responsible' for me, and about it not being fair that if we broke up I'd be homeless, and she'd feel guilty. I told her that nothing could be as bad as how I'd felt all that night before, lying next to her, knowing she didn't want me there, and that I'd go to Celia's for two weeks, and after that I'd figure something out. I told her I loved her, and I'd miss her, and I'd never forget her, but she was never gonna be happy with me, and knowing that, I was always gonna feel like nothing because of it. And I deserved more than that – than feeling like nothing – especially when I'd only ever been kind to her, and tried to make her happy, and she'd ignored all that and concentrated on the things I wasn't giving her. I laid it on pretty thick, looking back. Totes one-sided, and with no right to reply, as I turned my phone off straight after. Cos I've always been one for melodrama, so if you're gonna go, I guess you should go big.

Back in the present, in reality, in Wood Green, I'm down in the park. It's called Duckett's something or other, it says so on a metal arch thing as you walk through, but that's the only real perimeter to it – there's no fences around it to protect it from the road, so it's the sort of place Emma wouldn't like me walking our dogs, but Celia's okay with me walking hers here. I keep her dog on that extendable leash thingy at all times though, cos her dog is mental, and I don't know it enough to guarantee that it won't run off on me, so it's academic. It's a biggish park – right across from Turnpike Lane tube station, which I've spent a lot of time in over the past year, as everything in my life seems to flow through there by accident. It's how I used to get from Hackney to Celia's, via Highbury and Islington; it's also on the way to Millie's place. There was some girl with blue hair I met that time I was single for five months – she lives in the next street behind Celia. The redhead girl I met on okcupid who's jolly and northern and likes to take in waifs and strays and collects Lego figures – she lives here too, but up the other way, up a hill that Celia calls 'the ladder'. I've had lots of adventures in Haringey, or in Finsbury Park. I know the area well enough now to give tube directions off the top of my head to tourists. Not bad for a filthy immigrant. Wood Green is choc a block with immigrants. That's why there's so many great places to get cheap takeaways here. And, up that road, towards the Overground that takes me to Leytonstone, every other building is a lovely middle eastern restaurant, and it's always alive with noise and fun every evening, cos the Turks and the Mediterranean people there love to eat out with their whole families, regardless of the hour, and the vibe is always good, cos they're Muslims, so no one's boozing and getting lairy, it's just laughing dads, chattering mums, and cute, runny-aroundy kids. My favourite things about London usually have nothing to do with actual Londoners. But I guess we're all Londoners, when we live here. Except me, anymore. Because I have to go today. And I don't want to.

There's three parts to the park. The bit where you go in first, by the traffic lights and junction, which is always a busy part. The middle, which has an adventure playground that's also always busy, either with parents and their small kids in the morning, or lots of loitery teens in schoolbags and uniforms after three. Then there's the third bit, which is a big open space, which usually has one or two people giving their dogs a good old run about, and the odd tramp sitting on one of the two benches to the right. Today I'm the odd tramp on the bench. I walked the dog earlier. I picked up some very strong cider on the way down here, in that way of mine where it doesn't matter how drunk I already am, I always need to be drinking something while I wait for the effects of the last one to hit me. If I don't have something more to drink, I panic, cos maybe that means I've stopped for the day/evening/night, and I never do that. I stop when I pass out, usually. That's become standard procedure. On those tickbox parts of internet dating profiles, where it gives you a few options under 'Drinking', it only says things like 'Yes, Sometimes, Socially, Rarely, Never'. There's no option that says 'Alone, until I lose consciousness and wet myself'. Which is a pity, cos that might get me some higher match percentages.

I'm not the only one on a bench down here. There's two shifty looking blokes in black puffa jackets on the other bench, with angry looking haircuts. I don't know what the marketing for puffa jackets is, but I feel like, no matter where you go, for the last 25 years, if you see someone wearing a puffa jacket, you're probably going to get stabbed. A sweeping generalisation on my part, obviously. But I like sweeping generalisations. They're quicker. And anyway, I've lived in places where everyone wore puffa jackets, and none of them looked like they weren't going to stab you. The proof is in the pudding. Except it isn't; *the proof of the pudding is in the eating*, is the real thing you're supposed to say, but no one cares about that sort of thing in our new, *post-truth* world. This cider is way too strong, even for me. I say 'even for me' as if I'm some sort of seasoned drinker, but I'm not. I'm shit at drinking. I just do it a lot. There's a difference. The puffa boys are getting up now, which is good, cos when they leave, I'll be less nervous. Except they're not leaving. They're coming over to me.

*****

Of course, I've tried not to contact Emma. That's what they say you should do, the people on the internet. Stay away, give them time to miss you. I already knew that, though. I already had to do those things while I was still with her, cos she'd get annoyed at me for texting her or emailing her while she was working. Anything that reminded her I didn't have a real job and was sitting around, wasting my life, when she had no spare time, and would love some, so she could do all the things she wanted to do. She brought that up a lot – her lack of spare time. Even when I was living with Andie for five days out of seven and only saw Em at the weekends, I was still infringing on her spare time, when she could have been making a bookshelf out of old apple boxes, or looking on eBay for antique school chairs. I always seemed to be in the way. We did spend time together, but it was usually her dragging me off to do something, or to meet people she wanted to meet, so I could sit there, sober, while everyone else drank. Whenever we really did spend time – just me and her, wasting the day, watching TV shows, eating nice food I cooked, it still felt like she was watching the clock and wondering what things she could be *achieving* if I wasn't there, taking up time and space. I tried to understand. I constantly listened, even when nothing was being said, and made little changes, did little things to please her. But it was all one way. I'd change, or do something to surprise her (not too much of a surprise – a good surprise was usually, 'Hey! I read your mind via telepathy and figured out you'd really like to go do this thing that only you want to do, so we're going to do that thing today! Surprise!'), and she'd like that, but she never did anything like that in return. But then again, I never really wanted to do anything interesting, I just wanted some time with her, doing nothing, so maybe she had a point.

My stuff is still at hers; a little bit of stuff, but also all I own in the world. I took a small suitcase with me, and that's probably going to be the new everything I own in the world, because I can't really go back. I unfriended her on Facebook, without blocking her, and the other day I noticed that I had an event coming up, which was weird, cos I didn't remember saying I was going anywhere. Turns out she'd added me to something before the split, and had forgotten to take me off after. It was a housewarming/slash birthday party, in Leytonstone. I guess she has the house in tip-top shape now, no small thanks to me, and it's time to show it off. I dunno why that event notification killed me so much, but it did. I still didn't cry. I still haven't at all. But that – well, it's like – she can warm the fucking house all she likes, with all her fancy friends, and prosecco, and a fire pit in the garden that I dug and planted for her. It's not going to be a home anymore, without me. I'm bitter now, and I don't like it. It's to be expected, though. There's stages, and you can't fast track your way through any of them. But I've at least tried not to contact her, so that's something at least.

*****

I'm in the puffa boys' flat, or one of their flats, I'm not sure which. They have names now; Grant and Danny – both of them are proper Essex geezers, even though they're from London, but it's all the same, really. They came over and asked me for a fag to make a joint, and we got talking. I wasn't sure if they were friendly or not, but I chatted away like the drunk that I am, offered them a can each, and we ended up walking back here, cos they said they had some drugs, and I have ages yet before I have to get to the airport, and I really want some drugs.

Their place is above a kebab shop, around the corner from the tube station. It looks like a drug dealer's flat, and it almost definitely is. Grant is the older one, even though he's really short. Danny is his younger cousin. I'm riding on a wave of drunkenness, cos these are the last sort of people I'd ever associate with while straight, but that's what drink does sometimes. Gets you into adventures. Sometimes it gets you killed. But I'm still alive, so far.

"So, what's your poison, Steve mate?" says Grant. I've done the Steve thing again. That's a worry. The Steve thing hardly ends well, but maybe this time will be different. You have to have hope, don't you?

"Eh, I like anything. Everything," I say.

"Weed?" says Grant, again.

"Everything except weed."

"Hahaha, you're mental, mate," he says, in that way stupid people call you mental or mad, when you haven't said anything remotely insane. Danny's playing Grand Theft Auto on a PS4 with what must be a 50-inch plasma telly. Apparently, crime *does* pay. The glass coffee table between us and him has so much drugs on it I'm almost getting high just looking at it. Pills, powders, veritable *sacks* of cannabis, and some funny looking glass pipes; thin, with a bubble at the end.

"Yeah. Oh, I used to take these," I say, picking up the only legitimate narcotic on the table – a blister pack of capsules.

"Thorazine, mate? You some sort of schizo, is it? Hahaha. Ay, Dan! Dan!"

"What?" says the younger fella, pausing the game in the middle of a car chase.

"Steve here's on the Thorazine, mate. He's a fackin 'eadcase, innit. Hahahahaha."

"Yeah, mate. Cool," Danny says, and unpauses with a screech of tires from the Dolby surround. He's not much of a chatter. I'm not sure when I'm supposed to come back into this conversation.

"Yeah, I… I used to. Don't take them anymore," I say, cos that's true.

"Oh. Cured, was you?" Grant is picking through the baggies of powder on the table like a music geek looking through old vinyl in a record shop. It's mostly white stuff, or off-white crystals, but there's a few brown bags too, which I assume is heroin. I think about how I've never tried it – apart from that time with the opium and the traffic light dragon – and then I try and shake the thought, cos that'd be a road I'd go down and never come back, given my personality.

"Yeah. Something like that." They'd put me on them a long time ago. I must have been eight years old. Never told me what they were for, just said I had to take them, and they'd help me sleep at bedtime, and not have so many bad dreams. I had been having a lot of bad dreams, after the Fiona thing, at the seaside. I'd kept taking them all the way up to a few years ago. By then, I had the internet, and could look up what they were for. They were for lots of things – bi-polar, dissociative personality disorder, borderline, and schizophrenia. None of which I actually had, I decided, so I just came off them, right before I moved to Jim's. The doctor I had back then was tied up with the old address, with the ex and the kid, so I never got any letters asking me why I hadn't come back for check-ups, or why I hadn't picked up my prescription. I didn't miss the tablets anyway. One night, when I was in Jim's, drunk, I had this weird, almost religious experience. I was standing in front of the mirror, not looking at it, just doing something else. And I looked at myself, but without making eye contact with my own eyes. Sort of like the way you do those Magic Eye pictures. I looked through myself, with unfocused eyes, and when they refocused by themselves, it was like I was still looking at me, but someone else was looking back at me. And I'm not sure if I heard a voice out loud, or in my head, but it said 'You're doing fine. You're doing okay. You're doing the right thing'. And I didn't know if it was God, or if it was me, but I believed it. That was the night I'd come back from the place with the trees under the bridge, so I kind of needed that reassurance. I needed that voice. I've tried to do that mirror trick again, lots of times, to see can I see that person again – whoever he is; maybe it's another me, maybe it's God, or the Devil. Maybe it's Steve. Maybe Steve is God. Maybe I'm God. But I've never been able to see it again.

*****

I don't know how long has passed since I got here. I'm sucking on one of the glass pipes now, and burning the bubble end with a lighter, like Grant showed me. I don't know what this drug is. I think it's Meth. Or maybe Crack. Every time I ask someone they tell me and then I forget and when I ask them again they just laugh, and I've stopped asking now, cos there's a voice in my head telling me that the next time I ask, they won't laugh, they'll be angry, and I'll be in trouble, and I don't want to be in trouble. Whatever this stuff is, it's amazing, like nothing I've ever taken before. It's like MDMA, but a million times stronger. I don't even feel like I'm on Earth anymore. Or in my own body. Grant's had some too, and so has Danny, now. I like them. I love them. These past three weeks have been a living hell, and now I suddenly feel great – more than great. Nothing feels bad when I think about it. Not Emma, not Millie, not that tramp whose name I've forgotten, not the guy from Grindr that I met up with two days ago and strangled in the park – not cos he was gay, just cos it was the quickest, safest, most anonymous way to get someone new to... well, there's no need to go into the details. I'm glad I'm leaving today though, because Millie's been in the local news – missing, of course, not dead; the tramp has definitely been found by now, but there's been nothing on him. The Grindr guy, he might have been found too – I don't know. And there's nothing to connect any of them – nothing to say they were all done by one person, cos there's no pattern, they all happened in different places, etc. But I connect them all, so it's better that I'm going, just in case. Just in case I'm not the chosen one. I don't know why I used that phrase, or if I've used it before. I can't remember things, sometimes. Or I remember them wrong. Sometimes I remember stuff that hasn't happened, as clear as if it really did. And then I don't know if it did or it didn't, cos how can you tell? That's the definition of insanity, when you can't extinguish fantasy from reality. I thought the wrong word there. I think it's cos I was staring into space, and the only thing in my field of vision was that red thing for putting out fires that I can't remember the name for. I make myself laugh, then I stop, in case anyone heard me. I look around.

Danny's in a soft chair, looking really relaxed, with one of the pipe things in his hand. Grant is in the doorway between here and the next room, talking to someone on his phone. He's doing a weird, soft voice, so I think he's talking to a woman. I need a piss, so I ask Danny where the toilet is, and he doesn't look at me or say anything, but somehow I know where it is anyway. I go past Grant in the doorway, and it's a tight squeeze, even though I'm short, and he's tiny. He stops the conversation for a second and looks at me with really glassy blue eyes.

"Everything all right, mate?"

I look back at him with what must be a very fucked expression, cos he chuckles and raises both his eyebrows at me. I can barely stand up, but only when I'm standing still. When I move, it's like I'm gliding.

"Yeah, man. I'm sound", I say, and carry on past him. In the background I can hear him talking about me to the person on the other end of the phone. A girl. I could do with a girl right now. Whatever this shit is, it's making me feel super fucking horny, as well as happy. I lock myself in their toilet and sit down on the seat. A few seconds later I've got my dick out, beating the living hell out of it, and every single stroke feels as good as the orgasm from a normal wank. If wanking feels this good, I can only imagine how good sex feels. I close my eyes and think of fucking Emma, and then that gets too bittersweet, so I switch to Millie, and that's good for a while, til I remember, so I go back to a few years ago, and Ellie, and that works, cos that was great, and dirty, and filthy, and beautiful, and it had a happy ending. When I come it feels like I'm shooting out bullets of fire, and my whole skull almost boils with the pleasure. This drug is fucking amazing. I clean up with someone's facecloth that I run under the tap, cos I'm too wrecked to find the bog roll.

On the way back to the living room, I have a nose in the kitchen. My eyes almost pop out of my head (they were sort of doing that anyway I think, to be fair) when I see their countertop/breakfast bar. It's wall to wall death, even more than the coffee table inside the other room. Hunting knives, baseball bats with nails in them, machetes, actual swords, an axe, and, right at the end, a real gun. A pistol. Black thing. I don't know what it's called, so I go to have a closer look at it, see if it has a name or something, when a voice comes from behind me.

"Oi oi! What you doin' in 'ere?" It's Grant, and I'm not sure if it's an angry voice or just his normal voice. I can't tell right now. I've only just met him, after all. And I'm hopped up on goofballs.

"Uh, I'm just… looking," I say, cos it's all I can say, and it's true.

"Just looking? Just lost is what you are, Stevey boy. C'mon, I've someone for you to meet, mate."

"Yeah? Okay." I go with him out the door and leave the crazy arsenal behind. I think that phrase popped into my head because Grant's wearing an Arsenal top, and cos I'm crazy. Or I'm not. I can never tell, even less so now. Maybe I should have kept taking my tablets.

*****

It's even later now, and I've had more of the stuff in the pipe, cos I'm me, and I never know when I've had enough, or too much, or when it's time to stop. Grant's woman is with us now – her name's Cassie, and she's not doing any drugs, cos she's pregnant. She's gorgeous, but everyone probably is when you're on this shit. But she is anyway, I think. I tell her it a few times, and they all laugh at me, and I don't know if that's good or bad, cos I hate that thing where you're doing drugs with people and they all seem straight compared to you, so you get paranoid, and you don't enjoy it. They're all as fucked as me though, I think, except pretty, pregnant Cassie. It looks great on her, the bump, the boobs, she looks like she's still thin at the same time as being fat. I tell her all of this, cos I have no filter now, and she laughs in a nice way, and Danny sniggers, and Grant laughs in a way that I'm still not sure about.

"You can have a tickle if you like, Steve mate. My treat," he says, nodding at her. I'm not sure if he's being serious, and now I don't know if he literally means for me to tickle her, or if it's Essex slang for sex. It's not like I can ask. Cassie whacks him on the arm.

"Oi! Don't I get no say in it?" she says, then turns and gives me a wink. Or she mightn't have. My vision is getting worse as we go on, as is my ability to tell hallucinations from the truth.

"Pffft, you're 'avin a tin bath, intcha? Shut your mouth, 'fore I shut it for ya," Grant says, and lights up the end of his glass pipe again; the bottom of it has gone from see-through to black in a couple of hours. Mine's less black, but I think I've had fewer hits than him. I just smile at both of them and sink back into the couch, feeling nice, and happy, and horny, and hopeful. Maybe he was being serious. That would be nice. My hard-on pushes against my jeans like it's going to rip through the material any minute. I spot one of my cans of cider on the table, and grab it, cos I'm suddenly really thirsty.

*****

My dick is in Cassie's mouth and it's like the most beautiful sight ever. Better than any porn. I can barely see, to be honest, I've had so much of this stuff now, but it's like I can see on a bunch of whole different levels, so that doesn't matter. I dunno how much more time has passed, but it's still bright out, so that's okay. I look down again at her head, which is hanging over the edge of the mattress, so I can get my cock into her throat. That's the kind of sex it is – she's not exactly giving me a blow-job here, it's hardcore, rough, running mascara stuff. But it feels amazing. When she chokes too hard I take it out and let her breathe, but not for too long before I put it back in, cos that's how they do it in porn. I'm not even close to coming – this stuff is like Viagra, the control I have over myself with it. When I was in the toilet having that wank, I came, but only because I wanted to. If I hadn't wanted to, I could have carried on. Same as what's happening now. Carrie makes another 'ock' noise and I slide out again, looking at the strings of thick spit all over my shaft and feeling like a real porn star. I look down the other end and see Grant fucking Cassie hard, with her legs over his shoulders, and I get another amazing wave going through me that almost makes me shoot there and then. Looking down at her gorgeous face, or what I can see of it from this angle, I see the fringe of Danny's hair beyond her right shoulder, and I remember that he's lying under her, fucking her arse while Grant fills up the other hole, and I wonder how I forgot that was happening, and I remember that I'm really, really fucked, so it's understandable.

I pull out again, wondering are we gonna switch sides in a bit, or have we already and I've just forgotten it, and I catch sight of Cassie's eyes for a second, and there's something weird about the expression, but then I'm back in and it's gone, and I look back at Grant, who's laughing now, or smiling – whichever one it is, it doesn't look nice. It's sort of scary, or sinister, and I shudder, not from pleasure, but from something inside me that's trying to give me a message. The room smells like fucking, and there's no sound except the squelching of lube and the slapping of skin on skin, and the sound of Cassie gagging. She's really gagging now – choking. I think she's choking. I pull out, and not just spit comes out this time, she sort of retches a bit, and now I'm gagging, and her face is a mess, even more than it was, and now I suddenly feel something different. I feel like this isn't so great, or sexy, or beautiful; that there's something else. I keep myself out of her mouth, and use the side of my hand to wipe the stuff off her face. Cassie looks right into my eyes and all of a sudden I know what's wrong. She doesn't say it out loud, but she mouths two words to me. Just two words.

"Help me."

I come away from her, walking backwards towards the bedroom door, still naked, still hard as a rock, cos my dick isn't being controlled by my emotions right now – if it was, it would have retracted inside me completely, trust me. And Grant looks over in a sort of menacing way, or a friendly way, I can't tell anymore, and says:

"Awight, mate? Where you off?"

"Toilet," I say; still standing to attention, and a bit embarrassed about it, now that sense is flooding back to me.

"Just piss in her, mate. All she's good for anyway," says Danny's voice, cos I can't really see the rest of him. I feel my fingernails digging into my palms and my teeth biting down on the inside of my bottom lip, and neither of them are drug-related.

"Hehe, nice one, bruvva. Back in a tick," I say, and get out of there before anyone can say anything else to me. I can hear Cassie now, though. The noises she's making aren't good ones. I need to fix this. I need to fix it fast. I didn't know. Did I know? Do I even know now? Am I just imagining it? Did I imagine her saying to help her? I don't know. I don't know anything. I just… it feels bad. It felt so good a minute ago, but now I can't remember how it started. If it was consensual. Or if Grant just made her do it. Made her do us. I don't know, but something isn't right. Nothing is right anymore. I remember the kitchen, and I feel good for the first time in a few minutes. Well, not good. But okay at least.

*****

"Bit chilly or summink?" Grant says, when I come back in, wearing my trousers. I haven't put a top on or anything, but I'm still the most dressed person there.

"Haha, nah mate. Bit shy, you know?" I say, going back over to take my place by Cassie's head. She opens her eyes and sees me, looking half-confused, half-scared.

"That's you fuckin' Irish, am I right?" he says, still thrusting away at her crotch, never missing a beat. I shiver a little from the cold steel inside the back of my waistband.

"Yup, all that Catholic guilt," I say. Then I grab Cassie's head by her ponytail and use all my strength to jerk her body over to the left, leaving Danny's surprised face completely exposed. Before anyone can do or say another thing, I reach behind me for the machete and bring it crashing down into his skull, through the socket of the right eye. Blood sprays up, covering my face and drips down my bare chest. It's boiling hot, and it smells like old metal. Cassie screams, and rolls herself over to one side, and I swear I hear both of their penises come out of her, but that's probably my mind playing tricks. I look at Grant, who's frozen to the spot for a second, and then he says:

"Mate, what the FUCK????"

I reach behind me again and pull out the pistol. I still don't know what it's called, I forgot to check, and point it at his face. He looks astonished, then bemused, then he starts laughing, loud, and uncontrollably. I don't understand. Cassie's in a foetal position on the ground beside the bed now. Danny's twitching and gurgling, but he's no danger. He's fucking done. I'm still looking at Grant, and I want to say something clever or pithy now, but I have nothing to say, so I just squeeze the trigger, and brace myself for the kickback and the deafening noise. There's a click, then a silence, and then Grant says, still smiling:

"Would help if there was some bullets in it, mate."

I feel the life pouring out of me. I didn't know. I wouldn't even have known how to check. He starts to come towards me, and I have to think fast, cos I'm dead now. He's not gonna let me leave here alive. I can't think of anything, so I just throw the gun at him. And he doesn't have the reaction speed to get out of the way, so it whacks him, right on the temple, but he doesn't go down. He keeps coming at me, staggering, like a zombie. The slower ones, from the George A Romero films, not the new, fast ones. I don't know what else to do, so I rush him, and knock him over.

Now we're both on the ground, wresting, struggling; me in just my trousers, him naked, still with a fucking hard-on, and I don't know if that's the drugs, or just because all of this shit excites him. I'm heavier than him and bigger than him, but I think he's stronger than me. He's trying to take me out with headbutts, but he's missing so far. I need to end this, but I can't hit him, or strangle him; my hands are both being used to keep him down, and that won't be for long. He throws his head back for another shot at smashing my nose, and I see my chance – my only chance, so I take it. I clamp my teeth around the bit of his neck that I think has the big artery; I'm just guessing right now, and I'm not thinking straight at all, but it's all I've got. I bite hard, and I keep biting, until I'm through the skin, and I know I'm in the right place, cos my mouth fills up with thick, hot liquid, and I know it's blood, cos it tastes like the stuff you get at the back of your throat when you have nosebleeds. And some of it's in my throat now, but I keep biting, and it's okay, cos I'm on top, so the gravity means most of it is just pouring out of my mouth and back onto him, and now the room is full of his screams, and I don't stop until they stop, and then it's over, and I'm shaking, and I think it's okay now. I think I fixed it. And I sit there for a long time, not moving or talking or thinking. And then Cassie comes over to me, and gives me a fag and a light. I need to say so many things to her, but she just hugs me and shushes me, like the way your mum would.

And then I cry, for the first time since I walked away from Emma; for the first time in a long time. And it's good. It's so good that I stop worrying about how I'm gonna get out of here, how I'm gonna need to shower, to change into new clothes, to square things with Cassie about what she's gonna tell the police, if she tells them anything at all – maybe she'll just leave like I'm gonna leave – she doesn't live here, after all. I cry, cos it makes me feel better, it makes all the bad come out of me, it makes me feel like a person again. And then I go to my jacket to get my phone, cos I have no idea what time it is now, and I have to get on a plane later, and go back to Ireland, where I don't know what I'm gonna do next, but at least it'll be a new start. And you never know what's around the corner.

Twenty-two

Today, Limerick, Orla

I'm at the train station. In the buses bit. We're getting a coach. Orla's not here yet. But she will be. I stop for a second and wonder if she mightn't come – if she couldn't go through with it, and my heart sinks. But I wouldn't blame her. It's all crazy. I dunno if I'd be able to do what she's doing. But she is doing it. She'll be here. It'll be okay.

It's been three weeks since that day and night in the hotel. And everything has gone so quickly. It's been all her, too. It had to be. I couldn't push it, even if it's what I want. What I've always wanted – me and her, together. And now that it's happening, it still doesn't seem real. When I see her, though – when she walks around the corner with her suitcase, then it'll be real. I want a cigarette now, but I haven't had one in a fortnight. Or a drink, either. It turns out I can stop, apparently. I've been very good. Because I have a reason to be, all of a sudden. No holes that need to be filled anymore. Having her is everything. And I do have her, as long as she shows.

We've been talking non-stop since. We've met up a few times, not for long or to do anything major; just to be together, and maybe to steal a kiss, when we were sure no one was looking. All of this has been her plan, and she's serious about it. She's leaving him. Today. And she's already got somewhere to go. For both of us to go – in England, which couldn't be more perfect for me, cos I get to go home, to my kid. Well, near enough to her, anyway. She has a sister who lives in Kent who'll put us up until we get on our feet. I haven't argued with her about it – we don't argue, I can't even imagine us arguing, although you always think that at the start of things, I guess. This isn't just a thing, though. This is like nothing I've ever known before. Except it is, cos I knew her before. But not like this. Not all the way, like I know her now. I thought nothing could ever match the way things were with Emma when they were good, so much so that I was prepared to put up with the shittiness just so I could keep the good stuff. But the good stuff with Orla is even better. And there's no shittiness. She feels the same. That's why she's leaving. That's why she doesn't care about quitting her job or not seeing her friends. She just wants to be with me. And she wants me to be happy, and she knows I'll be happier over there, where I can see my kid. She doesn't have kids, so she's the one who can lift right out, she said. And I didn't argue with her, but I did make certain she was sure. And I've been making certain for three weeks now. And I think she's sure. If she turns up. And she will. I should stop worrying about it. And anyway, it's been three weeks, and that was time enough for the bodies to start showing up around Limerick. She even said something to me about it – about how Limerick was becoming so dangerous it would probably be good for us to get away. And she was right about that, sort of. Staying here might get very dangerous for me, cos Limerick isn't London, and maybe the police do things differently here. Maybe my luck is going to run out.

*****

"Would you love me if I had nothing?" I ask, when we're on the coach, heading for Dublin.

"What, you mean like now?"

"Hahaha, touché." She has a point. I'm really happy, just sitting next to her like this. It's bliss. And not just because of where we're heading, what we're about to do, what we're… embarking upon. I just love the here and now of her being next to me. It's wonderful. She's wonderful. I'm very lucky.

"No, I understand, really I do. You don't have to worry. I'm not her. Look at what I'm doing. Look at what I did today. Would I be doing any of that if I wasn't sure. If I didn't really love you?"

"No. No, I suppose not. I'm sorry." I'm still not sick of her saying she loves me, I don't think I'll ever get tired of hearing it. This is all I ever wanted. Not just her – all I ever wanted was to love someone and have them love me back. To have someone who's loyal, and in cahoots with me, always. Who thinks it's me and her against the world. And I know that's not pragmatic or realistic, and it's overly romantic, and the way a 20-year-old looks at the world, but maybe we weren't so wrong to think like that when we were 20. Maybe we were right, and we just hadn't met the perfect person yet. And maybe we got older, and some of us got harder, and more cynical, and gave up on that dream. I think I did too, but I was wrong. Cos I have it now, after so much shit and pain and whatever else. Maybe the good things do come to those who wait.

"Now it's me having to tell you not to say sorry, yeah?" She squeezes my hand a little harder. It's been locked in hers since we put the seatbelts on. I feel ten feet tall just touching her like this. It's beyond comprehension, even though I comprehend it completely. It's perfect.

"Apologies for my sorrys, boo," I say, not even feeling silly for calling her that, like I'm in a hip-hop song from 2002 or something.

"Boo-boopy-doo," she says, before pointing at the window and shouting "Sheeps!" in a way that makes the old lady across the aisle from us give her a stern look over the top of her reading glasses, and making Orla giggle and move a little closer to me.

"Sheeps are excellent. And Moo Cows," I say, wondering if she remembered to keep the Diet Coke in her shoulder bag and not leave it in one of the suitcases that we put in the baggage compartment. She must have spotted me looking, cos she takes the bottle out from the bag under her feet and says:

"Looking for this?"

I nod at her with a smile, cos I've been smiling ever since she arrived, and the noise as I open the bottle reassures me that, on top of everything else that makes her perfect, she's also not one of those people who don't close bottles of pop properly, letting all the fizziness go flat.

*****

The drive to the airport takes about three and a half hours, but it flies by, cos we're thick as thieves, talking about everything and nothing. It's just like the old days, when we used to do this in pubs, with our respective girlfriends/boyfriends glaring at us from across the room, and strangers assuming we must be on a date, or already be an item, cos the chemistry between us was so obvious. It's different now though, cos it's finally legit. We don't belong to other people anymore. It's just me and her. Against the world. And it feels amazing. We go through the toll road that I know means we're not far from where we're going, and I get a weird wobble, a little pang in my chest, when I remember that everything isn't quite as perfect as I keep thinking it is, but I shake it off, cos it's okay. It's gonna be okay. It mightn't be, but I have to believe in myself. I've come so far in these three weeks. I've changed so much. I've fixed so much. I have a past. I have demons. I have things that might catch up with me one day, sure. But I have her now, and that makes all of that easier to cope with. Or it will, when I have to cope with it. But maybe I won't have to. There's definitely one thing I have to cope with, of course, but if this is meant to be, I'll find a way.

"Penny for them?" she says, doing a bad English accent. It takes me a second to register that it was her saying it.

"Huh? Oh, nothing. Just thinking."

"Thinking about me, was it?" There's that smile again. How many years did I miss seeing that smile? I'm determined that I'll never have to miss it again. We're on the open road now, and I can see the towers in the distance. Nearly there.

"Always."

"D'awww. You *lie*, but you're a good liar, and you lie about nice things, so I'll leave you off." She kisses me on the cheek, and I remember that time all those years ago, when she kissed me on the cheek, and I thought it was the best day of my life. Maybe today's the best day of my life, though. It feels like it.

"Thanks, can I have another one of those?" I say, wanting more than a peck on the cheek this time.

"If I must, ffffffffff." She's read my mind too, cos it's a proper kiss this time, and I can't see the old lady with the glasses with my eyes shut, but she's probably horrified by us two thirtysomethings, acting like horny teenagers, on the bus to Dublin Airport.

*****

She didn't confront him or anything, the husband – *James*. She said there was no point. She said they hadn't been together properly as husband and wife for a long time – that he barely touched her anymore. That was hard for me to believe. Not because I thought she was lying, just because I can't imagine anyone being able to touch her any time they want, and choosing not to. I know they say no matter how gorgeous you think she is, someone somewhere is already sick of her shit, and I used to agree with that. But she's Orla. I spent years wanting to touch her, when I couldn't. To think someone else basically had her on tap and didn't bother makes me really angry in one way, but obviously really glad in another. His loss is my gain. And this afternoon he's going to come home to a Dear John letter on the living room table, and he'll have his whole life to regret not making things right when he had the chance. I don't feel sorry for him. Fuck him. That's life. I've been on the wrong end of unfair things for most of my life, it's good to be on the right end for once. Cos that's what 'life isn't fair' really means. You say it to people to make them feel better about life shitting on them, but life isn't fair for the people who win, either. That's sort of the point.

We're in a café at the airport, cos it's a while before the flights, and we don't have bigger luggage to check in. I feel like I've spent most of the last year in airport lounges, but I've actually never been in this one before. We're only here because she booked her ticket first. She said she'd have booked mine for me too, but she didn't feel right doing it without making sure that I was going to come with her. That she was leaving no matter what, so wanted to leave it up to me, no pressure. I booked my own the second she told me, though. It was ludicrous to think I wouldn't be going with her – there was no way in hell that was what was going to happen, but I sort of understood where she was coming from. And anyway, it solved one little problem I'd had in my head for a bit. So maybe everything happens for a reason.

"Are you looking forward to it?" I ask, enjoying the latte, cos caffeine is pretty much the only vice I have left. Not that I'm complaining – I don't want to drink or smoke.

"Which part?"

"Oh, I dunno. All of it, I suppose." I'm excited myself, and a bit nervous, and worried, but that's all perfectly normal, I suppose.

"Yeah! I have a job interview lined up, I told you that, yeah? Course I did. And we'll have somewhere to stay – you'll like Laurie, my sister, she's sort of like me, but a bit madder – and there'll be plenty of room, cos it's just her in that big house now. It'll be great. And it'll be us, you know. Together. Doesn't that sound exciting?" She looks at me all open and honest and pretty and adorable.

"Sounds amazing. It'll be amazing, all of it, I'm sure." I'm biting my fingernail while looking at the clock on the wall behind her. About 30 more minutes before we need to go to security, I reckon. Then we'll be out of here. I just need to figure something out first, and it's getting me a little stressed out.

"Are you okay?" she says, taking a sip of her coffee. She has it black. She did back then, too. It hasn't ruined her teeth, they're still pretty white, if a little crooked. I like that, though. I like her crooked teeth and her slightly funny nose. They make her even more attractive.

"Me? Oh yeah. I'm grand," I say, slightly annoyed that she can see straight through me like that, and wondering what else she sees when she looks at me sometimes. I shake the feeling off.

"Good. Cos you know, if you have any second thoughts…" She's not actually joking. I can tell, cos she's not smiling, but on top of that I can see she's doing a brave face to hide the sadness that would come out if I looked even for a second like I was considering what she's offering.

"God, no. No second thoughts. D'mind me, I'm just a bit…"

"Yeah, me too. It's okay." She squeezes my hand and now I feel bad. Really bad. Like there's a black cloud coming over me, and my lungs are filling with smoke and soot. I swallow but there's no spit in my mouth. I squeeze her hand back, a little too hard, and stop when I realise. I hope she hasn't noticed the way my mood went so dark just there. I look in her eyes and they're smiling, so I think it's okay.

*****

Half an hour later we're walking up to the security gates. They're automated, so it's just a barcode on a printout, or in my case, a barcode on the Android app, and there's no need to show anyone your passport or even interact with any humans until it's time to go through the metal detectors. The queue at the departure gate and the bit where you get on the actual plane is the only time anyone looks at your passport, I think. I've never flown from here. We both get through with our bags, and that bit's over, at least.

"You look stressed. You hate that bit, do you?" Orla says, once we're out the other side and into the departure longue proper.

"Uh, yeah. Yeah, it just gives me anxiety. Crowds and stuff, and not knowing quite where you're supposed to stand, or if you have to take off your-"

"Shhhhh, my little baby. Tis all over now," she says, giving me a hug, and I want to cry, for a whole load of reasons, one of them being relief, I guess. And I wasn't really lying about not liking this bit. I'm definitely glad it's over. We're dragging our bags on their wheels through all the fancy shops, not planning on buying anything, although Orla does pick up some silly Irish souvenirs to bring for her sister, mainly as a joke, cos her sister is as Irish as she is. Then we spot the gate for our flight is open, so it's time to head down to the queue. I get the nerves again, and my stomach feels funny.

"Did you tell me you don't like flying? Was that you?" Orla asks me, once we're standing waiting to board. They haven't walked down the queue yet, checking the boarding passes, I notice, which is strange, cos the flight is in five minutes, according to the monitors above.

"Huh? No, I'm, well, I do get a bit nervous, yeah. I used to be really travel sick when I was a kid, in cars and buses and stuff, so I never wanted to go on ferries or planes." I say that, but going on a plane was never really an option. We never went on foreign holidays when I was a kid. Same with ferries, really. I was 23 the first time I went on one of them.

"Hmmm, no, this was someone terrified of them, definitely. Must have been someone else. Is this plane delayed then?" She squints up at the screen. It still says five minutes, but it also says 'Last call', and there hasn't been any call, and there isn't anyone manning the desk. It's weird. I feel worried again, but not sure about what, specifically.

"I'm not sure. Let me ask this guy," I say, tapping some fella in a uniform walking past.

"Yes?" He sounds foreign. Probably Polish. Foreign and a bit gay. It's amazing how much you can tell from one word.

"Ah, do you know if our flight's on time, like? There's no one on the desk, and the woman who comes down and-"

"Ahhhhh, this one, yes? Okay, yes. This flight, it is on time, but we are short of the staff. Soooooo, there will not be this woman come to check boarding passes first. In minute now, someone is come to the desk, and when this come, then you can go on plane. And, uh, this up here, this desk, you will show passes with, uh, lady that is there. Yes?"

"Oh, okay," I say, giving him a thank you expression, like a grown-up would.

"Everything is okay yes now fine?"

"Everything is more than okay yes now fine, thank you," says Orla, nearly making me giggle. And, before the guy even leaves, the woman comes to the desk, and the queue starts moving. I look at Orla, and if it's even possible, she looks prettier than I've ever seen her look.

"You okay?" she says, blinking her big cartoon eyes at me. The light coming through the big window beside her is making her look like she has a halo around the top of her lovely red hair. I don't think I've ever loved her more. I look up and see we're about fourth in the queue.

"I really need the toilet, sorry," I say, and step out from under the ribbon, taking my bag.

"What? Will I keep your place for you?" she says, looking very confused.

"No, you're grand. You can't do that. I'll just join the end of the queue. I won't be long, honest. And we're sitting together anyway, so no worries." The toilets are right across from where our queue is, I'm already half way to them.

"Can't you wait until we get-" She gives up mid-sentence when she realises I'm not gonna change my mind.

Inside I find a cubicle and just about lock it before I drop to my knees and vomit up everything I've drank or eaten that day. Definitely couldn't have waited to get on the plane to do that; they don't even open the toilets on there until they're already in the sky. Wishing I had a bottle of water, and cursing airport security, Osama bin Laden, and all the rest of them, I drink some water from the tap, and clean up my face with some tissue paper. I look at myself in the mirror and say

"You're okay. It's okay. It's gonna be fine." My stomach lurches a little again, and I wonder if I should go back in the cubicle, but then I remember that the flight is leaving straight away, and the public address doesn't seem to be calling out anything at the moment. When I get back to the queue there are only about ten in front of me, and I'm through the gates with no fuss whatsoever, and I feel almost okay again, walking quickly out to the plane.

*****

"You worried me earlier, you know…" Orla says, a little later, when we're somewhere over the Irish sea.

"I did? How?" I know what she means, but sometimes it's better to drag out a conversation, in case you need time to come up with some answers.

"With the whole last minute rush to the bogs thing, stupid." She gives me a nudge with her shoulder.

"Ah, yeah. Sor- Yeah, I didn't mean to worry you. Why were you worried, though?"

"Cos I thought you might be doing a runner, you eejit. Why else?"

"Oh. Oh, right. No, I wasn't gonna do a runner. I just…"

"Needed a piss, yeah. We'll have to see about getting you a new bladder once we're in England, yeah? They're probably free on that NHS thing ye have over there." She's smiling again now, and I'm glad she is. I'm smiling too, cos the worst of today is over, I think. I can stop worrying. For a while, at least. For today, definitely.

"I'll have a word with my GP," I say, thinking how I haven't had a GP since before I moved to Jim's, cos I'm never sick. Well, I'm never ill, anyway.

"Sound. So, Laurie texted me. She says she'll pick us up from the airport herself, no need to bus it or get the train. Isn't that nice of her?"

"Yeah. She seems sound, all right," I say, wondering what this woman's actually going to make of me – the guy who came out of nowhere and wrecked her sister's marriage. But it's all worked out already between them, according to Orla. She must approve of it all. Otherwise she wouldn't have offered to put her up. But you never know, with people. Especially family. Lots of poisoned chalices get offered when it comes to family. And being told you're welcome to stay somewhere isn't always what it seems. I should know; I just left somewhere that was the place I grew up in – my real home, and lots of times it felt like anything but.

"She is! And she's dying to see you, too," Orla says, holding up the cheese and ham panini she ordered earlier, and scrutinising it like she's the health inspector or something.

"Oh yeah?" I say, a weird feeling suddenly in my stomach again.

"Yeah! Here, look for yourself." She puts the panini down, and picks up her iPhone, showing the screen to me. There's only one sentence in the text:

Oh, and tell that Steve fella of yours I can't wait to meet him.

And there it is. That one little problem I had to cope with. The reason I couldn't go through the gate with her and open my passport next to her. The reason I've been so stressed all day. But I have to believe in myself. I've come so far in these three weeks. I've changed so much. I've fixed so much. I can fix this. I've stopped everything, nearly. I give her hand the biggest squeeze I can, and hope that this time, I can finally stop me.

The End

Afterword

Well, now. Yes. Quite. Wasn't that a lovely story? Thank you again for buying one of my actual novel book things. You may not think you're making much of a difference, but you really are. It's the difference between me selling a book, and me not selling one. If you got lucky and read this book for free, for some reason, be a sport and throw a review for it on Amazon. Reviews are a writer's bread and butter. Although I don't eat bread anymore. And I'm off dairy. So reviews are my... potatoes.

This book was quite different to any of the ones I've written before. I wanted to try new things with narrative and structure – prove a few personal points about the rules of writing, etc. I wanted to see if I could manipulate the reader's emotions and get them rooting for the bad guy, if he even was the bad guy, that is. I wanted to write something entertaining, and gripping, and surprising, and emotional. Which is what I always want to do, when I start a book. So maybe it isn't that different after all. Except it totally, totally is. So, when you're telling a friend about it tomorrow, and recommending that they check it out (or warning them never to read it), think carefully about how to describe it, in a nutshell. And then please write that description down, and email it to me, because I haven't a clue myself. Just don't accidentally give the ending away. I still haven't forgiven the person who ruined The Sixth Sense for me in 1999.

Acknowledgements

Thanks to everyone who's ever read, bought, or reviewed a Ciarán West book, to everyone who's supported, encouraged, or put up with me over the last few months. Thanks to my Mum for her patience and her kindness, to my brother for his advice and his help, to the rest of my family for miscellaneous deeds. Thanks to God, Sophia Bush, and Dean Koontz, in no particular order. Thank you for the music, thanks for the memories, thanks!

Printed in Great Britain
by Amazon